RAIN DOGS

A Detective Sean Duffy Novel

RAIN DOGS

Adrian McKinty

SEVENTH STREET BOOKS®
AN IMPRINT OF PROMETHEUS BOOKS
59 JOHN GLENN DRIVE • AMHERST, NY 14228
www.seventhstreetbooks.com

Published 2016 by Seventh Street Books®, an imprint of Prometheus Books

First published in January 2016 by Serpent's Tail, an imprint of Profile Books Ltd., 3A Exmouth House, Pine Street, London EC1R 0JH; www.serpentstail.com.

A portion of chapter 1 appeared in the 2015 summer fiction issue of *Radio Silence*.

Cover design by Jacqueline Nasso Cooke
Cover images © Philip Lee Harvey / Media Bakery (lake)
and Martin Siepmann / Media Bakery (castle)

Inquiries should be addressed to
Seventh Street Books
59 John Glenn Drive
Amherst, New York 14228
VOICE: 716–691–0133
FAX: 716–691–0137
WWW.SEVENTHSTREETBOOKS.COM

20 19 18 17 16   5 4 3 2 1

Library of Congress Cataloging-in-Publication

Names: McKinty, Adrian, author.
Title: Rain dogs : a Detective Sean Duffy novel / Adrian McKinty.
Description: Amherst, NY : Seventh Street Books, an imprint of Prometheus Books, 2016.
    | Series: A Detective Sean Duffy novel
Identifiers: LCCN 2015037617 | ISBN 9781633881303 (softcover) |
    ISBN 9781633881310 (ebook)
Subjects: LCSH: Detectives—Northern Ireland—Fiction. | Murder—Investigation—
    Fiction. | BISAC: FICTION / Mystery & Detective / Police Procedural. | GSAFD:
    Mystery fiction.
Classification: LCC PS3563.C38322 R35 2016 | DDC 813/.54—dc23
    LC record available at http://lccn.loc.gov/2015037617

Printed in the United States of America

Humiliation, unhappiness, discord are the ancient foods of heroes.

—Jorge Luis Borges, *On Blindness*, 1983

CONTENTS

1: The Most Famous Man in the World   9

2: The Theft That Wasn't   21

3: Lizzie Fitzpatrick Redux?   43

4: Mr. Underhill   54

5: The Strange Suicide of Lily Bigelow   64

6: The One Shoe   83

7: Interviewing the Finns   89

8: The Killing of the Chief Super   98

9: Wiping the Whiteboard   110

10: The Preliminary Autopsy Report   117

11: Interviewing Mr. Underhill Redux   126

12: East to the Smoke   137

13: Jimmy Savile's Caravan   156

14: Kinkaid   163

15: Tony McIlroy's Detective Agency   174

16: The Brothel   186

17: Ed McBain's Notebook   196

18: Finlandia   201

19: Constable Hornborg's Story   213

20: On the Ice   221

21: Mercury Tilt   229

22: Closing the Net   233

23: The Famous Carrickfergus Fifteen-Pub Crawl   251

24: The Ministry Man   266

25: Breaking the Case   276

26: Lifting the Prime Suspect   281

27: How He Did It   284

28: The Oakman Surprises Everyone   290

29: *Kami No Itte*—The Divine Move   295

30: What Defeat Tastes Like   307

31: It's Not the Leaving of Liverpool That Grieves Me   312

32: *The Helsinki Times* (5 Months Later)   319

Afterword   327

About . . . Adrian McKinty   329

1: THE MOST FAMOUS MAN IN THE WORLD

Even the fulminating racists on the far side of the police barriers were temporarily awed into silence by their first sight of the Champ as he stepped nimbly—*lepidopterously*—from the bus onto the pavement in front of Belfast City Hall. He was bigger than ordinary men, physically, of course, but there was an aura about him too. Ten years past his prime, heavier, greyer, and with what was rumored to be early onset Parkinson's, this was still the most famous man on the face of the earth. He was wearing Adidas trainers, a red tracksuit, and sunglasses. He was flanked by two Nation of Islam handlers in dark jackets and bow ties, and a pace behind them was the Reverend Jesse Jackson, a celebrity in America, but a largely unknown figure here.

The Champ ascended the dais and the crowds surged forward to get a better look. And in cop-think: *the better for some nutter to get a bead on him—to throw a bottle or a brick, or to line up a concealed pistol.* He was loved, yes, but he was hated too, and he had sown equal parts enmity and adoration since his first title fight against the hapless Sonny Liston. Over the years the enmity had diminished, but it still lingered here and there in the hearts of those made vulnerable by the diseases of racism, patriotism, and religious fervor.

The Champ took off his sunglasses, tapped the microphone, took a step back, and shadowboxed. Cheers rippled through the crowd. This was what they had come to see. "Look at his feet!" someone said in front of me—a sage and pugilistically astute observation. The Champ danced like a kid, like the skinny kid who had outfoxed Zbigniew Pietrzykowski at the Rome Olympics.

He had the crowd in the palm of his hand and he hadn't even spoken yet.

It was a cold, clear day and it couldn't have been shot better by Néstor Almendros: sunlight illuminating the Baroque revival columns behind the Champ's head, and the clouds parting to reveal an indigo sky the likes of which were frequently to be found loitering over the Champ's hometown in a meander of the Ohio River, but which seldom troubled the heavens over this muddy estuary of the Lagan.

He stopped boxing, grinned, and an aide gave him a towel to wipe his forehead. He attempted to unzip his tracksuit an inch or two, but his hand was unsteady on the zipper and the aide had to help him. But then the Champ smiled again, strode confidently forward, grabbed the microphone stand, and said: "Hello Ireland! I'm so happy to be here in beautiful Belfast at last!"

The audience was momentarily baffled by the statement. None of them had ever previously considered the notion that Belfast could be beautiful or that anyone would have come here voluntarily and upon arrival, would have been happy with this as their choice of final destination. Yet here was the most famous man on earth saying exactly that. Belfast's default demotic was sarcasm, and everyone liked a good joke, so perhaps the Champ was only kidding?

"Yes, sir, it's a lovely winter day and it's wonderful to be here in beautiful Belfast, Northern Ireland!" the Champ reiterated, and this time there was no doubt about his sincerity. The crowd, oddly moved, found itself roaring its approval.

He had shadowboxed, he had waved, he had lied and told them their city was aesthetically pleasing. He could have run for mayor on a Nation of Islam ticket and won on a first-round voice vote of the council.

The other policemen began to relax a little, but I wasn't so easily taken in. I was up on a raised platform with half a dozen other cops, the better for us to keep an eye on the small group of National Front skinheads yelling abuse from the protest-pen that had been rigged up for them next to Marks and Spencer. No more than twenty of them in total, but with a wig or a hat they could easily have infiltrated the crowd—although that level of ingenuity was probably beyond their mental capacity.

Another quite separate protest group was the Reverend Ian Paisley's elderly band of evangelical parishioners far down on Royal Avenue, who were not happy about the appearance of a famous Muslim spokesman in the capital city of Ulster, God's true Promised Land. They could be heard singing their discontent in dour Presbyterian hymnals and determinedly joyless psalmody. Wherever Paisley went there was always an element of unselfconscious surrealism, and today he had brought with him a gospel choir, a gaggle of schoolgirl accordionists and a moonfaced kid on a donkey shaking a tambourine.

The Champ ducked from a phantom left hook and then took the microphone stand again.

"Abe Grady, my great-grandfather, walked from Ennis, County Clare, to Belfast in 1860. In Belfast, he took ship to America. He crossed the Atlantic Ocean and found a country in the midst of Civil War. A land where my other great-grandparents were slaves. We've *all* come a long way since then and it's great to be back home!"

More roaring from the crowd.

"But I heard, I heard that some folks here aren't happy that I came here to Belfast to see you today? Is that true?"

Cries of "No!"

"No, I see 'em. I see 'em over there!"

Defiant cheers from the National Front contingent below us.

"I see 'em. Look at them! Oh man, they so ugly, when they look in a mirror the reflection ducks."

Laughter.

"They so ugly that when they go into a haunted house they come out with an application!"

Roars of laughter.

"They so ugly that when they go into the bank, the bank turns off the security cameras!"

A great howl of laughter and cheers.

The Champ let it die away until there was only silence.

"Now they're quiet, huh? I don't hear them. Oh boy, they think they can outwit me? I'm so pretty. I'm so fast! I'm so fast that last night

I turned off the light switch in my hotel room and I was in bed before the room was dark!"

More laughter.

"He's doing all the old classics," a sergeant grumbled next to me.

"If you even dream of beating me you'd better wake up and apologize!" the Champ said, and took a step back to do some more shadow-boxing. The crowd was deliriously pleased.

The Champ wiped his forehead again and waved. Jesse Jackson waved. The lord mayor waved and, pushing his way to the front like an eager schoolboy in Cuban heels, Bono waved.

The Champ talked some more about his Irish roots and his grandmother and great-grandmother. He talked about growing up in Kentucky in the era of Jim Crow. He got serious.

"Service to others is the rent you pay for your room here on Earth. The fight is won or lost far away from witnesses—behind the lines, in the gym, and out there on the road, long before I dance under those lights. Only a man who knows what it is like to be defeated can reach down to the bottom of his soul and come up with the extra ounce of power it takes to win when the match is even. . . . Now I know you got problems here in Belfast. I know it. But believe me, there's no problem that can't be solved by the human spirit. You got to work together. You gotta work hard! We're all brothers and sisters, no matter our creed or color. Someday this will be a peaceful island! And that day is going to come because of people like you! Thank you, Belfast, and God bless you all!"

"Ali! Ali! Ali! Ali!" the crowd chanted and cheered. The Champ acknowledged them and waved good-bye. He turned and an aide put the towel around his shoulders and began guiding him toward the bus.

"Is that it?" the copper next to me was saying.

"I think so," I said.

I was glad. The riot gear was making me sweat and already my boxer shorts were drenched. I'd be happy to get it all off, put in my overtime claim, and go home to Carrick.

But then as he was making his way between the crash barriers toward the bus, the Champ suddenly stopped in his tracks, shook his head, turned, and walked back onto the stage. He peered out over the audience and then walked down the steps at the front of the stage into the adoring crowd.

"Jesus! He's gone walkabout!" I barked into the radio.

"We know!" a dozen voices yelled back into my earpiece

The crowd surged toward the Champ. Thousands of them. Young, old, Catholic, Protestant. . . . His two handlers were swamped immediately. Swept away.

"I've lost him! I can't see him!" desperate voices yelled into radio mikes.

For an uneasy thirty seconds we wondered if he had been trampled, if maybe we should fire in a couple of tear-gas canisters or baton rounds . . . but then we all spotted him again, just across the street from us.

He was slowly shaking hands and making his way toward my position.

"He's coming to Donegall Place," I said into the radio.

"Who is this?" a voice asked in the earpiece.

"Duffy."

"He's coming toward you?"

"Yes."

"Get him back on the bloody bus, Duffy!"

"How?"

The reply was lost in a blizzard of static.

The Champ moved through the crowd, "like a cinder through the snow," the peeler next to me said. Fame was his protection. He wasn't a politician or an actor, but he was sporting royalty and people gave way before him. Arms reached out to touch him, others were holding out notebooks and scraps of paper which he signed with pharaonic detachment.

"This is DI Duffy, we'll need more uniforms at the east side of Donegall Place. Could be trouble. He's heading straight for the National Front demonstrators behind the crash barriers."

"Roger that, Duffy, I can send you half a dozen men."

"We'll need more than that!"

Confused radio traffic now. Panic. Fear.

"He's going to get into it with the bloody National Front!"

"They're going to lynch him!"

"We need reinforcements!"

Normally, the Champ had handlers with him at all times, to prevent lunatics throwing sucker punches in the hope that they could acquire infamy by coldcocking the great Muhammad Ali.

And now, without handlers or aides or policemen, he was walking right up to the racist NF protestors outside Marks and Spencer.

"There is no black in the Union Jack!" the National Front were chanting—nervously—as the crowd followed the Champ toward them.

What on Earth was he doing? Did he think he could reason with them? Ali's spiel wasn't going to play with this lot. Ali's spiel worked on the postmodern ear. Ulster had barely entered the twentieth century.

Yet still he advanced.

Finally, I could see a couple of RUC Land Rovers heading toward us, bringing the much-needed reinforcements, but they were going to be too late—the Champ was going to get to the National Front protestors before they did.

"Come on," I said to the sergeant. "We've got to go down there."

"Into that lot?"

"Yeah."

"No way."

"That's an order."

"Says who?"

I pointed to the inspector's pips on my shoulder. "Says me."

"You're going to get us both killed . . . sir."

We climbed down off the platform just as the Champ reached the crash barriers.

A dozen seething skinheads in parkas, skinny jeans, and DM boots were yelling at Ali like caged laboratory animals. Ireland—the land of Charles Stewart Parnell and Daniel O'Connell—had been brought to this happy state whereby Ian Paisley and a skitter of foulmouthed skinheads were the spokespeople for the disaffected.

The Champ found the skinhead leader, fixed him with his eye, and waved his hand for silence.

The crowd hushed and held its breath.

"Listen to me! Listen to me," the Champ began. "I took an easy shot. I called you ugly and I made everyone laugh. You riled me up. I heard the war music. But then I remembered to be humble in the face of mine enemies and to trust in the mercy of Allah. I'm here in the spirit of peace and brotherhood."

The skinhead stared at him, amazed.

The Champ leaned over the crash barrier and put out his hand.

That big right hand.

That big right hand that had floored Foreman in the eighth.

That big hand right that was shaking with Parkinson's.

The skinhead froze. His mouth opened and closed. And then his arm began to raise. He couldn't help himself. It was magnetism. It was kinetic. His eyes were wild. He turned desperately to his friends. *I can't stop myself. . . . I mean, don't you see who this is? Sure you can talk about Gene Tunney or Joe Louis or Jack Dempsey, but this is The Greatest!*

His arm lifted. His fist unclenched. He shook hands with the Champ. *I'm shaking hands with Muhammad Ali.*

"What is it you don't like about black folks?" the Champ asked.

The skinhead was tongue-tied.

"Come on, answer me like a man!"

"I, I . . . I . . . You shouldn't be in our . . . this is our . . ."

"Son," the Champ said, "if all you have is a hammer, everything looks like a nail. . . ."

And you could see it in the skinhead's eyes.

This was it. Saul to Paul. Right now. Instantly. This wasn't Donegall Place, this was the royal road to Damascus.

The Champ destroyed the National Front contingent with a handshake and a grin. We'd never seen anything like it.

"Never seen anything like it," the sergeant said. This was the opposite of what happened when the Kennedys came. The Kennedys brought bad voodoo, Ali brought good.

"Duffy, are you still there?" the radio voice asked.

"Yeah."

"We've got the bus around to Royal Avenue, get him down to Castle Street."

"OK."

The sergeant and I escorted the Champ to his bus, which had moved to the junction of Royal Avenue and Castle Street. He was exhausted now. But he took the time to thank the sergeant and me.

He shook *our* hands. And his grip was strong. The sergeant got an autograph, but I was too starstruck to think of that.

I walked back to Queen Street Police Barracks where I'd parked my Beemer and said hey to some grizzled old cops who looked like rejects from Jim Henson's Creature Shop.

I got in my car and drove along the A2 to Carrick Police Station.

Everyone was more or less gone except for Lawson up in the CID room and the chief inspector lurking in his office. I decided that I would avoid both of them. I put in my overtime claim and quickly looked at the duty logs. It had been a busy day. Muhammad Ali had come to Belfast, robbing the station of half its staff, and back in Carrickfergus the secretary of state for Northern Ireland had been showing visiting dignitaries around the old ICI factory in Kilroot. The bigwigs were from Sweden, the rumors being that either Volvo or Saab were going to set up a car plant. It was pro forma stuff. Every new secretary of state pretended he was going to "save Northern Ireland" by encouraging investment, but in fact the new investment always went to marginal electoral constituencies in England.

Outside to my Beemer. Home to Coronation Road in Victoria Estate.

I parked the BMW in front of my house: Number 113, a three-bedroom former council house that sat in the middle of the terrace.

"Hello, Mr. Duffy."

It was Janette Campbell, the jailbait daughter of the thirty-something, chain-smoking, dangerously good-looking redhead next door. Janette was wearing Daisy Dukes and a T-shirt that said *Duran Duran* on it. She was smoking Benson and Hedges in a way that would have cheered the heart of the head of marketing at Philip Morris.

"Hello, Janette."

"Did you see Muhammad Ali right enough?"

"Yes, I did," I said, wondering how *she* knew where I'd been today.

"Me boyfriend Jackie says Tyson could take him easy."

"Your boyfriend is an idiot, Janette."

She nodded sadly and offered me a ciggie. I declined and went inside my house.

There was the smell of cooking from the kitchen and there were three suitcases in the hall.

Beth was in the living room, coiled on the sofa like some exotic cat, an ocelot, perhaps, reading Fanny Burney's *Letters*.

"How's the Fanny Burney?"

"The burny fanny's much better, thanks. You know, since I started taking the antibiotics," she said with a grin.

"That gag must be fifty years old," I said, and sat beside her on the sofa.

"Here's a brand-new one, Janette next door told it to me: Why do French chefs make omelets with only one egg?"

"I don't know."

"Because one egg is *un oeuf*."

I put my face in my hands and let the riot helmet drop to the carpet. Beth poked me between the folds of my body armor.

"Well?" she said.

"Well what?"

"*Well*, did you meet him?"

"Who?"

"The Champ—as you've been annoyingly calling him all week."

"It wasn't really about meeting *him*. I was just there to do a job is all."

"Ha!" she said with obvious disdain. "As if you didn't pull every string you could. You said 'Ali' in your sleep last night."

"Did not," I said, blushing.

"How was his speech?" Beth asked, handing me a still-cold can of Bass.

"Speech was fine. What's with the suitcases?"

"Moving out."

"*You're* moving out?"

"Yes."

"What? When?"

"Tomorrow morning. Rhonda's brother's coming for me."

"Tomorrow?"

"We've discussed this, Sean."

"We have?"

"You've known all along that this was only temporary. I have to be near the university, my classes. And this, frankly, is probably the least interesting street in the least interesting town in the world."

"It's had its moments in the last few years. Trust me."

"Yeah, well, it's not for me."

I drank the rest of the beer and took the book gently out of her hands. Beth and I had been going out for nearly seven months, and she'd been living here for the last few weeks. Sure, there was an age gap, but I wasn't dead yet and I made her laugh and we got on well. We'd met at the Stone Roses concert at the Ulster Hall, but apart from an affinity for Manchester bands we had little in common. She was a Prod from a wealthy family, who, after working for her da for a few years, was now doing a master's degree in English at Queens. Short red hair, slender, pretty, with a boyish androgynous body, which, if you know me at all, shouldn't surprise you. Her legs were long and strong, and there was something about her deep green eyes.

"I thought we had a good thing going here, Beth?"

"Do you ever listen to me? I mean, ever? I told you this was just until Rhonda got the wee house on Cairo Street."

"I thought that fell through."

"No. It didn't."

"So that's it? We're . . . what? Breaking up?"

"Come on, Sean. Has the weed destroyed what's left of your noggin? We talked this over two weeks ago."

"Yeah, but I thought things had changed, you know? I thought you might want to stay. We've been getting on so well."

"There's no future for us, Sean. In a couple of years you'll be forty."

"You'll be thirty!"

"It's not the same. Look, we'll still be friends. We'll always be friends, won't we?"

"*Friends*. Christ."

She put her arms round me and kissed me on the cheek. "Come on, Sean. You didn't think I was staying here permanently?"

"Actually, I sorta did."

"Oh, Sean, sweetie. . . . Look, you must be starving, let me give you your dinner. I made it special, so I did. A last supper."

Cooking was not one of Beth's talents, but it didn't matter. It was hot and it would have taken a culinary genius to screw up an Ulster fry.

"How do you like it?" she asked, watching me eat.

"It's good."

"You don't think the potato bread is burnt?"

"That's the way I like it."

She leaned over and kissed me again. "You say all the right things."

I put down the fork. "Stay. Stay here with me. You won't regret it."

She shook her head and got a beer from the fridge. "Come on, let's watch the news and see if we can spot you in the crowd."

Ali's Northern Ireland peace initiative was the lead story. He was forty-six years old, but he was made for the telly, standing out like a black Achilles among the pasty, blue-white Micks.

"Oh my God! There's you!" Beth screamed delightedly, and it *was* me, coming down from the platform with the sergeant.

"You *were* on the TV! I don't believe it! You're famous."

"Yup. I'm famous."

"Now get in there, famous man, and do the washing-up while I finish off me packing."

I did the dishes and went out to the garden shed. I rolled a fat joint with a leaf of sweet Virginia tobacco and a healthy flake of Turkish black cannabis resin.

I'd smoked half of it when I saw that it was snowing. Sunshine in Belfast in the afternoon, snow in Carrickfergus in the evening. That was Northern Ireland for you. I finished the weed, and when I went back in Beth had added two toiletry bags to the three suitcases in the hall.

"That's it?" I asked.

"That's all of it."

"Let me lend you some records. Rhonda probably doesn't have much and I've seen your collection."

"Nah, it's OK, Sean, I'm not into that stuff."

"What stuff?"

"Old stuff. Elvis and crap like that."

"Bloody hell, have I taught you nothing? Lemme play something for you."

She groaned as I put on my rare bootleg of the *From Elvis in Memphis* sessions, where hit followed hit in the King's last great flowering. You know the stuff I mean: "In the Ghetto," "Suspicious Minds," "Kentucky Rain" . . .

"And to think that this was recorded in the same month as *Let It Be*, the last Beatles album—it's crazy, we've got the end of the fifties and the end of the sixties recording at exactly the same time," I said.

She sighed, shook her head, and smiled that lovely Beth smile. "I'm going to miss you, Sean Duffy."

Later that night I lay there in the double bed, looking at her pale cheeks in the blue light of the paraffin heater.

"Honey, I'm going to miss you, too," I said.

2: THE THEFT THAT WASN'T

Phone. Early. Its insistent ring through a fog of post-pot lethargy. *Brrrrriiiinnnggggg.*

"You see? This is why I have to move in with Rhonda. No one ever calls her. Ever."

"She sounds like the life of the party."

"You can talk."

"Do you want me to get it?"

"It's obviously for you, Sean."

"Maybe it's some kind of emergency with your da?"

"That's a nice thought. Go and get it. Your beeper's going as well."

Normally, I would have wrapped the duvet about me and burrowed into it and gone downstairs like a Russian soldier in Stalingrad, but I couldn't take the blanket from her, so, shivering in my pajama bottoms, I jogged along the landing and down the chilly staircase to where the phone was ringing madly in the hall.

I picked up the receiver. "Hello."

"Inspector Duffy?"

"Yup."

"Sir, it's me."

"What time is it?"

"It's just after six thirty, sir."

It didn't feel like six thirty, but when I opened the front door, sure enough there was a band of light in the eastern sky and the milkman had been and left two bottles of silver top. It was a chilly morning and there was frost in the front garden and a sprinkling of snow on the Knockagh. I brought in the milk and closed the front door.

"Is this early-morning phone call about a case, or are you just in the mood to chat, Lawson?"

"Oh yes, sir, I wouldn't have—"

"Fine. I'll go into the kitchen. Wait a minute."

I carried the phone into the kitchen, turned on the radio, and put two pieces of bread in the toaster. "Gimme Shelter" was getting its millionth play on Atlantic 252, but because they were pirates broadcasting from a boat in the Irish Sea they didn't have to pay the Stones anything, which made you feel a little better about it.

I attempted to turn on the shiny new kettle. The one Beth had bought. A really fancy job whose element looked like something from the engineering deck on *Star Trek*. Beth came from money. Not exactly *Scrooge McDuck swimming through the gold coins in his vault* money, but pretty comfortable. I looked at the clever piece of equipment and remembered Beth's words. "*It couldn't be simpler, Sean. You push the blue button and then the red button and the light goes green and the water boils.*" But when I pushed the blue button nothing happened, and nothing happened when I pushed the red button either, and there didn't appear to be a green light anywhere on the infernal device.

"Damn it."

"Sir?"

I gave up on the kettle, lit a ciggie, and buttered and marmaladed the toast. "Tell me about the case, Lawson."

"Well, sir, there's been a theft at the Coast Road Hotel."

"A theft?"

"Yes, sir."

"A burglary?"

"No. A wallet went missing from a guest hotel room."

"Was there violence?"

"No."

"How much money?"

"Approximately twenty pounds and credit cards."

"Is this the real Detective Constable Alexander Lawson, or is this perhaps some other detective constable, a constable who is new to the ways of Carrickfergus CID?"

"It's me, sir."

"It must be an imposter. Because there's no way the real DC Alexander Lawson would ever have woken me up on a Sunday morning to deal with the theft of twenty quid from a room in the Coast Road Hotel. Where is he? What have you done with the real Lawson, you fiend!"

"Sir, it is the real me!"

"And you've called me up because you are unable to handle a petty larceny?"

"I'm sorry, sir."

Beth had come downstairs now and was looking at me from the hall. "Give me a minute," I said to Lawson and put my hand over the receiver.

"Who is it?" Beth asked.

"It's Lawson."

"Is he the one who looks like he puts on latex and gets spanked?"

"That's Dalziel."

"Well, it must be a good case for this hour of the morning," she said.

"It's a theft. I'm not going."

"You should go, and then I can be safely gone when you get back," she said.

"There's no need for you to leave this early. You've got all day. Relax. Have some breakfast. Put the kettle on for us."

She folded her arms and shook her head.

"I'll help you move," I said.

"No. You won't."

"Seriously, there's no rush, honey. Some of your stuff's in the wash. And I shelved your records alphabetically in our . . . my . . . the collection," I said.

"Donate the clothes, keep the records, I'm switching to CDs anyway."

"CDs are a fad."

"Fads are a fad."

"What does that mean?"

"Look, Sean, we're over, OK?"

"Over like the Roman Empire's over, or over like Graeme Souness and Liverpool are over?"

"Who's Graeme Souness? Actually, it doesn't matter. Go to your case, Sean. Better for both of us," she said.

"Beth, please. . . . You'll be contributing to a stereotype which from your literary theory essays I know you hate. The policeman with dependency issues *and* girlfriend trouble. Come on, cliché city," I said.

"Everything isn't always about you," she said, kissed me on the cheek, took one of my slices of toast, and went back upstairs.

"At least show me how to work the kettle!" I shouted after her. I took my hand off the receiver. "It looks like I'll be there in ten minutes, Lawson," I said.

I dressed in jeans, black polo neck, black leather jacket, then got my gun and went outside to the BMW. I checked underneath it for mercury tilt switch bombs, didn't find any. I was about to get in the car when I remembered that I needed to get the riot gear spray-cleaned at the station, to get the whiff off it. I went back inside, got my riot gear, put it in the backseat of the car, locked it, and returned a final time.

"I'm leaving," I shouted upstairs.

"Look after yourself, Sean," she said.

"That's it?"

"*C'est tout.*"

I closed the front door, checked under the Beemer, got inside, and drove down Coronation Road and along Taylor's Avenue.

"Beth! Jesus! How can you do this to me? What went wrong?" I said to the good-luck Snoopy she had stuck on the dashboard. Snoopy kept his own counsel and I was still nonplussed when I parked in front of the Coast Road, Carrickfergus's only hotel.

Lawson was standing outside, waiting for me.

"I'm very sorry about this, sir, only the chief inspector told me to call you," he said, as soon as I got out of the car.

"The chief inspector is here?" I asked, surprised. He occasionally showed up when there was a murder. But a theft case?

"Yes, sir. And Chief Superintendent McBain and you just missed Superintendent Strong."

"Oh shit. What the hell's going on, Lawson?"

"Perhaps you should come inside, sir."

"All right."

We went inside the rather smart seaside hotel that would have been thriving but for the fact that this was bloody Carrick and bloody Carrick during the bloody Troubles.

"I noticed the riot gear in the backseat of your car, sir," Lawson said.

"Yes?"

"I heard you were on crowd duty at the Ali event yesterday?"

I gave him a hard look. Was he taking the piss? His eyes were steady and there was no trace of a grin.

Probably wasn't trying to mess with me. He was a good lad, Lawson. Handsome if you liked cadaverous and pale (and if you did, I could sell you a morgue pass for a tenner). He was tall and blue-eyed, with dyed blond hair that he had gelled into a series of gravity-defying peaks. Sergeant McCrabban and myself had ordered the gel out ages ago, but he had been surreptitiously sneaking it back in over the last couple of months. Today he was wearing a sober, well-tailored, dark-blue suit with brown oxfords and a dark-grey raincoat. He was observant, too. *The riot gear. Damn it. I should have put it in the boot.* As a detective, I considered myself above such things as crowd control, and I encouraged the other detectives in Carrickfergus CID to think likewise: "*esprit d'corps, boys, we're a special breed, selected not for our muscle, but for our nous*." Very fine talk, and yet I had begged Superintendent Strong for the Ali detail, and now Lawson had caught me red-handed.

"Yes, I was up at the Ali event. It was a favor for Strong, he wanted an experienced hand."

"Of course, sir," Lawson said, serenely.

Inside the hotel we were met by an exhausted-looking Chief Inspector McArthur and a rosy-cheeked, ginger-haired concierge.

The chief inspector shook my hand. He was a trim, blue-eyed, dark-haired Scot, younger than me, something of a highflier, but still very much in the adjustment phase to war-torn Ulster.

"Thank God they found you, Duffy. It's action stations here," McArthur said.

"What's happening, sir?"

"Someone lifted a wallet from one of the guest rooms."

I looked at Lawson. Had everyone in the world gone completely mad?

"A wallet, sir?"

"It must have been one of the cleaning staff or something," McArthur muttered. "Chief Superintendent McBain is upstairs with them now, trying to calm things down. It's a very volatile situation."

"I don't think I'm really getting this, sir. We're talking about an ordinary wallet here, are we? Not a magical wallet that dispenses wishes?"

"It was nicked from Mr. Laakso's room! It's the dignitaries, Duffy," McArthur said, lowering his voice to a panicky stage whisper.

"The dignitaries?"

"The Finns."

"From the factory visit?"

"Yes! That's why me and you and the chief super are all here at this unholy hour! What did you think was going on?"

"I don't know. Some kind of Masonic thing?"

"Masonic—This is a serious matter, Duffy."

"I thought it was Swedes, sir. Volvo, Saab, that kind of thing," I said.

"No. Not Swedes. Finns, Duffy. Phones, not cars."

"Why are these VIPs staying in Carrickfergus, not Belfast?"

"They're going out to the old Courtaulds plant. I suppose it's convenient," McArthur explained.

Carrickfergus had an embarrassment of abandoned factories that had been set up in the optimistic sixties, closed in the pessimistic seventies, and were on the verge of ruin now that we were in the apocalyptic mideighties.

The concierge interposed himself between us, looking miffed. "It's not about convenience, gentlemen. This is one of the best hotels in Northern Ireland. We had the England football team here two summers ago, so we did," he insisted in a broad, camp West Belfast accent so grating that it could be banned under several of the Geneva Protocols. "And may I just add, gents, that the possibility of a wallet being stolen from one of the hotel rooms by one of my staff is very, very unlikely indeed, so it is."

"Why is that?" I asked him.

"We're a small establishment, sir. At this time of the morning, it's just myself and the night porter. Just us. The cleaning and breakfast staff have only just arrived now. And *I* didn't take the wallet, and Joe has been at the front door the whole night."

"What's *your* name?" I asked him.

"It's Kevin, Inspector. Kevin Donnolly. Kev, if you want."

"OK, Kevin, and you're the concierge, are you?"

"I'm the manager!"

"Are you quite sure that there are no other employees on the premises at this time of the night? What if someone's hungry or something?"

"We do it all. There's only Joe and myself until the breakfast staff come in."

"Hmmm. How many rooms are there here in the hotel?"

"Nine on the first floor and six on the floor above. Mr. Laakso's room was on the first floor. The Castle View Suite."

"Who else has the master key to the rooms?"

"It's not keys in the suites. We've made those very classy, so we have. All the suite rooms have been converted to keycards and the only person with the override card to all the suite rooms is myself."

"Was Mr. Laakso sleeping alone?"

"Yes."

"Could he possibly have had a guest? A young lady, perhaps?"

"Mr. Laakso is an, uhm, elderly gentleman. He did not sign in a guest."

"And no one was sent up to his room?"

"Definitely not! That sort of thing doesn't happen in this establishment."

"Does Mr. Laakso's room connect with any other rooms?"

"Oh yes, there are two rooms on either side of him, both occupied by members of his staff."

"So if the wallet wasn't taken by the hotel staff, it's either been mislaid or it's been taken by another member of the delegation?" I suggested.

"Almost certainly mislaid, Inspector. Happens all the time. Once or twice a week. Of course not everybody's so quick to yell 'thief!' and call out half the police force at ungodly hours of the day and night," Kevin said.

We could see Chief Superintendent John Edward "Ed" McBain coming down the stairs now. He was a twitchy, lanky, stork-like man with a defiant early-seventies-style comb-over. He was the operational commander over all the police stations in East Antrim and one of the few brass hats that I got on quite well with. I always let him beat me at snooker at the police club, and once Sergeant McCrabban and I had actually found his missing pooch before it either got itself run over, or, as his wife, Jo, had predicted, "fell into the clutches of those Satan worshippers you read about in *The News of the World*." Ever since then, big Ed McBain had been eternally grateful to Carrick CID.

He shook my hand in a sweaty, uncharacteristically hesitant grip. He was pale and looked deeply irritated.

"Good to see you, Duffy," he said.

"You too, sir."

"Heard you met Muhammad Ali, yesterday."

"Word gets around doesn't it, sir?"

"Overrated. All mouth. A fighter not a boxer."

"If you say so, sir."

"I *do* say so, Duffy."

He stared at me, Lawson, Kevin, and the chief inspector for a moment.

I very deliberately examined my watch. "Maybe I should go up and inspect the crime scene, sir?"

"Good idea." He pointed upstairs and lowered his voice to a whisper. "They want us to pull out all the stops. Is that clear?"

"Yes, sir."

"Finns here to save the country's bacon. You wouldn't have thought we won the war, eh?"

"Weren't they, uhm, on our side, sir?" I asked.

"No they weren't! Not at first, anyway. Come on, let's go up."

"It's a crime scene, sir," I said to McBain, nodding my head toward the chief inspector.

McBain got the drift. He put his hand on McArthur's shoulder. "You'll have to wait down here, Pete. This is CID business," he said.

McArthur looked upset. "Oh. Is it? Oh.... All right. I'll just take a seat then, shall I?"

"That would be best," McBain said.

I wasn't *just* trying to fuck with the chief inspector . . . upstairs *was* a de facto crime scene and we didn't need any well-meaning amateurs poking around in it.

McBain led Lawson and myself up the wide, elegant staircase, past prints, watercolors and various framed cartographic representations of Carrickfergus from the previous eight centuries.

"No technical ability, Duffy. That's his problem."

"The chief inspector, sir?"

"Ali. A brawler. A puncher. A big puncher."

"What about his feet, sir? Surely—"

"His feet! His feet, you say? Well, yes. . . . His feet. Good point, Duffy. Very good point. He could dance, couldn't he?"

"Yes, sir."

"Must have been quite something to see him in the flesh. And we got him in and out alive, which is more than you can say for the Memphis Police Department with Martin Luther King."

"Er, what?"

"OK, here we are, Duffy. Now, when you're with the Finns I want no lip from you, OK? What's past is past."

"What do you mean?"

"The wife's father was on the Murmansk convoys. You just have to bite your tongue, don't you? Do the full Basil Fawlty, OK?"

"The Basil—"

"Don't mention the war."

"Sir, I wouldn't dream of—"

"Course you wouldn't, you're a professional. Now, you, what's your name, son?"

"Lawson."

"You likewise. I want the pair of you to appear to take this very seriously indeed. Tell them we'll be turning over every stone, eh?"

We both nodded.

At the top of the stairs we were met by four men and a woman.

The woman was a tiny, bird-like thing, very pretty. She said that she was Miss Jones and explained that she was a liaison official from the Foreign Office. She introduced us to the delegation. A small, stooped, sixty-year-old bald man in black pajamas was Mr. Laakso. He was standing next to a tall, trim, hollow-cheeked, grey-faced, blue-eyed man with dyed black hair, also about sixty, or perhaps a little older. This apparently was Mr. "Elk." The final two men appeared to be identical twins: slim, blond-haired youths of about nineteen or twenty. One of them was wearing a pink kimono-style silk robe that would have gotten him stoned to death as a "poof" if he'd stepped outside in it.

I shook both the older men's hands.

"Mr. Laakso, nice to meet you, Mr., uhm, Elk was it?"

"Ek," the grey-faced man corrected me, shaking my hand like he wanted to break it.

"Ek," I said.

"It means 'oak' in Swedish," he said.

"Swedish? Now I'm confused, I thought you were all Finns," I said, cheerfully.

"We are," Ek said, intensely annoyed by what clearly was some kind of faux pas.

He was a geezer, but he had shaken my hand with the grip of an ex-serviceman—a shit-kicking drill sergeant perhaps.

"And may I present Nicolas and Stefan Lennätin?" Miss Jones said. Close up, the boys were pale, willowy, handsome, with dark-brown rather unintelligent eyes.

"What can you tell me about the particulars of the incident?" I asked Mr. Laakso.

"Mr. Laakso left his wallet by his bathroom sink last night before he went to bed. This morning it was gone," Ek said, before Laakso could open his gob.

"What time did he go to bed?" I asked.

"Mr. Laakso went to bed at some time after eleven p.m. and woke this morning just after five, alerting me," Ek replied for his boss.

"Make a note of that, Lawson," I said.

Lawson flipped open his notebook and wrote this information down.

"I'd like to see the crime scene, if I may," I said to Mr. Laakso.

"I would expect so," Ek said, curtly.

Lawson and I followed Ek past half a dozen guests who had come out of their rooms to see what all the commotion was. We entered Mr. Laakso's bedroom, a large, tastefully decorated suite with a rather impressive view of Carrickfergus Castle to the south and County Down and the Galloway coast of Scotland to the northeast. We were trailed into the room by a worried-looking chief super and the rest of the delegation.

Nicolas and Stefan had begun to giggle and were whispering confidences to one another. I nudged Lawson so that he would take a note of that, too.

Ek led us into the large bathroom, which was luxurious by Northern Ireland standards: marble bath, marble sink, shower, bidet, Italian-tiled floor and walls.

"This is where the wallet went missing," Ek said. "Now, if you will excuse me, I have more pressing concerns to attend to."

"Of course. Observations, Lawson?" I asked my junior colleague.

"Water spill on the floor. Soap suds on the mirror. It doesn't look like the cleaning lady's been through, not that they were supposed to be in this early, anyway."

"What about the sink? What do you notice about that?"

Lawson peered into the sink.

"Uhm, there are shaving hairs in the sink. No one has cleaned this sink since yesterday."

The chief super peered into the sink and nodded. "I'll bet you this sink was designed by a woman or a man with a beard. Look how flat the bottom is. You'd be hard-pressed to wash your stubble away after shaving. And, uhm, yes, as you say, it hasn't been cleaned today," he muttered.

I turned to Mr. Laakso. "Where exactly did you leave the wallet?"

He pointed to a little shelf near to the toothbrush holder. Definitely no wallet.

"And when did you last see the wallet?" I asked.

"Last night before I went to bed," Mr. Laakso said in perfectly serviceable English.

"And you didn't hear any intruders?"

"I heard nothing."

"And the door to your room was locked?"

"It was locked," Mr. Laakso agreed.

"And the adjoining rooms?" I asked.

"Locked, I believe."

"Who was staying in these rooms?"

"Nicolas and Stefan."

Was that another smirk on Nicolas's face? He was staring at his twin brother, both of them on the verge of giggles. I walked to the first adjoining door. It was unlocked. I walked across the room and tried the second adjoining door. It also was unlocked.

"I'd like permission to search these rooms, if I may?" I said to Mr. Laakso.

He looked at Nicolas and Stefan. A rapid conversation in Finnish followed between the three men. When it concluded, Mr. Laakso said something to Miss Jones, who scowled at me. "Is there a problem?" I asked her.

"Mr. Laakso resents greatly the implication that any of the dele-

THE THEFT THAT WASN'T

gation are somehow connected with the theft of Mr. Laakso's wallet. Mr. Laakso rejects this idea as preposterous. Mr. Laakso wishes you to restrict your investigation to his room, which the thief undoubtedly entered using a pass card," she said.

"Can you tell me whom the rooms belong to?" I asked.

"The one over there is my room, that one is Nicolas's room," Stefan explained.

I gave him a long look. The smirk was widening on Nicolas's face. I had had just about enough of this nonsense.

"Perhaps, then, if you could all leave and give us space to search Mr. Laakso's rooms thoroughly?" I suggested.

"*Ulos!*" Laakso said. When they were gone, I looked under the bed and in the drawers and in the cupboard. When this superficial examination failed to undercover anything, Lawson and I divided the room up between us and did a thorough shakedown, but that also failed to turn up the wallet. "That settles it, then," I said.

"Settles what?"

"It was Nicolas."

"Why? Some kind of practical joke?"

"Who the fuck knows? Come on, let's get out of here," I said. "There's been enough wasting of police time for one morning."

We went back outside the room where Mr. Laakso was waiting with the two boys, Miss Jones, and the chief super. Ek had buggered off, but half the landing was out trying to see what was going on. *This would be the time to sneak into a room and steal somebody's wallet,* I thought. Hovering nearby was an attractive young woman ominously holding a notebook. She had a black bob, rosy cheeks, and lovely green eyes; even though she was wearing a scruffy black T-shirt and unflattering flannel pajama bottoms, you could tell right away that she was a stylish foreigner, not a frumpy Mick.

"Reporter at six o'clock," I muttered to Lawson.

"Where . . . oh yes."

"Right gentlemen, Miss Jones, I think that concludes the preliminary inquiry. I am going to leave you in the capable hands of Constable

Lawson here, who will take statements while I coordinate the rest of this case from the station. You can return to your rooms after the statements have been made, and hopefully we'll get this resolved as soon as possible."

The Finns seemed happy enough with that.

"Of course I could call a forensic team down from Belfast and we could take fingerprints of the area around your sink, Mr. Laakso. The thief might have inadvertently left a print," I said, looking at Nicolas.

Mr. Laakso stole a nervous glance at Stefan and Nicolas. Now he, too, understood what had happened with the wallet. He winced. Calling the police had clearly been a mistake. The dynamic was obvious in the little group. Laakso was the head of the delegation, but Stefan and Nicolas were the sons or grandsons of the powers that be back in Finland and were thus pretty much unassailable. I stifled a yawn. I had seen shit like this before a million times. None of it was remotely interesting.

"I do not think that will be necessary. I have full faith in your abilities," Mr. Laakso said.

Of course you do. I nodded to Chief Superintendent McBain. "I'll take my leave, sir," I said.

"Very good," McBain said.

The woman in the black T-shirt stopped me at the top of the stairs.

"I heard all the commotion. What's going on?" she asked, in a lovely Home Counties accent reminiscent of Anna Ford off the TV news.

"Are you a reporter?" I asked.

"How can you tell?" she wondered.

"The notebook and the pencil are a bit of a giveaway."

"Lily Bigelow, the *Financial Times*," she said, offering me her hand. I shook it. "What's a nice girl from . . ." I began.

"Woking."

"Woking, doing in a place like this?"

"I'm covering the Finnish trade mission to Northern Ireland. I suppose for the week I'm the *FT*'s Northern Ireland correspondent."

"I see."

"So what happened?" she asked, gesturing back down the corridor.

"Mr. Laakso misplaced his wallet. It'll show up," I said.

She bit her pencil. "So you're saying that it's not a story."

"Either that or I'm part of a sinister cover-up."

She folded up her notebook and put her pencil in her pajama pant pocket, which is what I wanted. This was a non-story and Carrick CID didn't need to get a mention in any of the English papers.

"Unlucky you, eh? Editor comes over and says, 'Lily we've got a foreign assignment for you,' and you're thinking Hong Kong, New York, Paris, and you end up in bloody Belfast," I said.

"I actually asked for this job. But I'm used to privation. You know what happened to Woking, don't you?" she said with a tragic look on her face.

"No," I said.

"Totally wiped out by the Martians in the *War of the Worlds.*"

I grinned. Pretty *and* funny. I wouldn't forget Beth in a hurry, but a drink or two with an attractive English journo wouldn't hurt.

"And they've rebuilt it since then, have they?" I asked.

"Partially rebuilt."

"Got rid of all that red weed?"

"They had to pull it all up, the kids were smoking it."

"What are you doing later?" I asked, chancing my arm.

"Visiting the Courtaulds factory with the delegation."

"I've been out there. Lovely place. Watch out for the septuagenarian security guard with the shotgun and the itchy trigger finger."

"Sounds great."

"What are you doing *after* the factory visit?"

"Carrickfergus Castle."

"That's exciting, too. And after the castle?"

"Typing."

"And after the typing?"

She shrugged. I gave her one of my cards, crossed out the work phone and wrote my home phone number. "If you want to go for a drink or something?"

She smiled. "Kind of unlikely, I'm on a story."

"But if the story doesn't pan out, or you get it done?"

"Maybe."

I'll take a maybe, I thought, and as I was rummaging in my brain for something funny or charming to say as a parting sally, Ed McBain stuck his big face in.

"Ah, I take it you're the reporter? Among other duties I'm the senior press liaison officer here, Chief Superintendent McBain," he said.

I left them to it and went downstairs feeling depressed. Chief Inspector McArthur was still there sitting glumly on the leather sofa by Reception.

"Did you find the wallet, Duffy?" he asked.

"Not yet, sir," I said. "Lawson's taking statements."

I called Kevin over.

"Does anyone on your staff have a theft conviction?" I asked him.

"No! I've read all the CVs myself. Nothing like that. Unemployment's so high in Carrick, we have our pick of the staff."

"That's what I thought."

The chief inspector looked at me anxiously. "Do you think you'll find the wallet, Duffy? The chief super is quite worried about the impression we're giving off here."

I concealed another yawn. "The arc of the universe is long, sir, but it bends toward justice."

"Does it, really Duffy?"

"So they say, sir."

"*They* haven't been to Northern Ireland though, have they?"

"No, sir. Well, I must be off."

"Good-bye, Duffy."

"Good-bye, sir."

I went outside. The sun was well up over the blue line of Scotland. I walked to the Beemer and looked underneath it for bombs. There weren't any, so I unlocked the driver's side door. I was about to get inside when I saw another BMW pull in behind me. New one. Black. Personalized plate: "McIlroy1."

Out of the Beemer stepped Tony McIlroy, late of the RUC and now of Scotland Yard. Tony was my age, but he didn't look it. He was tanned and fit and his clothes hung well on him even at this ungodly hour. His hair was wavy and black without a trace of grey, and his eyes were clear and bright as always. He was wearing a sharp tailored midnight-blue suit, fancy brogues, and a really expensive-looking shirt. His watch was gold. Life across the water clearly agreed with him. He'd been a chief inspector in the RUC Special Branch, but Northern Ireland hadn't been a big enough stage for his talents and he'd moved over the water to join the Old Bill. We'd met up and had a drink in London during the Lizzie Fitzpatrick case, just before my rendezvous with destiny and a couple of kilos of Semtex in Brighton. . . . Always ambitious was Tony, but a real character, somebody who left an impression, not like all the other boring-as-shit peelers around here.

"Well, if it isn't Sean Duffy!" he said, grinning.

"What in the name of God are you doing here?" I asked, genuinely pleased to see him.

"I could say the say the same, mate," he said, shaking my hand.

"Well, this *is* my manor," I said.

"Still?" he asked, surprised.

"Yeah," I replied defensively.

"Jesus, Sean, I thought you'd be a chief super in Belfast by now," he said.

"Nope, still a humble detective inspector. Tip of the spear. I like it," I said, trying to sound like I believed it.

He nodded dubiously. "Come on, Sean. . . . You can tell me," he said, and gave me a little dig on the shoulder.

I sighed. "It's been a tough few years, mate. Problems with the boys upstairs, you know how it is."

He shook his head, took a silver cigarette case out of his jacket, and offered me a ciggie.

"Nope. Trying to cut down," I said.

"Let me guess. You're going out with a nurse?"

"Just trying to cut down. Bad for you. Yul Brynner, you know?"

"Sad," he agreed, lighting up. "So you're still a detective inspector. Well, well, well. And you were the best of us. This bloody country. They don't know talent when they see it. You should be running the CID, for heaven's sake."

"What about you, mate? Still in the Met? I suppose you *are* a chief super . . ."

"You didn't hear?"

"Hear what?"

Tony shook his head. "I resigned. I'm off the force completely. I'm running a private security firm now. Back over here for now. Private security is where the money is. Lot of contracts with American firms, the government, that kind of thing," he said.

"Resigned from the Met? Jesus, I didn't hear that."

"Six months now."

"And you're back living over here? What about Liddy? I thought she hated it over here."

"Liddy and I went splitsville," he said, ruefully.

"Bloody hell. I'm shocked. You always seemed to get on so well," I said, and I *was* surprised, for although Tony was a notorious ladies' man, Liddy came from money and her father was a well-connected Tory MP who could have advanced Tony's career in the Met all the way up to commander, or even higher. Obviously, the sweet, long-suffering Liddy had finally had enough of his shenanigans, or possibly caught him more or less in flagrante. The rest wasn't difficult to compute: bitter divorce/angry father-in-law/gloomy portents about Tony's future with the Yard/no possibility of a transfer back to the jilted RUC/ergo the private sector . . .

Now it was Tony's turn to sigh. "Liddy? Yeah, sometimes people just grow apart don't they, mate?"

"Private security, eh? Is there money in that?" I asked, looking at the new Beemer.

"Like you wouldn't believe, son. That's why I'm here this morning. Apparently one of my clients has been robbed. This place was supposed to be safe."

"Mr. Laakso? I've just been dealing with that."

"My firm's in charge of security for the whole delegation. Here, take a look at this," he said, handing me a card.

McIlroy Security Services
The #1 Northern Irish Private Security Firm
"We Never Sleep."
Founder Anthony McIlroy, ex Det. Chief Inspector, Scotland Yard
Tel. Belfast 336 456

"Nice," I said, giving him the card back.

He shook his head. "Keep it, we're always looking for people, Sean. Someone like you? We'd jump at the chance to have you. What are you earning now?"

It was a vulgar question and he saw the disgusted look on my face.

"No, don't tell me, I can guess. We could pay you twenty percent more, plus bonuses."

"How many people do you have working for you?" I asked, pocketing the card. Anthony might be a good man to know if the RUC's bullshit finally forced me to resign. Again.

"We're new, Sean. Just a start-up. Half a dozen, all told. But we're going to double in size by the end of spring. Double again by the end of the year. And we're hoping to open a Derry office in July. Security is the one growth industry in these troubled times. You can't make an omelet without shoving some eggs in the back of a van and smacking them around, eh?"

"I like the Pinkerton quote on the card."

Tony grinned. "Bit cheeky, eh?"

"I like the car even more."

"Oh yeah. She's a beaut. The 535i. '87 model. 3.4 liter, 6-cylinder engine."

"What's your top speed?"

"I've had her up to 125."

"I've done a ton and fifteen in mine and I thought I was flying."

"I took her apart and put her back together. Engineering degree comes in a bit more handy than your ... what was the wanky thing you studied, philosophy?"

"Psychology."

Tony looked at his watch. "Well, I suppose I'd better get upstairs and find this wallet."

"Already cracked that case, mate. My *psychology* training. Check in Nicolas Lennätin's room. Some sort of joke, it seems."

"Oh really? Great."

"Hey, let's go for a drink later, catch up, eh?"

He sucked his teeth. "I can't this week. Security for the delegation and then I'm flying to London."

"Another job?"

"Sort of. Signing the papers on the old D-I-V-O-R-C-E. Glad to get it behind me at last. Shit, you've no idea, Sean. Liddy's da's lawyers. ... But I'll call you, OK?" he said.

"Yeah, mate," I agreed and we warmly shook hands again.

He waved and ran inside the hotel.

Poor bastard. Nice to see Tony after all these years, but I didn't envy him his life. At least a real cop occasionally got to push around the great and the good, but a private dick had to be polite to every arsehole in the room. Who'd want that? I'd stand him a round, though, Tony was an old friend and those were hard to come by.

I drove back to Coronation Road and went inside the disturbingly empty house.

No Beth.

I went upstairs. Her stuff was gone from the wardrobes and there was a note on the bed. I unfolded it.

This is my number: Belfast 347 350. Please don't call. I'm not coming back. If anyone rings up looking for me, please pass on the number and my new address: 13 Cairo Street, Belfast. These last few months have been lovely, Sean, and you're a nice man and I'm sure you'll find someone your own age to settle down with. All my love, Beth.

As these things go, it wasn't a terrible note. A terrible note was "Fuck You, Sean Duffy" attached to a half brick that gets thrown through your BMW windscreen.

The "someone your age" crack hurt, though. It was a ten-year gap, which was pretty much insurmountable, except if you were those love-birds Charles and Diana or Van Morrison and the reigning Miss Ireland, Olivia Tracey. But I was no Van Morrison, nor a prince of Wales.

I avoided pouring whisky into my coffee, but I did go out to the shed and have a puff or two. At nine o'clock the phone rang.

"Hello?"

"Sir, it's me."

"What is it, Lawson?"

"The cleaners found the wallet, sir. Nothing was missing."

"Where was it?"

"It was under the bed in Mr. Laakso's room."

"We looked under the bed, didn't we, Lawson?"

"Yes, sir."

"There was no wallet under the bed, Lawson, was there?"

"No, sir."

"All right. Case closed. Type up the report and give it to the chief inspector."

"Mention your suspicions of young Mr. Lennätin in the report?"

"No, I don't think so. That would be a potential charge of wasting police time and we want this to go away, don't we?"

"Yes, sir. What about your friend, sir?"

"What friend?"

"Mr. McIlroy, sir."

"He's at the station, is he?"

"Yes, sir. What should I tell him, sir?"

"Oh, you can tell him everything. He's a good copper. Or was, anyway. Don't let him recruit you, Lawson, by the way. You're young, you've got your whole career ahead of you. You're not washed up like me and him."

"No, sir."

"And remember this is my day off, Lawson. If anything else happens, call Sergeant McCrabban."

"He told me not to call him. He said it was lambing season."

"It's always bloody lambing season with that one. Call him. He's duty officer."

"Yes, sir."

"I mean you can handle it all, yes?"

"Yes, sir. . . . Except you know, with the chief super hanging around . . ."

A long silence down the phone.

"Am I really going to have to come in on my off day?"

"No, sir, I. . . . But, well, he makes everyone nervous."

"All right, all right, let me have a long nap and a shower and I'll come in after lunch, OK?"

"OK, sir."

I hung up. An extra edition of the *Belfast Telegraph* flopped through the letterbox. On page 2 there was a picture of me escorting Muhammad Ali onto his bus. I called up the *Tele* photo editor and ordered an 8 × 10. I'd frame it and put it up in the kitchen, and if anyone ever asked me what I'd done with my life I'd say, "Come here and take a look at this, mate, look, it's me and the Champ."

And with that happy thought I broke out the Bowmore, smoothest of the Islays, got a blanket, and settled down on the sofa in front of the record player as Ella Fitzgerald decanted some of that old-time religion and lulled me over into a well-earned nap.

3: LIZZIE FITZPATRICK REDUX?

I woke up around one in the afternoon and called Beth at her new number.

"Hello?"

"Hey Beth, I just wanted—"

"Didn't you read the note? I told you *not* to call me! Jesus."

"You forgot your extra-sensitive toothpaste. You know how upset that makes it."

I could hear her grinning, but she still hung up.

I rang again. "Beth, listen, I just want to see if you're OK."

"Fer fuck's sake, I'm fine. Don't call again. *Please*, Sean. You're making it hard for both of us."

Phone slam. OK, I get the message.

I showered, dressed, skipped lunch, and went into the station.

The chief super was still lurking there and everyone *was* on edge. But he was happy to see me. He shook my hand. "Good work, Duffy, your team cracked the case."

"Apparently so, sir."

I took him into my office and poured him a Glenfiddich and soda, which I knew was his tipple of choice.

"That fellow McIlroy was hanging around after you left. Do you know him?"

"I did, sir, when he worked for us."

"He said he knew you. He said he was a friend of yours."

"Yes, sir. Although I haven't seen him in a few years."

"I remember him too. Highflier. He left us, went across the water to join the Met, didn't he?"

"Indeed."

"Didn't work out though, did it? Divorce and a scandal is what I've heard. Now he's back here and set up business for himself, eh? As if we don't have enough problems without private bloody detectives and private bloody security firms. I don't approve of that sort, Duffy. I don't want him poaching my tax-payer-trained officers."

"No, sir. I already told young Lawson that we—"

"The VIPs will be gone tomorrow and once they are gone, we'll give Tony McIlroy and the likes of Tony McIlroy short shrift. You hear me, Duffy? Friend or no friend."

"If you say, so, sir."

"I do say so, Duffy."

He finished the Glenfiddich and got to his feet.

"Well, everything seems to be in hand here. I'm having a coffee with that reporter—I'll tell her we've cracked the case and then I'll head back to the old homestead in Glenoe, Duffy. I expect I'll run into you at the police club."

"Yes, sir. At some point, sir."

"See you, Duffy."

"I'll see you soon, sir," I said as he left my office, not knowing, of course, that I would never see the poor bastard again.

It was a dreary day at the station. Nothing was on the board and Lawson and I caught up with the paperwork until it was quitting time.

Kenny Dalziel wanted to see me, so I called him on the internal line.

"Sergeant Dalziel."

"How do you keep an idiot in suspense?" I asked, and hung up.

Childish, I know. The temperature dropped and it began to sleet as I drove back to the sad, cold, empty house on Coronation Road.

I lit the paraffin heater and put on the telly.

Maybe this *was* for the best. Beth with someone of her own age. Me with someone my own age. Try to mind-flip it. An opportunity to grow for both of us. Everybody wins. I remembered an old and typically dark Harland and Wolff joke: "Life is all about perspective. The sinking of the *Titanic* was a frigging miracle to the lobsters in the ship's kitchens."

The mind flip didn't work and I found myself lurking around the telephone, waiting for the cute reporter, Lily, to call; but, unsurprisingly, she didn't.

Beans on toast. The inane void that was the BBC 1 TV schedule. *A Question of Sport*. Beans on toast and *A Question of Sport*—hardly the examined life.

A Valium and a vodka gimlet. Paraffin fumes. Death-sleep and then: *Briiiinnngggg*.

Another early-morning call. Burrow down the stairs, wrapped in my duvet. Snow falling outside again today.

I picked up the phone, dropped it, picked it up again. "Yes?" I said trying to convey in that one syllable as much world-weariness as I possibly could.

"Sir?"

"I don't believe it! It can't possibly be you again, Lawson. Not two days in a bloody row."

"Sir, there's been a, well, I suppose it's a suicide, or an accident, or possibly a murder, hard to say at this stage. . . . Suicide, if you had to pin me down."

"I'm duty detective today, am I? I know I definitely was *not* duty detective yesterday."

"No, sir, I'm very sorry. It is you. I wouldn't have called you, otherwise."

"You know it's snowing outside?"

"I see that, sir."

"Whereabouts is the crime scene?"

"Carrickfergus Castle, sir."

"Well, I won't have any trouble finding it. Forensics on their way?"

"Already here, sir."

"Are they indeed? What time is it, Lawson?"

"I waited until seven before I called you, sir."

"Thank you for your compassion. Who found the body?"

"The caretaker found the body just after six and called us."

"What caretaker?"

"The castle caretaker."

"Didn't know there was a castle caretaker."

"There is. He has a cottage inside the castle. Mr. Underhill. He lives there."

"And what was he doing up at six in the morning?"

"He does a full inspection of the castle first thing before opening the doors at seven."

"The body was found *inside* the castle?"

"Yes, sir."

"Wait a second, I'm carrying you into the kitchen."

I put two slices of bread in the toaster and two scoops of Nescafé in my Liverpool FC mug. I faced down the sinister-looking kettle and attacked its various buttons.

"The gender of the victim?"

"A woman, sir."

"Do you have a cause of death, or do the Forensics boys need more time?"

"I don't want to step on anyone's toes, but the cause of death seems pretty obvious, sir."

The toaster popped and I lifted out a slice of toast.

"Don't keep me in suspense, Lawson."

"Blunt force trauma. It looks like she jumped off the roof of the castle keep into the courtyard below."

"How big a drop is that?"

"Ooh, uhm, a hundred feet?"

"That'll kill you."

"Yes, sir."

"The body was found, exactly where?"

"In the central courtyard just in front of the keep itself. Do you know where that is, sir?"

I'd been inside Carrickfergus Castle briefly once, but that once was enough to get the gist of the place. "Yeah, I know where that is. How long has she been lying there?"

"That's a rather interesting question, sir. The caretaker gets everyone out at five to six and locks the front gate. Then he does a full check of the castle to make sure all the visitors are out and accounted for. Then he does another quick check of the building at ten, before he goes to bed."

"And she wasn't lying there in the courtyard at ten?"

"No."

"He inspects the entire castle before he locks the doors at six?"

"The time line is important, sir. He gets all the visitors out, inspecting the castle for stragglers and then he locks the front gate."

"And the front gate is locked from when until when?"

"The front door is locked from six p.m. until seven a.m."

"What kind of a door?"

"Thick, heavy, medieval."

"Is there any other way in?"

"Over the external walls, but . . ."

"But what?"

"They're sixty feet high . . . and six feet thick."

"I see."

"And the entire castle is illuminated by spotlights all night, so anyone putting up a sixty-foot ladder . . ."

"Secret tunnels, secret doors?"

"No secret tunnels, no secret doors. The castle is built on the bedrock. No one's tunneling through that. I've checked with the caretaker about that, anyway, the only way in is through the front door, which was locked."

I buttered my toast and when the kettle decided to boil of its own accord I poured my coffee. My head was beginning to perk up now, and I was visualizing the situation clearly in my mind's eye.

"He calls time, he does an inspection to check that all the visitors have gone and locks the gate. And then he does another lookeyloo before he goes to bed and everything seems fine. Yet when he wakes up this morning, a little over an hour ago, he finds a woman's body in the central courtyard, in front of the keep, with her skull smashed in."

"Yes, sir."

"How does *he* think she got there?"

"He has no idea, sir."

"He just found her sprawled there in the castle courtyard?"

"Yes, sir."

"Is he lying?"

"That would certainly be one explanation."

"And what would the others be?"

"I haven't thought of any others yet."

I finished the toast and took another swig of coffee.

I had a sudden and rather unpleasant flashback to the summer of 1984 and the Lizzie Fitzpatrick case. Similar setup happening to the same CID detective *twice*?

Never in a million years. This kind of lightning did not strike twice.

"Can you think of any other explanation, sir?"

"Uhm, off the top of my head . . . a stowaway clinging to the undercarriage of a plane falls out when it's coming in to land at Belfast?"

"I suppose that's not impossible, sir."

"All right, I'll admit that you've piqued my interest, Lawson. I'll be over in fifteen minutes."

I hung up.

I showered, shaved, put on a suit and tie, and looked out my heavy wool coat. I checked under the Beemer for bombs. There were no bombs, but my battery was dead because I'd left the lights on. I phoned the Automobile Association and they said they'd send someone out. I called Carrick Cabs, and the taxi arrived a couple of minutes later.

The driver had on Radio 1, which was giving us Kylie Minogue's "I Should Be So Lucky." Within a few seconds, Miss Minogue's sunny Antipodean vocals and the chirpy lyrics had brought out my dark, misanthropic side. By the song's second verse I was already longing for an IRA ambush, and by the second chorus I was dreaming of a rogue comet strike that would reset the entire evolutionary clock *à la* the KT boundary extinction event.

Carrickfergus Castle was in front of us now, with the lough on the left-hand side and the lights of Belfast behind. There were a couple of dirty cargo boats out on the water, a big Soviet tanker, and two army Gazelle helicopters hovering over West Belfast.

Funny that in my nearly six years in Carrickfergus I'd only been in the castle that one time for fifteen minutes and that had been on my first day here to satisfy my curiosity. I'd never really thought about it since. It was always just something that was there. A grey-black castle that had been the center of Anglo-Norman power in Ulster for nearly seven hundred years, until the rise of Belfast in the nineteenth century.

I paid the cabbie, and Lawson met me at the car park entrance with one of the trainee detective constables they were always sending to us because Carrick was a relatively safe posting for a trainee and they were unlikely to get killed in the first few weeks on the job —something which was always bad for morale.

The trainees were usually rubbish, and I was glad to see the back of them when they rotated them out after a few weeks. Lawson, however, was good. He had passed for sergeant, and if there hadn't been a glut of RUC detective sergeants, he would have been promoted long ago. Across the water he'd probably be a detective inspector already, although perhaps his incorruptibility would have held him back.

He handed me a hot beverage in an insulated paper cup.

"Thanks. What's this?" I asked.

"Coffee, sir."

"You made it?"

He shook his head. "The forensic team brought flasks of tea and coffee down from Belfast with them. And doughnuts and buns and Danish pastries."

"That's very well organized and together of them."

"They're a very well organized and together bunch, sir."

"Are they? Just because they bring baked goods doesn't necessarily mean they know what they're doing. Mr. Kipling makes mistakes, doesn't he? Battenberg cake, for example. Nobody likes marzipan."

I looked at the skinny, spotty trainee wearing a suit jacket miles too big for him. "And you are?"

"Detective Constable Young," the trainee said, and added, "Uhm, sir."

"Have we met before?"

"Only briefly, sir."

"How long are you here for?"

"I'm here until Friday, sir."

I looked at Lawson. "What's the point of that? He won't have time to pick up anything."

"Don't know, sir."

"Do you like Battenberg cake?"

"No, sir."

"See, Lawson?"

"He's probably just agreeing with you, sir. I'll bet if you'd said you didn't like Bakewell tart he would have said he didn't like that, either."

I looked into Young's naïve, baleful, trusting face. "Do you like Bakewell tart?"

"Oh yes, sir! It's one of my favorites," he said.

"Everyone likes Bakewell tart, Lawson. Well, *Trainee* Detective Constable Young, why don't you tell me about the crime scene as we walk over there?"

"What about it, sir?"

"Your thoughts, observations?"

"The victim is in her, uhm, twenties. Or thirties. Maybe forties. Maybe fifties? Cause of death seems to be the fall from the roof of the big bit in the middle."

"Anything else occur to you, Constable Young?"

Young shook his nervy face from side to side.

"Lawson?"

"Well, sir, if your airplane theory doesn't work, I think the central puzzle here, sir, is how she got into the castle to kill herself, if indeed it was a suicide. And if it was murder you have to ask yourself how the murderer managed to escape. So I looked for a ladder leaning up against the castle walls or perhaps concealed nearby."

"And did you find one?"

"No."

"We'll have to canvass for witnesses to discover if anyone saw anything untoward," I said. "Young, there's a big cargo boat tied up in the harbor. Get on board and see if anyone saw anything last night. They usually have someone on watch all night in those boats."

"Yes, sir."

"And when you're done with that, go to every shop and flat along the seafront and ask them if *they* saw anything unusual. Write everything down in your notebook. Legibly."

"Yes, sir," he said, and stood there.

"Run along!"

Young jogged off in the direction of the harbor.

I yawned. "Most of that will be a waste of time, but it'll keep him out of our hair," I said. "Now tell me about the CCTV footage. The castle must have some and there's definitely a camera overlooking the harbor."

Because of the Troubles, CCTV cameras had become commonplace in Northern Ireland over the last few years. It was a boon for the RUC: one of our few advantages over forces from other parts of Britain.

"The castle does not have CCTV. It's a listed building and they weren't allowed to put any up. There *is* a CCTV camera on the roof of the harbormaster's office that faces the harbor and, crucially for us, the castle. I already have a constable over there looking at the footage. Nothing so far, I'm afraid."

"No one tumbling out of the sky?"

"No, sir."

"If someone did put a ladder up against the walls it'll be on the tape."

"Yes, sir. The harbormaster says that the camera covers the entire south side of the castle."

"And the north side?"

"Well the castle is roughly oval-shaped, and the entire north side juts into the sea . . ."

"So not only would you need a sixty-foot ladder, but you'd need a sixty-foot ladder on a boat."

"In the full glare of the spotlights and exposed to the traffic on the Marine Highway and anyone walking along the seafront."

"I wonder if the cameras at the police station and those at the Northern Bank would cover the north side of the castle?" I mused.

"I'll have someone check it out, sir."

"But the easiest way is still through the front gate. Pick the front gate lock and there's no need for a ladder at all. The Northern Bank camera would cover that, too, wouldn't it?"

"Yes, sir. But as, uhm, you'll see, that wouldn't really help."

"What do you mean?"

"Better to show you, sir, when we get there."

"Mysterious. What else, Lawson?"

"No sign of a sexual assault on a cursory look at the victim."

"Forensics wouldn't let you have more than a cursory look?"

"No, sir."

"So what makes you think that she wasn't sexually assaulted?"

"She was fully clothed, sir."

"Wearing?"

"Stylishly dressed. As far as I'm able to judge. Black skirt, black tights, wool sweater, pricey-looking shoes, nice green scarf, very expensive-looking leather bomber jacket, black with red piping."

"Too stylishly dressed for these parts?"

"Could be, sir."

"Tarty?"

"I don't think she's a working girl, sir. Although you can never tell."

"ID?"

"There's a handbag, but it was partially under the victim's stomach and Forensics wouldn't let me move her to get a look inside."

"She jumped holding her handbag? Why would she do that, do you think?"

"So that we could identify her? It's not uncommon for jumpers to jump with their suicide note and their ID on hand. Or maybe she threw the handbag down first and then jumped and landed on it."

"Was there a suicide note?"

"No."

I looked at Lawson thoughtfully. "You seem pretty convinced that she jumped, then."

"Yes, I think so, sir."

"On the phone you said that if you were pushed you would say that we were looking at a suicide rather than an accident. Why?"

"It must have caused her a lot of trouble to get into the castle. If she didn't go in over the walls somehow, she must have slipped off a tour yesterday and hidden when Mr. Underhill was doing his rounds. She goes to all that trouble, goes to the top of the keep, and then accidentally falls off the roof? Unlikely."

"And why not a murder?"

"Where's the killer?"

"Presumably you've searched?"

"Oh yes, sir."

"And has anyone left since you arrived?"

"Absolutely not. And I've had someone on the gate since we got here."

"And the caretaker?"

"Doesn't seem like the murdering type."

"They never do."

We had reached the massive castle gatehouse now. A WPC was standing there behind a POLICE LINE DO NOT CROSS tape. I finished the coffee and threw it in the rubbish bin near the entrance. I straightened my collar and ran a hand through my hair.

"All right," I said. "Let's go and check out this crime scene, shall we?"

4: MR. UNDERHILL

We couldn't get through the gate because a big forensic officer was dusting the lock for fingerprints. He was wearing a white boilersuit, and he was so bloody enormous that he was like a cloud with feet. But before I could hit Lawson with this *cloud-with-feet* observation, the kid had taken out a map and was shoving it in my face.

"Sir, we're here. As you can see, this is the front entrance of the castle and the only way in and out," Lawson said.

"Yes, I see," I replied and tapped the big forensic officer on the shoulder.

"DI Duffy, Carrick RUC, can we just take a look at this lock for a second?" I asked him.

The big forensic officer nodded. "Be my guest, pal, but don't touch anything."

"Any prints on the gate so far?"

"Oh, only about a million."

Lawson and I examined the lock on the front door of the castle. It was an enormous, old-fashioned cast-iron job that you couldn't pick with conventional tools as the tumblers were just too big; but like every lock in the world, with the right equipment, it *could* be opened.

"Give me a couple of days to think about it and I reckon I could make a skeleton key to turn this," I said.

Lawson looked at the lock. "But it would be easier just to steal the real key and make a clay impression of it."

"Where does the caretaker keep his key?"

"On a hook in the ticket office."

"And he can't be in there all the time, can he?"

"Nope."

"So maybe we don't need those sixty-foot ladders after all."

"Well—"

"Or maybe the caretaker's just a liar. Not necessarily a murderer. How about this: he has some girl over, is showing off the roof of the castle, there's an accident, invents this 'mystery' to cover his tracks."

"He seems pretty credible to me, sir, but obviously a full interrogation is warranted," Lawson said.

We walked through the castle gatehouse and under the spiked iron portcullis into the castle proper.

"Sir, this is what I was talking about, the portcullis," Lawson said.

I looked up. "Fascinating."

In front of us, I could see half a dozen white-boilersuited forensic officers going about their business deeper in the courtyard.

"About the portcullis, sir—"

"Who's the lead FO today?" I asked.

"A Chief Inspector Payne, sir?"

"Jesus! Frank Payne. As fine an example of nominative determinism as you'll ever get, Lawson."

Lawson smiled. "I get it," he said. *Yeah of course he got it, but I wouldn't have thrown the nominative determinism crack to Crabbie or anyone else in Carrick RUC.*

"He's one of the good guys, Lawson, but, uhm, a bit prickly. Best not poach on Payne's turf, or go asking him stupid questions. I'll interview the caretaker while we let them finish their job."

We went inside the caretaker's cottage, which lay just behind the castle's ticket booth. Cozy little one-bedroom bungalow with all mod cons.

The caretaker's name was Clarke Underhill—a sprightly enough old chap in his late sixties. Ex–Royal Navy. Scottish. Grey hair. Slight frame. Unmarried. Been in this job for a decade. I introduced myself and ran all of Lawson's questions by him again.

"When did you find the victim?"

"The first thing this morning when I went for a walk around the castle."

"What's your usual morning routine, Mr. Underhill?" I asked.

"I usually wake up at 5:30, or a wee bit later and make a cup of tea. Normally I go for a wee walk around the courtyard and the battlements. Then I open the gate, bring in the milk, lock the gate, get the ticket booth ready, and then open up properly at 7:00."

"Very early for tourists."

"It's the way we've always done it. Sometimes a coach will stop at 7:30 on its way up to the Giant's Causeway."

"And this morning? Anything strange? Any noises during the night?"

"No. My alarm clock woke me up and I listened to the World Service while I made my tea and I went for my wee walk and then I saw her."

"The victim."

"Aye. Lying there by the keep."

"Dead?"

"Aye. Deed as a doornail."

"Did you touch her?"

"Why would I do that for?"

"To see if she was still alive?"

"No. I didnae go near her. To be honest I thought that maybe . . ." His voice trailed away.

I looked at Lawson. He shrugged.

"You thought what, exactly, Mr. Underhill?" I asked.

"Well I wasnae sure if she wasn't maybe, you know . . . a wraith."

"A what?"

"A wraith."

"What's a wraith?"

"A specter. A banshee."

"You thought the dead girl might be a ghost?"

"Aye. I did."

"A ghost in a leather jacket?" Lawson asked.

"This building's been here for eight centuries and the well was a site of pilgrimage for eight afore that. I've seen and heard of some very strange things here in my time," he said, his voice assuming a kind of defensive John Laurie cadence.

"Anything like this before?"

"No, but the caretaker afore me, old Mr. Dobbin, he saw Buttoncap by the well."

"Buttoncap is?"

"A soldier. A red coat. Hanged at the Gallows Green in 1798."

"Last night no strange sightings or noises?" I asked.

"No. Nothing out of the ordinary."

"No sign this morning that someone had tried to break into your cottage?"

"Nothing like that."

"And the key was on its usual hook?"

"Yes."

"At what point this morning did you determine that the deceased was not a supernatural being?"

"Fairly soon thereafter. She didnae speak when I spoke to her and she didnae move and I soon kenned that she was deed. So I went in and called the poliss."

"Are you sure the castle was empty when you locked up at six o'clock last night?"

"Yes."

"Are you sure the castle was completely empty when you did your final inspection at ten p.m.?"

"Yes."

"And this morning the gate was closed?"

"Oh yes."

"In that case, how on Earth do you think someone could have gotten into the castle between ten and six this morning?"

"No idea."

"Mr. Underhill, are you sure you didn't invite the young lady to spend the night with you in the castle last night? Show her the dungeons, secret passages, things like that?"

"My days of entertaining young ladies are long behind me, Inspector Duffy," he said with a steady eye.

"*See?*" Lawson said with a nod, and I had to admit that Mr. Underhill was pretty convincing. Still, I'd make him do a written statement, and then I'd let McCrabban have a few hours with him in Interview Room 1 later on today.

"Is the front gate the only way in and out?" I asked.

"Yes."

"And who has the key to the front gate?"

"I do."

"Duplicate?"

"There is a spare key—"

"Aha!" I said, looking at Lawson.

"In the National Trust head office in London," Underhill continued.

"On, er, my own initiative I checked with the night security people in the monuments department at the National Trust HQ and apparently the key to Carrickfergus Castle is still in the monuments office. Hanging there on its hook. But, as Mr. Underhill will explain, the key isn't really an issue anyway," Lawson said, proud of himself for following this particular evidentiary rabbit down into its burrow.

"That's a pretty stupid system, don't you think? What if you had a heart attack in here at night when it was locked up? How would the emergency services get in to rescue you?" I asked Underhill.

"They wouldnae. I'd be dead," Underhill said with grim satisfaction. "You couldnae even get through the door with fireman's axes. It's two-foot-thick oak. Four-hundred-year-old oak. Designed to resist a siege. It would take them half a day to get through that with axes. Not that it would do them any good, anyway. At night I lower the portcullis to keep it in working trim. Lower it every night. Raise it every morning."

"The portcullis? That iron spikey thing?" I asked.

"That's what I was going to tell you, sir," Lawson said. "The portcullis makes the issue of the key and the lock irrelevant."

"Can you show me, Mr. Underhill?"

"Certainly."

Lawson and I walked back into the gatehouse, which was a rectangular structure about fifteen feet by ten. It was walled on two sides with the big oak door at the front and the portcullis in the rear. The cumulus-like forensic officer had moved on, giving us a clear picture of the geography.

"Stay there, gents!" Underhill said.

Underhill lowered the heavy cast-iron portcullis behind us with a long chain that wound round a capstan.

"Christ! How much does that thing weigh?" I asked, when the enormous portcullis reached the ground.

"Two and a half tons."

"What's it made of?"

"Cast iron."

"You lowered it last night like normal?"

"Yes."

"And you can't lift it up from below?"

"Try it."

I tried pushing it up with my hands, but there was no bloody way.

I turned to Lawson. "Well, this is a pretty picture isn't it?"

Lawson nodded. "You pick the lock or steal the key to the front gate. You get into the gatehouse, but that's as far as you can get, because there's a portcullis in the way."

"A two-and-a-half-ton portcullis."

"With spikes at the bottom."

I examined the portcullis. It had been freshly painted in the last month or two and there were no strange markings where someone had tried to lift it up with a hydraulic jack, or break through with welding gear.

"You think you could wriggle underneath those spikes?" I asked Lawson, but he could tell I was only being rhetorical.

"You see, in the old days the enemy army would break down the front gate of the castle, but then they'd be trapped here in the gatehouse and from above—see that little hole in the ceiling—they shoot arrows or fire muskets or drop boiling oil down on them," Mr. Underhill said.

"Hole in the ceiling?"

"Up there, look. The murder hole."

Twenty-five feet above us there was a trapdoor in the ceiling. Lawson raised his eyebrows and gave me a nod. Could be the way our killer and our victim got into the castle. Pick the front lock and bring a ladder and go up through the murder hole.

"Can we take a look at this 'murder hole'?" I asked.

"Certainly," Mr. Underhill said.

He raised the portcullis again and we walked back into the castle proper.

"This way," he said, and led us up a spiral staircase to the room above the gatehouse—a dank, cold, stone-walled little cubby.

"If you brought a ladder, maybe you could get up to the murder hole and into the castle this way?" I asked.

Underhill shook his head. "Well, I suppose in a previous time you could have done that but that trapdoor to the murder hole has been sealed for decades. Welded shut for safety reasons. Kids kept falling through it and breaking their legs."

I looked at the welds on the cast-iron hinges, and Underhill was right—they were solid and they hadn't been tampered with recently.

"Could you make it through the arrow slots?" Lawson asked, pointing out several smaller rectangular holes in the floor for firing crossbow bolts and arrows.

Underhill shook his head and put his arm through, to show that his shoulder would get stuck. Even an anorexic contortionist couldn't get through the arrow slots. At their widest they were barely six inches across.

"What do you think of those welds on the murder-hole trapdoor, Lawson?" I asked him.

He examined the welds and shook his head.

"Secure and not recently messed around with," he said.

"Make sure Forensics takes a photograph of those welds and the lowered portcullis."

"Will do, sir," Lawson said. "It more or less eliminates foul play from the inquiry, doesn't it, sir?"

I turned to Underhill. "OK, so they didn't come through the gate. How else could someone get in here?" I asked.

He shrugged his shoulders. "I wouldnae have the foggiest."

"Lawson, any suggestions—as bizarre as you'd like."

"Your plane theory sir, uhm, hot air balloon? Hang glider? Helicopter? Microlight?"

"One of those pneumatic grappling hooks they used at Pont Du Hoc on D-Day?" Underhill contributed.

"And our old friend the sixty-foot ladder," Lawson said. "But all that would show up on the CCTV from the roof of the harbormaster's hut, wouldn't it, sir?"

"Or the CCTV at the Northern Bank and the cop shop."

I lit a fag, took two deep puffs, and tossed it. "No more cigarettes for me this morning, Lawson. Remind me."

"I will, sir."

I rubbed my chin. "How do you get your murder victim to get on the hang glider with you?"

"And how would the murderer escape, sir? Getting out's going to be much more difficult than getting in. You can slip in with the crowd of regular tourists and perhaps hide from Mr. Underhill on his nightly inspection, but how do you get out?"

"It all depends on how secure the front gate has been since the portcullis was lifted this morning," I said, looking at Underhill and Lawson.

Lawson saw where I was coming from.

"Mr. Underhill, what did you do after you found the body and called the police?"

"I covered her up, of course!"

"And after that?"

"I said a wee prayer and I waited by her body until the police came."

"And how long was that, Mr. Underhill?" Lawson asked.

"Oh, it wasnae too long. Ten minutes?"

"And then when DC Lawson arrived you opened the gate?" I asked.

"Aye. I raised the portcullis and opened the front gate to let youse in."

"You didn't open the portcullis and the gate before we came—are you sure about that?" Lawson asked.

"I'm sure."

"What about getting the milk?"

"I didn't get the milk this morning. It's still out there."

"Can the portcullis be lowered from the gatehouse or outside the castle?" I asked Underhill.

He shook his head. "No, it can't."

I turned to Lawson. "What time did you get here?"

"About six fifteen, sir."

"And what did you do *exactly*?"

"I met Mr. Underhill and went to look at the body."

"And the front gate?" I asked him.

He smiled at me and I sighed with relief.

He hadn't fucked it up.

"I've had WPC Warren on the front gate since the moment we got here. No one has left the building without going past her."

I patted him on the shoulder. "Well done, son."

"When Mr. Underhill gave me the particulars over the phone, I knew we were looking at a weird one, sir. Anyone would have done the same thing," Lawson said, giving me a significant look.

Did *he* know about Lizzie Fitzpatrick? No. It was before his time. McCrabban had helped me on that case, but Crabbie never told anybody anything.

Lizzie had been murdered in the Henry Joy McCracken pub in Antrim—a pub that was locked and bolted from the inside. Or so we had been led to think. It was a very unusual case anywhere, but especially unusual in Ulster during the Troubles, where murder was never that baroque or complicated.

I was no expert in the statistical analysis of the type of cases to be expected by a Northern Irish homicide detective, but surely it would be stretching the confidence limits to suggest that an incident like that could ever occur again to the same peeler. I was not the brilliant but exceptionally statistically unlucky Dr. Gideon Fell, nor was I the equally unlucky Hercule Poirot; no, I was the plodding, *ordinary*, Detective Inspector Sean Duffy of the humdrum RUC. And we dour-faced RUC men didn't go in for weird statistical quirks or coincidences, which meant that unless someone was deliberately messing with us, this had to be an *ordinary* suicide in a rather out-of-the-ordinary location.

I shook myself from the reverie. "Right, Lawson, let's get moving, we'll call Sergeant McCrabban at home and tell him to get down here with as many people as possible. Any warm body will do. And if Sergeant Mulvenny isn't at the station, we'll call him at home too. We'll need the K9 unit."

Mr. Underhill was looking at us, perplexed.

"What's going on?" he asked.

"The thing is, Mr. Underhill, if this was a murder and not a suicide, then the murderer is still inside the building," Lawson explained.

"But I searched the place last night," Underhill protested.

"Mr. Underhill, unless something strange shows up on the external video footage, you obviously missed at least one person on your search. Possibly two," I said.

"I had a friend who spent the night with his girlfriend in the Great Pyramid in Giza," Lawson said. "That's how they did it. Snuck in, hid from the security guard locking the place down, spent a terrifying night in there, came out in the morning when the place was filling up with tourists again. You bunk off the tour and hide from security. Easy as pie."

"Is it possible someone did that?" I asked the caretaker.

Underhill rubbed his chin. "Aye, I suppose . . ." he conceded.

"And since Detective Constable Lawson has had someone watching the front gate since just after you lifted the portcullis, then a murderer can't possibly have escaped, can he?"

"No!" Mr. Underhill agreed excitedly.

"Hence the K9 unit," I said. "If there is a murderer lurking in here, we'll find him. And if not, well, I'm afraid either you did it or it's almost certainly a suicide."

Mr. Underhill nodded sadly. "Her ghost will be a troubled spirit, no matter how she died. She'll haunt the place for decades, maybe centuries."

"Fortunately for us, troubled spirits, wraiths, and banshees are not within the jurisdiction of Carrickfergus CID," I said.

5: THE STRANGE SUICIDE OF LILY BIGELOW

Lawson and I went outside the castle to question WPC Warren. She was a new recruit and not a detective, but she was not one of those time-serving eejits from the part-time reserve either, so hopefully she had her shit together.

"WPC Warren, I'm Detective Inspector Duffy, I don't think we've formally met, yet," I said, and gave her what I hoped was a friendly smile.

"No, sir, I don't think so," she said in a pleasing South Belfast accent.

She was very young, with a pert blond bob under her kepi. She seemed alert enough.

"Are you cold?" I asked.

"I'm fine, sir, I've got my gloves and scarf. I've heard it's going to snow again later."

I looked at the darkening sky. "I wouldn't be surprised. Now listen to me, Warren, you've been on duty here since six fifteen this morning?"

"Yes, sir."

"Right here at the entrance to the castle?"

"Yes, sir."

"You haven't slipped away for a toilet break, or a cup of coffee, or a wee smoke or anything? I won't be cross with you if you did any of those things, I just need to know."

"I've been right there, sir, I haven't moved!" she said, indignantly.

"Good. Now has anyone come out of the castle in the time you've been standing here?"

"No, sir. . . . Well, apart from you and DC Lawson, sir. And two men from the forensic team."

"Apart from *police officers*, has anyone else entered or left the castle?" I reiterated.

"No, sir," she said.

"Are you quite sure?"

"Oh yes, sir."

"That's very good, Warren. Now we're going to conduct a thorough search of the building with sniffer dogs, and until that search is over, no one is to leave the castle without my express permission. Is that understood?"

"Yes, sir."

"Good work, Warren, keep it up."

Lawson and I walked down to the police Land Rover in the castle car park.

"Was I sufficiently encouraging with her, Lawson? I take my pedagogical role seriously, at least I do after I've had my coffee."

"You were very encouraging, sir. I'm sure Warren was inspired," Lawson replied. I looked for satirical intent behind those blond eyebrows, but he was stony-faced, the cheeky bastard.

We called the barracks and ordered in the K9 unit and as many PCs as the duty sergeant would let us have without endangering the station's security. Then I got Sandra on the desk to call McCrabban and tell him to get down here pronto. It was well after seven now, so he'd be done milking the pigs, or plucking the cows, or shagging the sheep, or whatever it was one did on a farm.

Within the hour, McCrabban appeared, along with Sergeant Mulvenny and his dogs and a dozen PCs who'd had nothing to do back at the station. I split us into three teams, with a detective leading each team. We went back into the castle, found Mr. Underhill, and told him our plan of conducting an exhaustive search of every conceivable nook and cranny in the place.

He produced an archaeological map and explained the layout of the place in detail. It was not a particularly large structure: a courtyard, a ruined "curtain" wall, two sets of dungeons, and cannon emplacements complete with half a dozen large, nineteenth-century cannons. The main building was the twelfth-century Norman castle keep from which presumably our Jane Doe had fallen or jumped. We went through all the floors in the keep, the spiral staircase and its flat roof. The keep was packed full of local history stuff: Carrickfergus's first fire engine, prehistoric pottery found in the area, medieval tapestries, and so on. There was a military museum on the top floor, which had uniforms and weapons from across the centuries. An old well on the lower level would have been a terrific place for a psychopath to hide, but the well was covered with thick, impenetrable Perspex that hadn't been tampered with.

"What about secret tunnels? Priests holes? Hidden rooms? You're always hearing about secret tunnels in places like this," I asked Mr. Underhill.

"As I was telling Detective Lawson, there are no secret tunnels in this castle. We're built over black basalt. No one's tunneling through that. No one was able to tunnel through that in eight centuries of sieges. I doubt very much someone managed to do it last night," he said definitively.

"Secret rooms that someone with insider knowledge might know about?"

"There are no secret rooms. There have been half a dozen archaeological digs in the castle and nothing like that has ever been found."

Sergeant Mulvenny and his dogs discovered no one hiding anywhere in the castle: not in the dungeons, not the keep, not the courtyard, not the gatehouse.

"Sorry, Duffy. There's no killer in this place. We've looked all over. She must have done herself in," Mulvenny said in a Scouse accent so dense and incomprehensible that I made a mental note to suggest him for the post of media relations and civilian liaison officer.

"Do you think your dogs could tell me where she spent the night, at least? She must have been hiding somewhere?"

Big Mike Mulvenny scratched his brown beard and nodded.

"Maybe, Duffy, maybe. I'll see what I can do."

While this search was continuing and the forensic team continued to work, I had McCrabban and Lawson review the CCTV footage from the harbormaster's office and the rear entrance to the Northern Bank.

An hour later, Detective Sergeant McCrabban's dour visage told me that this exercise had borne little fruit.

"No one came in over the walls," he said with certainty.

"Are you sure?" I asked. "This is probably going to be very important at the inquest, Crabbie."

McCrabban explained that the castle had been clearly illuminated all night by spotlights. During this time, there had been no ladders leaned up against the wall, no balloon landings, no UFOs, no microlights, nothing out of the ordinary at all.

"A couple of seagulls came and went. And I think I saw an owl at one point," Crabbie said.

"A massive, human-sized owl?" Lawson asked.

Crabbie shook his head. "Nope. An owl-sized owl. No human being came over the walls into Carrickfergus Castle last night," he said, confidently.

"What about the bank's footage, Lawson?" I asked.

The CCTV from the Northern Bank apparently told a similar story on the seaward side and at the front gate.

"After Mr. Underhill locked up last night, no one came near the front gate until I showed up this morning," Lawson said.

I looked at both of them. "And Mike Mulvenny's K9 teams found no one hiding in the castle, which means, gentlemen, that she must have done what Lawson's friend did: slipped off one of the tours, hid in the castle somewhere last night, and jumped off the keep roof sometime between ten p.m. and six a.m."

Lawson and McCrabban both concurred.

"Did the actual jump show up on the CCTV footage?" I asked.

"The angle's wrong for the harbormaster's camera," Crabbie said. "If she'd come to the south part of the keep, I would have seen her, but if she just went up there and jumped off the north wall, the camera wouldn't have caught her."

"I'll check the footage again, sir, but I don't think the Northern Bank's cameras are positioned high enough to cover the roof of the keep. Didn't notice on a preliminary view, anyway," Lawson said.

"We're going to have to go through all the footage from last night again and again, until we're satisfied," I said.

"Are there any actual eyewitnesses?" McCrabban asked.

"Our fine trainee detectives are canvassing the area, but there's none so far," I explained.

"I suppose we'll also have to go to the keep roof, then, and have a thorough look round there, eh?" I said.

"I'm not a big fan of heights," Lawson said nervously.

"Me neither, actually," I agreed, and Crabbie looked at us as if we were a big bunch of jessies.

"I'll lead you up there," Mr. Underhill said. "The thirteenth step in the spiral staircase is a trip step."

We climbed the narrow medieval spiral staircase inside the keep. It was lit by electric lights, but even so, without Mr. Underhill's help we would have been caught out by the trip step, which was half as big as the other steps.

"What's the purpose of the trip step?" Lawson asked, stubbing his toe.

"To trip up invading knights running up the stairs," Underhill explained. "The Normans did it in nearly all of their castles."

I avoided coming a cropper on the trip step and reached the keep roof just as the snow began to fall again.

"Bloody freezing," I said, buttoning up my coat.

"It's some view though, eh?" Crabbie said, turning up the collar on his wool trench coat.

Indeed it was. Despite the snow clouds you could see clearly down the chilly lough all the way to Scotland across the even chillier Irish Sea. Belfast lay to the south and east, and beyond the city were the foothills of the Mourne Mountains.

"Forget the view, let's look for some evidence," I said. "Let's line-walk the roof. Mr. Underhill, do you want to help?"

"Aye, I'll help," he said.

"We'll form a line and slowly pace out the roof in sections. Walk next to Sergeant McCrabban, and if you spot anything that isn't bird shit, let us know."

We line-walked the roof and found nothing. It was extremely windy up here, and the roof had been blown clean of snow, cigarettes, and potential suicide notes.

"If she'd left a note, it would have blown away," McCrabban observed.

"Aye."

I walked to the north wall of the keep and looked down into the courtyard where the forensic officers were continuing their work.

"She must have jumped from here," I said, gingerly peering over the four-foot-high keep wall. I looked for cigarette butts, a pen, ash, chewing gum, anything at all, but there were no clues.

"Thoughts?" I asked Lawson and McCrabban.

"She probably didn't hang about. No cigarettes or matches or anything. She came straight up and just jumped," Lawson said.

McCrabban shrugged. "We don't actually know that. She might have been up for hours, thinking about it. Like I say, we're in a CCTV blind spot on this side of the keep."

"If she was up here for a while, pacing, thinking about it, could she possibly have slipped into a frame or two?" I asked.

He lit his pipe. "As you say, we'll have to go through the footage carefully, but I didn't notice her at all."

The spiral staircase exited near the north wall of the keep, so she could have come up and jumped without being captured by either CCTV camera at the harbormaster's office or the Northern Bank.

I looked down into the courtyard again.

Dizzying.

So easy just to slip over the edge. End all your bloody problems in an instant. Girlfriend trouble. Career trouble. Drink problems. Give Chief Inspector Payne a story to tell for years: "Here I was, investigating a bloody jumper and fucking Duffy—always an odd fucking fish and no mistake—jumps from the castle keep almost bloody braining me . . ."

"Let's get down from here, lads, we'll send up an FO to see if they can get prints from this wall," I said with a shiver.

Back in the courtyard, none of the search teams turned up any hidden suspects, clothes, or murder weapons, so I had no choice but to send them all back to the station.

Sergeant Mulvenny had at least some interesting news from the dungeons.

"Well, Duffy, don't make me swear on it, but it's possible that your Jane Doe spent the night in the dungeon near the gatehouse."

"Oh yes?" I said.

"Don't get your hopes up too high. If she did spend the night, there wasn't any physical evidence, but one of the dogs seemed to get quite excited down there."

"Excited how?"

"Well, I asked the FO—Chief Inspector Payne—if I could let Moira, my best bitch, sniff the body, and he said OK, cos he was nearly finished, and Moira got the scent and I took her all over the castle again. Sometimes it's better in the snow. You wouldn't think it, but there something's about a scent carrying in the snow."

"And?"

"Well, anyway, Moira had the lass's scent and she was calm until we got down to the dungeon, but down there she barked and whined a bit."

"She barked and whined?"

"Aye."

"And that's proof the dead girl was down there at some point?"

"No. I wouldn't say that that was proof that the lass was in the dungeon at some point last night, but she might have been."

"Can you show me where you're talking about?"

Mulvenny took McCrabban, Lawson, and me to the dungeon near the gatehouse. It was a dank little hole, twenty feet by ten feet, in a hollowed-out fissure in the bedrock. There were iron rings hammered into the wall, where, presumably, the prisoners had been chained. Formerly, there had been a door that locked the dungeon from the outside, but this door had been removed and concrete steps had been added to provide easier access for tourists. The dungeon was slick with moss and had the revolting sulfur stench of centuries of urine.

"Are you sure Moira could smell anything over this stink of piss?" I asked Mulvenny.

Mulvenny shrugged. "I think so."

"Maybe she smelt another dog, or one of the visitors?" McCrabban asked skeptically.

"I don't think so."

"Is she in heat?" McCrabban asked.

"Definitely not," Mulvenny said. "And she's normally pretty reliable."

"I can't imagine spending the night down here," McCrabban said.

"And, don't forget, Mr. Underhill says he checked down here," Lawson added.

"Checked how, I wonder?" I said. "A quick scan with a flashlight or a real, solid look around the room?"

"I think we should ask him," McCrabban said.

"Well, thanks, mate. Good work," I said, shaking Mulvenny's hand. We traipsed back to Mr. Underhill's cottage, where he was in the middle of giving a formal statement to a PC. We took a smoke break outside until it was done. Lawson wasn't a smoker, so he pulled out a Walkman and clicked in a cassette while Crabbie relit his pipe and I lit another ciggie.

"Sir, you told me to watch the cigarette count," Lawson said.

"Oh yeah," I said stubbing the ciggie out and putting it back in the box. "Whatcha listening to on your machine?" I asked, for a distraction.

"The new U2 album," he said, innocently.

I rolled my eyes.

Lawson saw the eye roll. "Just because it's popular doesn't mean it's not good," he protested.

"What's the record called?"

"*The Joshua Tree.*"

"Stupid name."

"It's really ace. You wanna listen to it?"

"What's the difference between listening to U2 and shitting yourself? . . . If you shit yourself you'll smell but you can deal with the self-loathing," I said.

"Oh, sir, that's just a recycled Depeche Mode joke!" he protested.

I coughed and shook my head ruefully. I used to have better material. Crabbie noticed the cough and took me to one side. "You look a bit rough. Are you OK, Sean?" he asked, in what for him was a bold venture into the realm of the personal. I could never tell with these crazy Presbyterians whether he was just being polite or whether this was an opening for me to spill all my troubles.

"Didn't sleep well, mate. Beth's left me."

"Is she the young one?" Crabbie asked.

"Yeah."

"Well, I'm not surprised," he said.

"Neither am I . . . well actually, I am surprised. I thought things were going OK."

"She was quite a bit younger than you, wasn't she?"

"Ten years—is that a lot?"

Crabbie considered it. "Insurmountable, I would have thought."

The PC finished taking Underhill's initial statement, and we went inside the cottage and sat opposite the old man at his kitchen table. He looked quite tuckered out now by the interviews and the questions and the hike up and down the stairs. But still he got up and offered us a cup of tea. "Really, it's no trouble. It's good tea. It's from Yorkshire," he insisted.

We assented to the tea and Crabbie lit his pipe. "Didn't know you could grow tea in Yorkshire," Lawson said to himself.

Crabbie was flipping through his notebook as he smoked. "Could someone have raised the portcullis last night without Mr. Underhill noticing?" he asked.

"We've been through all that. It makes quite a racket, Crabbie, and more importantly, it can only be raised and lowered from the inside. This morning, Mr. Underhill found it exactly where he left it last night."

Mr. Underhill brought our tea and biscuits, and I went through his written statement. It wasn't different from what he had already told us.

"Mr. Underhill, I wonder if you would mind showing us exactly how you carried out your search last night. Grab your flashlight and show us exactly your routine, please," I said.

We went outside into the now-strengthening snow.

We followed him through the courtyard and the gatehouse and the keep. Without commenting, we watched him go down the steps into the dungeons. He flicked the light around both dungeons and then walked back up to the courtyard again.

"You search the dungeons every night exactly like that?" I asked.

He nodded.

"That was pretty fast, Mr. Underhill. If someone had been hiding in the left-hand corner there, do you think you would have seen them?"

"Aye, I think so. I know this place backward and forward, anything out of place and I'll ken it. That's why Buttoncap doesnae try his tricks with me," Mr. Underhill said.

"Who's Buttoncap?" McCrabban asked.

"The castle ghost," Lawson explained.

"Why do you check the castle twice before going to bed? Surely once would be enough, no?" I asked.

"It's always been that way. Old Mr. Dobbins did it that way and Mr. Farnham afore him, and afore that it was the army way. An inspection at six and one at ten. It's always been done and I'm not going to buck tradition."

"This second inspection. Do you go up to the keep roof for that one?"

Mr. Underhill shook his head. "No, not usually. I do check the dungeons, though and the courtyard!"

"And last night, did you go up onto the keep roof?"

"No I cannae say that I did."

"But you checked the courtyard, and just to reiterate there was nothing unusual?"

"No."

"Thank you, Mr. Underhill."

I waited until he had walked back to his cottage before turning to the lads.

"Well?" I said to Lawson and McCrabban.

"Aye, she could have been hiding in the dungeon. Up against that back left-hand wall. He wouldn't have seen her," McCrabban said.

Lawson nodded. "I agree with that."

"And that's what the dogs think, too," McCrabban reiterated. "She bought a ticket, hid in the dungeon, waited until the coast was clear, and then went up to the keep roof."

"And at some point after ten she jumped," I said.

"We know where she hid, where she jumped, we just don't know why she did it," Lawson said.

When we got back to the courtyard I could see that the Forensics boys were finally done. They'd stripped off their boilersuits but were still unmistakable as cops because of their good teeth and bad haircuts—RUC men got free dental and somehow, invariably, always ended up at the worst barber in town. Interestingly, terrorists also had bad haircuts, but that was because their fashion sense had been frozen around 1973—the era of the Che screen print and the Red Army Faction wanted poster. Chief Inspector Payne, the big, bald fifty-something forensic officer, had lit himself a cigarette and was taking off his boilersuit with controlled aggression. He put his hand out to catch the snowflakes, as if noticing them for the first time.

"I suppose we'd better have a chat to Frank Payne," I said, reluctantly.

"Nothing else for it," Crabbie agreed.

Payne looked up when we approached.

"Ah, Duffy," he said without any warmth.

"Long time, Frank," I replied. "These are my colleagues. I think you've met Detective Sergeant McCrabban, and this is young Detective Constable Lawson."

Payne gave a curt nod to McCrabban and Lawson. "Nice day, eh? Fucking freezing, so I am. Calling us out at this time of the day, in a blizzard, no less. Your men should have covered the whole crime scene with tarpaulin. Sloppy work, Duffy."

"Hardly a blizzard, Frank, a—"

"Did you send one of my boys up to the roof of the keep, Duffy?" he asked, narrowing his eyes.

"Aye, to see if there were any prints on the ledge where she jumped. Or, you know, anything that we might have missed. You guys in Forensics are always a bit sharper than us regular CID," I said.

"Don't try to butter me up, Duffy. If you want one of my men to do something, you ask me first, OK?"

"OK, Frank."

He spat on the cobbles and took another draw on his ciggie. A Gallagher's long, by the nasty pong off it.

"I heard you went to see Ali," he said to me.

"Christ, you'd think there'd be some other gossip in the RUC besides me doing a routine bit of crowd-control duty."

"What the hell was Ali doing over here, anyway?"

"He was on a peace mission with the Reverend Jesse Jackson."

"Bloody hell. Muhammad Ali and the Reverend Jesse Jackson bring peace to Northern Ireland! PR stunt. That's all it was, Duffy. Jackson's running for president. Did you know that? Needs the Irish vote, that's what they said in the paper."

"If it's in the paper, it must be true."

"Ali's overrated, anyway."

"You think Muhammad Ali is overrated as a boxer?" McCrabban asked, incredulously.

"He was OK, McCrabban. Just OK. Look at Tyson. Now there's a brawler for you. He's got the hunger. Murder ya for a Cup-a-Soup, so he would."

"I don't think they have Cup-a-Soup in America," Lawson said.

"No Cup-a-Soup indeed. Who doesn't like soup in a cup? Jesus. The point is, Ali talked his opponents to death. Tyson just knocks 'em out," Payne said.

"That's what made Ali so great. He used psychology," McCrabban protested, but Payne cut him off with a snort.

"Psychology! Listen to him! Psychology, he says."

This was the kind of rubbish peelers talked about when they didn't have a case to focus their attention, but I'd had enough of this blather. "Time's pressing, Frank, do you want to walk us through the crime scene?" I asked.

"If you insist," he said, reluctant to leave the shelter of the overhanging battlement.

Payne, Lawson, McCrabban, and I walked over to the body. It had been covered by a grey Forensics blanket, which would have to serve as protection until they came to take her away for the autopsy.

". . . that's why they call it the sweet science. You have to get in your opponent's head. It's never been about who hits the hardest . . ." I heard McCrabban muttering to Lawson as we crossed the courtyard.

Payne bent down and took the blanket from the dead woman's body.

She was face down, and her head was half smashed in. She was wearing a rather chic black leather jacket, and underneath that, a black wool sweater and a white blouse with a green cotton scarf. Black skirt, black tights, a single slip-on pump, and thin black leather gloves completed the ensemble.

"Where's the jacket from?" I asked.

"The label said 'Dolce & Gabbana—Milano.' Never heard of them," Payne said.

"Me neither," I confessed. "But things ain't cheap in Milan, are they?"

I looked at the shoe. It had a half-inch heel on it, so it wasn't completely impractical, but there was something about it I didn't like.

"How come both her shoes didn't come off? Those are slip-ons, right? Wouldn't the impact smack both of them off?"

"Not necessarily. The force shook one shoe off, but not the other. That's not so uncommon if she belly flopped. More proof it was a suicide, actually. If she'd changed her mind she might have tried to land feet first."

"Death would have been instantaneous?" I asked.

"Absolutely. She busted open like an egg. She wouldn't have felt a thing."

"No sign of foul play?"

"There's no blood trail anywhere. We searched with the UV, so I'm fairly confident in saying that this is where she jumped and the body has not been moved."

"What else?"

"Tox report off already. Medical examiner will have to tell you about sexual activity."

"Fibers, hairs?"

"Everything we found is off to the lab, nothing out of the ordinary."

"Signs of domestic abuse, drugs, anything like that?"

"No, but again the ME will give you a fuller picture."

"Time of death?"

"Tough to estimate body cooling because of the low ambient temperature, but one of my men inserted a rectal thermometer when we first got here and it gave a reading of 27 degrees."

I did the calculation in my head. A dead body normally lost about 1.5 degrees centigrade per hour from a base level of 37 degrees centigrade. A loss of 10 degrees would put death at roughly around midnight, or maybe a little after.

"So death about twelve o'clock?"

"Aye."

I sighed and looked at the dead girl. "So, what do you reckon, Frank?" I asked.

"She topped herself. Why, I don't know. That's for you to find out, if you can."

"If we can," I agreed.

"How many suicides do you get a year, Duffy?" he asked.

"A few," I conceded.

"You ever find out why they do it?"

"The last three suicides we dealt with were all peelers. Blew their brains out with their side arms. Of course we had to write them all up as 'death by accidental discharge of a firearm.'"

"Pressure from the union?" Payne asked.

"Aye, and from upstairs. Suicide invalidates life-insurance policies and it's bad for morale."

"That it is," Payne agreed.

I looked up at the keep roof. "If you were going to kill yourself, would you jump from here, Frank?"

"It's the tallest building in Carrick that the general public has access to," he said.

"And she would have been certain to die?"

"Doing a bit of mental arithmetic ... after ninety feet of free fall, your maximum velocity at the pavement would be about seventy-six feet per second, uhm, that's about fifty-two miles per hour. Maybe take off one mile an hour for wind resistance because she was belly flopping. . . . A person weighing a hundred pounds hitting the ground at, say, fifty miles per hour would experience a force of about a ton exerted on their body for about a tenth of a second. That's certain death, I think."

"I expect you're right."

"Aye, Duffy, she knew what she was doing and she picked a good spot to do it. Away from prying eyes or people trying to talk her out of it."

"No chance she fell from the wheel well of a passing plane?"

"No. She would have sprayed all over the courtyard."

"Lovely image. Anything else you can tell me, Frank?"

"Do you want to know the victim's name?"

"You know her name?"

"Follow me," he said, and led us back to the overhang and a portable table and chairs where her bag and effects had been laid out. He handed me a set of latex gloves. I put them on and he gave me an evidence bag that contained a purse. Inside were a couple of credit cards, a driving license, and a photo ID for the *Financial Times*.

"Lily Emma Bigelow," I read off the ID and, shocked, handed it to Lawson.

"Jesus!" he said, stunned. "We met her, didn't we, boss? Your woman from yesterday!"

I explained the context in which we had met Lily Bigelow to McCrabban and Chief Inspector Payne.

"She didn't seem depressed to me," Lawson said.

"Or me," I agreed.

"She was very good-looking," Lawson added.

"Not anymore," Payne said with a malicious cackle that turned into a coughing fit so severe it almost made you believe in karma. When he'd recovered, he said good-bye and he was followed out of the castle by the rest of the forensic team.

Lily's bag contained nothing else of note. A few tissues, a pencil. I put the evidence back in the bags carefully, and we walked up the steps to the battlements to survey the crime scene. No new insight from up here.

"No notebook among her effects," I said to Lawson and McCrabban.

"Probably back in her hotel room," Lawson said.

"We'll have to check for that. That's probably where she left the suicide note, if this wasn't a spur-of-the-moment job."

"She was English?" Crabbie asked.

"She was. A journalist with that delegation visiting Carrick. Speaking of which. . . . Shit! We'll need to question all of them before they leave town. Where's my head today? Lawson, run up to the Coast Road Hotel and tell the manager that no one's to leave until they've given a statement about their whereabouts last night."

"And their knowledge of the whereabouts of Lily Bigelow?"

"Yeah, that too. For as much of yesterday as they can remember. Take as many reservists as you need to write down statements. On my authority. We'll need to get all the statements now. If they're all going back to Finland, we might not get another chance."

"Yes, sir."

"And make sure no one goes into her hotel room until I get there."

"Of course, sir," he said, and scurried out of the castle.

I sat down on the cold steps and looked at McCrabban. "Is someone coming to take the body away, or is she just going to lie there all morning?" I asked him.

"I'll go see, Sean," he said.

He came back a minute later. "They'll be here in half an hour to take her up to Belfast for autopsy," he said.

I stared down at the body again. There was something not quite right about this crime scene, something that I was missing, but try as I might I couldn't figure out what it was. Had Beth's departure frazzled me, or was it just thirteen long years of this exhausting profession in this exhausting land?

The snow was getting heavier. Crabbie's lips were turning blue.

"I'll watch over the body until they come for her. You best run along, mate," I said.

"What do you want me to do?"

"Log the evidence. Secure the CC footage. Find that bloody trainee detective constable whose name I've forgotten. Later we'll search Lily's room for a note. Women are more likely to leave a note than men in cases like this. And then help Lawson get those statements in. Make sure no one leaves the Coast Road Hotel until we get statements from them. Statements and phone numbers and addresses, even if they're in bloody Finland. Notification of the family, if you get the time. The *FT* will have her next of kin on file, no doubt. Oh and can you send someone with a Land Rover to wait for me outside? I had to get a taxi here, my car's banjaxed."

"What happened?" McCrabban asked.

"Battery."

He nodded sadly. "It's not your day, is it? Broken-down car, girl-friend leaving you."

I coughed a nasty smoker's cough and sputtered. "At least I've got my health."

McCrabban smiled. "I'll send a Land Rover and we'll see you later."

He turned to go and then looked back at me. He didn't say anything.

"What?"

"I know what you're thinking about," he said.

"What am I thinking about, Crabbie?"

"You're thinking about the Lizzie Fitzpatrick case."

I nodded. "I was, earlier."

"We can talk about it or not talk about it. It's entirely up to you, Sean."

"If it's not a suicide we may need to talk, but I think it is a suicide, isn't it?"

"Looks that way," he agreed. He brushed the snow off his lapel. "I'll head off, then," he said.

When Crabbie had gone, I rummaged in my inside pocket for that old roach I knew was in there. About an inch left in the spliff, which would be good enough. I lit it and drew in the Turkish black.

There's something inherently cinematic about snow falling in an enclosed space. And this was snow falling into the enclosed space of the courtyard of an eight-hundred-year-old castle. Snow tumbling from an early February sky onto the covered form of a beautiful, dead English girl who had jumped to her death. Poor lass. I looked at the thin little blanket covering Lily's body. Her feet were sticking out, one foot in the little black shoe, one foot bare. There was, I thought, surprisingly little blood around the body. Payne was surely right, though. She didn't die from internal bleeding. Death would have been instantaneous.

Snow was accumulating on the blanket folds.

And then, quite suddenly, I was crying.

Sobbing for all the lost daughters and missing girls.

"Shit," I said, and let the joint drop to the flagstones with a hiss. It lay there in the courtyard with all the other rubbish from our presence this morning. Snow drifting down onto cigarette ends, latex gloves, plastic coffee cups, yellow photographic film wrappers, dog shit from the K9 unit.

I stood up and came down the steps and walked over to the body.

"Why did you do it, honey? You had it all going for you . . ."

I lifted the blanket to look at her. Her dark hair, her pretty face smashed on the left side and strangely untouched on the right. Her arms were by her sides. Her left eye was open: no longer emerald it was blind, bloodshot but transfigured by the Mystery. A snowflake drifted onto her lip, another into her half-opened mouth. Strange that she hadn't put her hands up to protect her face. Even the most determined suicide generally protected their face—it was instinct, you just couldn't help it. But maybe that's why she had jumped at night. In the dark she wouldn't have seen the ground coming.

Yes. That had to be it. Because this couldn't be anything else but suicide.

I let the blanket fall again and checked that no one was looking. "*Sancta Maria, Mater Dei, ora pro nobis peccatoribus, nunc, et in hora mortis nostrae. Amen,*" I said quickly and made the sign of the cross. If she was Catholic, it would help; and if she wasn't, it wouldn't do any harm.

I saw the men arrive from the Belfast morgue. I waved to them. They were young guys whom I didn't know.

"This the stiff?" one of them asked, a greasy-haired character with long sideburns that he probably thought made him look like Elvis.

"This is the victim, yes. Her name was Lily Bigelow. I knew her. So, you know, be careful with her, OK?"

"We always are, boss, always are," the young man lied, and to feel better about things, I chose to believe him.

6: THE ONE SHOE

I nodded to WPC Warren, still protecting the crime scene, and walked down to the car park, where a Land Rover was waiting for me.

"I'm Constable Stewart, sir. Your lift, sir," a chubby, young constable said while attempting to hide a cigarette behind his back.

"Thanks," I said getting into the passenger's side.

Stewart tossed the ciggie, missed first gear twice, but eventually got us going up along the seafront toward the Coast Road Hotel.

"This is you, sir," he said, pulling up in front of the Coast Road. I was about to get out when a sudden thought hit me.

"Jesus!" I said, and jumped back into the Land Rover's cab.

"Sir?"

"Back to the castle, son, and step on it and stick the bloody siren on!"

"Sir?"

"No, shift over, I'll drive."

We swapped seats, and I put the siren on and got the Land Rover up to 70 mph on the short run back to Carrick Castle. I parked it right outside and ran past WPC Warren into the courtyard.

The men from the morgue had just loaded Lily's body onto a gurney but hadn't begun wheeling her outside to their van just yet. I lifted the blanket and looked at her feet. One shoe was still on, the other off and inside an evidence bag. I examined the shoe in the bag and the one remaining on her foot.

"I knew something was up with those bloody shoes. Look!" I said pointing at her feet.

"What's the matter?" Elvis Sideburns asked.

"She's put her left shoe on her right foot!" I said, showing them the shoe in the bag.

"She wasn't thinking straight. She was topping herself," Elvis Sideburns said.

"Aye," his mate agreed.

I looked at Stewart.

He shrugged. "Your mind's not in the right place when you're killing yourself is it, sir?" he said.

"Go and relieve WPC Warren at the gate and tell her to come over here. And don't let anyone leave the castle without my say-so," I said.

Warren arrived a minute later.

"Sir?" she asked.

I explained the situation to her. "You ever put your shoe on the wrong foot?" I asked her.

"Never," she said.

"Aha!" I said, and looked triumphantly at Elvis and his mate.

She looked up at the top of the keep. "How did she get up there?" she asked.

"Only way up is the spiral staircase."

Warren bit her lip.

"What?" I asked.

"If I had to walk up to the top of the keep in heels like these, I probably would have taken my shoes off," she said.

"To climb up the stairs? The heels aren't that big."

"I've been up that staircase. You can't climb it in any kind of dress-shoe heels. So you take them off. Stands to reason. That trip step thing they have. You'd take your heels off."

"So she takes them off for the staircase, and then when she puts them on again she puts them on the wrong feet? I don't buy that," I said.

"Maybe she kept them off until she walked across the keep roof and then she put them on before she jumped. She wanted to her look her best, didn't she? I'd wear me good shoes if I was topping myself," Elvis said.

"Who asked you? Come on, Warren, follow me up the stairs."

We walked back up the spiral staircase onto the keep roof, where the snow had made conditions quite treacherous.

"What do you think now, Constable Warren?"

"Where did she jump from?" Warren asked.

"Just here," I said. "Don't go near the edge. It's very slippy. We don't need another calamity today."

"I don't know, sir," Warren said. "It's possible that she kept her shoes off, held them in her hand, and just slipped them on before she jumped. She sat there on the edge with her legs dangling over the side thinking about it. . . . I really don't know."

"And could she have put them on the wrong feet?"

"I don't know."

I began to have doubts myself. How could anyone else have put Lily's shoes on, apart from Lily herself?

"I suppose it was dark. And if she didn't actually walk in the shoes . . . and she was in a highly emotional state, wasn't she?" I muttered, as much to myself as to WPC Warren.

"Yes, sir."

"Take your shoes off and put them on the wrong feet and tell me what it feels like."

WPC Warren put her shoes on the wrong feet.

"Well?" I asked.

"They feel different, sir, but if your mind was disordered . . ."

I sat down on the roof and tucked my coat underneath me. I closed my eyes, took my DMs off, and put them on the wrong feet. I stood up and walked around for a bit. It was an odd sensation, but perhaps not as odd as I'd been expecting. Was that good or bad? Did I want this to be a murder?

"Why put the shoes on at all? Why not just toss them over?" I asked.

"I don't know, sir. . . . How did one of the shoes come off?" Warren asked.

"Forensics says the force of the impact blasted one shoe off, but the way she landed the other one stayed on," I explained.

Warren nodded. I opened my notebook. "Just to be clear, Warren, you think it's possible that she *could* have mistaken one shoe for the other in the dark?"

"Uhm. . . . I suppose so, yes it's possible. If she wasn't walking in them."

I nodded and let the information sink in.

"Because if someone else put those shoes on Lily Bigelow's feet, well, then this is probably a murder."

I looked at her for a good ten seconds, but she didn't answer.

"You're the expert on women's feet and women's shoes up here."

"I don't know, sir. . . . I suppose, yes, the most likely explanation is that she took the shoes off to come up the stairs and kept them off until just before she jumped and didn't notice or didn't care."

"All right. Fair enough," I said—my voice a curious mixture of relief and disappointment.

"Phone call for you, Inspector Duffy!" Mr. Underhill yelled from back down in the courtyard.

"Coming!" I yelled back.

"OK, lads, you can take her away," I said, reaching the bottom of the steps.

I walked into the caretaker's cottage and picked up the phone. "Hello?"

"What's the story, Duffy?" Chief Inspector McArthur asked.

"Oh, it's you, sir."

"Aye, it's me. Duffy. Several of your men have just showed up at the Coast Road Hotel and prevented everyone from checking out."

"Those are my orders, sir."

"What's going on, Duffy?"

"Sir, do you remember that journalist we encountered the other night? Actually, you might not have met her, she was with the delegation?"

"I remember her. What's she done?"

"She's apparently killed herself."

"Killed herself?"

"Yes, sir. Jumped from the top of the keep in Carrick Castle."

"Oh my God! . . . Killed herself. . . . And you're sure it's not a murder?"

"If it was a murder, there's only one possible suspect and we're taking him into custody...but none of us in CID think it was a murder at this stage of the investigation."

"Why only one suspect?"

"No one else could have gotten out of the building, and we've just searched the place thoroughly."

"Suicide, though, Duffy. She seemed pretty happy to me. I said hello to her after you left. Women are an enigma though, aren't they? Impulsive. Always bursting into tears at the drop of a hat. Hormones. Menstrual cycles. That kind of thing."

"Possibly, sir, but this particular suicide had the air of planning and premeditation about it."

"Did you talk to her the other night, Duffy?"

"Yes, sir."

"What were you talking about?"

"Nothing really."

"Did you ask her out, Duffy? The truth ..."

"I gave her my number but she never called it."

"Are you sure?"

"Perfectly sure."

"Thank God for that! An added complication we don't need."

"No, sir."

"All right, so I understand why you have to question the delegation. It can't be dodged. Not if we want to avoid a bollocking from the coroner, but can you make it sharpish, Duffy? Hardly their fault that a journalist staying in their hotel decides to kill herself."

"No, sir. Unless they're implicated somehow."

"How could they be? You're not suggesting it was an assisted suicide or anything like that?"

"Well, obviously we can't rule anything out, sir. But at least at this stage of the inquiry I think they're probably in the clear. I'm going to check the CCTV footage personally; so far it looks like she decided to stay behind in one of the dungeons after the castle closed for the night. She hid from the caretaker until after dark, made her way to the top of the keep, and then jumped off."

"No accomplice because the accomplice couldn't have gotten out?"

"That's exactly right, sir. There was a portcullis and a locked front door preventing any egress from the castle, and if he couldn't get out, then he's still here. And he's not still here. We've done several searches and I'm confident he's not anywhere in the castle."

"It's a big place, that Carrickfergus Castle."

"Not that big in terms of your actual hiding places. We've searched it from top to bottom several times. And I had Sergeant Mulvenny come out with his K9 teams. Nothing."

He breathed out heavily in relief. "So unless something turns up, it's an ordinary suicide."

"Looks like it, sir."

"Excellent Duffy. . . . You're a dedicated copper, wish I could say that for all the peelers in my . . . uhm, well, best leave that thought unsaid. I'll let you get back to work. Like I say, don't keep the delegation waiting. Question them, get statements, but make sure they all get their flights and aren't inconvenienced. The last thing I want today is a phone call from the chief constable or, God save us, the secretary of state."

"Understood, sir."

I walked WPC Warren back outside the castle gate with me.

"Listen, Warren, just to be on the bloody safe side I'm going to have Mulvenny come back here with his dogs one last time. He won't like it, but I want to be one hundred percent sure. That shoe thing has unnerved me. Until Mulvenny gives you the all-clear, you're to stay here, OK? No one in or out, apart from cops or coroner's men with IDs."

"OK, sir."

"Do you mind staying? It's a cold morning."

"It's overtime for me, sir, so there's that."

"Good job. OK, Constable Stewart, back to the hotel for us."

7: INTERVIEWING THE FINNS

We drove back to the hotel and I found McCrabban and Lawson. I told them about the shoe and Warren's opinion of the matter, and neither of them seemed particularly worried by this new piece of evidence. But I still made the phone call to Mulvenny and asked him to have one more look through the building just to be on the safe side. I thought he'd be furious, but he said his dogs loved a bit of a run in the snow.

McCrabban and Lawson had taken statements from all the guests on the top floor, none of whom had anything to contribute to the case.

They had also taken statements from Miss Jones, who didn't remember seeing Lily after the visit to the castle. Mr. Ek recalled seeing Lily at the castle but didn't remember seeing her at dinner that night in the hotel. Laakso had a similar recollection. "Stefan and Nicolas were no help at all," Lawson said.

"Why's that?" I asked.

"Because they've already left. Went home yesterday afternoon."

"Before the castle trip?"

"Yes. Just after breakfast."

"Sent home for playing silly buggers with Mr. Laakso's wallet, I'll bet. Well, that's them off the hook. I'll want to interview Ek and Laakso again, separately," I said.

"I think they're packing now. They're in a rush. They've got planes to catch," Crabbie said.

"Nevertheless. We've got a coroner to answer to down the line."

Laakso first in the upstairs bar. Me talking. Lawson and Crabbie observing.

"When did you last see Miss Bigelow?"

"I don't remember. I think she went with us to the castle."

"Did you notice if she slipped away from the group?"

"I did not notice that. But I would not blame her for doing so. I would have gotten away if I could. My knees on those stairs! I think they forget that I am sixty-four years old!"

"After the visit to the castle, you did what?"

"We made our own way back to the hotel. I walked along the seafront, returned to the hotel, had dinner, and went to bed."

"Were there any functions you had to go to last night?"

"No. Thank God. Last night was a free evening. I had my food, if it can be described as food, as early as possible and went to my room."

"And did you notice Miss Bigelow in the hotel last night?"

Laakso shook his weary head. "I would not have noticed if Diego Maradonna had been demonstrating football trick shots in the dining room. I was utterly exhausted. These trips are getting beyond me."

"Did you notice anything strange about Miss Bigelow's behavior? Any strange questions? Anything out of the ordinary?"

He shook his head. I tried a few other lines of inquiry, but it was no good, Laakso had apparently no information about Miss Bigelow's whereabouts or mental state.

Mr. Ek had the same story. He remembered Lily joining them for the visit to the old Courtaulds factory, but she hadn't made much of an impression there, or elsewhere, on the delegation's visit to Northern Ireland.

"She didn't interview you about the trip?" I asked.

"She asked a few questions on the first day of our visit here, but as the trip went on she grew less interested, I think," he said.

"Why was that?" I asked.

"I do not know. Either she had information enough to make her story or she knew that there was no story to make."

"Anything strange, or out of the ordinary, about her behavior?" Crabbie asked.

Ek shrugged. "I was looking after Mr. Laakso. I wasn't paying attention to a British newspaper reporter," he said.

"A very pretty female newspaper reporter," I said.

"Even a pretty female one," Ek said. "My role here was to look after the concerns of Mr. Laakso and the two young Mr. Lennätins, not to worry about the state of mind of young English reporters."

"Of course, but you would have noticed if she was crying or anything like that, surely?" I said.

"Why would I have noticed that?" he asked, a little irritated. He looked at his watch to hurry me along, which made me want to hurry even less.

"Sir, we are trying to determine why a young lady may have committed suicide," I said.

"We have no idea why she committed suicide. Why don't you ask her boyfriend?"

"What boyfriend?" I asked.

"Young ladies like that always have boyfriends."

"So you admit that you noticed her looks," I said.

He sighed. "Do you think I could get a drink if this is going to take much longer?" he said.

Aye, how about a pint of answer my fucking-questions, you in-a-hurry Swedish-Finnish fuck, I thought. "Tea, coffee?" I asked.

"How about a brandy?" he said.

"Get him a double. And the same for me and for you and McCrabban, if you want," I said to Lawson. McCrabban shook his head and Lawson came from the bar with a couple of doubles.

"I got cognac," Lawson said, unsure if he had done the right thing.

"Very good," Ek said, and drank with satisfaction.

He leaned forward and patted me on the knee. "She was pretty. So what? Pretty girls die every day. Prettier girls than this one."

"Well, yes . . ."

"What do you mean?" Lawson asked.

"In Leningrad once, I saw a room full of dead girls. Beautiful girls. Fifteen, twenty of them. All dead."

"When was this?" Lawson asked, aghast.

"'42, or perhaps '43. Most of the school had been evacuated before our advance. Why had these ones stayed? Had they missed the truck? Had they not been given the information? We didn't know."

"Who killed them?" Lawson said.

Ek shrugged. "The Commissars? The SS?"

"If I could bring you back to Miss Bigelow . . ."

"I do remember something. You should always give your interview subjects a little brandy. It makes everything flow."

"I'll bear that in mind. What do you remember?"

She asked several questions during the factory visit."

"What questions?"

"She asked the civil servants about the asbestos roof. She wondered if it was a safe work environment," Ek said.

"I've been in that old factory; it's not a safe work environment," I said with a smile.

Ek nodded. "It was an entirely unsuitable place for what we have in mind," he said. "That was obvious to everyone."

"Did she have her notebook with her when she was asking these questions?" I asked.

Ek shrugged. "I do not remember," he said, absently.

"And when did you see her last?"

"I think at the castle. But I was not paying attention to her. It was raining and cold. None of us had umbrellas. The fools running the trip had not thought to get us umbrellas. I was worried for Mr. Laakso. I was glad when he got back to the hotel. I did not notice if Miss Bigelow was with us or not."

"You made your own way back to the hotel yesterday?"

"Yes. We could spend as much time in the castle as we wanted after the formal tour, but I did not think it was so interesting a place, so I came back to the hotel. Mr. Laakso does not like me to help him as I am a little bit older than he, so I went briskly to the hotel to wait for him and make sure he arrived safely. He arrived shortly afterward."

"And Miss Bigelow?"

"I did not see her."

"At dinner last night?"

"I did not eat dinner last night. They have been stuffing our faces this whole time. I went to bed. I would have swum if this hotel had a swimming pool, or if the beach was not so filthy."

"A little chilly for swimming," Lawson said.

Mr. Ek laughed. "Who are you talking to? You are talking to Finns!"

"In the castle, did Miss Bigelow seem distracted, or sad, or unhappy in any way?" McCrabban asked.

"Who knows? Who knows what is going on in anyone's heart? Not you. Not I. She was quiet. Ask her boyfriend, perhaps he will tell you about her mood, if he can."

"Your English is very good," I said.

"So it should be, after two decades in America. But my accent is not so good. A little hard to understand, yes?"

"Your accent is fine."

He looked at his watch. And now I did want to hurry, what with him being so cooperative and everything.

"After the castle visit, did the group have any more functions planned? Was Miss Bigelow's absence remarked upon?"

"We had a late breakfast with the Northern Ireland Better Business Bureau this morning. In my opinion, they need a better Better Business Bureau. Those men know nothing about business. Anyway, Miss Bigelow did not attend this function for obvious reasons."

We asked him a few more questions, but it was clear that the colorful Mr. Ek couldn't help us, either with Lily's whereabouts or with her state of mind.

I looked at Crabbie and Lawson, but they had nothing to add.

"Detective Lawson will take your contact details in Finland, but after that you're free to go," I said. I looked at my watch. "And I think you'll still make your flight and your connections."

Ek nodded, stood, and shook my hand. "This was an ill-omened visit from the beginning. I knew it would be a waste of time, I am just sorry that it ended in such a way. Please pass on my condolences to the young lady's family. From all of us," he said.

"I will," I said. Just as Ek was leaving, Tony McIlroy came into the conference room. He was bleary-eyed and harassed-looking. He made a beeline for me.

"Sean, mate, you've got to let my clients go. If they miss their connections they'll be stuck in the UK for another night," Tony said.

"No 'hello'?" I asked, somewhat irritated by the brusqueness of his manner. He wasn't my senior anymore. He wasn't anybody's senior anymore. He was nothing.

"Sorry. Hello, Sean. Look, what's going on here?"

"Lily Bigelow, the journalist with the deleg—"

"Aye, I know all that, but why are you interviewing my clients? They have planes to catch. They're important people, Sean!" he said, raising his voice.

"It's a slow process, Tony. You know what it's like."

"What process? She bloody killed herself, didn't she? That's what everyone's saying."

"That's for the coroner to decide. Our job is to gather the evidence. *All* the evidence, and that means interviewing your clients, which, you'll be happy to know, we have just wrapped up."

Tony sighed with relief. "So they're off to get their flights?"

"They're off to get their flights."

"Thank God for that! Laakso's people in Helsinki have been calling me all morning! Jesus," he said.

Tony suddenly seemed to notice McCrabban and Lawson for the first time. His cheeks reddened. He had embarrassed himself in front of them.

How the mighty had fallen, I thought. *There but for the grace of God and a girl from MI5 go I . . . That's what happens to ex-policemen. Grubbing around for your weekly paycheck, kowtowing to the clients, eating shit sandwiches left and right. The private sector, my arse.*

"Uhm, I suppose I'd better go and help them out to the airport," Tony said.

I shook his hand. "Yeah, mate, I'll see you around."

"See, Lawson, you think it's all quoits on the deck, wanking to *Readers' Wives* and U2 'music' blaring all day long, but that's the private sector for you: grim. See Tony's face? Harassed. You're better with us," I said, when Tony was out the door with his clients.

"Sir, I never thought about leaving. I—"

"Yeah, don't think about leaving. Think about Lily Bigelow's shoe, or Lily Bigelow's notebook, or why Sergeant Dalziel has a giant rubber cock in the bottom drawer of his desk."

"Why does S—"

"Cos I put it there. Now, get back to work."

We interviewed the remaining hotel guests and the manager, but no one had seen Lily come back the previous evening, and no one had noticed anything out of the ordinary about her behavior.

I called up the *Financial Times* and got Lily's next of kin from Personnel. Unfortunately, it was a complicated business. Her parents had divorced. Her mother had emigrated to South Africa, and her father was living in Norwich. She had a flatmate but the flatmate was on vacation. I called up the local peelers, and they found her father on the electoral roll. I explained the situation, and the Norfolk Constabulary said that considering the nature of the news they would call on Mr. Bigelow in person. If Lily's father was up for it, I asked them to ask him about her mental health and to call me back with the details. Presumably they had nothing else to do in Norwich, because they said that they would send out a "team of detectives" and something called "grief counselors" and get back to me later in the day.

"She liked a wee glass of wine with her dinner. She sat by herself, sometimes reading a book," Kevin, the manager, said, leading us up to her room.

"Did she seem depressed at all?" I asked.

Kevin nodded. "There was a sadness about her, sitting by herself with her wine. She was very pretty. Such a shame. Boyfriend trouble, more than likely."

"She told you that?" I asked.

"No, no, but you could tell," he said.

We stopped outside her room.

This, we all knew, would probably be the moment of truth.

I distributed latex gloves, and Kevin put the key in the door. This was not one of the suite rooms with the new keycards.

"Maybe call Forensics in?" Lawson suggested.

"Forensics would be furious to get called in for something like this," I said, and Crabbie concurred.

We went into Lily's hotel room.

Freshly made bed. Clothes in the wardrobe and the drawers. Portable Olivetti electric typewriter on the desk. Toiletries in the bathroom. An empty suitcase and a typewriter carry case on the suitcase stand. Nothing of interest anywhere. Lily had traveled light.

No note in the typewriter. No note anywhere in the room. We did a thorough search but found nothing. In the bathroom we found aspirin, Nembutal, and Valium. Nobody knew what Nembutal was, but we'd find out.

"No note and no sign of that notebook, either," McCrabban said.

"Aye, I don't like that missing notebook," I agreed. "I saw her writing in it."

McCrabban's grey face contorted into a sort of scowl. "I don't like it either, Sean. The shoe on the wrong foot, the missing notebook. It's almost enough to make you start to wonder, isn't it?"

I turned to Lawson. "I asked Mike Mulvenny to have one final search of the castle with his dogs. Do me a favor and find out what he came up with, eh?"

Lawson nodded and left the room. When he was gone, I closed the door on Kevin, who was still hanging around in the hall.

"Lightning doesn't strike twice, Crabbie."

"You're referring to Lizzie Fitzpatrick," he said, lowering his voice and giving me a significant look.

"I am."

He gazed out of the window at the black lough and the castle beyond.

"No note, a missing notebook, a shoe on the wrong foot," he said to himself.

I sat on the edge of Lily's bed and let him think it through.

"But on the other hand, a lonely lass and absolutely no way anyone else could have been involved," he said.

"Aye," I agreed.

Lawson came back with news about Mike Mulvenny.

"He says he didn't find anyone hiding in the castle. He's a hundred percent sure. He made sure to tell me it was 'a hundred percent sure, not ninety-nine percent sure,'" Lawson said.

"That's the fourth search we've done now, Sean," McCrabban said. "Three with dogs. There's no murderer in the castle."

"Tell the big Scouse git thanks. And call him Sergeant Mulvenny not 'big Scouse git.'"

When he returned, Crabbie and I had thoroughly searched the room, finding nothing of interest.

"Still no notebook, Lawson. I want you to take half a dozen PCs and search all the bins in the castle, all the bins in the center of Carrick, and go through all the bins in the hotel."

"Yes, sir."

I called up Carrick Cars, the only vehicle rental place in Carrick, and found that Lily Bigelow had rented a Ford Escort for her stay in the town. "What sort of mileage had she done?" I asked.

"I'll check. . . . Log says twenty-five miles."

Twenty-five miles seemed rather a lot when you considered that she was traveling with the delegation most of the time in Northern Ireland civil service transport. Why bother to hire a car at all? Side trips? Tourism?

"She leave anything in the car?"

"No."

"I'll send an officer to examine it; we're looking for a notebook."

I decided to go with the officer myself, but there was nothing of evidentiary value in the vehicle. I put on rubber gloves and joined in on the rather revolting search through the bins in the center of Carrick. No notebook.

When we got back to the station, I noticed that Lawson had written Lily Bigelow's name on the incident room whiteboard in blue pen. Blue pens were what we used for accidental deaths, suicides, and deaths from natural causes.

He saw me looking at the pen. He picked up the red pen. Red pens were for homicides and suspected homicides.

"Nah, you were right the first time. The blue pen for now," I said.

8: THE KILLING OF THE CHIEF SUPER

Station buzz. A violent death. An English girl. Eyes on this one. Media. UTV. The BBC. Maybe journos from over the water.

Downstairs to Interview Room 2. Start the tape recorder. Mr. Underhill, please state your name and date of birth and how long you have been in your current occupation. No leading questions. Let him talk, let him digress if he wants. Lawson watching me. Crabbie watching me. A nod to Lawson, a nod to the Crabman, a nod to Mr. Underhill. No need for good cop/bad cop. *Never* a need for good/bad cop. Good cop/bad cop seldom worked. The statement spooled into the tape recorder. Lawson made notes. Crabbie made notes. I looked at the notes.

We tried to crack Mr. Underhill's time line. It didn't crack. We tried to crack his certitude on the locked front door. That didn't crack, either. We tried to crack the punctiliousness with which he performed his job. No dice there either.

A constable brought in Mr. Underhill's criminal record: a drunk and disorderly in Glasgow in 1955, a drunk and disorderly in Portsmouth in 1961 and again in Portsmouth in 1964. That was it.

"Did you kill Lily Bigelow?"

"No, I didnae! How many times are you going to ask me that?"

"Did you touch or move Lily Bigelow's body after you found her dead?"

"No."

"You like the drink, Mr. Underhill?"

"I havenae touched the stuff in twenty years."

"This inspection that you did . . . do you wear glasses, Mr. Underhill?" Lawson asked.

"Never needed to!"

"When was the last time you had your eyes tested?"

"I donae remember."

Lawson led him outside, asked him to read the number plate of a car in the car park and the bugger could do it. We couldn't crack his story, we couldn't crack his time line, we couldn't crack his confidence that the castle was locked and bolted all night. No way in, no way out.

We released him and told him that we might need to talk to him again.

We spent the rest of the afternoon going through the CCTV footage and conducting wide source interviews.

The CCTV camera pointing at the rear entrance of the Northern Bank was by far the most helpful. It covered the Marine Highway and the entrance to the castle, and its twenty-four hours of tape was more than sufficient for our purposes. We spotted Lily going into the castle with the delegation at 4 p.m. the day before. There was a confusing mass of people leaving the castle at a quarter to six, when Mr. Underhill kicked out all the visitors, but when we freeze-framed and meticulously examined the tapes we didn't see Lily among them. Not that we could have. Lily had stayed behind when Mr. Underhill closed the castle gate and lowered the portcullis. She had stayed behind to kill herself, for reasons that were still obscure.

We interviewed the two civil servants from the Northern Ireland Office who had taken the delegation to the castle. They had nothing helpful to add—had known that Lily was joining the tour, hadn't noticed that she hadn't exited with the Finns. They'd been so intent on getting Mr. Laakso up and down the castle's spiral staircase without breaking his neck that they hadn't noticed anything else.

Norwich police called us back at four. I put them on speakerphone in the CID incident room and a chatty Chief Inspector Broadbent filled us in on all the gloomy details of the notification. Mr. Bigelow was devastated. He lived alone, his son from a previous marriage was in America, his ex-wife was in South Africa. Lily was all that he had. ... She had taken the train up from London to see him once a month. No, he hadn't noticed anything out of the ordinary, or any change in her behavior, but it was true that she hadn't been that happy since the break-up with her boyfriend, Tim, the previous year. They'd been going together since college, and after the break-up Lily had been quite upset.

"Who broke up with whom?" I asked.

"It was complicated, her father says," Broadbent explained. "He works for Lloyds. He got offered a promotion to the office in New York. He wanted her to come with him. She tried to get the *FT* to transfer her but they wouldn't do it. New York is for senior reporters only and she was very much a cub. Apparently they had a big row, then they made up and Tim proposed. She thought about quitting her job and going to live with him in America, but in the end she decided to stay in London. They tried the long-distance relationship thing for about half a year, but it didn't work out. Tim met someone else, apparently, and the relationship fizzled out."

"This Tim fellow still in New York?" I asked.

"Yeah."

"Full name, contact number?"

"Tim Whalen. I don't have a contact number. You think he might have some insight into the case?"

"I have no clue, but if I was going to top myself over a broken heart, I think I'd try one last communication with the ex," I said.

"Well, I'll see if I can track down a phone number, and if I can I'll get it over to you," Broadbent said.

"Good."

"What will I tell them is the official cause of death?"

"Uhm, we don't have an *official* cause of death at the moment. There will be an autopsy later today, but barring anything out of the ordinary, we'll be tagging this one as a suicide."

We talked for another ten minutes or so, but nothing pertinent came up. Mr. Bigelow had phoned his wife in South Africa, so I was spared the necessity of that notification. While I was on the phone, Lawson called BT and got them to fax over the list of every phone call that was made from the Coast Road Hotel in the previous twenty-four hours, which was smart work.

He was a good copper, Lawson, almost too bloody good, and we lived in fear that he'd be nicked by a big Belfast command, or by the Fraud Squad, or Special Branch.

Crabbie, Lawson, and I worked our way through the list of calls. All local, save a few to England, half a dozen to Finland, but none to America.

We bagged Lily's gear and put it in the evidence room.

"Shouldn't we send it to her father?" Lawson asked.

Crabbie shook his head. "We'll have to hang onto it until after the coroner's inquest, and we'll need to keep that CCTV footage too. If the coroner asks to see it, we'll have to be prepared to show it to him."

We got a call from the medical examiner in Belfast, asking if any one of us wanted to attend the autopsy, which would be getting under way within the hour.

I turned to Crabbie.

"Not me," he said. "I hate those things. Always have."

"Well, I don't want to go," I said.

We both turned to look at Lawson. He was horrified.

"Oh come on, not me. I'm still new here, aren't I? And it's snowing. What if I faint? Let the station down?"

"What do you think, Crabbie, will we let him off, just this once?"

"I think we will," he said.

I explained to Lawson that the medical examiners generally disliked it when cops attended the autopsy and only ever asked out of courtesy. There was an unspoken rule that we didn't poach in their terrain and they didn't poach in ours.

"You can go on home, lads. There's nothing much going to happen now, I would imagine. I'll hold the fort," I said.

"But you've been on since the first shift," Crabbie objected.

"It doesn't matter. And besides I don't want to go home. Depressing back there. Cold, empty house."

Crabbie emptied his pipe into the litter bin and cleared his throat. He looked nervous and I could tell he was about to launch another bold, doomed Edwardian exploratory expedition into my private life.

"A girl your own age, Sean, I could ask Helen, uhm . . ." he said, before his voice trailed off into an embarrassed silence.

I looked at him. "You're right, of course," I agreed. "Thanks. Maybe I'll take you up on that. Go on home, the pair of you, the roads are going to get bad soon."

Later. My office. Darkness. Heavy snow outside. Traffic slowed to a crawl on the A2. Fog horns from ships out in the lough. My car had been fixed and rather cheekily I'd sent a constable to my house to pick it up and drive it to the barracks, reminding him to look underneath for bombs, to go easy on the clutch, and to bring me the Steve Reich album from the backseat.

He'd returned safely and I looked at the record. Interesting artwork on the sleeve. A painting by someone called Henry Darger. Have to check him out. I took the record out of the press and examined it for imperfections. Number twenty-two of a pressing of a hundred, it said on the label.

Twenty-two of a hundred? They hadn't told me that in HMV. Did they even know? I might have got a bargain here. I put the record carefully back in its sleeve. This was too rare to play on my office equipment.

Instead, I found Steve Reich's *The Desert Music* and put it on. I closed my eyes and after a few bars I wasn't there. I wasn't in Carrickfergus, or this office. I wasn't in 1987; I was wherever *The Desert Music* was taking place: some ashy grey wasteland, where, no doubt, just out of sight Sisyphus was pushing a boulder up a volcanic slope.

A knock at the door.

Chief Inspector McArthur.

"Come in, sir, have a seat," I said.

He sat down. I went to the drinks trolley and poured him a glass of Jura, which he took with thanks.

"Shouldn't you be on your way home?" he asked.

"I'm just waiting for the preliminary autopsy results on Miss Bigelow. ME might call me. Sometimes they do. Sometimes they don't."

"I see. Any trouble with the Finns?"

"Nope. And they all caught their planes, so the NIO is happy."

"Excellent."

"They were quite an eccentric bunch. Think the civil servants were glad to see the back of them."

McArthur shook his head. "That's the wrong attitude, Duffy. We'll all be delighted, I'm sure, if they decide to build their mobile phone plant here rather than in the Republic."

"Oh yeah, of course, sir," I said.

"This is very good whis—"

The phone rang. I picked it up.

"Uh huh? . . . Yes. . . . We had noticed that. Tell him thank you, anyway."

I hung up and looked at McArthur. The whisky had dulled his wits slightly and he was grinning like a simpleton.

"What was that about?" he asked.

"The ME's nurse passed on a note to us from the doctor. He wanted to know if we'd noticed that the victim's shoe was on the wrong foot."

"Wrong foot?"

"The victim had her left shoe on her right foot. I thought, initially, that there might be something untoward about that, but my mind was somewhat put at ease by WPC Warren."

"How was that?"

I explained our theory about Lily walking up the spiral staircase and the keep roof barefoot, only putting on her shoes to jump.

"So definitely a suicide then," he said.

"It's *looking* that way."

"As long as we can rule out the castle ghost, I'm happy," he said with a wink.

"Yes, sir, there was no supernatur—"

"Chief Inspector! Chief Inspector, are you still here?" Mabel was yelling from her desk.

"I'm down here in Duffy's office," McArthur called back.

"Oh, sir, I thought you'd want to know immediately!" Mabel said, running breathlessly into the room.

"What is it?"

"It's Chief Superintendent McBain, sir!" she said.

"What about him?"

"Turn on the news, sir!"

I turned on BBC Radio Ulster.

". . . At the scene of a car bomb in the village of Glenoe, County Antrim, that happened late this morning."

I looked at Mabel, who was crying now.

"How do they know that it was McBain?" I asked.

"I confirmed it with district," she said.

". . . the victim is reported to be a senior police officer. No paramilitary group as yet has claimed responsibility, but our security spokesman Dermot Clawson says that the mercury tilt device bears all the hallmarks of the IRA . . ." the newsreader continued.

I turned off the radio in a state of shock. Ed McBain was one of the good guys. I'd known the big ganch for years.

"Jesus Christ! I was just talking to him yesterday," I said.

"Me too. We should get up there! It's insane that the BBC are there before us. Happened this morning and we're only finding out about this now?" McArthur said.

I shook my head. "Glenoe village is not in our jurisdiction, sir. That's why we haven't heard. It's Larne RUC. Their case."

"Even so, we should offer our help!"

"Uhm, they're a bit of an awkward bunch, sir. I'll call them up and offer our assistance, but I doubt they'll take it."

A sobered, grim-faced McArthur nodded and went to his office. A sobbing Mabel went with him.

The phone on my desk was ringing.

"Duffy, CID," I said.

"Sean, did you hear the news?" Crabbie asked.

"I did. Horrifying."

"Mercury tilt switch bomb under his car."

"That's what they're saying."

"You let your guard down for a minute and you get blown up. I'm coming in," Crabbie said.

"There's no point, mate. It's Larne's case. You stay home."

"Aye, OK. He was a good copper, wasn't he?"

"That he was," I agreed. "All right, Crabbie, I'll see you later."

McArthur went to get a coat and I put in the courtesy call to Larne RUC. A new DI that I didn't know, named Armstrong, surprised me by saying that "We would love your help, Inspector Duffy."

"What?"

"We'd love your help."

"Wouldn't I be getting in the way?"

"Oh, no, not at all. We'd love it if you came down, Duffy. You knew McBain, did you?"

"I did know him. In fact I was talking to him about a case only yesterday."

"Well then, I'm sure they'd be glad of your assistance at the crime scene."

I hung up and looked at the phone suspiciously. Chief Inspector McArthur popped his head around my office door. "Anything new, Duffy?"

"Yeah. Uhm, I was wrong. Larne RUC say it's fine if we go down there. Say they need all the help they can get."

"Oh, OK, I'll go with you, if you don't mind."

". . . All right. We'll take my car."

I told Mabel to fill Lawson in on all the developments and we drove up the Beltoy Road to Glenoe.

It was a treacherous night with the snow and sleet, and none of the roads in the hill country had been gritted. Fortunately, the Beemer kept us on the straight and narrow; I kept the speed down to a steady fifty and we arrived at Glenoe in one piece. Pretty little place, Glenoe, with a steep road up past whitewashed cottages to a small deciduous wood with a famous waterfall.

Not pretty tonight, though.

McBain's Volvo scattered over half the village. One of McBain's legs clearly visible on the roof of a house.

Dozens of cops from Larne RUC, the Belfast Forensics Unit, and Special Branch. Dozens of media. Ambulance men, even some sol-

diers from the local UDR base. A perimeter had been set up in front
of McBain's house, which was a neat Georgian manor at the top of the
hill. The mercury tilt switch had evidently gone off almost immediately
after he had pulled out of his driveway.

I parked the Beemer and got out.

I introduced myself and the chief inspector to a constable guarding
the RUC DO NOT CROSS tape and he let us through. Larne RUC
hadn't done too bad a job. They'd set up spotlights and a generator, and
they were giving the boilersuited forensic officers a wide berth to do
their business.

I walked past the wreck of the Volvo. The rear of the vehicle was
completely gone, and the rest was like some kind of abstract sculpture
that Ballard might have liked. A headless torso covered with a blanket
was in the driver's seat.

"Poor bastard," I said.

McArthur nodded.

I recalled a dozen little kindnesses that Ed had shown me and his
other junior officers. Eccentric, old-fashioned, but such a decent man.
. . . I had to take a minute to swallow a sob.

We walked up the gravel path into the house and were immediately
intercepted by DCI Kennedy, a red-faced, passed-over, fifty-year-old
chief inspector whom I'd encountered a couple of times before. Each
occasion as unpleasant as the one before. "What are you doing here,
Duffy?" Kennedy asked.

"I was told that you might need some help."

"Help from you? I'd sooner have Myra Hindley babysit our Kevin."

"That's a bit of—"

"Who told you we needed your help?"

"Armstrong, at your station."

"He's new. He doesn't know anything. You can fuck off, Duffy. You
can fuck off back to Carrick where you belong."

McArthur gave me a wide-eyed look.

"See here, Kennedy, this is my gaffer, Chief Inspector McArthur,"
I said, pointedly.

Kennedy turned to McArthur and looked him in the eye. "You can both fuck off. We don't need your help."

I didn't want to make a scene in front of so many people, so I put my arm around McArthur's shoulders and led him outside.

"What was that all about?" McArthur asked, amazed.

My cheeks were burning. I was angry at myself. "I had a feeling they were going to be like this," I mumbled.

"Is there friction between Carrick and Larne CID or something?" McArthur asked, finally becoming aware of our long-running feud.

"There have been a few jurisdictional disputes over the years, that's all. Kennedy is just an ignorant bloody bastard. Everybody knows it."

We walked past Mrs. McBain, still sitting in the back of the ambulance with a blanket around her shoulders, apparently unhurt, holding a mug of tea. She had a cut on her forehead, but it must have been from flying glass from the shattered house windows. There was no way she'd been in that Volvo.

"Joanne?"

She remembered me from the police club and the missing dog.

"Inspector Duffy," she said.

"I'm so sorry, Jo. We all loved Ed, as you know."

She nodded, sniffed. "I suppose, you'll want a statement, while it's fresh in my memory, before I forget," she said.

"God, no, I just wanted to say hello and see if there was anything I could get you," I said, a little surprised that Larne RUC hadn't already taken her statement.

"He didn't *always* check, in answer to your question. His knees were bad. It hurt to bend down and look under the car. Today he didn't check. He was in a hurry. That phone call."

"Phone call?"

"Someone called very early. After six. Eddie said he had to go straightaway, and a few moments after he left I heard the bang. We're at the top of the hill. Any direction you go from here, the mercury will flow and set the bomb off. I knew what had happened immediately. Eddie had described it to me often enough."

She started to cry, and I sat next to her and gave her a hug. I handed McArthur the empty teacup. "Get her another," I whispered. "Milk, lots of sugar."

She sobbed on my shoulder for a full ten minutes.

"Do you have somewhere to go tonight? You can't stay here," I said.

"I'll stay with Mary, she's on her way over," Joanne said.

"Have they notified Jack, Noel, Richard, and Suzanne?" I asked.

"Yes. They're flying back tonight."

"They'll be a comfort."

She turned to look at me. "The chief constable's coming down. I don't want to have to deal with him, can you tell him that I'd rather be alone with my children and my sister?"

"Of course. I'll take care of it."

McArthur arrived back with a new mug of tea, his raincoat covered in snowflakes.

"Mrs. McBain wants to wait here until her sister arrives to take her away. She doesn't want to have to deal with the chief constable, who is on his way down from Belfast. Can you make some calls, sir?" I asked McArthur.

"Me?"

"Yeah, you."

"I'll try," he said.

When he'd gone, Mrs. McBain took her second cup of tea and sipped it.

"They'll never catch them, will they, Sean?"

"You never know, Jo."

"Eddie always talked about it. Unless there's forensic evidence, or you can trace that phone call to a listed number, but they'll have used gloves and called from a phone box, won't they?"

She knew of which she spake. Unless they'd left a fingerprint somewhere on the device, there was next to no chance of catching the bombers. And no one who was clever enough to build a mercury tilt switch bomb would be stupid enough to leave a fingerprint.

"We'll do our best, Jo. We owe him that," I said.

McArthur returned, and we sat with her until her sister arrived and took over.

On the way back to the Beemer, I saw Frank Payne of the Forensics Unit having a smoke and a sandwich simultaneously.

"Long day for you, Frank," I said.

"So much for Muhammad Ali's peace mission, eh, Duffy?" he said venomously.

"Maybe James 'Bonecrusher' Smith will show up with a peace plan next week," I said.

Payne cackled and slapped me on the back. "You're a comedian, Duffy. Well, back to work, we still haven't found McBain's head yet."

"I saw one of his legs up on—"

"Yeah we've tagged that one. We're almost completely done now. But the head . . . you don't want some wee girl to go out playing in her Wendy house and find Eddie McBain's head grinning at her, eh?"

"No," I agreed.

"Eh, Duffy, ever have sex while camping? It's fucking intents. Get it? Get it?"

"Yes," I said, and walked to the car.

"Are all forensic officers as disagreeable as that chap?" McArthur asked me on the road back to Carrick.

"They can be, sir, but Frank Payne brings being an arsehole to a whole new level."

9: WIPING THE WHITEBOARD

The funeral was a full-dress affair at a little out-of-the-way churchyard on Islandmagee. The chief constable came down, as well as the secretary of state for Northern Ireland and, in a surprise move, the Irish foreign minister. All the media saw the Republic of Ireland foreign minister's presence as an optimistic sign of inter-Irish cooperation or something, but in fact it was because he and McBain had played rugby together at Trinity.

They found Ed McBain's head, but it was still a closed-casket affair. It rained, of course. Apocalyptic, cold, cleansing rain from the Irish Sea. The band got soaked, their brass instruments going flat, and the funeral march sounded even more doleful than usual. The honor guard was drenched. Superintendent Strong, a beardy Glaswegian roughneck, gave Ed a fine eulogy, and everyone felt that if Strong got promoted to chief super, he'd probably be an adequate replacement.

I saw Tony McIlroy at the wake. He came over and bought me a drink.

"You know we were among the last coppers to have seen Ed McBain alive," he said. "That theft nonsense at the Coast Road Hotel."

"I expect you're right," I said.

"Poor Ed. He was so worried about not letting everyone down. Showing Northern Ireland in its best possible light to that bloody delegation. Poor bastard. See the newspapers? Publishing that photograph of his torso in the car? Jackals, the lot of them."

"Aye," I agreed.

Tony sighed and sipped his Guinness. "You're not on the McBain case, are you?"

"Me? No. Larne RUC. They'll balls it up, of course."

"Why do you say that?"

"Because they always do."

Tony laughed. "What *are* you working on now?"

"The Lily Bigelow suicide."

"Christ, that was something, wasn't it? Quite the ill-starred trip for our Finnish friends. Or to use the parlance of the civil service, 'an utter fucking debacle.' That nonsense with the wallet, the shitty condition of the factory site, a suicide. And after they got back to Helsinki they're bound to have heard about Ed McBain's death, too. I'm no fortune teller, but somehow I don't think Lennätin will be setting up a mobile phone factory in Carrickfergus any time soon."

"I think you're right about that one, Tony," I said.

"And between you, me, and the gatepost, it was always going to be Dublin rather than Belfast because the corporation tax is that much lower down there. That's what Laakso told me. To quote a great Irishman, 'there's no future, there's no future for us.'"

"So why did you come back here?" I asked.

"I was made to feel very unwelcome in England, if you know what I mean."

"I know what you mean."

"There's no future for you in the RUC either, mate. Look at you, stuck at Carrick all these years. They don't appreciate you. Why don't you quit and come and work for me? Or set up on your own?"

I shook my head ruefully. "You know how many times I've written my letter of resignation? You know many times I've actually tendered it? I'm a joke. Even to myself now. No, I won't be quitting anymore. I'll be staying until I get my pension."

"Or until they blow you up like poor Ed."

"Yeah, or until they blow me up like poor Ed."

"Well, you have my card, let's go out for a proper drink, OK?"

"OK, Tony."

After an obligatory hour at the wake, I picked up McCrabban and Lawson and we all drove back to Carrickfergus in the Beemer.

We changed out of our dress uniforms and back into our ordinary clothes. Slow day at the office. We refused to charge an old lady shop-lifter, and that just left a kid, all of thirteen or fourteen, waiting for us in the cells, who'd been lifted driving a stolen car. After further investigation we discovered that this was his nineteenth car-theft offense in the United Kingdom. He was a gypsy who moved with a clan of travelers all over Northern Ireland, the Republic of Ireland, England, and Europe, so it was highly likely that in all he had stolen hundreds of vehicles.

"We have to dispose of this case today, Sean. Social Services say that if we keep him in the cells any longer they'll take it to a higher authority," Crabbie explained.

"What does that mean?"

"I don't know."

"Habeas corpus?"

"I don't know, Sean."

"All right, let's go and see the little shit."

Downstairs to the cells. The little shit was not so little. Six-footer. Ginger bap, sleekit look to him, but not unintelligent. Killian, he called himself. He spoke Irish better than English so we conversed in both languages.

"You were stopped in a stolen car, Killian, not for the first time," I said.

"I was given that car in exchange for a horse, I wasn't to know it was stolen," he said.

"And the other eighteen times you've been charged with car theft?"

"Eighteen times charged, but only one conviction."

"And for that you got two months in an English borstal," I said.

"Which I escaped from the second night I was there."

"Did you? That wasn't in the file."

"No, they were probably too embarrassed to put it in the file. But it's true enough. You can check into it."

"I believe you," I said. I passed him over my cigarettes and lighter. He lit himself a cig, expertly palmed four others, and passed the box and lighter back.

I sighed. "What are we going to do with you, Killian?"

"You can't hold me. Social Services are going to put me in this place called Kinkaid. Heard of it?"

"No."

"Easiest nick in Ireland to get out of. You just walk through the gate. I'll escape from there, steal a car, and be back with my Pavee by tomorrow."

"We could charge you with conspiracy. I suggest to Special Branch that you're part of a car-theft ring that aids the paramilitaries, I get you sent to an adult prison. Special Branch will keep Social Services out of it."

"Why would you do that?"

"To teach you a lesson and stop you stealing cars," I said, switching back to English.

"That seems a bit of a disproportionate response," Killian said.

"Maybe I'm the disproportionate-response type."

"You don't seem the disproportionate-response type," Killian said, blowing a smoke ring up toward the ceiling.

"Why's that?"

"You speak Irish and you're Catholic, I'd say that you've had your fair degree of shite from the RUC and are probably on the side of the underdog, which, in this analogy, would be me."

I bit down a grin and thought about it. *Not a completely unlikeable kid.*

"You know, *is minic a gheibhean beal oscailt diog dunta*," I said, which made him laugh.

"You're not allowed to do that anymore, are you?"

"Nope. We're not. Listen, son, if Sergeant McCrabban lets you go with a caution, could you at least promise me not to steal any more cars in my jurisdiction? In Carrickfergus?"

He stubbed out his cigarette, stood up, and offered me his hand.

"On my solemn word of honor," he said. "We're going over to England next week anyway and we'll probably be there for a bit."

He shook my hand and then Sergeant McCrabban's hand. I made

him give Sergeant McCrabban his watch back and we let him go with
a caution.

We walked back up to the incident room.

"Another case resolved," I said. "If only *his* name was up on the
whiteboard."

"What was that thing you said to him in Irish that made him
laugh?" Crabbie asked. "*Is minic* something?"

"*Is minic a gheibhean beal oscailt diog dunta.* It means 'an open
mouth often invites a closed fist.'"

"That it does," McCrabban agreed. "That it does."

I went home to the empty house on Coronation Road for lunch and
made myself a pint glass vodka gimlet. Vodka, lime juice, soda, ice—four
simple ingredients that conspired together to make most of the world's
problems go away. Certainly after two of them, easy on the soda.

I read *The Making of the Atomic Bomb*, which Beth had got me for
my birthday, along with an original 1953 pressing of *Tosca* from EMI—
the one with Maria Callas, Tito Gobbi, and Giuseppe Di Stefano. One
of the few birthday presents from anybody that I'd actually wanted.

Back to the station in the pouring rain, with the Maria Callas
under my arm.

Lawson came into my office with a sheet of fax paper.

"What's that?" I asked.

"Stomach contents report from the pathologist."

"Stomach contents? Where's the full autopsy report?"

"Hasn't arrived yet," Lawson said.

"What's the holdup?"

"Uhm, I don't know. I did call them, sir. Apparently there's some
kind of problem. The pathologist is carrying out more tests."

"Why?"

"They wouldn't tell me."

"How long until the preliminary autopsy report?"

"I don't know, sir."

"Well, find out, Lawson. You can't let these people run roughshod
over you. You're a policeman."

"I'll try to find out, sir."

"Bet the lazy bastards haven't written it yet. Never heard the like of it. Stomach contents, indeed," I grumbled. "Let me take a look at that."

I called Crabbie in, and all three of us read the report together. Lily Bigelow's stomach contained the usual food and drink, plus white wine, gin, aspirin, Nembutal, and Valium.

"Nembutal and Valium. Just like we thought. Did you ever dig up the facts on Nembutal?"

"I did. It's a prescription antianxiety medication, also sometimes used as a sleep aid," Lawson said.

"What happens if you mix Valium and Nembutal?"

Lawson flipped open his notebook. "Well, typical applications for pentobarbital (Nembutal) are as a sedative, a hypnotic, a pre-anesthetic, and it's also used for control of convulsions in emergencies. In the UK there's widespread use of it as a veterinary anesthetic agent. Pentobarbital-induced coma is sometimes used in Casualty in patients with acute liver failure. Lily presumably used it as a sleep aid."

"What about its use with Valium?"

"There doesn't appear to be a lot of research into its contraindicators with Valium, but I called up a Doctor Quine at the QUB Medical School, and she said that it was potentially very dangerous indeed. With, I'm quoting here, 'the potential to induce a hypnotic state, paranoia, trance, mood swings, and depression.'"

"And when mixed with alcohol?" I asked.

"Alcohol exacerbates the side effects and contraindicators of both medications."

"There you have it," Crabbie said. "An already-depressed young woman takes too many of those magic pills and she's away with the fairies."

"If it wasn't for the missing notebook, I would wholeheartedly concur. That notebook never showed up, did it?" I asked.

Lawson and McCrabban shook their heads.

"What about this Tim fellow? The ex-boyfriend?"

"I spoke to him," Lawson said.

"And?"

"He says he didn't break her heart. He says she was all right last time they spoke," Lawson said.

"People called Tim always say that."

Lawson stood there looking at me.

"OK, young Lawson, get on to the pathologist and tell him to hurry his arse up. No more delays. We may nearly be case-closed here. The chief inspector would like that. A dastardly car thief and a suicide on one day."

"Case closed?" McCrabban asked when he had gone.

"Case closed until the inquest. But we can probably clear all this stuff from the incident room and put it down in the evidence room."

"And wipe the whiteboard?" Crabbie asked, dubiously.

"No, not yet, Crabbie. Let's not tempt fate. When we get the autopsy report, things will probably be a lot clearer."

10: THE PRELIMINARY AUTOPSY REPORT

Check under the car in the pouring rain. No bomb.

Leathum's newsagents: *Guardian*, *Times*, packet of Marlboro, Mars bar.

Drive into work. Up to the office. Space heater on to warm the place up. Record player on to cover the racket. Mussorgsky, played loud.

Mars bar, cup of coffee, ciggie. Walk to the incident room.

A nearly empty whiteboard. Wow. Savor it. Just one name: Lily Bigclow.

Nothing to do. Middle of the Troubles with its capital T. And nothing to do. This must be what it's like to be a copper over the water.

Coffee cup. Papers. Stopwatch. Pen. *Guardian* crossword. Start the watch. Solve the clues. Pen down. Stop the watch. Four minutes, four seconds. Reset the watch. *Times* crossword. One down: "Spinning might make her clothes fall off." Bit racy for the *Times*. Answer: Ecdysiast. One across—

"Inspector Duffy!"

Mabel's voice.

"What is it?"

"Big letter for you, brown envelope, I think it's from the pathologist."

"I've been bloody waiting for that. I'll come and get it in three minutes."

Two minutes, forty-five seconds later: pen down, stop the watch.

I said good morning to Mabel, picked up the envelope, and carried it to Crabbie's desk. "Join me for a little read?" I asked.

"Finally. What took them so long?"

I opened the envelope, skimmed it, groaned.

"What is it?" Crabbie asked.

"They've ballsed it up," I said. "Overworked patho. Or drunken one. Or incompetent one. They've ballsed it up, mate."

"What have they done?"

I handed him the report. "They've screwed up everything. Time of death. Cause of death."

Lawson appeared from the break room with a mug of tea. "Is that the pathologist's report?"

"They say she died between five p.m. and eight p.m. on the seventh. And they've written 'homicide,' look!" Crabbie said, and slid the report across the desk.

"That can't be right," Lawson said, putting down his tea and examining the report. "It's not logical. Until six o'clock the castle was full of people, and if she jumped between six and eight, well, that means that Underhill lied."

"And if he's lied, it probably means he killed her. But it's definitely not right. I guarantee you the time of death is a typo. The forensic officer on the scene and my good self put the time of death at midnight."

I dialed the City Hospital.

"Dr. Beggs, please, pathology."

I got put through quickly. "This is Dr. Beggs."

"Hello, Dr. Beggs, this is DI Duffy from Carrickfergus RUC. I'm the investigating officer in the death of one Lily Bigelow in Carrickfergus Castle on the morning of February eighth. Listen, I've just received your autopsy report. Two things. First of all, you've written 'homicide' where it should be 'suicide,' and it looks like there's a typo on it relating to the time of death. I'm afraid you're going to have to fix that before we send the files to the coroner's office. If there's an inconsistency between the autopsy report and the RUC report, the coroner is going to kick up a right old stink."

"Let me look up the case. Hold on a moment, please," he said in some kind of Geordie accent.

I put my hand over the receiver and whispered to Crabbie. "He's looking up the file. . . . He's a Geordie."

He came back on a minute later. "Inspector Duffy?"

"Yes. Do you mind if I put you on speakerphone and bring in my two colleagues, DS McCrabban and DC Lawson?"

"Not at all. Now, what seems to be the trouble, Inspector?" Dr. Beggs asked.

"You've written 'homicide' and the wrong time of death down on the report."

"No, I haven't."

"Yes, you have."

"No. I haven't."

"You've written between five p.m. and eight p.m. on February seventh, but the forensic officer on the scene and I estimated the time of death to be between midnight and 12:45 on the morning of the eighth."

"Your estimate was incorrect."

I sighed. "Dr. Beggs, the forensic officer took a rectal temperature reading before seven a.m. He recorded a body temperature of just under 27 degrees, which is a 10 degree drop in body temperature. At the standard rate of cooling of 1.5 degrees per hour, that would give a time of death between midnight and 12:45 a.m. Since this was a cold night, I'd say that was a conservative cooling estimate and more likely she died between midnight and one a.m.," I said with a look of moderate satisfaction on my face. Crabbie grinned at me, sharing the pleasure of putting a know-it-all doc in his place.

"Your estimates are mistaken, Inspector. She died between five p.m. and eight p.m. on the seventh."

"She jumped from the keep at Carrick Castle, and the castle was full of people until six p.m. and they didn't notice any jumper. The night-watchman, a Mr. Underhill, inspected the castle grounds at ten p.m. on the seventh, and he didn't notice any jumper either, so you can see why we're convinced here that our estimate for the time of death is correct and your estimate is, as our American cousins say, wildly off base," I explained, patiently.

Dr. Beggs cleared his throat. "Have you got a few minutes, so I can take you through my reasoning?"

"Of course."

"I can see this is going to be an issue at the inquest, so I'll have an intern type this up for you as well and send it by messenger before we hand in the full report."

"That would be much appreciated."

Dr. Beggs cleared his throat again. "Well, Detectives, as you're probably aware, the two important unknowns in assessing time of death from body temperature are the actual body temperature at the time of death and the actual length of time the body has lain before it was discovered. Body temperature cannot be a useful guide to the time of death when the cadaveric temperature approaches that of the environment, or over the linear part of the sigmoid cooling curve. Any formula that involves an averaging of the temperature decline per hour may well give a reasonably reliable approximation of the time of death, however when the initial temperature may have been elevated or when environmental factors are such as to insulate a body—"

"Dr. Beggs, the body was not insulated and there's no evidence for a higher than normal body temperature so—"

"The pictures I have from your own forensic team show a body with snow on it, which can be an effective insulator. But let's leave that to one side. The presence of Nembutal, Valium, and caffeine in the victim's stomach and blood leads me to the conclusion that the core temperature of the victim was most likely elevated. The sigmoid nature of the relationship between the temperature of the cooling body and that of its environment should be kept in mind. And to quote a recent study I have in front of me: 'Simple formulae for estimating the time of death are now regarded as naïve. These include the well-known Simpson formula, which says that under average conditions the clothed body will cool in air at the rate of about 1.5 degrees Celsius an hour for the first six hours. Experience with this formula has shown serious errors and can now no longer be trusted, especially in the presence of extreme cold, where oxygen-deprived body tissue may be preserved for longer periods than was previously thought possible.'"

"So you're saying the cold made the victim's body cool slower? That doesn't make any sense," I said, beginning to think that Beggs was some kind of crackpot.

"If I may continue, Inspector. . . . The best-researched and documented method for assessing time of death from body temperature is that of Henssge. This is a nomogram method rather than a formula. The nomogram corrects for any given environmental temperature. It requires the measurement of deep rectal temperature and assumes a normal temperature at death of 37.2. Henssge's nomogram is based upon a method that approximates the sigmoid-shaped cooling curve. Extreme cold can both radically hasten or retard body cooling. All of this is moot, however, because your forensic officer did not take a deep rectal temperature."

"He didn't? How do you know that?" I asked.

"Because I phoned him and asked him. Chief Inspector Payne entrusted this task to a trainee forensic officer who did not place the thermometer deep within the victim's rectum. Prudery and a misguided attempt to protect the victim's modesty has produced bad data."

"I see."

"When a deep rectal temperature has not been taken, the variables increase markedly, which is why we use other, more accurate, methods," he said, significantly.

"What methods?"

"There are several, but in this case the relevant ones were liver temperature and the progression of rigor."

"Go on."

"Like I say, I'll have an intern type this up for you and send it over, but if you'd like the details now—"

"Please."

"When I performed my autopsy at 6:13 p.m. on February eighth, Miss Bigelow had a liver temperature of 17 degrees Celsius, which was room temperature. Using more accurate formulae, this would suggest a time of death between five p.m. and eight p.m. on February seventh. Furthermore, at the time of autopsy, I found that the process of rigor mortis had ended and, indeed, was in regression. This is very unusual before twenty-four hours after death. This, too, would place the time of death between five p.m. and eight p.m. on February seventh."

"All right, so perhaps we were mistaken about the time of death, but I don't see how that gives you a homicide diagnosis."

"Ah, yes, that's a different matter and is explained by the issue of livor mortis."

"Go on . . ."

"As I'm sure you're aware, livor mortis is the pooling of blood within the body, which occurs when the heart stops beating and blood pressure ceases to exist. In this situation, the blood falls to whatever parts of the body are lowest in relationship to the surface the body is resting on. As the body cools and the natural cellular processes cease, the blood becomes fixed in a certain position. In general, livor mortis is fixed a few hours after death. Mortis causes areas of pressure to appear as white areas on the body. Bra straps, belts, and other clothing can cause blanching in the areas under pressure. If a body is found fully clothed in reasonably tight clothing but no blanched patches are seen, this can suggest that the body was redressed after death. It can also suggest movement of the body after death. Lack of livor mortis signs on the parts of the body not at the lowest point of the body at rest strongly suggests the body *has* been moved after death. This was the case with Miss Bigelow."

"What?!" Lawson and I exclaimed together.

"The lack of blanching around Miss Bigelow's brassiere suggests to me that she died in a sitting position or was placed in a sitting position shortly after death and the body was subsequently moved. She certainly died from massive head trauma, but not, I suggest, from a fall from the castle keep. She was killed by a heavy blow, or possibly blows, to the head and left prone or in a sitting position for several hours before the body was thrown from the roof of the keep in an attempt to make a murder look like a suicide."

"That's not possible," Crabbie said.

"Oh, it's possible, all right. Very possible. I wonder, too, why an experienced detective inspector and an experienced forensic officer didn't notice how little blood was found around Miss Bigelow's body."

"There was blood all over the shop! She was drenched in blood. It was horrific," Lawson said.

I groaned. "No. There was certainly blood, but not enough," I replied.

"Indeed. Miss Bigelow's femoral artery was ripped from her chest in the impact after her fall. If she'd been alive, I believe there would have been more blood than appeared in the crime scene photographs we were supplied with. Four pints might have pumped from a wound like that. I'm sorry to be so graphic at this hour of the day."

"It's OK."

"I should stress, however, that this finding is my own personal view. My colleague, Dr. Paley, who was assisting, did not agree with this interpretation, and our final report to the coroner will reflect that."

"Dr. Paley agrees with the police estimates of the time of death?"

"No. Dr. Paley agrees with me about the time of death. That's not in dispute at all. She died between five p.m. and eight p.m. on the night of the seventh. Dr. Paley, however, disputes my interpretation of the livor mortis evidence and whether there was insufficient blood at the alleged crime scene. He feels that the body was too badly damaged in the fall to reach any kind of conclusive result about livor mortis and blood loss."

"I see. But *your* interpretation is that the livor mortis results and the lack of blood around the body are evidence that this was probably a homicide."

"Probably, but not definitively," Dr. Beggs said.

"And there was the shoe," McCrabban said. "The killer put the shoe on the wrong foot. You saw it, Sean."

The fucking shoe. Yes. The lack of blood. And the shoe.

"Well, thank you very much, Dr. Beggs. This certainly puts a new complexion on our case. . . . Was there any sign of sexual activity that you could discover?" I asked, thinking of possible motives now.

"Miss Bigelow had had no sexual relations in the previous forty-eight hours, nor was the body violated post mortem, as far as I can see. There were no ligature marks, or signs of other violence or of intravenous drug use."

"OK. Well, thank you. We'll be in touch if we need further help."

"My pleasure, and you should have the full typed report by the end of the week."

"Thank you."

I hung up and looked at Lawson and McCrabban.

"What now, gentlemen?"

"Search me," Crabbie said. "This has knocked me for six."

"Lawson?"

He shook his head.

I took a sip of coffee and looked through the police-station window at the grey, forbidding castle just a few hundred yards away along the seafront.

"Are those two trainee detectives still with us?" I asked Crabbie.

"Nope. They've been rotated up to Belfast now," he said.

"OK, then, we'll have to do this ourselves. We've got to reexamine those CCTV tapes of the castle between five p.m. and six a.m. when Constable Warren was put on the front door—if there was really no way anyone else could have gotten into or out of the building after the doors were closed, then nice Mr. Underhill must have killed her."

"What's his motive?" McCrabban asked.

"I don't know. Lily, unbalanced by her meds, decides to escape from the dreary castle tour. She hides somewhere and when he comes to do his inspection Underhill finds her. They get into an argument, he hits her, kills her. Maybe the meds make her pass out, Underhill finds her, tries to rape her, she wakes up. Maybe the meds make her pass out, she wakes up, can't get out of the castle because of the portcullis, finds Underhill's house, goes inside and finds him fiddling the books, reading kiddie porn. . . . Could be a million things."

"Apart from the D&Ds he hasn't much of a criminal record. Distinguished navy career, been in this job for ten years . . ."

"If these autopsy results are to be believed, and I for one found Dr. Beggs very convincing, then not only is Underhill lying about his inspections, but if she was killed then he's probably the one who did it."

We looked at the CCTV tapes until our eyes were aching, but it was no go. No one entered or left the castle between 5 p.m. and 6 a.m. when Warren went on the gate. After that, Sergeant Mulvenny's K9 unit had thoroughly searched the place from top to bottom and no one was hiding in the castle. There were no secret tunnels or any other ways in or out. That could only mean that Underhill was the killer.

We took a tea break and I called a case conference in the incident room. "Gentlemen?" I said.

"Underhill can't have been telling us the whole truth," McCrabban said with his cold Vulcan logic.

"I concur," Lawson said.

"Let's bring him in again."

11: INTERVIEWING MR. UNDERHILL REDUX

As exotic as Lily Bigelow's death had been, it had been quickly forgotten about. The papers and the TV had moved on to the murder of Chief Superintendent McBain and the murders of two part-time policemen on farms along the border, which happened a couple of days later. The media were calling this a new IRA campaign to assassinate vulnerable policemen.

When we drove to Carrick Castle there were no reporters, no TV crews, no police tape. The castle was open for business and Mr. Underhill was selling tickets in the ticket booth. I arrived with a small forensic team that I sent down to the dungeons to see if they could gather any evidence. Bit late for that, but you never knew . . .

"Oh, hello, Inspector Duffy, are you here to do more investigating?" Underhill asked as we approached the ticket office.

"Clarke Underhill, I am arresting you for the murder of one Lily Bigelow. You have a right to remain silent, but a court or jury may draw an adverse inference if you fail to mention any fact on which you later rely upon in your defense, this fact being one which you could reasonably have been expected to mention when being questioned under caution."

"What are you talking about? I didnae kill that wee lassie."

McCrabban produced a set of handcuffs and turned Underhill around.

"Wait a minute, laddie! At least let me get the patrons out of the castle and lock the place up!"

I nodded to McCrabban. "Aye, but go with him, we don't want him doing a runner or jumping off a battlement."

An hour later and Underhill was safely ensconced in Interview

Room 1 at Carrickfergus RUC. He had a jug of water and the tape recorder was running, as per the instructions of the Police and Criminal Evidence Act (NI Order).

Bog-standard procedure. We took Mr. Underhill through his written statement, looking for inconsistencies.

There were none.

We showed him the preliminary autopsy report and explained its meaning to him.

"Lily Bigelow almost certainly did not commit suicide. She was murdered and the body was moved. She was murdered between five p.m. and eight p.m. on the night of the seventh. Therefore, either someone murdered her before six a.m., when you say you found the dead body, or *you* moved it in front of the keep to make it look like a suicide for reasons of your own. Or you found her alive and hiding, murdered her, and then moved her body in front of the keep. The most logical possibilities, Mr. Underhill, are that you killed her, or you moved the body, or both. Which is it?"

"I didnae do any of those things. First of all, I was at the ticket office the whole time, until a few minutes afore six. Dozens of people must have seen me there. Then, at a quarter to six, I made the announcement that the castle was closing and I walked through the building and locked up."

"All right, so you didn't kill her between five p.m. and six p.m. That was always an unlikely scenario because of the lack of opportunity, the possibility of being seen, and the noise a murder may have made. But from six p.m. until eight p.m. you had the whole place to yourself."

"Why would I kill her? That's ridiculous! And I didnae see the wee lassie until the morning! If I'd seen her alive, I would have let her out of the castle. Why in the name of all that's holy would I have killed her?"

"You were angry that she was hiding in the castle? You tried to force yourself upon her?" I suggested.

"At my age! You're joking."

"I've seen you lift up that two-ton portcullis. You're stronger and more virile than you look. Certainly a match for young Lily."

Underhill looked at us incredulously.

"A child could lift that portcullis with the chain and pulley! Everything I have told you is the truth. The first time I set eyes on her was when I saw her dead. I never laid a finger on her!"

"Did you give her a ticket to go into the castle?" I asked.

"Hoots, man! Apart from that! Aye, I gave everyone in that group a ticket, but after that I never saw her again."

I stared at him, got up from the desk, nodded, poured him a glass of water, poured myself a glass of water, sat down again. Slow him down a bit. Gently, now:

"Clarke, we know it wasn't anything malicious. She wasn't interfered with. There was no sexual motive. Here's what I think happened. . . . You found her hiding in one of the dungeons; she was mentally unbalanced from mixing her medications. She attacked you, she scared the shit out of you. You clobbered her, just once, her head banged against those low dungeon walls. You couldn't believe it. She was dead. Dead as a doornail. You left her there, went to your office to get a drink. 'What have I done?' You went back to look at her, she was still dead. 'I didn't mean to kill her, but they'll put me away.' Your mind was racing and then you concocted a plan. She jumped off the keep. Who knows why? Women are mysterious. They're always doing weird things. You dragged the body up to the top of the keep. You put her shoes on the wrong feet and you pushed her off. You didn't even look at her. Wait until morning. Have a drink. Go to bed. It'll be all right in the morning. . . . Is that how it went down, Mr. Underhill?"

He put his head in his hands.

Crabbie gave me a look. *I think you nailed him, Sean.*

A tap on the glass through the one-way mirror.

I went outside to see what it was. Forensics team.

Blood on one of the dungeon walls. A tiny speck of blood that they'd sent off for analysis, but no hair, or any other physical evidence that Lily had been down there. We'd need that confession, or a clever barrister might sway the court . . .

Back into Interview Room 1.

"Well, Clarke? Manslaughter, not murder. The DPP will offer you four years if you plead guilty and save the Crown the expense of a trial. Four years? The prison service will let you out after two and a half. He could even take it to a jury, couldn't he, Sergeant McCrabban?"

"Aye, Inspector Duffy, he could. Self-defense. He was being attacked," Crabbie said.

"Self-defense? A jury might buy that, who knows? Not guilty. Zero jail time. But tell us the truth, now, Clarke. Lying will make you look guilty. Make you look like there's something to hide. The truth! Come on. Out with it, man."

He lifted his head from the table and stared at me through tears. Blue-eyed, old-man, bleary, sea-dog tears.

"I didnae kill her. I didnae lay a finger on her!" he said defiantly, and banged the table so hard the tape recorder jumped.

An hour of this.

Tag team.

Me and Crabbie out. Lawson in. Me back in again.

A couple of trainee detectives in, just to mix things up.

Night fell on Belfast Lough.

The snow flurries turned to cold, hard rain.

The regular cops went home to their beds.

"Take him down to the cells and let him stew. Suicide watch. He's the type," I said to the duty sergeant, and Carrick CID went home to their beds, too.

Next morning.

Take in the milk. Out to the car after no breakfast. Check underneath for bombs. None. Straight to the station. Wake up Underhill. Interview Room 1. The same questions over and over. Tell us the truth, tell us the goddamn truth, you lying bastard.

"Only you could have killed her. Only you could have moved the body. There is no other explanation. And don't mention the fucking ghost."

"I didnae do it. I didnae do it."

Water jug. Rolling tape. Cigarette smoke drifting up to the acoustic baffle ceiling panels.

Lawson and McCrabban in. Duffy out.

Morning bleeding into afternoon.

Rain and fog.

Football scores on the TV news. What day is this? Saturday?

"Can I see you in my office, Inspector Duffy?"

Swivel round in the office chair. The chief inspector. He was in a bristly, confident mood that I didn't like. He'd obviously been reading one of those books on people management.

"Have a seat."

"Come with me to *my* office, Duffy."

"OK."

The chief inspector's office. Only a little bit nicer than mine. Sea view, black-and-white photographs, some kind of ancient walking stick that he, no doubt, was dying to be asked about . . .

"Guess what Superintendent Strong sent me?" the chief inspector said.

"Oh no, not one of his wife's Dundee cakes?"

"No. Look!" he said, and took a pair of boxing gloves from a drawer. They were cheap red training gloves with a squiggle written on them.

"Ali was autographing gloves before he left. People were just buying gloves out of the Athletic Stores and he was autographing them with a felt-tip pen. You know how much a signed Muhammad Ali set of boxing gloves goes for?"

"No."

"About 300 quid. You buy a 30 quid pair of boxing gloves, Ali signs them, there you go, you've made 1,000 percent profit, just like that."

"I see."

"Strong sent me these. He's pleased with the work we're doing over here. It's a reward for all of us, you know."

"Is it?"

"They'll probably promote him to chief super and give him Eddie McBain's job."

"Fascinating."

"Do you see what I'm saying, Duffy?"

"I think perhaps you could be a tiny bit less opaque, sir."

"It's about Mr. Underhill . . ."

"What about him?"

"See, I had to talk to Superintendent Strong about it, and I couldn't really explain the case to him. First of all you tell me that this is a straightforward suicide, now you're telling me it's a murder. You've got an elderly suspect down there who denies everything and doesn't look like a murderer to me."

"It is probably a murder. We were—*I* was wrong about the suicide."

"Has Underhill confessed?"

"No. As you say, he's been strenuously denying his guilt."

"It's been twenty-four hours and he—"

"He hasn't asked for a lawyer yet."

"No, he hasn't *asked* for a lawyer. . . . But we're going to play this one by the book, Duffy. It's been twenty-four hours. You're either going to have to release him or charge him."

"If that's what you want, we'll charge him, then. Why are you so concerned, sir? Clarke Underhill's a nobody. No one's going to give a shit if I keep him here all week."

"That's where you're wrong, Duffy. Until it was transferred to the National Trust, Carrickfergus Castle was owned by the Ministry of Defense. Mr. Underhill is still technically employed by the Royal Navy, and not two hours ago, Superintendent Strong had an inquiry about him. A phone call from the admiralty. In London."

"You're joking."

"I'm not joking. The Navy Legal Services office are sending a solicitor down from Belfast to represent Mr. Underhill, and they want to know if you are going to charge him or release him."

"Like I say, sir, we're going to charge him."

"They are demanding that all questioning cease until his legal representative arrives."

"We can wait."

McArthur shook his head. Coping with pressure from upstairs wasn't his forte. Coping wasn't his forte. "So you don't have a confession?"

"No, sir."

"Do you have any actual evidence that he killed the girl?"

"Forensics was a bust, sir. No fluids, hair, or clothes belonging to Lily Bigelow in Mr. Underhill's cottage. Nothing of Mr. Underhill's on the body. There was one blood speck on a wall on one of the dungeons that is still off for analysis."

"Do you have a motive?"

"No."

The chief inspector looked irritated. "So what do you have?"

"We have the CCTV footage and the preliminary autopsy report. Mr. Underhill was alone in the castle and he either killed Lily, or he moved the body, or he's lying about being alone in the castle."

"You've no murder weapon, no motive, no confession, no forensic evidence linking him to the girl's death."

"But we have logic. We have the autopsy report about the time of death, and we have the fact that the body was moved and that no one else could possibly have killed her."

"You think that's enough to bring to this to the DPP's office?"

"I do. It's our job to arrest the suspects. It's their job to prosecute, and it's a jury's job to determine their guilt or innocence. And as a non-terrorist murder, this case is going to a jury."

He looked at me closely, his dark eyes for once flashing a kind of animal intelligence.

"So you're confident that Underhill killed her?"

"I'm not confident. But I can't see any other explanation. When his solicitor arrives, we will charge Mr. Underhill with murder."

The solicitor arrived.

A trim, dark-haired, clever-looking woman wearing a Royal Navy uniform. Lieutenant Commander Long, she called herself.

She blustered about his lack of legal representation, the lack of evidence, the fact that her client denied his guilt. She demanded that we release him immediately and apologize for the inconvenience we'd put him through. Instead of doing any of that, we charged him with murder.

The DPP, Sir Barry Shaw, was notified and he sent down his goons, who took Mr. Underhill into their custody, photocopied all our case files, and transferred him out of our jurisdiction.

And that was that.

We heard later that Commander Long had immediately applied for bail for Mr. Underhill and her request had been granted by a sympathetic judge. By nightfall, Underhill was back in his cottage at Carrickfergus Castle.

That was a surprise, but we had done all we could. It was out of our hands now.

The boys weren't happy.

We all knew something was very wrong with the case.

I took them down to Ownies for dinner and a pint or two of the black stuff. I found a nook in an upstairs snug overlooking the Scotch Quarter.

Another cold, rainy night. Low cloud ceiling. No stars. Ships on the lough sounding fog horns every few minutes . . .

Dinner of lamb chops and mashed potatoes.

Bushmills whisky and Guinness.

Talk of football and music and the flicks.

Lawson was the first to broach the case. "Now, I don't think he did it."

Silence. A look from Crabbie.

"Sean, do you think we should have a wee talk about the Lizzie Fitzpatrick case?" McCrabban said.

I finished my pint and nodded. "Maybe you're right, mate."

I turned to Lawson. "Sergeant McCrabban knows some of it and he's probably guessed the rest. What I'm going to tell you doesn't go further than this room. Is that understood?"

They both nodded.

And I told them everything. The approach by Annie Fitzpatrick. My investigation into the locked-room mystery surrounding Lizzie's death. How through a process of luck and deduction I had determined that she had been murdered and who had done it. I even told them what happened next, even though I'd signed the Official Secrets Act regarding that portion of the episode. The Brighton Bombing. Poor misguided Dermot McCann. . . . And the epilogue: Annie Fitzpatrick taking revenge on the person I identified as her daughter's murderer.

Lawson's eyes were big when the story ended.

Crabbie said nothing. He merely nodded. Clearly, the deep old file had put most of it together already.

"So you see, gentlemen, policemen in Northern Ireland do not get two locked-room mysteries in one career. The odds would be astronomical . . ."

"Aye, you're right there, Sean. It's always the simplest explanation, isn't it?" Crabbie said.

"Amen to that," I agreed. "One murder like that in a police officer's case book is all right. But two? Two is *de trop*, as Maigret would say. Two is coincidence piled on top of coincidence. I'm an RUC detective, not Miss Marple or Gideon Fell. No, Lawson, Underhill is a very convincing liar, but he's a liar nonetheless."

Lawson took a sip of his pint of Guinness and slowly shook his head.

"Well . . ." he said, and his voice trailed away.

"Well what, son?"

"You know my dad is a mathematician, right? And I did a couple of A-levels in math."

"So?"

"Well, it's not necessarily about you, sir, but on the other hand, it could be all about you, in which case Bayes' theorem is worth considering. Either of you, uhm, know about Bayes' theorem?"

"New one on me. Crabbie?"

"Never heard of it."

"Bayesian mathematics shows the relation between two conditional probabilities which are related to one another. Uhm, should I go on?"

"Continue."

"Well, uhm, Bayes' theorem expresses the conditional probability, or posterior probability, of a hypothesis H—its probability after evidence E is observed—in terms of the prior probability of H, the prior probability of E, and the conditional probability of E given H. It implies that evidence has a stronger confirming effect if it was more unlikely before being observed. Am I, er, making any sense at all?"

"I'm not sure I'm quite hanging in there," I said, and I could see he'd lost Crabbie.

"Well, according to Bayes' theorem, the fact that you dealt with a locked-room mystery once before might, in fact, be relevant in deciding whether this particular crime—the murder of Lily Bigelow—is also a locked-room mystery."

"How so?"

"Let's assume that Mr. Underhill is not the real killer."

"OK."

"And let's assume that the real killer knew that you were likely to be lead detective in any case of homicide to occur in Carrickfergus. If he knew your case history, including the Lizzie Fitzpatrick case, he could formulate an elaborate murder plot with the knowledge that you and Sergeant McCrabban would not think it possible for any one RUC policeman to encounter two locked-room mysteries in the course of his career. You are not, as you say, Gideon Fell."

I took a sip of Bushmills. "That would be pretty diabolical," I said.

"Indeed," McCrabban agreed. "And that's Bayesian mathematics, is it?"

"I've given you the gist," Lawson said, not wanting to explain that he'd given us the "idiot's version."

"It's certainly a nice idea," I said. "And I definitely want you to keep thinking laterally, Lawson, but you also have to learn not to overcomplicate things. There are two problems with your theory."

"Only two?" Crabbie said.

"Problem one: Look around you, son. This is Ulster in 1987—the criminals are not that smart. They get away with so many murders because they know that no one will ever testify against them. Your sophisticated diabolical murderer is quite a rare animal round these parts. Problem two: The killer can only be Underhill because anyone else could not have gotten *out* of the castle, or hidden himself any-where *in* the castle. Because we searched that bloody castle from top to bottom and there was no killer. He did not hide in a priest's hole, or get over the walls, and the dogs found no trace of anyone else but Lily Bigelow and Clarke Underhill."

"I'm not suggesting that Mr. Underhill didn't do it," Lawson said. "What I'm suggesting is that the possibility of you getting two such similar crimes in your career needn't worry you. If you take a Bayesian approach, the statistics aren't quite as formidable as they seem."

I smiled at him the way one did with a precocious child. "Well it's certainly food for thought, Lawson. Food for thought."

12: EAST TO THE SMOKE

Office. Window. Lough. Coal boats. Rain.

McCrabban and Lawson sitting there on the sofa, Gregorio Allegri's comforting (for a Catholic) *Miserere* on the record player.

"I don't like it," I said.

"What don't you like?"

I pointed at Lawson. "He has put a seed of doubt in my head. A seed which has grown into a virulent little shrub of doubt."

I was sitting with the Lily Bigelow file in front of me.

Crabbie took a sip of tea.

Lawson ate a biscuit.

They both knew a second shoe was going to fall. No pun intended.

"It's not sitting right, is it?" I said.

I waited for the scorn and the dour Presbyterian skepticism, but instead Crabbie nodded slowly. "I feel it too."

"You feel it too?"

"Yes."

"But what is it?" I asked.

He thought for a long time. "It's the fact that Underhill has refused every deal that's been offered to him by the DPP. He's not pleading guilty to manslaughter, he's not pleading self-defense. He wants to go to trial," Crabbie said. "That sounds like the play of an innocent man."

"Or a crazy man," Lawson said.

"Or a crazy man who killed a girl and convinced himself that he's an innocent man," I added.

"And yet . . ." said McCrabban.

"And yet . . ." I agreed.

"If Underhill didn't do it, who did?" Lawson asked.

"How many suicides do we get a year?" I asked.

"No idea," Crabbie said.

"Me neither. But it would be interesting to find out, wouldn't it? I think we'll do another little statistical analysis on the number of suicides, murders, and accidental deaths that Carrick CID has had to deal with over, say, the last ten years."

"To what end?" Lawson asked.

"I don't know," I admitted. "Let's reconvene here in two hours, when we have the figures. I'm sure it will be interesting. Lawson, will you do the heavy lifting?"

"It'll be actual heavy lifting, sir, those seventies files are down in the basement," he said.

"You are the youngest," McCrabban said.

He sighed.

"And use those math skills of yours, Lawson," I said. "I'd like you to break down the suicides by gender. I'd like to know how many women committed suicide in, say, the last ten years and the manner of their deaths. And your Bayesian diabolical murderer. . . . I'd also like to know exactly how many elaborate murders we've had to deal with. Non-terrorist-related murders. Murders where they tried to get away with it by passing it off to look like either suicide or an accident. Have you got that?"

"An analysis of the suicides and the murders? I'll get right on it," he said.

I stared at my teacup and then at the ships out on the lough, and when that got boring I read the sports pages in the papers. Hugh McIlvanney, as usual, with some good observations on the beautiful game.

It took Lawson an hour and a half to get the statistics and type up a little presentation on his Apple Mac. He came into the conference room with renewed vigor.

"I told you it would be interesting," I said.

"Yes, it was," he agreed.

I called Crabbie back in.

"You sit here," I said, moving from my seat behind the desk.

Lawson sat in my seat and gave us both a copy of his report.

"Summarize the data for us, will you?" I asked.

"Well sir, in our area of jurisdiction, Carrickfergus CID, from 1977 to 1987 there have been 52 murders, 51 suicides, and 152 accidental deaths. Almost all the accidental deaths were house fires, road accidents, accidents in the home, and drownings."

"The number of suicides seems high."

"Twelve of the suicides were police or army officers who killed themselves with their personal weapon. There were eleven more of these deaths categorized as accidents," Lawson said with a significant look at me and McCrabban.

"How many female suicides in the last ten years?"

"Nineteen, sir."

"How did they die?"

"Seven by hanging, four by jumping from a high building, two by gunshot, two by gas, two who jumped in front of a train, one who drowned herself, and one who burned her house down around her—that was Mrs. Donaghy from just last year, sir."

"I remember the case," I said, frowning—an unpleasant murder-suicide that had taken Mrs. Donaghy's two infant boys, as well.

"We also had a case back in 1981 that you initially categorized as a suicide and re-categorized as murder. Girl hanging in Woodburn forest. Jane Doe it said on the file, but I think you ID'd her later," Lawson said.

"That *was* murder. An unsolved murder," Crabbie said. "Although possibly attributed to Freddie Scavanni."

I added nothing, for neither Lawson nor McCrabban knew the full extent of my involvement in Scavanni's subsequent death.

"And then there's the case of Sylvie McNichol, which we also initially thought may have been a suicide, but was actually also a murder," Lawson said.

"Aye, the wee girl who supposedly gassed herself in her car, but was really done in," McCrabban said.

"How could I forget?" I said.

"And Michael Kelly himself. A case everyone initially thought was a suicide, but in fact was also a murder," I added.

"So what does that amount to, Sean?" McCrabban asked.

"How many non-terrorist-related murders in the last ten years?"

"Twenty-three," Lawson said. "Of which eight were domestic violence."

"So we've dealt with fifteen non-terrorist, non-domestic-violence murders, and of those, three of them, one fifth, were cases where the murderer tried to make it look like a suicide. One fifth, gents. Now I know what you're going to say, Lawson, you're going to say that the sample size is too small to be statistically significant. Go on, say it."

"Sir, the sample size is too small to have any significance whatsoever," he said.

"But the fact remains that we've all encountered cases like this before. Men who have killed women and tried to cover up their deed by making it seem like the quote-unquote 'silly bint' topped herself."

Crabbie tipped his pipe into the wastepaper basket.

"What are you getting at, Sean?"

"In Carrickfergus there have only been four suicides committed by women who have jumped off tall buildings in all of the last ten years," I said, looking at McCrabban.

"Rare," he agreed. "But not unheard-of."

"And then we have Lawson's Bayesian theory about Lily Bigelow's death," I suggested.

"Where's all this leading?" McCrabban asked.

"It's leading to this: I think, for the sake of all our consciences, we need to look into the possibility that Lily was murdered by someone else. Don't roll your eyes at me, Crabbie. We won't spend a lot of time on it and we'll keep it from the chief inspector, but we'll keep working at it unless something else pressing comes up."

"How could a different murderer have done it?" Lawson asked.

"I don't know. We'll need to think about that. I want to investigate motive. Why would anyone kill her? We'll look at boyfriend trouble, job trouble. Crabbie, I want you to call up the *Financial Times* and speak to Lily's boss and see if you can get any of her friends on the blower."

"No problem."

"And Lawson, you and I will try to figure out a way of reverse engineering Lily's death. If we were going to kill her in those circumstances, how would we do it? First of all, let's just make one hundred percent sure that the locked-castle problem really *is* a locked-castle problem."

The incident room, an hour later.

I had just had a very interesting phone call from a Professor Wallace of Queens University Belfast's archaeology department. Carrickfergus Castle definitely had no secret rooms or secret tunnels. He had done the survey himself, back in the seventies. Locked-room scenario confirmed.

"Lawson, any thoughts in that big brain of yours?"

Lawson shook his head. "I couldn't think of anything reverse-engineering-wise. We're ruling out magic, are we?"

"Yes."

"Crabbie?"

McCrabban looked troubled. "I had a very strange wee chat with Lily's boss on the phone. Weird, evasive, I didn't like it at all. He said he would call us back."

"Maybe he was just busy?"

"Not everyone can stop work at the drop of a hat to talk to a copper, but it seemed to be more than that."

"If he doesn't call back today, we'll try him first thing in the morning."

He didn't call back, and after this bit of excitement the rest of the day ebbed away in rain and coffee and cigarettes.

A sad, damp, lonely night back at Coronation Road.

A knock at the door. Mrs. Campbell from next door standing there in a rather fetching red dress. She appeared to be wearing makeup and her hair was elaborately done up. She was holding a Tupperware container.

"Hello, Mrs. C. Are you on your way out?"

She adjusted her hair. "No. Not at all. I was just wondering. . . . I couldn't help but overhear. . . . Well, what I mean is, your girlfriend having gone . . . would you like some dinner? Lancashire hotpot. I'd invite you over, but Kenneth's having one of his turns."

I took the Tupperware container. "Thank you. Be nice to have some good grub."

"I know. She wasn't much of a cook, was she? You could smell the burning skillet through the wall. Look at you. You're skin and bones. You're better off, Mr. Duffy, if you don't mind me saying. She had airs and graces. . . . Anyway, I thought you might be hungry."

"Thank you, Mrs. Campbell. This looks good."

"I must be off. Kenneth, you know?"

"Thanks again."

TV and Lancashire hotpot and the drink and the dark and the rain . . . that was it, was it?

That was life now?

Yeah, I think so.

Next morning.

Corduroy jacket, white shirt, brown tie . . . miserable seventies look to go with my miserable seventies mood.

Phone light flashing in my office.

Line one.

"Duffy, CID."

"Oh hello, my name is Andrew Graham, uhm, am I speaking to the police officer in charge of the Lily Bigelow, uhm, investigation . . . ?"

"Yes. The case is now with the DPP's office, but we're taking another look at the evidence ourselves."

"Are you the chief investigating officer?"

"Yes."

"I was Lily's editor at the Irish and Scottish desk. I, uhm, spoke to your Sergeant McCrabban yesterday, and he said that if I had any information relating to Lily's death I should contact you."

"Do you have any information relating to Miss Bigelow's death?"

Silence.

"Sir, do you have any information relating to Miss Bigelow's death?"

"I might have, yes."

"Well do you, or don't you?"

There was a pause on the line.

"Please continue, sir, I'm listening," I said.

"Well, that's the thing, you see, who else is listening? We heard it was suicide and now your sergeant is saying that it was murder. If Lily was, uhm, well, if Lily was murdered, then that puts a different complexion on things, doesn't it?"

"I can assure you no one else is listening and what you say to me will be in complete confidence."

"Well, yes, it's not just me being alarmist, though, is it? There's also the question of slander. We're dealing with some very well-connected people here. People who have sued newspapers in the past for much less."

"Sir, I don't know what you're talking about. Perhaps you could just come to the point."

"Well, the point is that we were cleaning out Lily's desk and one of our techs came across the file she was working on before she left for Belfast. He shouldn't, of course, have read her work, but he did. And then he came to me. And I, uhm, had a look into it, and, well, in the best interests of the paper I just decided to leave it. Until your sergeant called again yesterday and, well, it's a tricky dilemma for us, isn't it? Legally, I mean."

"Mr. Graham, I'm none the wiser."

"Look, it's all on the computer. I took this to Legal Affairs and they made me contact counsel immediately. Counsel, as you can imagine, was horrified."

"What council? What are you talking about?"

"Peter Carter-Ruck. Now you must understand, Inspector Duffy, none of us here know anything about it. Lily never discussed this story with us. Indeed, she would not have been allowed to pursue this story had she brought it up with me. It's my belief that she asked to cover the

Finnish visit to Northern Ireland entirely because of this private story that she was working on. A story which came from the tip line—not the most reliable of sources, as you can imagine."

"Can you hold on one moment, please, sir, I'm going to see if my sergeant has come in yet. I'd like to bring him into this call and put you on speakerphone if I may."

I found Lawson and McCrabban in the incident room.

"Lily's employer. He says she was working on a story that might have a bearing on her death. Important people involved. He's scared."

"Shit," Lawson said.

I led them into my office, took Graham off hold, and put on the speakerphone.

"Please continue, Mr. Graham."

"Continue? No, you haven't been listening. Mr. Phipps and Mr. Carter-Ruck have been quite insistent on that. We've got nothing more to say, Inspector. Lily, apparently, was working on a scurrilous story on her own time. A story that would never have been printed in the *Financial Times*. The story is on her computer with sketchy details and is quite preposterous. It's not so much a story as a series of bullet points, most of which are libelous. I do not wish to recite the story over the phone to you, nor do I wish to print it out and fax it to you. I have consulted with counsel, and Mr. Carter-Ruck says that if we were to print this out here, in this building, and were its contents to leak, the *Financial Times* could be held legally accountable in a potential defamation suit. It is the advice of counsel, therefore, that if you believe that Lily's computer may have evidentiary value, then you or your representative should come and take the computer away. If you do not believe that the computer has any bearing on Lily's death, then we have been advised to destroy the machine before the *Financial Times* can become implicated in a libel suit."

"How big is this computer?" Lawson asked.

"It is a 1986 model Macintosh Plus," Graham explained.

"About the same size as the ones we use in the office. We could fit that into a moderate-sized sports bag," Lawson said.

"Let me get your number, Mr. Graham. I'm going to have to call you back in half an hour. Is that OK?"

Graham gave me his number, and I hung up the phone.

"Well, lads, this is a fair old to-do. Thoughts?"

"Peter Carter-Ruck is that guy who's always suing *Private Eye*. If he's telling the newspaper to destroy the computer, then the stuff on it must be incendiary," Lawson said.

"We have to get them to print it out and send it to us," Crabbie said.

"I agree," Lawson said.

I called Mr. Graham back. "You're going to have to print out whatever's on those files and send them to us," I said.

"No. We're not going to do that. Mr. Carter-Ruck has made it clear to us that we are not to print out anything from Lily Bigelow's computer in this building. Mr. Carter-Ruck says that if you wish to impound said computer and print out its contents at a police station, then we would have no objection to that."

"I'll call you back in ten minutes," I said, and hung up.

"We gotta get that computer," Lawson said.

"Aye," Crabbie agreed.

Five minutes later, in the chief inspector's office.

"I know it's expensive, sir. But the DPP will call us negligent if we don't get our hands on all the evidence."

"The DPP doesn't have to pay for it out of his budget. You don't understand the budgetary pressures we're under. Have you seen Dalziel's memo about the use of toilet paper? We're using more toilet paper in this station than in any other barracks in East Antrim."

"That may be true, sir, but I bet we have the cleanest arseholes."

The chief inspector frowned. "...And you have your suspect anyway. What this can possibly add to the case, I don't know..."

I let him grumble on as it gave the useless ponce something to do.

An hour and a half later.

Belfast Harbor Airport.

British Midland BM34 to Heathrow. It was one of those buy-two-get-one-free deals, so just to annoy Dalziel, all *three* of us went.

Black cab to the *Financial Times* offices. Security surprisingly intrusive and our warrant cards inspected and queried.

On the second floor we were met by Mr. Graham, a dour, brittle-looking man with a perpetually runny nose, and by the senior Home News editor, Jason Phipps. Phipps dismissed Graham and said that he would take it from here. He led us to a rather charming office with a view of St. Paul's.

Phipps was a tall, balding, impressive individual with a voice so soft it was difficult to hear him. He was dressed in a three-piece suit that would have seemed dated several decades earlier. An actual bowler hat was resting on a hat stand in one corner. In 1987, with computers and Murdoch and Thatcher and Space Shuttles and cut-throat competition, you would have thought that Phipps's type would be extinct, but apparently not.

His secretary brought us tea and biscuits.

"We've read that you've already made an arrest in Lily's case," Phipps said.

"Where did you read that?"

"The AP wire. The case has been referred to the DPP. You've arrested a Mr. Clarke Underhill?"

"That's correct."

"Some sort of sexual motive?"

"Why would you say that?"

"Lily was very, uhm, attractive and this Underhill was an older man who lived alone in some sort of castle?"

"We're not at liberty to discuss the details of our investigation, or our case against Mr. Underhill. And we're not completely ruling out suicide," I explained.

"Well, as you can imagine, when we first heard that this was a suicide, all of us were a little skeptical, I must say. She seemed a fairly confident, happy girl," he explained.

"What about the boyfriend trouble?"

"Well, yes, I heard a little bit about that later. Employees are not encouraged to discuss their personal issues in the office."

"Did you know she was on various medications, including Valium?"

"No, I didn't know that."

"Did you know she was taking Nembutal?"

"No, what is that?"

"A sleep aid. What about her work? How was that going?" I asked.

"Her work was fine. She came straight to us from Girton, so naturally she was a little bit raw, but she was shaping up rather nicely."

"Girton?"

"Cambridge. A first in economics."

"And what did she do for you?"

"Piecework. Reshaping AP stories, co-writing longer articles, a little subediting, things like that."

"Any lead stories, front-page scoops, anything along those lines?"

"Heavens, no! You need about four or five years on the inside pages before we would let you near the front pages at the *Financial Times*. A story on our front pages can shake the very foundations of the market. Other papers can print what they like, but we have to be extremely circumspect in what we say."

"Tell me what you found on Lily's computer."

"I'll take you to her desk. We've sent her personal effects to her father, but her computer . . . well that's another story. It's a very valuable piece of equipment, and it would have been entirely within our rights to have had the memory 'wiped,' I believe the term is. Counsel, however, has advised that it is too late to do it now that it has become a police matter."

He led us out of the office to Lily's desk in a corner of the newsroom. It had been cleared, and the only thing left was the Mac.

"All her work was on this?" I said.

"Everything she wrote for the paper. Yes. The incriminating document apparently came from Lily's work on the tip line."

"Tip line?"

"One day a week we have our junior reporters man the tip line. It's a phone number where ordinary members of the public can call us with news and potential leads."

"You get a lot of stories like that?"

"We get a lot of tips, yes, but very, very few stories. As I have explained, Inspector, everything that goes into our paper has to be thoroughly researched first. Researched and vetted. It's not an exaggeration to say that the future course of world capitalism is dependent upon accurate information coming from within these walls."

"So why have a tip line in the first place?"

"It's a useful experience for the reporters, sorting the wheat from the chaff and very occasionally it does throw up a useful story or two."

"What sort of story?"

"Mostly financial irregularities. That's why someone would call the *FT* rather than the *Sun* or the *News of the World*. Often, however, they call us just to blow off steam about bad management practices within their organization."

"And what was this tip that Lily found that has gotten you all worked up?"

"Ah, yes, Lily's tip. . . . As soon as you see what she wrote, you'll appreciate why I wouldn't let Mr. Graham discuss this over the telephone, or why Mr. Carter-Ruck wouldn't let us print it out in this building. Let me get it for you . . ."

He turned on the computer, sat down at the desk, and used the mouse to click through the files. The system was exactly the same as we used in Carrick, and in a second he had found the file he was after.

"Here we go. Please do not press print. Read it and take it away with you. We will get you to sign a receipt and an indemnification document, if you don't mind. Counsel requires it. We have no idea who gave her the tip over the tip line, or what they said. She certainly did not come to us with this. A few days after this file was made, she asked if she could cover the visit of the Finns to Northern Ireland. Mr. Graham consented. It was a good business story and he thought she could get her feet wet in the field, so to speak. I assure you that we had no idea that Miss Bigelow apparently had a hidden agenda."

As he kept talking, I read what Lily had written in a file marked:
Tip 30/1/87

From the tip line: 30/1/87
Man. Twenties(?) Irish accent.
Kinkaid(?) Young Offenders' Institution – Belfast
Unknown Children's Home – Richmond
Prostitution/Boys

Cyril Smith MP, Sir Anthony Blunt, Unknown Sinn Féin MP,
Unknown Conservative Minister, Sir Peter Hayman, Unknown
Official Unionist MP dossier from Geoffrey Dickens MP to
Leon Brittan MP when latter Home Secretary (1984). Dickens
condemned by House of Commons but claims substantially
accurate? MI5? Govt?

Patron of Kinkaid YOI Jimmy Savile OBE. Savile on board
of governors. Savile aware of claims? Savile many visits to N.
Ireland/Rep. Ireland.

Savile will deny/sue. Smith will deny/sue. Paramilitaries. Celebrities. Finnish business delegation visit Belfast in February.
Setting up phone factory. Peter Laakso?

I stared in astonishment at the document for a moment before
flipping open my notebook and copying it down word for word.
"As you can see . . ." Phipps said.
"This is incredible stuff," I said.
"Paranoid, crazy stuff," Phipps countered.
"Did you follow up on any of this?"
"Of course. We are a newsroom, after all. And lurking in the back
of my mind was the electric possibility that Lily was killed because of
this. But, naturally, it was all bunk. Innuendo, rumor, gossip, stories
even *Private Eye* wouldn't publish."

"I seem to remember that Geoffrey Dickens thing," Crabbie said.

"Dickens made quite the fool of himself in the House of Commons. You can look it all up on *Hansard*. He claimed that there was a pedophile ring operating at the highest levels of British government. He had no proof whatsoever. He handed a so-called dossier to the Home Secretary and of course no action was ever taken. It was an attempt to smear various homosexual MPs. The sort of thing they did in the early sixties."

"Jimmy fucking Savile," I said, whistling.

"The wife doesn't like him," McCrabban said.

"Oh, come on. He dines with the Prince of Wales. He's a kind of godparent to William and Harry. Mrs. Thatcher has him round for tea every Christmas. Don't you think someone like that would have been seriously vetted before now? If there was a hint of anything untoward, he'd be out on his ear," Phipps said.

"So you think Lily asked to go to Northern Ireland to follow up on this tip?" I asked Phipps.

"It seems obvious now, doesn't it?"

"A conspiracy," Lawson muttered.

"This elderly gent in the castle doesn't seem like the sort of chap MI5 would hire to do its dirty work," Phipps said.

"Well, he is ex-navy, like Commander Bond," Lawson said.

"Bond is MI6," Phipps muttered.

"OK, Lawson, start packing this thing away. We'll take it with us."

Lawson had brought a big Adidas cricket bag that was the perfect size to carry the Mac away with us.

"I'd like to talk to Lily's friends while we're here," I said to Phipps.

"If you must."

Standard chat with friends, colleagues. Lily was an even-tempered, eager young reporter who was well liked. One chubby, bespectacled, freckly character called David Moore seemed to be her best friend.

"Lily ever talk to you about some big scoop she was working on?"

"Scoop? No. Scoop around here? Lily had a scoop? I never heard about that. She was on the low-level business stuff," David replied, in a charming Black Country accent that wasn't very *FT*.

"How was her career going?"

"It was OK."

"What does that mean?"

"She was on the Irish and Scottish desk."

"Not exactly the Treasury beat?"

"No, not exactly."

"She ever mention her interest in covering the Finnish visit to Northern Ireland?"

"Not to me."

"She ever mention the Kinkaid Young Offenders' Institution?"

"No."

"She ever talk about Cyril Smith, or Anthony Blunt, or a Children's Home in Richmond?"

"No, what's this about?"

"She ever mention a secret dossier that had been passed to Leon Brittan?"

"No."

"She ever mention the name Laakso?"

"No."

"She ever mention Jimmy Savile?"

Moore frowned. "That's weird. Yeah, she did she talk to me about Jimmy Savile."

"Recently?"

"Yeah a week and a bit ago. Just before she went away."

"What did she want to know?"

"She asked how we could get an interview with him."

"And what did you say?"

"I said I'd no idea. I said you'd probably have to go through the BBC."

"And that was that?"

"Uhm, not quite. Later that day, she said that she found out that Jimmy Savile was living in a caravan at Broadmoor Mental Hospital."

"What?"

"She said that he was living in a caravan at Broadmoor Mental Hospital."

"Why was he doing that?"

"I have no idea. She obviously wanted me to ask her more about it, but, uhm, well, I'm not particularly interested in Jimmy Savile, to tell the truth. Never liked that program."

"*Jim'll Fix It?*"

"No, nor *Top of the Pops.*"

"She told you that Jimmy Savile was living at Broadmoor in a caravan and you said nothing?"

"I just said, 'Oh,' and left it at that. I wanted to stay friends with Lily, but I didn't really want to spend too much time talking to her. I've started seeing Sarah, Mr. Doyle's secretary, and she's a bit, well, you know ...'"

"Yeah, I know. Lily ever mention Savile again?"

"No. In fact, that was the last time I ever talked to her."

"Did you know Lily had prescriptions for Valium and Nembutal?"

"I did, actually. I saw her take a Valium once, down at the pub. I asked her if it was OK to take it with gin and tonic."

"And what did she say?"

"She said it was OK."

"You ask why she was taking Valium?"

"I didn't, but she offered an explanation. She said that she was slightly claustrophobic. She had the occasional panic attack on the Tube. Doc prescribed Valium. It really helped her."

"Where did she live?"

"Vincent Terrace. Angel. Northern Line."

"You've been very helpful, Mr. Moore."

Out of the *FT* with the Mac.

Taxi across town to Vincent Terrace.

Nice little second-floor flat on the Regent Canal.

Key from the landlady, Mrs. Singh, who lived on the ground floor. "Such a lovely girl. So quiet. So respectable. Very few gentlemen callers, if you know what I mean. Lovely girl. She got me flowers for my birthday."

Lily's stuff was in boxes. "Her father's coming to take it all away on Saturday."

At my request, Chief Inspector Broadbent from Norwich Constabulary had come down here already to go through her effects and found little that was pertinent. No harm in another look. We had a careful rummage through the boxes, but there was nothing here of evidentiary value. A few writing pads, yes, but nothing relating to the case. I looked behind the mirror and under the bed and in the secret compartments of jewelry boxes. Zilch. Her book choices were good, her record choices were better.

Lily was a bright young woman, slightly anxious, with a promising career.

"They say Lily was claustrophobic, Mrs. Singh, did you see any evidence of that?"

"Oh yes. Very claustrophobic. Lifts. She didn't do lifts. And she had to take a pill to go on the Tube. Northern Line, too. You know what that's like. Or perhaps you don't. Heights, as well. Hated heights."

I looked at McCrabban and Lawson.

She hated enclosed spaces and she hated heights. So she hid in a dungeon and jumped off the keep of Carrick Castle . . .

"What are you looking for?" Mrs. Singh asked.

"We're looking for a notebook, home computer, anything like that?"

"She had a computer at work."

"That's what Lawson's lugging around in that giant bag. . . . What about a notebook?"

"She did have a little notebook. Always took it with her. She would have taken that to Ireland. . . . That's what I told all the other detectives. They were very thorough. They came in twice."

"That is thorough."

"If they'd found anything, they would have sent it to us," Crabbie said.

"Unless they're part of the conspiracy too," Lawson said in a dark, melodramatic whisper.

"Can I use your phone, Mrs. Singh?"

Phone call to the House of Commons.

"I'd like to speak to the office of Geoffrey Dickens.... My name is Detective Inspector Sean Duffy of the Royal Ulster Constabulary."

A pause, a transfer. A young woman came on the line.

"Can I ask what this is about?"

I told her what it was about. At the world *pedophile* I heard the woman wince. Mr. Dickens is very busy today. Perhaps tomorrow? Mr. Dickens is busy all week. Perhaps you should take this up with your own constituency MP . . .

I hung up and looked at McCrabban. "One down, one to go. We'll never get another trip over the water on our budget."

"Why? Who are you thinking of seeing now?" he asked.

"What if we went to see Savile out at Broadmoor? Ask him a few questions about Kinkaid before we go up there ourselves."

"Are we going up there ourselves?"

"Oh, yes. I think we are."

"Jimmy Savile? Seems a bit of a stretch."

"Lawson here has always wanted to meet Jimmy Savile. I'm fixing it for him."

"I never said any such thing!" Lawson protested.

"Oh, I nearly forgot!" Mrs. Singh said. "Wait there!"

She went into a back room and, after what can only be described as a loud scuffle, came back with a short-haired domestic cat.

"Here," she said, giving me the cat.

"What's this for?"

"Lily's cat. Her father doesn't want it, and I can't keep it here any longer."

"What are we supposed to do with it?"

"You're the police. You'll think of something."

"What her name?"

"His name is Jet. He's about a year old. Hasn't been fixed yet. Full of energy."

I attempted to give her the cat back. "Take him to the RSPCA."

"You take him to the RSPCA."

"I don't want to touch him. I live in fear of *toxoplasma gondii*," I said, giving the cat to Lawson.

"What's *toxoplasma gondii*?" he asked, eying the cat suspiciously.

"It's a virus cats carry. Causes severe mental disorders and behavioral problems, especially in the young."

"I've got a travel cage for him, if you want," Mrs. Singh said.

"Yes, please," Lawson said.

Lawson put the not-exactly-thrilled Jet in the travel cage.

"What now?" Crabbie asked.

"Mrs. Singh, do you know where we can rent a car around here?"

She thought for a moment.

"There are a few places on the Pentonville Road."

13: JIMMY SAVILE'S CARAVAN

British road-map book. A rented Ford Sierra (no Beemers available). Lawson navigating. Crabbie in the back, minding the computer and the cat. Pentonville Road to the Westway, through Shepherds Bush to the M4. Out along the M4 past Windsor and Eton. Along the river. Through Wokingham to Crowthorne.

Rain pouring up the Thames Valley. The Sierra's window wipers squeaking unpleasantly and not doing a very good job. The heat system and defoggers not working well.

"See that? Never buy a British-made motor, Lawson. Always buy German or Japanese," I said.

"Don't listen to him, son, my Land Rover Defender runs great," Crabbie said.

Broadmoor Hospital.

Gate Lodge.

Guy with a ginger stache, ex-military, Cockney.

"What can I do for you, gentlemen?"

I showed him my warrant card. "We're police."

"Oh, is this about the bloke who went over the wall?"

"What bloke?"

"It's not? Oh. . . . Uhm. . . . Forget I said that. *Please*. What can I do for you, gents?"

"We're here to see Mr. Savile. We believe he's staying here?"

"Yes, he is! Not as a customer, mind you! I should stress that. Ha, ha. Nah, he's here in an advisory capacity, so to speak."

"Where would we find him?"

"He's probably in his caravan if he's not on the wards. Easy to spot. The little white van hooked behind the Roller."

"Behind a Rolls-Royce?"

"Yellow one. Yeah. Can't miss it. Sign out when you leave, gents. Easy to get in, trickier to get out, although some days you wouldn't think that."

We found Savile's caravan in the sodden and partially flooded car park. The grim hospital building was behind us, shrouded in fog, giving it a sinister aspect.

We parked the Ford Sierra, got out, knocked on the caravan door.

"Who is it?" Savile said from inside in his distinctive, weird, DJ voice that had only a few traces of his original Yorkshire accent.

"Detective Inspector Sean Duffy, Carrickfergus police."

"Who?"

"Carrickfergus police."

The caravan door opened. Savile looked very much like himself. He was wearing a red Adidas tracksuit, Adidas trainers, and—although it had been raining all day—sunglasses. His famous dyed locks looked more grey now than platinum, and underneath his tan there was significant weathering. He was holding a cigar in one hand and a Leeds United mug in the other.

"Carrickfergus? Where the fuck is that?" he said.

"Northern Ireland. Can we ask you a few questions about the Kinkaid Young Offenders' Institution in Belfast?"

"What about it?"

"Are you on the board there, by any chance?"

"Probably. I'm a director or on the board of a dozen homes and institutions around the country. So many I can't remember them all."

"Look, do you mind if we come in for a minute and talk? We're getting soaked out here."

"All of you?"

"Yes."

"There's not room. And you're all wet."

"Sir, I must insist, we're conducting a murder inquiry."

"What's that got to do with me?"

"Please. It's only a few questions and we've come a long way."

Savile shook his head. "All right, come in then. Wipe your feet on the mat, though, and don't sit on the sofa till I put some towels down."

We entered the dinky little caravan and waited while Savile put dish towels on the sofa before we sat on it.

"What are you doing here, Mr. Savile?" I asked. "In Broadmoor?"

"Officially, I'm here to cheer up the patients and the staff. Unofficially . . ."

"Unofficially?"

"Just between you, me, and the gatepost, Edwina Currie sent for me. Special investigation."

"What?" I said, incredulously. Edwina Currie was one of the Thatcher government's health ministers, the only prominent woman in the Cabinet apart from Maggie herself.

"I'm already on the advisory board, but sometimes I do the government a favor. Bit of a hush-hush thing, this, as it happens. Financial irregularities. I'm looking into it. I suppose you'll be wanting some tea. All right, then. I've no milk."

"No, that's not necessary, I—"

"I'm already bloody making it!" he snapped. "Can't you hear the kettle boiling?"

He began making three cups of black tea with one tea bag. It gave me the opportunity to scope out the caravan. Filthy curtains, a fold-out bed, a muck-encrusted range, and a series of signed photographs hung up all over the metal walls: Savile with the Beatles, Savile with the Stones, Savile with the Kinks, Savile with Gary Glitter. And, to show how connected he was, photographs of Savile with political and religious figures: Savile with Cardinal Basil Hume, Prince Charles, Margaret Thatcher, Charlie Haughey, and Pope John Paul II. He'd seemingly met everybody. Savile wasn't yet a knight of the realm or a papal knight, but with all his good works for hospitals and kids, both ennoblings were on the cards . . .

He gave me the Leeds United mug without washing it out first.

"Thanks. I had a feeling you were a Leeds fan," I said, smiling and taking the mug.

"Who gives a fucking toss about football?" Savile said. "And don't be asking for any biscuits. I'm down to me last packet of creams, and if you lot take two each, they'll be all gone."

"No, this is fine," I said.

Savile handed mugs to Lawson and McCrabban. "Look at the gurning face on him. All right, I'll give you a biscuit or something. Look as if you could do with something to eat," he said to Lawson.

"You there, turn on the radio, it's like a dwarf's funeral in here," he said to me.

I turned on a transistor radio while Savile started rummaging in a cupboard. Joe Cocker's "You Are So Beautiful" was playing and Savile immediately dashed across the caravan and turned it off.

"You like that, do you?" he said, accusingly.

"It's all right, I suppose," I said.

"Fucking shit song. 'You are so beautiful to me'? If I'd said that to some bird, she would have belted me."

"Written by Billy Preston, though. John Lennon called him the fifth Beat—"

"'Fifth Beatle,' he says, 'fifth Beatle,'" Savile muttered. "They bloody called Jimmy Tarbuck the fifth Beatle. And they called George Best the fifth Beatle and he played for United! I knew the bloody Beatles in the Stu Sutcliffe days."

"Oh! Who was your favorite?" Lawson asked.

"'Who was my favorite,' he says. He could throw a punch, could John. Of course they shot him in the back. If they'd tried to shoot him in the front he'd of nutted that bloke."

"Did you get to meet Elvis?" Lawson asked.

"You and your bloody questions. How old are you, son? Twelve? How did you get to be a policeman? No, I didn't bloody meet bloody Elvis! Do you know anything? Elvis never came to Britain. Well, once, but that was only Prestwick bloody Airport!"

Savile gave Lawson a nasty-looking piece of Swiss roll on a paper plate. "There, there's some food. Now what's this all about? I'm a very busy man, you know."

"It's about the Kinkaid Young Offenders' Institution, Mr. Savile. You are one of its patrons, aren't you?"

His memory seemed to come roaring back to him. "That place? Yeah. Brand-new. New ideas. Treat kids with a bit of respect. I raised a million pounds for it and they put me on the board," Savile said, and lit himself a cigar.

"Have you ever heard about any allegations of abuse there?"

"What kind of abuse?"

"Primarily sexual abuse. But anything? Violence?"

"No. Why, what have you heard?"

"It's probably nothing. It was an anonymous tip to a newspaper that—"

Savile fake-laughed so hard he almost coughed out his cigar.

"An anonymous tip to a newspaper about a home or a hospital I'm involved with? Are you joking? Hundreds of those flood in every bloody week. I'm a crook, I'm stealing all the money I raise, I'm a kiddie fiddler, I'm molesting them on *Jim'll Fix It*, I'm doing it all for me own good so Mrs. Thatcher will cut me taxes. 'Anonymous tip,' he says. Load of rubbish. They always say stuff like that about me. About anybody trying to do any good in this country."

"Geoffrey Dickens MP said—"

"Geoffrey Dickens! You should hear what Maggie says about him. Daft as a brush, he is. Dear, oh dear. Is that all you've got? An anonymous tip?"

"The journalist who was investigating this anonymous tip was possibly murdered and that's why we're following up on this," I said.

Savile conceded the seriousness of the point with a grunt. "Well, I don't know anything about that. I raise the money. They spend it. God knows what goes on after that."

The phone rang in the corner.

"Better take this," Savile said.

He picked up the receiver and listened for a second while a woman said something down the line. He hung up.

"Listen, gents. I always like to cooperate with the police, I've raised a king's ransom for the Police Benevolent Fund. I'm an honorary police sergeant in the Met. And as for Northern Ireland.... I was the one who brought the Radio 1 Roadshow over there. Everybody else was too bloody scared to go, but I insisted. The kids of Belfast need a bit of light and hope too, don't they? Me, as it happens. They'll always go after you if you do something good. They'll always be looking for ulterior motives. They'll always try and knock you down. Especially the fucking tabloids, 'scuse my fucking French. They love building you up and knocking you down."

"So, just to be clear, you've never heard of any allegations of abuse at the Kinkaid YOI?"

"Absolutely not! And if I did, I'd go straight to the police. Have you got a card?"

"I have," I said, giving him a card with my name and office number on it.

"I'll go straight to you.... Now I really have to go, the patients are in need of a bit of cheering up, and I'm the man for the job."

Savile went to a small safe he had sitting on top of a mini fridge, opened it, and removed several gold chains and gold rings. He put them on.

"Come on! Out! Outen zee!" he said, and he began herding us toward the door.

We went outside into the rain, but I wasn't going to let him get away quite that easily.

"We will be investigating Kinkaid YOI, and at some point we may want you to make a formal statement, Mr. Savile, so if you wouldn't mind giving us your phone number and permanent add—" I began, but he cut me off.

"Don't take that tone with me, young man. You know where I spent Christmas?"

"The North Pole?"

"The North.... Chequers! All right? Carol, Dennis, Mark, Maggie, and me. Right? I don't expect to be troubled again, about this or anything else, or you'll be getting a bloody call," he said. He shut the caravan door, locked it, and jogged across the car park toward the hospital.

We stood, looking at him until he disappeared into the fog.

"Thoughts, gentlemen?" I said.

"He's a bit different with the cameras off, isn't he?" Lawson said. "He's a bit of a . . ."

"Fuckface?" I suggested.

"Or words to that effect."

"He didn't seem particularly worried about the allegations," McCrabban said.

"No. He didn't."

I looked at my watch. It was four o'clock now. "We're not too far from Heathrow, it's just back along the M4. Home, gentlemen?"

Home, they agreed.

14: KINKAID

Heathrow to Belfast Harbor Airport. A landing vector straight down the lough and over the shipyards. As we were on the final approach, we could see a riot kicking off along the Falls Road. "Look at that," Lawson said, as we watched Molotov cocktails arc through the air and crash into riot shields. One of the joys of landing at Belfast.

We got our bags and grabbed a very disorientated and spooked cat from the "Oversized and Special" luggage area.

I picked up the Beemer from the short-term car park and drove the lads home, Lawson to Downshire in a fairly nice but boring part of Carrickfergus, and Crabbie way up into the country on a scrabble sheep farm beyond Ballyclare.

"Do you want to come in for a cup of tea? The boys miss their Uncle Sean," Crabbie said.

"Another time, mate. I'm shattered, gotta get to my bed. My best to Helen, of course. Oh and give them this, if Helen doesn't mind," I said, fishing three giant Toblerones out of a WHSmith bag.

"Oh no! I forgot to bring them anything from London! They'll be furious!" Crabbie said, genuinely upset.

"Say the Toblerones are from you, I won't mind."

Crabbie wrestled with the possibility of telling a white lie for a moment and shook his head. "No, I'll make it up to them. They'll be delighted to have this from you."

"All right, you big weirdo, see you tomorrow. Hey, do you want to keep the cat? Could always do with a cat on a farm, couldn't you?"

"Uh no, Fluffy would kill him. He's very territorial."

"All right, then."

"Thanks for the lift, Sean. Get some sleep."

"I will."

But I didn't go home. I went to the station, gave Jet some milk, and plugged in Lily's Mac to check that it was still running after the flight. It worked fine. I printed out her memo from the tip line and looked through the other files to see if there was anything the *FT* had missed. Nothing jumped out at me. Boring finance and business stories— second-string stuff. This tip must have come right out of the blue from God knows who.

I logged in to my computer and went through the server to the England and Wales crime database headquartered at the Met in London. In theory, this database was a godsend for anyone wanting to check on someone's previous criminal history, but in practice it almost never worked. Anytime Lawson or I had ever tried to access anything, the system had crashed or been so slow we had given up.

But, as I had suspected, at two in the morning it was a different story. I might be the only copper in the United Kingdom looking up someone's criminal history at this time.

The someone was Jimmy Savile, but, if the computer was to be believed, he was as clean as a whistle. No arrests, no pending investigations anywhere in England and Wales. He looked and acted creepy as hell, but that didn't necessarily mean he was guilty of anything . . .

I shut off the computer and yawned.

No point going home now. "If you're going to take a shit somewhere, try and do it over at Personnel or Traffic. Everybody hates those bastards," I explained to Jet.

I took my sleeping bag from the filing cabinet, laid it down on my office floor, and went to sleep.

A gentle hand on my shoulder.

"Wha—"

Sunlight flooding into the room. The smell of coffee. Lawson and McCrabban staring at me as if I were the baby Jesus.

"Sean, we made you some coffee and there's a Mr. Kipling's French Fancy for breakfast," Crabbie said.

"Thanks," I said.

I looked across the office to the Personnel and Pay Department, where someone was raising hell.

"What's going on over there?"

"Someone did a shit on Sergeant Dalziel's desk," Lawson said.

"Where's Jet?" I asked.

"Curled up over there, on your leather jacket, sleeping," Crabbie said.

"That's a very smart cat, that."

I told them about Jimmy Savile having a clean criminal record, and they weren't surprised. It was as Phipps said: If he really was spending Christmas with the Thatchers, he'd have been vetted to the moon and back. When you stopped to think about it, it was an absurd allegation.

I looked out of the window at the castle.

"If Lily was murdered by someone other than Mr. Underhill, it was a crime of opportunity," I said. "If she was murdered because of the investigation she was working on, a smart murderer would want to do three things. One: kill her to shut her up. Two: burn her notebook. Three: wipe the files from her computer. This hypothetical killer was able to do the first two of those things, but not the third. The murderer saw an opportunity to kill Lily and he took it, but he's not the Security Services or the Special Branch because he couldn't get into the *Financial Times* and get access to her desk."

"So he's a private individual," Lawson said.

"Or maybe silencing Lily was the important part of it. The allegations themselves don't mean anything, but a mouthy crusading journalist can wreak a lot of havoc," I mused. "Lawson, do me a favor, find out who else is on the Board of Trustees of Kinkaid YOI, and see if there's been any complaints about the institution of any kind in the last five years or so."

"There won't have been any complaints in the last five years. I had a wee look in the files this morning. The place is brand-new. Only been open since August," Lawson said.

"Well, check the complaint logs with the Sex Crimes Unit in Newtownabbey. Oh, and send out a constable to buy a litter box and some Whiskas. Do cats eat Whiskas, or is that just the advertising?"

"They'll eat Whiskas," Crabbie said.

"Good. Get cracking, lads. We've a lot of work to do."

I shaved with the electric and looked halfway respectable when we arrived at Kinkaid Young Offenders' Institution, up near the zoo on the Antrim Road, in a nice bit of parkland. A very modern institution indeed. No fences, extensive grounds, a large rectangular building in the Danish style. Lots of ruddy-looking teenagers outside playing football, others chasing each other through a massive climbing frame.

"It's not quite what I was expecting," Crabbie said.

"Easy enough for them to escape if they wanted. There's no fences," Lawson said.

"That's probably the idea. No fences means anyone can walk off at any time, which encourages a kind of collective responsibility. It's a very northern European penal approach," I said.

"It's optimistic," Crabbie said—a word he only ever used pejoratively.

We parked the Land Rover and got out. Our presence had excited no interest from the young offenders, and we went inside. A sign pointed us to Reception, where we encountered a secretary called Louise.

"We're here to see Betty Anderson," I said. "We did call."

"Oh yes, are you Inspector Duffy?"

"I am."

"She's waiting for you. I'll show you right in."

She showed us in to Ms. Anderson's office, which was sleek, minimalist, and modern. A computer on a large hardwood table, hardwood floors, swivel chair, CD player, throw rugs, a sofa, a metal bookcase with about a couple of dozen titles (mostly psychology and penology books, by the look of it), and a view down the Antrim Road to Belfast and the lough. It was an office to be coveted.

Betty Anderson was thirtyish, blond, with big brown eyes. She was dressed all in pink and consequently bore an uncanny resemblance to Lady Penelope from *Thunderbirds*.

I introduced myself, McCrabban, and Lawson. She invited us to sit down on the comfortable red leather sofa. Unasked, Louise brought us tea, milk, cups, saucers, and Rich Tea biscuits.

She spoke a little bit like Lady Penelope, too. Lady Penelope crossed with Fenella Fielding. She was clearly English and posh, and the only explanation why someone of her class could possibly be in Northern Ireland running a prison was missionary zeal.

"So what can I do for you, gentlemen?"

"We're investigating the possible murder of a reporter in Carrick Castle last week. Lily Bigelow? It's been on the news."

"Sorry, I try not to watch the news. It's so upsetting."

"Following an anonymous tip, Miss Bigelow appears to have been working on a story about the abuse of young people. This institution's name came up in her inquiries," I said, circumspectly.

"I'm sure you've checked your files and you'll have discovered that we have an exemplary record here. Not one complaint since the pilot scheme began last summer. Not one complaint. Not one abscondee. If that's not proof of our method, I don't know what is."

"What is your method, if I may ask?"

"We run the Nils Christie Scandinavian prison model, where, as I'm sure you know, recidivism rates are substantially lower than in the UK. The young men we have here under our care are treated with dignity and respect. We encourage them to read and play sports and games. We teach them woodworking and metal working and car mechanics. They leave here with a skill set, confidence, and, that most elusive of things in Belfast, hope for the future. We only have seventy-five boys here, but every single one of them is taking at least one O-level or CSE. Some are taking A-levels. We even have one boy who goes down to the University of Ulster every morning."

"And not one complaint of bullying, or harassment, or ill-treatment?"

"Not one."

"I didn't see any prison officers on the grounds," I said.

"That's because I don't employ any prison officers. I employ only teachers, gardeners, and social workers. Oh, and two nurses."

"The prison officers' union can't have been happy about that."

She laughed. "That might be the understatement of the year. In fact, if I was to hazard a guess where poor Miss Bigelow's anonymous tip about impropriety came from, I would guess the Prison Officers' Union of Northern Ireland, who have had it in for us from the start."

"They don't approve of your methods?"

"No. Beat them, bully them, lock them up, that's their approach—and you can see around you the society that that has created."

"Seventy-five boys. What ages?" I asked.

"Thirteen to nineteen. You won't find seventy-five boys on the premises today, however."

"No?"

"Twenty of them are outward-bounding in Scotland with the Prince's Trust."

"Prince Charles's organization?"

"Indeed."

"I've read that Jimmy Savile is on the board of governors?"

"The board of advisors. 'Governor' is a prison term we don't like to use. Here, take a look at this," she said, giving me a colorful brochure that began with a foreword written by Savile and Lord Longford.

"Mr. Savile helped raise nearly a million pounds for us and a sister institution we are building outside Dublin," Ms. Anderson said.

"What's your background, if you don't mind me asking?" I said.

"I took an MPhil in criminology at Cambridge, and I actually did my PhD with Dr. Christie at the University of Oslo."

"How did you get interested in this business in the first place?"

"My father is Lord Desmond. . . . Chairman of the Howard League for Penal Reform."

"Chip off the old block, eh?"

"Yes."

"I see you don't have walls or fences," McCrabban said, still trying to take it all in.

"That's correct. Anyone who wants to leave can just walk out of the door," Ms. Anderson said.

"And anyone who wants to can just walk right in," I said.

"Why would anyone want to walk into a prison?" Ms. Anderson asked.

"What happens at night, after the teachers and the gardeners and the social workers go home?"

"Oh, we have a skeleton night staff. We're not silly. We know boys will be boys. Mr. Jones makes sure they're all in bed by lights-out."

"I'd like to talk to this Mr. Jones, and I'd like to talk to some of the boys, if I may."

"You can certainly talk to Colin Jones, but I won't allow you to talk to any of the boys. I'm sorry, it's nothing personal. No policemen, no prison officers—it's just our rule. We want them to trust us, and they won't if we allow bullying by policemen and prison officers. Like I say, no offense," she said, smiling sweetly.

"None taken. What if I got a warrant to talk to your boys?" I replied, smiling equally sweetly.

"You'll have to get your warrant from the secretary of state for Northern Ireland. We've been set up under a special order of the Privy Council and are not subject to the ordinary judicial procedures. I was quite insistent on that. We can't have our young men being harassed by the RUC at all hours of the day and night."

"Tell me a little more about them. Where do they come from? How long are they here for?"

"They're all category three, low-supervision inmates. The youngest inmate we have is thirteen. The oldest is nineteen. We have three dorms, segregated by age. Although we call ourselves a YOI, we're more like an STC—a secure training center."

She was telling me about the place, not about the prisoners.

"Violent offenders? Thieves? Sex offenders? What?"

"Category three, Inspector Duffy, so that only includes one or two violent offenders. Mostly drug, robbery, burglary cases. Quite a few so-called joyriders."

"What about the paramilitary element?"

"Oh, we don't allow gangs in here. That sort of thing is strictly forbidden."

"And by forbidding it, it just goes away, does it?"

"Our methods have proved very successful," she said.

She gave us fifteen minutes more of this stuff before our time was up. She was a busy woman. We thanked Ms. Anderson and went to see Mr. Jones in his rather less impressive office in one of the prison dormitories.

We caught a few glimpses here and there of industrious, serious youths, walking to and from various classes. They were wearing their own clothes, chatting, seemingly at ease, but they stiffened when they saw us: outsiders, adults, authority . . . danger.

"Hello," I said to one of them.

"Arright," he said back.

Colin Jones was an amiable, grey-haired sixty-year-old with a doleful white moustache. He was an ex–prison officer who had been disillusioned by the system, retired, written a book about prison reform, and been recruited by Ms. Anderson.

"How long have you been working here?"

"Since the beginning. Since August."

"And how have you found it?"

"It's met and matched all our expectations. The place is running beautifully."

"No trouble?"

"No trouble of any kind."

"Tell me about the nighttime arrangements."

"Betty and the day staff are all usually out by six or seven o'clock, unless there's a special event on like a play or a performance. I stay in the dorm until midnight. Lights-out is at 10:30 p.m., but I stay for another half hour or so, to make sure there's no shenanigans."

"And then what?" I asked.

"Then I go home. I have a wee cottage on the grounds."

"Who watches the kids?"

"That's the beauty of the Christie model. The kids watch themselves. We train them in fire drills and other emergencies. Give them the responsibility. Works wonders. But they can always wake me up if there are any problems."

"Have there been any problems on any of your shifts?" I asked him.

"No. The kids are very well behaved here. The older ones know how lucky they have it. Keep the younger ones in line. And they know I don't stand for any nonsense. As I say, I turn the lights off in the dormitories at 10:30 p.m., and I generally don't hear a peep out of them until morning, when some of them get up for an early-morning run."

"Where do they go for the run?"

"Oh, some of them go up the Knockagh."

"They're allowed to leave the prison to go for a run?"

"Oh yes. Treat people with respect, and they'll treat you with respect. Don't you find that, Inspector Duffy?"

"That hasn't been my experience. Not one of them has ever absconded?"

"Not a one. Not yet. The method works."

He was generous with his time, and we all took turns asking him questions, and if Mr. Jones was to be believed they had built paradise on Earth here up the Antrim Road.

On the way out of Mr. Jones's office we walked through one of the rec rooms where they had books and newspapers. Improving newspapers only. No *Sun* or *Daily Star*. Just the *Guardian*, the *Times*, the *Daily Telegraph*.

And there, on a coffee table, an old copy of the *Financial Times*. Three weeks old.

Back into Jones's office, Columbo-style. "One more thing, Mr. Jones. Do you not get the *FT* anymore?"

"The *FT*? Nah, we only got that for Lenny. One of our gardeners. He liked to keep track of his BT shares. And now he's left, there's no point. Nobody reads it. Nobody can do the crossword."

"How old was Lenny? Twenties? Thirties?"

"Twenty-nine."

"Where would I find this Lenny?"

He looked out Lenny Dummigan's file. His address was in a flat in a tower block in Rathcoole Estate, but of course when *we* got there, Lenny had gone. The flat was empty and he'd scarpered.

"Moved to England or Scotland," his next-door neighbor said. "Closed down his bank account, cashed out, and moved."

"Why?"

"Had enough of it over here, I suppose. Don't blame him."

Lenny's only relative, his sister, hadn't even known he was out of the country.

We drove back to the station.

Interesting, that. Lenny vanishing. Gardener at Kinkaid. Good money. But then he quits and moves and decides to live on cash. Lenny, who reads the *FT* to check his shares.

Could this bizarre Scandinavian model really work in a society like war-torn Ulster? Norway, sure, where everyone was rich and there was virtually no crime. But here? Here, now? In the terrible midnight of the Troubles? Was it too good to be true, or were we just too cynical to believe it? Was Lenny a shit-stirrer or a whistle-blower?

When we got back to the incident room, Lawson, McCrabban, and I did a zealous search through the police files and the court records. Betty Anderson and Colin Jones both had clean records. Jones had gotten commendations for his work in the formal prison service. Still, everyone could be corrupted in Ulster, and prison officers in particular were vulnerable to threats against their families. Lenny Dummigan had only worked there for eight weeks before jacking it in.

"Do me a favor, Lawson. Put an alert out for Lenny Dummigan. I'd very much like to talk to him."

"If he's using cash and lying low in Scotland, I don't think he'll attract too much attention," Crabbie said.

"No," I agreed. "Something spooked our Lenny, though, didn't it?"

"Aye."

"Let's see if there's anything on the Interpol records on either Mr. Laakso, Mr. Ek, or the Lennätin boys."

We did the research and came up with nothing.

The sun had sunk behind the Antrim Plateau, and the station was clearing out. Chief Inspector McArthur came into the incident room to see what we were up to. I told him about the tip on Lily's computer and our experience of Kinkaid YOI.

"I'd like to see this anonymous tip you've all been so excited about," McArthur said.

I showed him the printout from Lily Bigelow's computer.

"Holy shit," he said, and pushed the printout back across the desk.

"Yeah," I agreed.

"Who have you shown that to?"

"Only you."

"Thank God for that. Jimmy Savile? Cyril Smith? The Home Secretary? It must be a load of nonsense, mustn't it?"

"Savile in particular seems an unlikely suspect in this kind of inquiry, sir. Apparently he's a personal favorite of the prime minister, so I imagine Special Branch have given him the old third degree."

"You talked to him, I gather?"

"Yes, sir. Rather an eccentric, sir. Abrasive. Not really his telly persona."

"But that doesn't prove he's a pervert."

"Quite."

"Tell me about Kinkaid."

"Odd place. Modern. Been running for six months. Some sort of pilot scheme. Only has seventy-five inmates, but it seems to be working. Ms. Anderson believes it will end recidivism among the young offender population and turn Belfast into a kind of Oslo on the Lagan."

"What's that extraordinary noise coming from your office, Duffy?"

"It's Lily Bigelow's cat. It was sort of foisted upon us. Are you a cat person, sir?"

"No. I'm not. Get it out of here, Duffy. We're not going to have a station cat. It's bad luck."

"It's a domestic shorthair, tabby, sir, no bad luck in that."

"Take it home with you, Duffy, or take it to the RSPCA. Your choice."

"Yes, sir."

And with that I said my good-nights, dismissed the lads, and took the cat to its new abode on Coronation Road.

15: TONY McILROY'S DETECTIVE AGENCY

Morning. A cat climbing onto my head and meowing. Shower, shave, skip breakfast, leave some tuna for the cat, check under the BMW for bombs. No bombs.

No bombs, but was that somebody watching the house from the bend at the bottom of the street? Guy in a parka?

No. My imagination. Why would anybody want to watch me? He was just a loiterer. Keep my eye open, though.

Inside the Beemer. Culture Club on Radio 1. Vivaldi on Radio 3. Dolly Parton on Downtown Radio. Downtown it is.

Up to the incident room. "Case conference, lads," I said. "Let's have it in Ownies," I said. "Breakfast there. My shout."

Ownies Bar, just down the street. As I've said many times: the best pint of Guinness in Carrickfergus—almost as good as 1950s slow-pour, sawdust-floor, Dublin-pub Guinness.

Ulster fry, Irish coffee—nice little hits of sugar, booze, caffeine, and fat.

We were in the upstairs snug overlooking the Marine Gardens, the lough, and the castle. Rain streaks in the window, white caps on the sea.

"Well, gentlemen?" I said after my second coffee.

"It looks like we've more or less run this fox to ground," McCrabban said.

"Lawson?"

Lawson wasn't sure what the fox-hunting metaphor meant, but his sentiments were the same as Sergeant McCrabban's: "Sir, I think the tip Lily got was a load of rubbish. There's no evidence at all of any kind of impropriety. Kinkaid YOI hasn't had a single complaint."

"There's nothing in the files," I agreed.

174

"The paramilitaries don't seem to be involved. Your woman seemed extremely respectable and on its board of governors are Richard Coulter and Jimmy Savile—two people with impeccable records. I know Savile rubbed us the wrong way, but he can't be involved in anything sinister. Lily is a smart lass, she realizes this whole thing is a wild-goose chase, is depressed already because of her meds, and decides to top herself," Lawson suggested.

"And the claustrophobia and the fear of heights?"

"The meds helped her get over those fears. That's what they're for."

"And the time line and the movement of the body?" Crabbie asked.

"Underhill lied about doing a meticulous inspection of the castle because he was drunk," Lawson suggested.

"And the livor mortis? Moving the body?"

"Either the doctor was wrong about that, or Underhill moved the body when he was drunk and moved it back again when he sobered up."

"It's not a very elegant solution," I said.

"No, it isn't," Crabbie said.

"But stuff elegance, Crabbie, we're talking about Belfast here."

We sank into silence and thought about it.

"I'll type up a report for the DPP suggesting all these various scenarios," I said. "Maybe if they lean on Underhill, he'll crack." I made an imaginary scale with my hands "Interfering with a body and wasting police time versus second-degree murder. I'd cop to it," I said.

"He might cop to it even if he didn't do it," Crabbie said.

"Aye, but if he didn't move the body and he didn't kill her, what *did* bloody happen, exactly?" I said.

"I dunno," Lawson said.

I finished my Guinness and stood up. "But we're agreeing that the Kinkaid angle is bogus?"

Lawson nodded. Crabbie did not.

"Come on, Sergeant McCrabban, sir, you know as well as we do that although pedophile conspiracies get all the ink, they're always, always, always bullshit. *News of the World* bullshit," Lawson said.

"First of all, watch your language," Crabbie said.

"Yes, sir."

"Secondly, you know who would know if anyone from the Finnish delegation was visiting the Kinkaid YOI—or anywhere else for that matter—for immoral purposes?"

"Who?"

"He'd have their full itinerary. He'd know their movements for every second that they were in Ireland."

"Who?"

"Your friend, Tony McIlroy, Sean."

I grinned. "You're right. Let's go have a wee chat with him and attempt to close the book on this case."

Back to the station. BMW instead of Land Rover.

The chief inspector summoning me to his office.

"Duffy!"

"Can't stop, sir, I've an appointment in Belfast. CID business. Don't worry, I took care of the cat."

"Duffy, you've turned in all your receipts. Sergeant Dalziel wants to know why all *three* of you had to go to London. He says you'll have to take the travel out of your budget, not the station budget."

"We got a three-for-two ticket. I'll take care of it. Really must go, sir."

BMW.

Crabbie sitting next to me in the front seat. Lawson in the back. Radio 3 playing Rachmaninoff. All that monotonous running up and down in the arpeggios. Who can stand it?

"Turn it off, Crabbie, will ya, mate?" I said.

"Radio 2?" he suggested.

"Aye, why not."

He flipped to Radio 2 and easy listening carried us up the A2 and the M5. "Your Cheatin' Heart" by Hank Williams as we pulled up in front of Tony's office on York Road. Me and Crabbie very much enjoying it, but young Lawson sitting in the back with utter incomprehension etched on his face.

The Blacklock Building was in an old cigarette factory near the docks that had recently been converted into cheap office space. High ceilings, lots of square footage, water views. It would take a hundred years to get rid of the cigarette pong, but you probably got used to it after a while. Plenty of parking, too, now that the factory was gone and the docks weren't exactly turning over a roaring trade. It used to be thriving in this part of town, not ten years ago, but now shipping containers lay rusting on wharves and the big cranes of Harland & Wolff shipyard were idle down on Queen's Island. The only things that weren't rusting were the rows of gleaming aluminum DeLoreans that had been sitting on the dock for four years in legal limbo.

Tony's office was on the top floor with a nice view right down the lough. The place looked good. He had a receptionist and a secretary, a Coke machine, and two comfortable sofas arranged around a coffee table. The walls were painted in pastels, and there was original art hanging on them.

"Can I help you gents?" the very pretty receptionist asked, putting down a nail-polish brush and a bottle of red enamel.

"We're the police. Has Mr. McIlroy got a moment?" I said.

"Have a seat, please, and I'll ask Donna if he's busy. Donna, is he busy?"

Donna looked up from *Cosmopolitan*.

"I'll go and see," she said.

"Tell him Sean Duffy's here to see him."

She told him and Tony burst out into the reception area with a big grin on his face. He was wearing a baggy blue suit, which I assumed was the style in London, but which none of us had seen in Belfast before. Clashing with the suit was a canary-yellow tie and pointy brown shoes, but I had the feeling that the clash was deliberate and this, too, was the fashion over the water. Should have paid more attention when I was in London.

He shook me warmly by the hand and, recognizing Crabbie from several previous meetings, shook his hand. I reintroduced him to Lawson, and we followed him into his office, which looked pretty good, too. Bright-blue paint job, big windows overlooking the harbor, paintings of Mediterranean landscapes, teak desk, leather sofa.

"Have a seat, lads. What can I do for you?" Tony said, sitting down at the desk, which was completely clear of executive toys, computers, or anything else, save for a phone, a notebook, and a couple of pencils—nice touch that: shrink-like, clients' needs to the forefront.

"Cigar?" Tony asked, opening the door of a humidor that had been cleverly built into his desk. He removed a box of very elegant-looking Cohibas.

"I don't mind if I do, Tony," I said, grabbing one.

Neither Lawson nor Crabbie wanted a cigar.

"Take theirs," Tony insisted.

"All right," I said, and took two more.

"I will take one, after all," Crabbie said, and although Tony's grin was fixed, I noticed that as the cigars disappeared from the proffered box he winced a little. It was a wince that conveyed a lot of information. As always, Tony put up a good front. The brand-new office, the business cards, the hair, the clothes.... And, yes, he was right. Private security was a growth industry in Northern Ireland. The security situation was tenuous, to say the least, and Ulster did have some wealthy people, but it can't have been easy to get a start-up business going in the Ulster of 1987. There were other detective agencies feasting on divorce work, and for the bigger contracts there were Securicor and Home Guard. Tony might have the contacts and money coming in, but he clearly couldn't easily afford to see pricey cigars disappear into the pockets of visiting RUC men.

We sat down on the leather sofa, opposite Tony. Behind him, through the continual Belfast drizzle, the car ferry was leaving for Liverpool.

"Oh! Drinks. Whisky?" Tony asked, and before we had a chance to say that we were on duty and really shouldn't, he'd poured us all a healthy measure of Islay.

We thanked him and got down to business.

"Tony, look, this isn't a social call, we've come to talk to you about Lily Bigelow's death," I said.

"Of course. I read you arrested that old geezer in the castle. Why would he do it? Not a sex crime, surely?"

"We don't know why he did it. We've turned the case over to the DPP, and I suppose he'll try to figure out the whys and wherefores."

"So what do you need from me?" he asked.

"Well, we've got this little additional wrinkle to the whole case. Apparently, Lily only came to Northern Ireland in the first place because she got a tip that the Kinkaid Young Offenders' Institution was being used as some kind of center for underage prostitution, and that the visiting Finnish delegation might be taken there on their trip to Northern Ireland. Have you heard anything about that?"

Tony looked amazed. "I was with them almost 24/7 for the three days they were here. I never saw anything like that. You met the Finns, Sean. Geriatrics and those two ridiculous kids. Don't think they're up to anything like that."

"It seems unlikely."

"What's this Kinkaid place? Never heard of it."

"Some sort of borstal. Quite an impressive place, actually. Very modern institution. No criminal records on the staff, and the board of governors includes prominent local businessmen and even a few celebrities."

"So where do I fit into this, exactly?"

"You must have the Finns' complete itinerary for the time they were in Northern Ireland. If we could run through that with you and eliminate the possibility that they went to Kinkaid, then, well, we can completely close the book on that part of the case."

"What'll that prove?"

"It'll prove that Lily came over here on a false lead, and that her death is unrelated to the anonymous tip she picked up at the *Financial Times*."

Tony looked puzzled. "I'm not following your logic, Sean. She gets an anonymous tip that the Finns are diddling little boys, so a huge conspiracy is put in motion to silence her by hiring a nearly seventy-year-old castle caretaker to murder her in a dungeon?"

"Uhm..."

Tony looked at McCrabban. "John, was this your idea?"

"We sort of all came up with it together," he said.

"Dear, oh dear," Tony said, getting up and rifling in his filing cabinet. He handed me the complete itinerary of the Finns' visit to Belfast.

I looked through the itinerary. From their arrival at Belfast International Airport, to their departure from Belfast International Airport, they had had a packed schedule of factory visits, luncheons with businessmen and civil servants, visits to sites of historical interest (Carrick Castle, the Giants Causeway, etc.), and formal dinners.

"As you can see, a pretty packed schedule, hardly time for satanic ceremonies and murders."

"What's this on the night of the sixth? It says 'Free: Entertainment.'"

I handed the schedule to McCrabban and Lawson.

And now it was Tony's turn to look uncomfortable.

"It was just a free evening they had. Really tight schedule. And they had the evening off. That was the evening of the theft, you remember?"

"The theft was in the middle of the night, Tony. What were they doing earlier in the evening?"

"How am I supposed to know?" he asked. "It was their free night."

"Dear, oh dear, Tony, you used to be a better fibber back in the day," I said.

He sighed, shook his head, and finished his whisky.

"Don't embarrass me, Sean. Can you ask those two to leave?"

"Detective Sergeant McCrabban and Detective Constable Lawson will be remaining for the rest of this interview, Mr. McIlroy."

"Oh Christ, don't 'Mr. McIlroy' me, Sean, we're mates. Colleagues, for crying out loud. And you know very well where the gentlemen went that night without me having to say it out loud. And it wasn't no home for troubled youths."

"Some of them might be troubled, mightn't they? And they are young. It was the Eagle's Nest, wasn't it, Tony?"

Tony shook his head in disgust. "If you knew all along, why all the games, Sean? I'm not some eejit off the street. I'm your mate. Or thought I was."

"Don't take the huff, Tony. Just tell us the story. Whose idea was it? Who went?" I asked.

Tony lit himself a cigarette.

"Well, look, you met all four of them, right? You know the dramatis personae, don't you?"

"Yup."

"OK, so Mr. Ek, he's the older guy, not the boss guy, but the kind of fixer guy, he says to me that the kids—the two boys—are looking for—" Tony began, but stopped when he saw that Lawson and McCrabban had taken out their notebooks and were writing down what he was saying in shorthand. "Come on, lads! Is that really necessary? Now my name's going to get sucked into this?"

"They're doing their job, Tony. Please continue."

Tony shook his head. "So Stefan and Nicolas Lennätin are bored as shit and they're looking for a little fun, so I suggested the Eagle's Nest up the Knockagh Road. Mrs. Dunwoody, you know? Nice lady. Good service. Bit pricey. But classy. So Ek says that sounds ideal and, much to my surprise, all four of them decide to go up there. Not just the two boys, but old Mr. Laakso and Ek, as well as Stefan and Nicolas. We won't fit in my car, but Ek has a car, so they follow me up to the Eagle's Nest, I introduce them to Mrs. Dunwoody, she says she'll take care of them. The price of drinks in there is shocking, so instead of waiting at the bar, I go back to my Beemer and have a bit of a kip."

"And then what?" I asked.

"When they're done, I take them back to the hotel, go to bed, and I get a phone call from Mr. Ek saying that someone has stolen Mr. Laakso's wallet from his hotel room. And I tell him to call the police and he calls you and we both arrive at more or less the same time."

Lawson had his hand up in the air.

"Yes, Lawson?"

"Sorry, what's the Eagle's Nest? I haven't heard of it," he asked, innocently.

"It's a brothel," I explained.

"A what?"

"A house of ill repute, a bordello, a bawdy house."

Lawson looked surprised and a little scandalized, which was nothing short of adorable. "I thought that sort of place was illegal," he said.

"Of course it's illegal. How could it be legal? Jesus," Tony snapped.

"So you took the Finns up to the brothel. Then what?" I continued.

"I took them to the brothel. I introduced them to Mrs. Dunwoody, and I went back out to the car."

"What time was that at?"

"I don't know. Nine, half nine, something like that."

"You didn't happen to notice if you were being followed up to the brothel?"

"Followed? What do you mean?"

"I mean was someone following you?"

"Well . . . yeah. Ek was following me in his car. He didn't know where the place was and I told him to follow me."

"Was anyone following Mr. Ek?"

"No. I don't think so. . . . You mean the reporter?"

"Yes. The reporter."

"Why would she?"

"Because she thought you were up to no good. She'd rented a car and there was a lot of mileage on it."

Tony thought about it for a few moments. "No, I'm pretty sure there was no one following us. That road's fairly isolated up to the Eagle's Nest itself. There was no one following us," he said, confidently.

I looked at Crabbie to see if he had any questions.

"How long were they at the brothel?" he asked.

"An hour?"

"Any complaints? Everyone happy?"

"No complaints. Everyone happy."

"Tell me about the wallet. It was never really stolen at all, was it?" I said.

Tony shook his head. "No, it wasn't. Some kind of practical joke by the twins on old Mr. Laakso, I suspect."

"What was the power dynamic there? How come those boys could get away with something like that?" I asked.

"Well, as I understood it, Laakso is the CFO—the chief financial officer—of Lennätin, basically the second-in-command of the whole operation. But he's not family. It's a family company, entirely privately owned. The CEO is old Mr. Lennätin. His two sons are on the board of directors and the two grandsons, who've just turned eighteen, have also been appointed to the board. According to Mr. Ek, this little trip was to give them some overseas experience."

"So the two boys can't be fired?"

"No, I mean technically Laakso was senior to them, but as they are Mr. Lennätin's grandchildren they're pretty much untouchable."

I thought about all of this for a minute.

"When you were driving back home from the brothel, did you notice any other cars at all on that long driveway road, Tony?" I asked.

"Nope. And you're right, Duffy. That is a long driveway back to the main road. And there were no cars on it. She wasn't on our tail, or if she was, she bloody lost us, not that we were going particularly fast."

"Any more questions, Crabbie? Lawson?"

They shook their heads.

I nodded, got to my feet. "We'll need to check this with Mrs. Dunwoody, but it looks as if there's nothing along this tangent. You understand why we had to investigate it, though? Anonymous tip, keen young reporter, possible murder, and that Mr. Underhill does not look like any kind of killer to us."

"What about his history? Sex crimes? Anything like that?" Tony asked.

"Nothing like that. Widower. He was in the navy for thirty years. Couple of drunken brawls in the street, that's about it."

"And the CCTV footage more or less rules out any third-party involvement, doesn't it?" Tony said.

I nodded.

"So why pursue this angle of the case at all?" Tony asked. "Waste of police resources, no? What's your gaffer say about all this?"

"Oh, he's not too happy. We flew over to London. Didn't have the budget for it. And Kenny Dalziel—remember that waste of space?—he's probably going to make me pay for it out of my own pocket in the end."

Tony nodded, and an awkward silence drifted into the room.

"Right, well, we'll be heading on," I said.

Lawson and Crabbie made for the door.

"Can I speak to you alone for a sec, Sean?" Tony said.

I nodded at Crabbie. "See you in the lobby."

When they were gone, Tony closed the door and sat on his desk in front of me.

"You really embarrassed me there, Sean. Treating me like a civilian. Making me look like a fool in front of John McCrabban and young Lawson there. I wouldn't have done that to you. We could have sorted this whole thing out over a drink or something. What's with the heavy brigade?" he said.

I acknowledged the truth of it. "I'm sorry, Tony. It's just this case. It's been odd. Something about it hasn't felt right from the start."

"What?"

"We made a few mistakes early on and we got humiliated by the medical examiner. And then there's the eerie echo of that Lizzie Fitzpatrick case we talked about in London."

"The girl in the locked pub."

"Exactly. So I'm thinking maybe Lily's death was suspicious and then the pathologist tells me that we screwed up the time of death and somebody moved the body and then we find out that Lily was working on some kind of pedophile case. You'd be seeing conspiracies, too," I said.

"You have to follow the leads, Sean," Tony said. "You're a pro. It's nothing personal, I know that."

"Thanks, Tony."

Tony offered me his hand. "OK, mate. No worries."

I shook the hand gratefully, and Tony leaned in and gave me a sort of half hug.

"We go back, Sean, don't we?"

"We do. And I'm glad you're back in Ulster, even under these circumstances. I don't have many friends, you know?"

"I know," he said.

I took the cigars out of my jacket pocket and offered them back to him. "These must have cost a fortune. Here, I'm not really a cigar smoker, anyway," I said.

"Jesus! Don't insult me even more! Keep the cigars. Look around you. Business is booming."

"Sure, Tony. And look, we'll have that drink sometime, OK?"

I found Crabbie and Lawson out in Reception. Donna had now finished *Cosmopolitan* and the receptionist had painted and dried her nails. Evidently the phone hadn't rung and no new clients had appeared the whole time we'd been in Tony's office. This made me feel even guiltier about the cigars, and I gave them to McCrabban in the Beemer on the way home, telling him that I was still trying to cut down on my tobacco.

16: THE BROTHEL

Trying to quit tobacco, possibly, but I was still a big fan of imported Moroccan hash, which brave smugglers risked life and limb to bring in from Marrakech only to have it taken from them by the customs or the paramilitaries, or me.

And hash only ever worked properly if you rolled it up in Virginia tobacco or shoved it into a cigar to make a blunt. That night I sat in the garden shed with the door open, smoking the hash and looking at the rain lash the back lawn.

I stared at the grass. Blinked slowly, drifted off to sleep for half a minute or so . . .

I opened my eyes again.

"That's odd," I said, and went to examine a slight indentation in the sod. There appeared to be a footprint there, belonging to someone else's foot. I bent down to look at it. Yes. A footprint and another one. Someone had come in over the hedge at some point in the last twenty-four hours. I measured my own shoe against it, and this foot was smaller than mine by a full size. I threw away the joint and followed the footprints. The person had come in over the hedge, walked to my back door and found it locked. Upon discovering that, they'd retreated back over the fence again.

"Ha," I said. "Everything's going to hell. Even burglars have no persistence these days."

I—foolishly as it turned out—dismissed the incident, went to bed, slept a solid eight, breakfasted, dressed, checked under the Beemer, and drove to the station.

Sergeant Mulvenny saw me at the coffee machine making a coffee-choc.

"Heard you met Jimmy Savile?"

"Aye, I did."

"Quite a week for you. Ali and Savile. Brilliant. What's Savile like when he's off the telly?"

"He's like an eclipse."

"What does that mean?"

"Shady as fuck."

I carried the coffee-choc to my office. Good line. And definitely shady, yeah, but not, *apparently*, criminal.

Mabel was looking for me. "Inspector Duffy? Inspector Duffy?"

I came up behind her. "I'm here. What are your other two wishes?"

She laughed and then lowered her voice. "Chief inspector's looking for you."

"You haven't seen me," I said.

But it was no good. He caught me as I was slipping into my office.

"Duffy, I've got a job for you," he said.

"A job! I'm sort of on a case, actually, sir. Bigelow: one more lead to follow up and then we can definitively call it."

"The reporter?"

"Yes."

"I thought you already *had* called it."

"Just one more lead to follow up and then I'll wash my hands and let the DPP run it."

"Where's this lead?"

"You don't want to know, sir."

He looked at me intently. "Where's the lead, Duffy? Not England again?"

"The Eagle's Nest. Mrs. Dunwoody's establishm—"

The chief inspector put up his hand. "You were right, Duffy. I don't want to know."

"I'll keep it discreet, sir."

The chief inspector nodded, sighed. "They'll never be back, of course, whole thing was a waste of time," he continued.

"Sir?"

"The phone factory. They won't be coming here. Did you read the *Irish Times* this morning?"

"Missed it."

"You have to keep abreast of current events. In this day and age it is vital for the modern police officer to keep abreast of current events."

"Yes, sir."

"Make sure you pass that on to young Lawson."

"Yes, sir."

"Anyway, it was in the paper this morning. Business section. Len-nätin are building their factory in the Republic. Five hundred jobs in the first phase."

"Sorry to hear that, sir."

"It was inevitable after everything that happened here. You know who'll be on the blower later today?"

"No, sir."

"If I'm lucky it'll only be the secretary of state for Northern Ireland."

"And if you're unlucky?"

"Mrs. bloody Thatcher. . . . Gimme one of your cancer sticks."

"I'm attempting to give up, sir. I don't have a pack on me."

"Some detective you are, Duffy. You stink of tobacco."

"Well, I might have a pack in my office."

We retired to my office, and the chief inspector sat in *my* chair.

"Anyway, about this job, Duffy. They shot a peeler up in Belfast this morning. Constable Pratt. Someone has to tell his ex-wife."

"Not me. I hate notifications."

"You, Duffy."

A dreary, depressing notification, as all notifications were. Pratt had been shot with a partner while on foot patrol in the center of Belfast. The two gunmen had shot both coppers simultaneously from behind and run off into the side streets. Headshots, close range, whole thing over in ten seconds. A neat job. The IRA were getting better at killing peelers, and we were getting worse at catching killers.

We drove up to Sunnylands Estate, wading through the rubbish, gangs of feral children, donkeys and horses tied to car bumpers.

Mrs. Pratt took it OK: a few tears, only a quarter-box of Kleenex.

"Have youse told Dorothy yet?" she asked bitterly.

"Dorothy is the new wife?" I guessed.

"Aye. The fucking bitch. He met her at the Gospel Hall, if you can believe it."

"I can believe it."

"She was leading the Bible-study class. 'Bible study,' my foot! What about the Second Commandment, eh?"

"Thou shalt not make a graven image?" Crabbie said.

"The adultery one!"

"That's the seventh," Crabbie explained.

"I'll bet she doesn't even phone me, the wee hoor. Well, I'm not phoning her, so I'm not," Mrs. Pratt went on.

Notification over, McCrabban and I drove up the North Road toward the Eagle's Nest. "At least she took it better than Mrs. McBain. Did you see her at the funeral? Very upset," Crabbie said.

"I missed Jo at the funeral. I must have been outside having a smoke."

"Helen was talking to her for a long time. They knew each other from church. Helen advised her to go back to work. Work is the cure, sometimes. She loves her job. Mrs. McBain that is, not Helen."

"I saw her the night of the bombing. Holding up remarkably well, I thought. Better than when her dog went missing."

"Oh yeah, the dog, I remember that. People get very attached to their dogs. City people. People who've never had to shoot a dog."

"What was Jo McBain's work? I don't think I ever asked her," I said, to change the subject.

"University lecturer. And she raised four children. Mostly by herself, what with Ed's schedule. All of them successful. Working over the water."

"And McBain was no slouch either, except that one slip. Didn't check under his car. Strange that, eh? Course that's the one slip that always gets you, isn't it? Ahh, here we are," I said, turning onto the semi-concealed private road that led up to the Eagle's Nest, County

Antrim's most exclusive brothel. Prostitution was illegal everywhere on the island of Ireland, of course, but the Eagle's Nest had been described as "paying off at a height so elevated you'd need Sherpas to come after them." Mrs. Dunwoody's clientele included judges, politicians, senior civil servants, and police officers of all ranks. Ahem.

"Been here before, Crabbie?" I asked, pulling up in front of the main house.

"Of course not!" Crabbie said, shocked.

"Mrs. Dunwoody is the lady running things. Don't bully her. Hobnobs with the great and the good. You'd be surprised."

"Have you been out here before?" Crabbie asked, deadpan.

"On a case, for the chief inspector," I explained. "Bit of a hush-hush affair."

"I imagine so."

Inside. A liveried butler who showed us to an anteroom. Mrs. Dunwoody recognizing me immediately, but with masterful discretion showing no visible sign of it at all. I formally introduced ourselves and told her why we were here.

She ushered us into her office, which was a plain little room with a rather nice view up the lane to the woods at the foot of Knockagh Mountain.

"Yes, I read about that young lady reporter's death. I heard you've arrested someone. A Scotsman."

"Yes. We have. We're pursuing a different aspect of the inquiry. Miss Bigelow seems to have come to the conclusion that the Finnish delegation visiting Carrickfergus may have been involved in some illegality."

"What sort of illegality?"

"We're investigating a possible pedophile link."

Mrs. Dunwoody rose to her feet, simmering with rage. The red wig on her head seemed to be ablaze, and all the goodwill from my last visit here had evidently evaporated. "I hope you're not implying that anything like that goes on in my house! All my employees are over the age of eighteen and can prove it."

"Mrs. Dunwoody, I'm implying no such thing. I merely would like you to tell me what the Finnish delegation got up to when it visited your establishment and if anyone happened to notice whether Lily Bigelow had followed them here."

Mrs. Dunwoody sat down again. "Miss Bigelow was never here! As if I would allow a reporter in my establishment!"

"Could she have followed the delegation down the driveway and—"

"That is quite impossible! Although we do not have a gate across our driveway entrance, we do have a gate lodge, and it is manned twenty-four hours a day. Each car passing by the lodge is noted and the security attendant radios ahead so that we can prepare a welcome for our guests."

"And the Finns came alone?"

"No, they were accompanied by another gentleman who used to be employed by the RUC."

"Yes, we know about Tony. Apart from the Finns and Mr. McIlroy, was there anyone else?"

"No."

"Are you sure? Do you want to check your files or—"

"I have a good memory, Inspector Duffy," she said, giving me a very significant look.

A young woman came in with tea and cake served on a silver tray. Mrs. Dunwoody was "mother" and poured us our tea. The cake was lemony and delicious, and the tea wasn't bad either.

"So the Finnish delegation and Mr. McIlroy?" I said.

"Mr. McIlroy chose to wait in his car," Mrs. Dunwoody said.

"Yes, that's what he told us."

"There were two younger gentlemen, Nicolas and . . . let me think. . . . Stefan . . . who went off with two of our young ladies. Everyone got along famously and they were well satisfied."

"And Mr. Ek and Mr. Laakso?"

"Mr. Laakso was introduced to all of our young ladies and our young men, but although charmed by what we had on offer, he did not feel inclined to partake."

"Why was that?"

"He was an elderly gentlemen and I assume he was rather tired by the burden of official engagements."

"And Ek?" Crabbie asked, finally overcoming his embarrassment at being here in the first place.

"I took it that Mr. Ek was there as a minder for Mr. Laakso and the two young gentlemen. He did not share in the custom of the house, either."

"So what did they do?"

"Mr. Laakso, Mr. Ek, Sandra, and myself played cards while we waited for Nicolas and Stefan. Mr. Ek taught Sandra and myself a card game called Paskahousu."

"Paskahousu? Never heard of it," I said.

"It is a Finnish game. Rather an amusing one. It means 'shit pants' in Finnish. It is a little like Spit, or Dummy, or Jack Changes. The object is to lose all one's cards."

"So you played the game and talked?"

"Indeed."

"Would it be indiscreet to ask what you talked about?"

"Not at all. Mostly about the war, actually. You may not believe it, Inspector, but I remember the war vividly."

"Surely you were far too young, Mrs. Dunwoody!" I said.

She laughed. "I was a young girl when the American GIs came. I remember Hershey Bars and chewing gum and the big camp they had at Sunnylands. General Eisenhower came to visit once. Mr. Ek's experience was quite different."

"Oh?"

"The Siege of Leningrad."

"It must have been awful. Starvation, constant shelling, the cold."

Mrs. Dunwoody looked at me as if I were an imbecile. "Mr. Ek was one of the besiegers. He was on the German side."

"Oh, yes, of course, Ed McBain told me that," I said, the history of the Second World War not exactly my strong suit.

"Mr. Ek told stories that could turn your hair white. Well, not mine, obviously," she said, laughing and adjusting her wig.

"What sort of stories?" Crabbie asked.

"Mr. Ek said he was in a commando unit in the war. They would hunt the Russian soldiers at night. Skin them. Behead them. Quite the tales, he told. I think he made most of them up. Poor Sandra had nightmares."

"And when Stefan and Nicolas finished upstairs, everyone did what, exactly?"

"They paid their bill and went home."

"Just as Mr. McIlroy said," McCrabban pointed out.

"No trouble with them at all?"

"No."

"And no sign of a reporter?"

"Absolutely not!"

I looked at Crabbie. He had nothing. I stood up.

"Well, thank you for your time, Mrs. Dunwoody. This was obviously something of a wild-goose chase," I said.

"Any time, Inspector Duffy," she said, somewhat mollified by our courtesy. I gave her my card. "If you can think of anything else relating to the visit by the Finns, or anything that might be pertinent to Lily Bigelow's death, please give me a call."

"I'll see you anon, Inspector," Mrs. Dunwoody said with a little squeeze of my hand.

Another well-dressed butler type showed us back to the car park.

It was lashing down, but the butler type had brought a massive black umbrella that kept us dry.

BMW back to Carrick.

Heavy rain.

Floods on the top road. Slow movement from the Seventh on the radio.

"What's it all about, Crabbie?"

He stared at me with alarm. "What? Life, you mean?"

"Aye."

"Endeavour to discover the will of God," he said firmly.

"And if there is no God?"

"If there is no God, well, I don't know, Sean. I just don't know."

I looked at him. As stolid a Ballymena Presbyterian as you could ask for. He'd do the right thing even if you could prove to him that there was no God. While the rest of us gave in to the inevitable, he'd be the last good peeler attempting to impose a little bit of local order in a universe of chaos.

Rain. Wind. The afternoon withering like a piece of fruit in an Ulster pantry. I made a sorry excuse for dinner, put on Joan Armatrading, made a vodka gimlet, and went to bed with a book.

Phone ringing. Downstairs in my dressing gown, Che T-shirt, Liverpool FC pajamas. "Hello?"

"That one slip you were talking about, Sean," Crabbie said.

"One slip?"

"With McBain. He didn't check under his car, and that's what killed him."

"So what?"

"They put the bomb under the back wheel behind the driver's side, where no peeler ever looks. It was a bigger bomb with more Semtex, so they could get him from back there. They placed it where no policeman would look, certainly not a policeman in a hurry."

"What have you found out, Crabbie?"

"You got me thinking, Sean. About Ed and that night. Not like him at all. So I asked Helen about it. What she and Jo had talked about . . ."

A chill spread over my neck.

"What did Jo tell Helen?"

"She said that the chief super was agitated all night after his talk with some journalist. And then, he quote, 'got that phone call first thing in the morning and immediately headed out of the door.' Without apparently checking under the rear wheel of his car."

"He was agitated after his talk with some journalist?"

"He was agitated after his talk with some journalist."

"Doesn't necessarily have to be our journalist."

"Not necessarily, no."

"We're going to have to talk to Jo McBain, aren't we?"

"We are, Sean."

"Bloody hell, Crabman, this additional little file I'm crafting for the DPP's going to need two volumes and an index."

"The DPP won't mind. He's an officer of the court."

"What does that mean?"

"His duty is to ascertain the truth, not to get convictions."

"Ah, Crabbie, if only that were as true in practice as it is in theory, what a world that would be."

17: ED McBAIN'S NOTEBOOK

Doorbell. It was early and my eyes weren't focused yet and Mrs. Campbell was a ginger blur, talking a mile a minute. She handed me a box. It felt too heavy for a cake and not heavy enough to be her ex-husband's head.

She sashayed down the path in a cerulean, satin dress. *Sashayed* being the correct word here. She was a melody. A melody from, say, Duke Ellington, if such an exotic metaphor could be permitted in Northern Ireland, or indeed in any country that had a sectarian civil war and men with guns flying about in helicopters.

"Bye," I said, and opened the box. It *was* a cake. I licked chocolate icing off my finger, closed the box, and lit a cig as it began to rain. There's a Ray Bradbury story somewhere about a planet where it rains so much it has driven everyone mad. Bradbury wrote it after spending a year living with John Huston in the west of Ireland, trying to write a screenplay for *Moby Dick*. Madness, rain, Ireland—it all fits.

Jet the cat appeared at my legs, whining. I finished the fag, tossed it into the palm pot next door, got the milk, went back inside, and made some tea for me and got Whiskas for the cat. He'd shat in the litter box, and I transferred the shit to the rubbish bin.

"Beth was a cat person, you know that? I'm more of a dog man," I said, stroking its back while it ate the Whiskas with evident pleasure.

I checked under the Beemer, picked up Crabbie and Lawson from the station, and drove to Belfast.

QUB.

The geology dept.

A secretary. "Dr. McBain is in a lecture. I don't know if she's going straight home after. It's been a terrible time for her, and no one expects her to keep her office hours."

"A lecture?"

"In Prentice Hall. It's a big space. You can slip in the back and wait for her without making any fuss."

Prentice Hall.

Dr. Joanne McBain pacing in front of the lecture theater, pointing at a complicated geological map of the North Atlantic region. A hundred bleary-eyed students who were, for decency's sake, trying to look interested.

The winding-up portion:

". . . ice lay a mile thick here, in a glacier that stretched from Scotland, over the earth's curve, across the Atlantic to Newfoundland. Britain and Ireland were tundra and ice back then: no men, no women, just mammoth, deer, wolves, tigers. All that gone now, but not forever. Remember that. This is the Holocene epoch. We are living in a brief warm window between inevitable ice ages. Think on that, ladies and gentlemen. Eventually . . . five thousand years, ten thousand, nobody knows, but eventually the ice will return and once again wipe the slate clean over much of the Northern Hemisphere."

"Yikes," Lawson said.

"Sounds good to me," I said, and Crabbie nodded his head in agreement.

When the lecture was done, we approached Jo McBain at her lectern. She had expended all her energy on her talk and now seemed frail and drained and broken. She put on a big jumper and hugged her flask of tea for dear life. I explained why we were here.

"You think his death is somehow connected to that poor girl's suicide in Carrick Castle?" Dr. McBain asked, dabbing at her eyes.

"I don't know if it's connected or not, I just want to know what it was that was troubling him the night before he died, if you can remember."

"He did seem upset that night."

"Did he talk about what was bothering him?"

"He said something about a young reporter."

"Did he mention her name?"

"I don't think so."

"What *did* he say?" I asked.

"Eddie never talked about his work with me. Well, hardly ever. He wanted to hear about my work, but he never brought his work home with him. He is . . . was . . . wonderful like that."

"He was very much respected in the force, Jo, and that's not true for all the senior officers," I said, truthfully.

She smiled and touched me on the arm. "You're very kind, Inspector Duffy."

"Sean, please."

"Eddie and I were very grateful when you found Bathsheba for us. Such a silly dog," she said with a sigh.

I gave her a minute and then tried again. "The reporter?"

"He was upset. He said some 'English reporter was going to cause them all a lot of trouble with her wild accusations.' Does that mean anything to you?"

I nodded. "Yes, it does."

"Did he say anything else?" Crabbie asked.

"No, I don't think so."

"Tell us about the phone call," Crabbie said.

"They called early, at around eight in the morning, I think. Eddie said he had to go. He went out to the car and, well, you know the rest."

"Did he talk about the call, who it was from, what it was about?"

"No. Maybe it was in his notebook. Did you see his notebook?"

"What notebook?"

"Well, like I say, he seldom talked about his cases, but I noticed him scribbling away in the notebook the night before he died."

"Where is this notebook?"

"Larne RUC took it. They would have called you, I'm sure, if there'd been something in it pertinent to your investigation."

"Not necessarily," I said, tactfully.

"Poor Eddie," she said, eyes watering.

"We all miss him," I said.

She smiled bravely, and I gave her a little hug.

"Well, thank you so much for your help in this difficult time, Jo."

"You're very welcome."

We walked back to the BMW.

"Larne?" Crabbie asked, as we checked underneath it for bombs and got inside.

"Larne," I agreed, with a heavy heart.

Larne.

Not the most aesthetically pleasing town in Ireland. Not one for the Tourist Board calendars, or the Guinness posters or the coffee-table books.

Working port, blue-collar—nothing wrong with that, but the big UVF mural on the A2 as you drove into town, in which a masked gunman promised "death to informers" perhaps wasn't the most welcoming of messages.

Larne RUC was a recently renovated, rather impressive, fortress on Hope Street (no irony intended). Larne had more manpower, money, and resources than Carrick RUC, and their district stretched from Whitehead all the way up to the Glens of Antrim. They even had a boat division and a separate wing for the harbor and British Transport Police. So you'd think they'd be a highly professional crew who had their shit together. You'd think wrong. All the young guys were good, but the McBain murder investigation was being run by CI Kennedy— a first-class arse, if ever there was one—and CI Monroe, who was an ill-natured, red-faced son of a bitch. Both of them were masons, promoted way beyond their level of competence through insider connections. To add that they were lazy, Catholic-hating scumbags would be obvious and redundant, but I've added it anyway out of spite.

It took an hour of tedious wrangling before Kennedy finally let us see Ed McBain's notebook, and another hour before he finally gave us his permission to photocopy the final page, which had relevance for our investigation.

All the hassle, however, was worth it.

The last page of the notebook was electric:

February 7th Carrick

Finnish delegation. Theft. Wallet. DI Duffy Carrick RUC called to scene. Good horse sense.

Talked to English reporter. Bigelow. FT. Accusations against Finns. Harald Ek the man to talk to. A fixer. Real operator. WW2 record. Mid 60's? Very good English. Spent a lot of time in America. Played cards with him. Finnish game. Paskahousu. Ek won every hand even against boss. Arrange to interview Ek before they fly out tomorrow. Delay flight if necessary. Interview Ek under caution if necessary.

We took the photocopied note back to Carrick RUC. I blew it up and pasted it on the whiteboard in the incident room.

"What are we going to do now?" Lawson asked.

"Kenny Dalziel's not going to like it," I said.

"Why?"

"Because we're going to have to interview Mr. Ek."

18: FINLANDIA

Two *Ylikomisario* (senior commissars) from the Central Criminal Police met Lawson and me at the airport. Crabbie was needed back at the fort to run the CID and check in on my cat, but to be honest I would have preferred him here rather than Lawson, who had listened to horrible music on his Walkman the whole way from Belfast to Heathrow and Heathrow to Helsinki. Horrible music from bands I'd never heard of. When I'd protested he'd skewered me with, "Come on, sir, you don't want to be one of those guys yelling 'Judas' at Bob Dylan because he plugs in an amp."

The two commissars introduced themselves as Alvar Akela and Aarno Ruusuvuori, which didn't help much. To further complicate things, they looked similar: big, beefy, blond-haired men about thirty. As liaison officers they weren't up to snuff either: their English was minimal and their bedside manner gruff and taciturn. They were dressed in the same sartorial mode as Detective Sergeant John McCrabban, who only ever wore a neo-Calvinist color spectrum that ranged from dark-grey to black. When they shook our hands, they gave me the old-fashioned hard-squeeze handshake, and their small talk, while we waited for our luggage, was nonexistent. If I'd been a conspiracy theorist I'd have thought that the Finnish police were trying to fuck with us from the get-go, but I've never been much of one for conspiracies . . .

We cleared Customs and, much to our surprise, Alvar, or possibly Aarno, took us to one of the domestic gates and gave us each an air ticket.

"What's all this about? I thought we were in Helsinki?" I said.

"Mr. Ek and Mr. Laakso have arranged to meet you in Oulu," Alvar said.

"Oulu?"

"Oulu."

"Where's Oulu?"

"North."

"But why Oulu?"

"Lennätin headquarters is in Oulu."

"I thought we'd arranged to meet them at a police station in Helsinki?"

"No," Aarno said.

"Change of plan. You will be met at airport by local police," Alvar said.

"I can only hope that they'll be as charming as you two."

Lying just a degree of latitude from the Arctic Circle, Oulu in February cannot be wholeheartedly recommended as a pleasant place to either visit or do police work.

The small Dash 7 aircraft, unnervingly and rather bumpily, touched down on a frozen runway that seemed to have just been freshly scraped from the forest. It was only 2 p.m. when we landed, but already the sun was setting.

"Vampires must have a field day up here," Lawson said gloomily.

The walk from the Dash 7 to the terminal building wasn't exactly Apsley Cherry-Garrard's *Worst Journey in the World*, but it wasn't a walk around the vicar's rose garden, either. Lawson and I were in suit jackets and raincoats, and the wind howling straight down on us from its icy prison at the pole was murderous. All the other passengers were in furs or heavy woolen overcoats.

"It must be twenty below," Lawson said, his lips turning blue.

"Courage, Lawson. Remember Captain Scott."

With morale-boosting talk like this, I kept Lawson's spirits up until we reached the terminal. A young woman in a gigantic fur-lined parka was holding a sign that said "RUC."

I introduced ourselves and she said that she was "Vanhempi Konstaapeli Signe Hornborg."

"That's easy for you to say."

Vanhempi Konstaapeli apparently meant "senior constable," although she was only twenty-three. She was another blond with short-cropped hair, rather eerie blue eyes, and a pixie-like upturned nose.

"Did you have a pleasant flight?" she asked, in utterly perfect English.

"It was OK," I said.

"Oh yes. Very pleasant," Lawson insisted.

"Is this your first visit to Oulu?"

"Are you a local?" Lawson asked, clearly smitten.

"Very much so."

After we retrieved our bags, she led us outside to her Volvo 240. Lawson jumped in the front and I sat in the back. We drove out of the airport and were quickly skirting a dense spruce forest. I could see glimpses of the town to the north and east, but we seemed to be heading in the other direction. Lawson asked Constable Hornborg about the nature of the landscape, and she was happy to oblige him in rather exhaustive detail.

"The land is rising due to post-glacial rebound, the forest are spruce and fir with some birch, there are nine hundred lakes in this province alone, many of which are linked to the Baltic Sea . . ."

I stopped paying attention and tried to figure out where the hell we were going. The town was definitely in the other direction. Far to the east, I could see glimpses of chimneys, factories, houses—we seemed to be making a beeline for the coast.

"Excuse me, Constable Hornborg, where are we heading?"

"To interview Mr. Ek and Mr. Laakso. I thought you knew? Yes?"

"Well, yes, but where exactly are we going?"

"Hailuoto."

"What's Hailuoto?"

"An island where Mr. Laakso and many of the Lennätin executives have their homes. Lennätin has an estate there."

"Shouldn't we be doing it at a police station?"

"Mr. Laakso has not been well. We did not want to put him to unnecessary stress," Constable Hornborg explained.

"An island. Are we taking a ferry?" Lawson asked, excited.

"The ferry does not run in the winter," Constable Hornborg said.

"How *are* we getting over there?"

"There is an ice road across the Baltic. Hopefully there will be enough light for you to see. It is really something."

"An ice road! Wow. Wait till I tell my dad, he loves things like this," Lawson said.

"In the future, because of the post-glacial rebound I was speaking about, Hailuoto will become joined to the mainland. All of Hailuoto was underwater only a few centuries ago."

We reached the ice road and it indeed really was something. A narrow stretch of frozen sea ice, reaching out five kilometers toward Hailuoto island.

"Do not put your seat belt on. If we somehow go off the road into the sea, we will need to make a quick escape from the car," Hornborg said. "You are supposed to have special tires for driving on this, but I don't use them," she said, comfortingly.

The sun set as we were on the ice, and as we drove off onto the island it was pitch black.

Ten minutes more on a windy road through more forest, and we arrived at a gate lodge that led to a massive house built in what, we would subsequently learn, was the "Finnish Deconstructivist" style. It looked as if a giant had stomped on a massive block of stainless steel and put triple-glazed windows between the gaps. It was all angles and points and curves. I rather liked it.

"Who lives here?" I asked Constable Hornborg.

"This is Mr. Ek's house."

"Impressive."

The guard at the gate waved us through, and we parked in front of the house.

"Would you like a cup of tea or coffee before the interview?" Constable Hornborg asked, as we walked toward the front door.

"Sorry, what?"

"Would you like a drink before the interview?"

"We're interviewing Ek and Laakso now?"

"Yes. Mr. Ek and Mr. Laakso are traveling to America tomorrow."

"We've just got off an international flight! We're in no fit state to conduct an interview," I protested.

"I'm afraid it is now or never," Constable Hornborg said, glumly.

"Oh, I'm sure it'll be fine, eh, boss?" Lawson said. "I mean, what other choice do we have? We can't go back to the chief inspector with no interview at all. He'll go ballistic. The expense, Sergeant Dalziel . . ."

I said nothing and, frowning, followed them inside.

We were met by a tall, cadaverous bald man in a black suit who introduced himself as Kevin Wilmot QC, Mr. Laakso's "legal counsel." Wilmot was an English barrister and had been brought in especially from London for this interview.

"Quite the firepower for a simple chat," I said to Wilmot, shaking his proffered hand.

"We just want to make sure that your interview is conducted within the parameters of Finnish law and the Police and Criminal Evidence Act," Wilmot explained, with a not entirely friendly smile.

I turned to Constable Hornborg. "Yes, coffee would be good and some food, if you can find any. I've had nothing since a very early breakfast," I said.

We went up an open-plan staircase to a large conference room overlooking what presumably was the water (although it was too dark now to tell for sure).

Ek, Laakso, two more Finnish lawyers, a female stenographer, several male assistants, and a female secretary were waiting for us. A tape recorder had been set up at one end of a large mahogany table, and one of the flunkies was filming the proceedings through a video camera on a tripod.

"Jesus," I muttered to myself.

"It's quite the setup," Lawson agreed.

"Aye, maybe it's a sign that they've either got money to burn or something to hide."

"Or both," Lawson replied.

We shook hands with everyone in the room and sat down at the head of the table. Ek and Laakso seemed friendly enough. Laakso had on a dark business suit, his grey face rather like that famous self-description of WH Auden: a wedding cake left out in the rain. Ek was svelte and relaxed in a black sweater, brown cords, and black loafers. Neither man looked particularly nervous.

Wilmot started the tape recorder. "If you'd like to begin, gentlemen, my clients have a very tight schedule," he said.

"Let's wait until we get some coffee. We've just finished a long journey," I stated firmly and said nothing while the tape spooled. There was an awkward five-minute silence until someone came in with a coffee pot and little cakes. I ate a cake and took a drink of coffee.

"My name is Detective Inspector Sean Duffy; this is my colleague, Detective Constable Alexander Lawson. We're investigating the violent death of one Lily Bigelow in Carrickfergus Castle on the night of February 7th, 1987, and the possibly related violent death of Chief Superintendent John Edward McBain in the village of Glenoe on the morning of February 8th, 1987. Both Superintendent McBain and Miss Bigelow were traveling with the Lennätin delegation on its visit to Northern Ireland from February fifth through the eighth. Mr. Laakso and Mr. Ek, I take it that both victims were known to you?" I began.

Neither Ek nor Laakso said anything.

Mr. Wilmot smiled with a cool sanguine indifference and opened a file. "We've done a little research on this case and into your investigation," he said.

"Oh?"

"We were able to get the files on both deaths."

"What files? From whom?"

"The attorney general has been in contact with your DPP."

"The attorney general of . . . Finland?" I asked, surprised.

"Just so. He is a friend of Mr. Laakso. The attorney general spoke to your director of public prosecutions, who was good enough to fax us your preliminary report on the case."

"When did all this happen?"

"Today."

"While we were in the air?"

"I believe so."

I looked at Lawson. Did he see what was going on? We were being dicked about. The question was, why? Just your casual corporate big-footery, or something more interesting?

"In Lily Bigelow's case you have arrested and charged a suspect, a Mr. Clarke Underhill?" Wilmot continued.

"Yes, arrested, charged, and released on bail," I said.

"And as I understand it, the nature of the crime scene implies that only Mr. Underhill could have committed the murder of Miss Bigelow."

"That would seem to be the situation," I agreed.

"Mr. Underhill seems to have been acting alone. No unusual amounts of money were paid into his bank account and he does not fit the profile of a 'hit man.'"

"All that is true," I agreed.

"Even if he were acting for someone else, which seems unlikely, Mr. Ek and Mr. Laakso had no relationship whatsoever with Mr. Underhill. Indeed, they met him only on one occasion, for a few seconds, when he gave them a ticket to visit Carrickfergus Castle."

"That would also appear to be the case," I agreed.

"We go on, then, to Mr. McBain."

"*Chief Superintendent* McBain."

"Chief Superintendent McBain was murdered with a bomb under his car that was planted by the IRA."

"We don't know who planted the bomb under his car."

"Mr. Ek and Mr. Laakso have no connection whatsoever with Mr. McBain, and I am sure you are not suggesting that they have a connection with a terrorist group," Wilmot said.

"No. I'm not going to suggest that."

"Perhaps you could explain, then, why this meeting was deemed necessary. Why you came a thousand miles to interview my very busy clients about two deaths which they could not possibly have any link to?" Wilmot said.

"I'll be happy to explain. Miss Bigelow was investigating a potential pedophile ring connected to a young offenders' institution in
Northern Ireland. We believe that she got herself assigned to cover
the Lennätin delegation's visit to Northern Ireland so that she could
further investigate these claims. Before she came to Northern Ireland,
she was given the name 'Peter Laakso' and a suggestion that he might
be connected somehow to the Kinkaid Young Offenders' Institution.
We know that on the night of February sixth Mr. Laakso, Mr. Ek,
and Nicolas and Stefan Lennätin visited an illegal brothel called the
Eagle's Nest. They may have visited other such places while in Ulster.
Miss Bigelow seems to have been sufficiently troubled to have a conversation about the activities of the Finnish delegation with Chief
Superintendent McBain. He was sufficiently intrigued, or perhaps
concerned, by her speculations that he wanted to interview Mr. Ek on
the morning he was killed. His surviving notebook says quite clearly
that he wanted to interview Mr. Ek. It is reasonable, then, that we
would wish to follow up on this possible connection between the two
violent deaths," I said, calmly and clearly.

Ek's face was a mask throughout all of this, but I noticed Constable
Hornborg raise her eyebrows at one point, which was interesting and
something, perhaps, to be followed up on.

"What do you wish to know?" Ek asked, in his perfect, ever-so-
slightly American-accented English.

"Tell me about your visit to the brothel," I said.

"The young men wished to visit such a house and Mr. Laakso and
myself felt obliged to go to keep an eye on them. They are the grandsons of David Lennätin, and it was our duty, my duty in particular, to
see that they did not get up to any mischief."

"Visiting a brothel didn't count as mischief?"

"No."

"Even though it was illegal?"

"Illegal, but not something the authorities would ever take note of.
Am I right in thinking that, Inspector?" Ek said.

"What did you and Mr. Laakso do at the brothel?"

"We played cards."

"Do you remember the game?"

"Of course. We played Paskahousu."

"And after the visit to the brothel, where did you go?"

"We returned to the hotel."

"What time was that at?"

"Perhaps around ten or eleven o'clock."

"Were you aware of anyone following you on this visit to the brothel?"

"No."

"Could Miss Bigelow have been following you?"

"Perhaps, but I was not aware of it," Mr. Ek said. He looked at Mr. Laakso, who shrugged.

"Mr. Laakso?" I asked.

"I was not aware of anyone following us," he said.

"Did Miss Bigelow ask you any questions about your brothel visit?" I asked.

"No," Ek said.

"No," Laakso agreed.

"She must have spoken to you at some point during the trip?" I said.

Ek shook his head. "That was what was so puzzling about her. She was traveling with us to do what we had been told was a feature story for the *Financial Times*, but she didn't ask many questions. She asked a question about the roof of a factory we visited, I think."

"How long have you been working for Lennätin Corporation, Mr. Ek?"

"Nearly ten years."

"And you Mr. Laakso?"

"Twenty years."

"What did you do before working for Lennätin, Mr. Ek?"

"How can that question have any bearing on your investigation, Detective Duffy?" Wilmot objected.

"I will answer him," Ek said, unconcerned.

"After the war, I emigrated to America and spent several decades there before moving back to Finland in the early 1970s."

"What did you do in America?"

"I was in the army."

"The American army?" I said, surprised.

"Of course."

"What, uhm, regiment?"

"The United States Army is not regimentally structured. I was in the 10th Special Forces Group. Commonly known as the Green Berets," he said with a touch of pride.

"The Green Berets? Did you serve in Vietnam?" Lawson asked.

"Oh yes," he said.

"That must have been heavy," Lawson continued.

"Indeed," he said warming to the theme. "And that was my fourth war."

"Your *fourth* war?"

"If I can interrupt you, gentlemen," Wilmot said. "We are somewhat pressed for time. Inspector Duffy, do you have any more questions relating to the matter in hand?"

"Just to clarify, Mr. Ek, Mr. Laakso, neither of you were aware that Lily Bigelow may have been following you the night you visited the brothel?"

"No," they both said.

"After the brothel visit, you returned to the hotel?"

They agreed that that was the case.

"Do you know why Chief Superintendent McBain may have wanted to talk to you?"

Neither had any clue.

I took them through the time line of their entire visit to Northern Ireland, but nothing jumped out at me. They seemed to have had minimal interaction with Lily Bigelow and, apart from the visit to the brothel, had not done anything untoward. They had been taken to several abandoned factories and brown-field sites and had been subjected to several working breakfasts, lunches, and one formal dinner with the secretary of state for Northern Ireland.

I looked at Lawson. "Any additional questions, Detective Lawson?"

Unhelpfully, Lawson had no additional questions and, jet-lagged and somewhat wrong-footed by the day's events, I couldn't for the life of me think of anything else.

Wilmot smiled. "Well, I think we're done then, gentlemen," he said.

He stood up. Lawson stood up. Ek and Laakso and the other lawyers stood up. I sat there. I didn't want to go. Not yet. I knew we had missed something. Ek and Laakso had pulled a fast one, but I couldn't think what it was.

"Inspector Duffy?" Wilmot said.

Reluctantly, I got to my feet.

We shook hands with everyone again.

"You have all the information you could possibly need," Wilmot said.

"Hmmm," I said.

"We'll make sure the attorney general tells your director of public prosecution about your professionalism and courtesy," Mr. Ek said.

I looked at Lawson. He wasn't being sarcastic was he? We had been professional and courteous, hadn't we?

I walked with Ek down the stairs.

"You have a lovely house, here," I said.

"I like it very much."

"Does Mrs. Ek like it too?"

"My wife, alas, died of cancer two years ago," Ek said.

"I'm sorry to hear that," I said.

Ek nodded grimly.

"Your children are nearby, at least?"

"We had no children."

We had reached the front door now. He offered me his hand again and I shook it. "I am glad that we have helped you sort this out, Mr. Duffy," Ek said.

Yeah, we had sorted it out.

Everything was fine. Everybody's story concurred. Everybody's story worked. The only person who could possibly have killed Lily Bigelow was Clarke Underhill, and Chief Superintendent McBain had, like dozens of police officers in the last few years, been murdered by terrorists, by way of a mercury tilt switch bomb.

"I'd like to talk to you again, if that's possible. And I'd like to talk to Nicolas and Stefan," I said.

"We are all very busy men."

Car drive back across the frozen sea.

Constable Hornborg strangely silent.

Snow falling on the windscreen of the Volvo 240.

"We go back home tomorrow, sir?" Lawson asked from the front passenger's seat.

"I suppose so."

"Should we do our souvenir shopping here? Or do you think we'll have a day in Helsinki?" Lawson wondered.

"We'll head straight back. Flight out in the morning and straight back to Belfast. I don't want Dalziel to have any excuse to think this trip was a boondoggle."

"No, sir," Lawson said glumly. "Only, you know, we're never likely to be back in Helsinki . . ."

I didn't reply. I was thinking about Harald Ek. He'd been perfectly credible, perfectly civil, but I just didn't like his bloody answers.

"It was a pretty successful trip, if you ask me, sir. We finally nailed down that lead," Lawson said.

"Did we?"

"Well, yes, sir. I think it's obvious now that Lily's death had nothing to do with the Finns."

"They certainly did give us all the right answers."

"That's what I mean. A rushed visit, but, you know, a successful one, sir, wouldn't you say?"

"It could be considered a successful trip from a political or diplomatic standpoint, but not, I think, as police work."

19: CONSTABLE HORNBORG'S STORY

Constable Hornborg left us off at the Finnair Hotel on the easy-to-remember street called Pakkahuoneenkatu, which was just down the road from the Lennätin Corporate Headquarters.

Although this was 1987, the Finnair Hotel was still stuck somewhere in the early seventies—its décor was very much of the orangey-brown sort, and the furniture was a squeaky plastic that smelled. Strange, unfashionable hotels in strange, unfashionable towns were often places of beauty and mystery, but not *this* strange, unfashionable hotel in *this* strange, unfashionable town.

The desultory hotel restaurant had an incomprehensible menu, and when we asked for steak it was reindeer steak with cloud berries and cold mashed potatoes. Actually, it wasn't bad and, properly cooked, or even heated up, it could have been OK.

The drink was rather good vodka. The background music was Finnish easy listening, which was surprisingly inoffensive.

"It's snowing," was Lawson's conversational gambit as he looked through the windows at the lifeless Pakkahuoneenkatu. But it wasn't his job to sustain the convo anyway—that was what I was supposed to do.

"Your name's Alexander, right?"

"Yeah."

"They ever call you Sasha?"

"No."

"They ever call you Sandy?"

"No."

"What do you they call you?"

"Alex."

"Bit of a boring nickname, no?"

"I suppose so."

"You did maths, you say?"

"Yes, sir."

"I'll bet at some point someone offers you detective sergeant in the Fraud Squad."

"I don't fancy that. I like general cases."

"If you're good with numbers, you should go the white-collar crime route. You can get up the promotion ladder pretty quickly there, too."

"Yes, sir."

"I brushed up on my Finnish humor before I left. Didn't get a chance to use it today. You wanna hear my joke?"

"Do I have a choice, sir?"

"Nope."

"OK, then, I would love to hear the joke."

"How can you tell the difference between a Finnish introvert and a Finnish extrovert? . . . When he's talking to you, a Finnish introvert looks at his feet. A Finnish extrovert looks at yours."

Lawson nodded.

"If you were Finnish, you'd be on the floor now," I claimed.

It wasn't a great conversation, but at least we hadn't resorted to football. The easy-listening music went off abruptly and an elderly man with a mysterious stringed instrument got on to a stage and began singing in Finnish. The singing was OK, but the mysterious stringed instrument could not possibly have been tuned for the human ear. By the time the old man was done, Lawson and I were the only customers left in the place. We gave him a round of applause, he bowed and came over for a tip. He seemed satisfied with a couple of the gold Finnish coins.

It was 8 p.m., but it was so quiet and dark now it felt like two in the morning.

A final round of the excellent local vodka and I got the bill.

Nothing else for it but to go to bed, I supposed.

I paid in the strange, colorful Finnish banknotes, left a tip, and looked up to see Constable Hornborg walking in from the street.

"Hello," I said. "You just missed the concert."

She was pale, nervous, twitchy.

"What is it?" I asked.

"They did not tell me all the details of the case that you are investigating," she began breathlessly.

"What do you want to know?"

"Everything."

We sat back down at a corner table, ordered three beers, and I told her the whole story. She listened intently, made notes, asked a few questions, and then decided that it wasn't safe to make notes after all and threw the paper in a rubbish bin.

"Now, why don't you tell us what the Finnish police don't want us to know about Harald Ek and Peter Laakso?" I said.

She swallowed. "You are right. This is a company town. Lennätin is Oulu. Oulu is Lennätin. Peter Laakso is the CFO. Harald Ek is head of corporate security."

"And the boys?"

"This is not about Nicolas and Stefan."

"Who is it about?"

She took a sip of her beer, wiped the foam off her nose, and continued.

"First, let me tell you about Ek."

I got out my notebook.

"Please, no notes, just remember," she said.

"OK."

"I don't know if you are aware of this, but there is a small Swedish-speaking minority in Finland, from the time when Finland was part of the Swedish Empire. These Swedes, sometimes, are more Finnish than the Finns, as the expression goes. Harald Ek is one of these Swedish-Finns. In 1939, Finland and Russia went to war. Harald Ek joined the Finnish army and quickly proved himself an able fighter. When the war with the Soviets was concluded in 1940, Ek had become an army captain. In 1941, following Operation Barbarossa, Finland joined with Nazi Germany to invade Russia. The Finnish army quickly captured the territory we had lost in the Winter War and our soldiers advanced on Leningrad from the north. Cooperation between the Finns and Germans was very good. So good, in fact, that thousands of the best young Finnish soldiers were trained by the Wehrmacht in Germany and others joined the Nordic legions of the Waffen-SS. Harald Ek was one of these men."

"He was in the SS?" Lawson said, shocked.

"The 11th SS Volunteer Panzergrenadier Division Nordland, to be exact. They fought in many desperate campaigns on the Eastern Front, including the final battle for Berlin, where most of them were killed."

"But not Ek."

"No, not Ek. Fortunately for him, he was captured by the Americans, who wanted to send him back to Finland to be tried for treason."

"Treason? I thought you said Finland was on Germany's side."

"Finland switched sides before the end of the war," Hornborg explained.

"Smart of them. OK, so he comes back to Finland, to be tried for treason . . ."

"He never makes it to Finland. He goes to America, marries a Finnish-American girl, and joins the US Army. He fights in Korea—"

"His third war, I've been counting," Lawson said.

"And is part of the original formation of the American Green Berets in Vietnam. In 1966, he is wounded at the battle of Lang Vei and invalided back to the United States. His first marriage has broken up by this stage, and he expresses the wish to move back to Finland. He is a hero to the American Special Forces (one of their camps is named after him), and the Americans fix things with the Finnish government so that he can return. He marries a local government official here in Oulu, and since the mid-1970s he has worked for the Lennätin Corporation. He is known to be tough, even ruthless, and he has powerful friends in the civil service and, depending on the administration, in the government."

"Would you say that he was a man who was capable of anything?" I asked.

"I think so, yes."

"Even murder?"

"He has no criminal record, unlike . . ."

"Unlike Mr. Laakso?"

She nodded.

"I looked Peter Laakso up on Interpol. There's nothing there."

"I am not surprised," she said.

"Tell us about him," I said.

"Peter Laakso comes from a very prominent Finnish family. His father was a member of parliament, both before and after the war. His uncle was on the supreme court. He himself was an MP in the 1950s. He was a very successful businessman before being recruited by David Lennätin in the late 1960s to improve the Lennätin Corporation's finances. The new team that David Lennätin brought in, including Laakso, helped turn the company from a small national concern to a multinational electronics giant. Phones, calculators, computers, radios, CD players."

"He must be getting up there. How old is Laakso?"

"Sixty-four," Lawson said, remembering his remark about his aged knees.

"He is no longer in charge of the day-to-day running of the company's finances, but he is still a very important figure in Lennätin, in Oulu, and in Finland."

"OK, so tell us, what did he do?" I said.

Hornborg swallowed hard, hesitated.

"That's why you came here tonight, Hornborg. To spill the beans, as we say in the UK. To tell us. So what did he do?" I asked.

"Three times in the 1960s and one time in the 1970s, Peter Laakso was arrested and charged with having sexual relations with minors. He was not convicted for any of these offenses. None of these cases came to trial, and if I was not from Oulu I would not know about them. The police records have been. . . . I do not know the word in English."

"Expunged?"

"Expunged."

"Boys or girls?"

"Young boys. I did not think to bring it up with you until I heard you talking about the young offenders' institution and the English journalist's suspicions. But I thought you should know what I know."

"You did very well to tell us. This is important," I said.

"How does this help us, sir?" Lawson asked.

"I think it finally provides us with a motive," I said.

Lawson looked puzzled. "How?"

"The Finns go to the Eagle's Nest brothel, they find that it does not cater to Mr. Laakso's needs. Tony takes the Finns back to the hotel, thinking that he's done his duty above and beyond, but Laakso is still looking for action—"

"At his age, sir? Surely not."

"Let me finish, please, Lawson."

"Yes, sir."

"Ek and Laakso have been told in advance of such a place that caters to Laakso's needs. They know exactly where to go. They shake off Tony, they slip out of the hotel, they drive up to this Kinkaid place. They visit Kinkaid, they drive back to the hotel, and on the way home they notice that Lily Bigelow has been following them the whole time. Lily has been waiting for this opportunity. She knows that Laakso has been given the name of this place and that at some point during the trip Laakso might go there. This is the proof she needs to make a story. But she's been spotted by Ek. Ek knows he has to silence her. He gets his opportunity the next day, on the tour in Carrick Castle, killing her with a blow to the head."

"Ek was back at the hotel with Mr. Laakso," Lawson said.

"He lied about that. He was with Lily, in the castle, killing her. It was a crime of opportunity. He had act to fast before she got a chance to write up the story for the paper, or tell anyone else."

Lawson was shaking his head. "It doesn't work, sir."

"It works. He kills her, he hides with her in the dungeon, he waits until the caretaker has gone to bed, and then he carries her to the top of the keep. At some point, her shoes fall off and he puts them back on, wrongly. He waits for his moment and shoves the body off the keep. He knows that everybody will think it's a suicide; and if they don't, the only suspect will be Mr. Underhill because no one else could have gotten out of the castle without being seen on the CCTV cameras."

"And how does *he* get out of the castle?" Lawson said.

"That part I haven't figured out yet."

"There are no secret tunnels or anything like that. We talked to the site archaeologists."

"I know."

"So how does he get out?"

"I don't know, Lawson."

"And how does this tie to Chief Superintendent McBain's death?"

"Lily had coffee with Ed McBain and told him of her suspicions. Ek knew he had to kill McBain as well, before he started an investigation."

Lawson was smiling at me indulgently. "So Ek concocts a plan to kill Lily Bigelow, magically escapes from Carrick Castle, goes back to his hotel room, somehow gets hold of two kilos of Semtex, spends the rest of the night making a highly complex mercury tilt switch bomb, drives to Glenoe, plants the bomb under the chief super's car, calls him from a pay phone, and kills him too?"

"It's possible."

"Sir, with all due respect, it's ridiculous."

"What's your explanation, Lawson?"

"Laakso and Ek come back from the brothel having found nothing to cater to their needs and being very old men, they *go to bed*. The next day, a depressed and slightly addled Lily Bigelow hides in Carrick Castle, where she thinks the keep might be a good place to commit suicide. She tops herself that night."

"And the livor mortis?"

"Underhill panics, moves the body, realizes he shouldn't have done it and lies about it to us."

"And the time line?"

"She jumps as soon as it gets dark and Underhill lies about doing his inspection."

"Because?"

"He's a lazy old drunk who doesn't give a shit anymore?"

"And her claustrophobia and fear of heights?"

"That's why she was taking the tablets."

"Listen, mate, it was you who got me thinking along these lines in the first place. You were the one who came up with up the bloody Bayesian analysis allegedly explaining why I could possibly have a Lizzie Fitzpatrick case and a Lily Bigelow case in one bloody career."

"Yes, sir, but—"

I got to my feet.

"They're leaving tomorrow, eh?" I said to Constable Hornborg.

"Yes," she said.

"It has to be tonight, then. What say you, Young Lochinvar? Are you going to come?"

"Where?"

"Netherby Hall, of course."

"Where?"

"We're going to interview Ek and Laakso before they leave. Our third interview with them. Third time's a charm, eh, Lawson?"

"Laakso has already gone. He flew to Helsinki when your interrogation was over," Hornborg said.

"We'll talk to the charming Mr. Ek, then."

"I don't think that is a good idea," Hornborg said. "There are certain protocols to be followed."

"We'll need your car, love. I don't think a taxi's going to take us across that frozen sea and wait for us half the night."

"I can't be involved, I have said too much already!"

"You're involved, Hornborg. Are you coming or staying, Lawson?"

Lawson got up with a predatory peeler's grin on his face. "Let's go, boss," he said.

20: ON THE ICE

Ice road over a frozen sea. A cold, clear sky.

Above us, the stars that make the Plough: Alkaid, Mizar, Alioth, Megrez, Phad, Merak, Dubhe... exotic, eastern names for an exotic, eastern night.

Oncoming headlights were looming toward us from the outer dark. By a weird optical effect they seemed to be coming right at us.

"This is a two-lane road, isn't it?"

"Yes."

Closer and closer and then, suddenly, a brief glimpse of a man and woman in furs before they entered their present, our past, in the rearview mirror.

"Everyone around here drives too fast," I said.

"Yes," Hornborg agreed.

"That thing you were saying earlier, does anyone really go off the road and into the sea?"

"All the time. Especially in the spring."

"What happens to them?"

"Usually they drown. Sometimes they die of shock or hypothermia."

"Good to know."

We drove off the dangerous ice road and onto the island.

Through the forest to Harald Ek's magnificent home. We parked in front, got out of the Volvo, and rang the bell. A big, burly shaven-headed factotum opened the front door. A rather different character than the butler who had met us earlier.

"*Mitä haluat!*" he demanded.

"*Tahdomme puhua pomollesi,*" Hornborg explained.

We went inside and upstairs to a large living room area overlooking the woods at the back of the house. Huge leather sofas, a gleaming hardwood floor, a roaring fire, and there was Ek in beige slacks and a black jumper, playing some sort of board game with another man. Not quite the scene of debauch I'd been hoping for.

"In light of the fact that we are both leaving tomorrow, I thought perhaps we could take this opportunity to ask you some more questions," I said, before Hornborg could get a word in.

Ek put down one of his game pieces and stood up. "I am not surprised to see you again, Inspector Duffy," he said "Sit down, please. Heikki will bring you drinks."

We sat down and Heikki, the shaven-headed man, brought us a carafe of vodka, a carafe of water, caviar, and crisp bread.

"Allow me to introduce an old, old friend, Jasper Miller. Jasper, this is Inspector Duffy of the Irish police and his comrade, Constable Lawson. And this young lady is Constable Hornborg of the Oulu police."

"Delighted to meet you," Jasper said in an American accent.

"How do you know Mr. Ek?" I asked Miller, conversationally.

"Old war buddies," Miller said with a grin.

"Which war? Mr. Ek has been in four of them."

Miller laughed. "Don't I know it! Harry and I were in Korea together."

"Let me see if I've got all the wars straight in my head, Mr. Ek. In the Winter War you fought with the Finns and in Korea and Vietnam you fought with the Americans and in the Second World War you fought with the Germans. In the 11th SS Volunteer Panzergrenadier Division Nordland."

Ek nodded. "That story is well known. I hope you didn't come here tonight to blackmail me with old news."

"Blackmail you into doing what?" I asked.

Ek took a sip of vodka and moved a game piece. They were playing the Chinese game Go, by the looks of it.

"I have been an officer in the Finnish army, in the Wehrmacht, and in the American army. My military record is public knowledge," Ek said.

"Where did you go after the Eagle's Nest brothel on the night of February sixth?" I asked.

Ek looked at me for a moment before placing another tile on the board.

"You know where we went, Inspector. We went back to the hotel."

"Are you sure you didn't go somewhere else?"

"Quite sure."

"I know about Peter Laakso. I know that *his* record isn't public knowledge."

"What record? What do you think you are talking about?"

"Laakso is a convicted pedophile."

Ek looked at Hornborg. "I don't know what you've been told, but Mr. Laakso has been convicted of nothing."

"Oh, that's right. He hasn't actually been convicted, has he? Arrested many times, but never convicted of anything."

"Rumor and innuendo. Rumor and innuendo perpetuated by Lennätin's business rivals."

"A twenty-year campaign of rumor and innuendo that included police investigations?"

"Finland, like Ireland, is a conservative country. Unlike America, or even Sweden, homosexuality is taboo here," Ek said. "If you wish to join those reactionary forces who have been trying to persecute Mr. Laakso, feel free to join them, Inspector Duffy. I expect no less from the Finnish police. Following our brief meetings, I had expected a little better from you."

"It is your move," Miller said.

"I never mentioned the word *homosexuality*. The word wasn't mentioned to me. But thank you for confirming the allegations, Mr. Ek," I said.

"I have confirmed nothing!" he barked, and finished another shot of vodka.

Constable Hornborg was looking nervous now and clearly wanted us to leave, but Lawson gave me an encouraging nod of the head. Through the gigantic glass windows, snow was coming down like cherry blossoms, floating in big, lazy flakes as large as popped corn.

"We returned to the hotel on February sixth. We know nothing about Lily Bigelow's death. As I have told you now, three times!" Ek said.

The music on the stereo had stopped and the room was spookily quiet. I stared at him and he met my gaze easily. Close up, Ek cut an impressive figure. Lean, long-jawed, clean-shaved, with a Samuel Beckett intensity of eye.

"I shall change the music," Ek said.

"Allow me to help. I'm a bit of a buff," I said.

We went to the CD collection and I picked out a Magnus Lindberg CD and gave it to Ek. He nodded and put it the player.

Lindberg's disconcerting *Kraft* began playing through the stereo's speakers.

I leaned toward him. "I know that you killed Lily Bigelow, or had her killed," I said in a low voice. "I know that killing's always been easy for you. How many civilians did you slaughter as the 11th Panzergrenadiers made their way back to Berlin? Eh?"

Ek grinned mirthlessly. "You have no idea who you are dealing with, Inspector Duffy," he said with black malice radiating from his eyes.

"You killed Lily Bigelow, didn't you?"

"What would be my motive?"

"To protect your boss's reputation after Lily Bigelow found out that he was consorting with rent boys, possibly supplied by the paramilitaries from Kinkaid Young Offenders' Institution. To protect Lennätin's investment in Ireland."

"Rent boys? Kinkaid? What are you talking about, Inspector Duffy? And murder? How could I, or anyone else, have killed poor Miss Bigelow? An impossible crime, Inspector Duffy. How would I have achieved this crime? Necromancy?"

"Even before you came to Ireland you had Kinkaid sussed out as a place that might cater to Mr. Laakso's interests, didn't you? You asked around. And it leaked. Somebody found out, and that somebody called a reporter. But the reporter underestimated you, didn't she? You saw her. You sussed *her* out. That missing wallet? Maybe that was staged to get Lily Bigelow out of her room so that you could go in there and look through her stuff."

"Nonsense."

"Killing her was foolish. An overreaction. Laakso was panicking, and panicked people make mistakes."

"What mistakes?"

"I'll find the mistakes, don't worry about that."

Ek's eyes narrowed. "Perhaps you are not so stupid as you look."

"Is that a confession, Mr. Ek?"

"A confession to what? A murder I could not have committed, for no reason at all?"

"Aha! I have you!" Miller said from the Go table. "Come over here, Harry. I am on the verge of the *Kami no Itte!*"

"I must return to my game, please excuse me, Inspector Duffy."

He crossed the room and sat back down at the Go board. I turned Magnus Lindberg up another notch and joined them at the table.

"You have made me lose my game, Inspector Duffy," Ek said in good humor. "Jasper here is on the edge of the *Kami no Itte.*"

"I don't think I'm familiar with that expression," I said, returning his smile.

"The word *Itte* has *te*—'hand'—as its root and can be directly translated into English as 'move.' The word *Kami* means 'divine.' Hence 'the divine move': the move whose sheer beauty inspires an almost religious awe in those who witness it."

I examined the Go board, but I was none the wiser.

Ek stood. "Our games are ended and I am tired. I have a guest to put to bed and I have a flight in the morning. I believe I am finished with your questions, Inspector Duffy," he said. He looked at Constable Hornborg. "And you should take these gentleman back to the mainland before the storm comes in."

"Yes. Thank you for your time, Mr. Ek, I know this was an unscheduled—"

Suddenly there was a yell from downstairs.

"*Se onsusi! Se onsusi!*"

"Heikki!" Ek yelled back.

The factotum came running up the stairs, carrying a Kalashnikov assault rifle. There was a rapid conversation in Finnish, before a gleeful Ek turned to us. "Would any of you gentlemen care for some sport?" he said.

"What's going on, Harry?" Miller asked.

"Heikki thinks he saw a wolf in the grounds! We've had reports that a pack chased a moose onto the sea ice a few days ago. Jasper? Inspector Duffy? Constable Lawson?"

"Yes!" Jasper said.

"We'll go with you," I said, grateful for another opportunity to take the measure of the man.

"Excellent!" Ek declared. "Heikki will get you both a coat and a gun."

We went downstairs, where Heikki handed Lawson and me an anorak and an AK-47 each. I had never handled one before, but Heikki showed me the basics while I put the coat on.

"Shouldn't we have a rifle for this kind of job?" I asked.

"No rifle!" Heikki grunted.

"Lawson, on second thought, maybe you should stay here," I said. "I don't want to be responsible for getting you shot."

"Floodlights!" Ek said, pulling a lever, and the entire wood at the back of the house was lit up by a brilliant white light.

I carried the AK two-handed and safety-gripped, the way I would carry an MP5, and followed Ek out into the trees.

The snow was heavier now and the fresh powder was difficult to wade through. My DMs were soaked in seconds.

"Tracks!" Ek exclaimed, and sure enough there were fresh paw prints in the newly fallen snow. Huge prints, bigger than any dog, and if I hadn't been carrying the world's most reliable assault rifle, I would have been nervous.

Ek was running now, but I kept up with him, and in half a minute we had left Miller behind us. For a sixty-something-year-old man he was impressively agile and strong.

"It's making for the ice. Heikki must have startled it! Come on!" Ek said.

I followed him down a wooded slope toward what must have been the shoreline. Through the snow I could see the lights of Oulu some five kilometers away over the frozen sea. Above and behind us, the big, grey snow clouds had covered the stars and moon.

"We are on the ice now!" Ek said, just ahead of me.

I couldn't see anything. Snow was in my eyes, I was breathing hard, and my socks were soaked.

"We must have lost it. If it has sense at all, it will have gone to ... There! My God! There!" Ek exclaimed, and a burst of gunfire startled me as a jet of flame shot from the barrel of his AK-47.

I saw something blur at his shoulder. Something big and grey.

It bounded past me.

A thick, white tail and a powerful back. The wolf, a beautiful metaphor of speed and power.

"Shoot!" Ek yelled.

I let it run past me across the ice.

Ek fired the rest of his clip.

"Shoot!" he yelled again and ripped the gun out of my hands; but it was too late, the wolf was gone.

"Why didn't you fire?" he snarled at me.

"I didn't want to."

"You *are* a fool, Duffy. A fool and a coward."

"I just didn't want to shoot the—" I began and stopped when I saw that Ek had turned and was pointing the AK-47 at me. There was a full clip in the weapon. At this range, half a dozen of those big rounds would rip me to pieces.

Miller was nowhere nearby. Hornborg and Lawson were back at the house. The whole thing would be a tragic accident. If I turned and ran, he'd spray me on full auto. I wouldn't get five feet.

I blinked the snowflakes out of my eyes and saw Ek grinning at me in the dark.

"I can see the future, Duffy—a closed-coffin funeral for you, I think. Do you have a girl? Will she weep for you?"

Yes. Beth would weep.

She'd look good in black.

Ek lowered the muzzle and pointed it at my heart, his face rigid behind that crude iron sight.

I was not afraid. Somehow I was not afraid. Through my trouser pocket I touched my wallet where I kept the postcard of Guido Reni's *Michael Tramples Satan*.

"In answer to your question: hundreds of civilians, Duffy. As we Panzergrenadiers marched back to Berlin. More than I can remember. In Leningrad, in Poland, in those final weeks on the Oder. Russians. Poles. Germans. Your death would not make me bat an eye."

The rifle. The muzzle. The iron sight. The steady hand of Harald Ek. In the background, the distant strains of Magnus Lindberg— perfect dying music.

The cold clawed at my face with dead man's fingers.

A thousand miles away, Morrigan the crow turned her harsh heathen head to the east.

"Sir? Sir?" Lawson called out to me, from the edge of the ice.

"Over here, Lawson!"

Lawson approached us, holding his AK-47. Ek lowered the weapon to his side.

"The wolf escaped," Ek said.

"Is everything all right, sir?" Lawson asked.

"It is now," I said.

Ek began walking back across the ice toward the wood. "Hurry, gentlemen, if Constable Hornborg is going to get you to your hotel room before the road closes, she will have to leave now."

I touched my wallet again. The patron saint of warriors, mariners, pilgrims, and policemen had protected me once more. Saint Michael and the timely appearance of Lawson with a Kalashnikov.

21: MERCURY TILT

Oulu–Helsinki–Heathrow–Belfast. Iain Banks's *The Wasp Factory* occupying the time.

Crabbie meeting us at the airport in a Land Rover. Me filling him in on everything: the pointing of the gun, the pseudoconfession, the pseudothreats. Lawson stepping in at the last minute. Crabbie was surprised but not shocked. Ek had given him a bad feeling, too.

While we'd been away, he had brought our inquiries about Kinkaid YOI to the RUC Sex Crimes Unit at Newtownabbey, but so far they hadn't got back to him.

We returned to the station for the interview with the chief inspector, and I made up a bunch of bullshit that would keep him happy: "We liaised successfully with the Finnish police and conducted our interviews with the competence and authority you would expect from officers in the RUC."

Sergeant Kenny Dalziel from Admin was not so easily impressed. "I don't know why *two* officers had to go to Finland. *Two* officers to follow up a potential lead on two cases, one of which is the responsibility of the DPP's office, and the other the responsibility of Larne RUC. We're going to get an internal audit over this little jaunt of yours, Duffy, oh, yes, mark my words, and you'll need to fill in Form 890 or I'll have your guts for—"

Tune him out. Tune them all out. Always.

Dalziel stopped speaking.

"Did any of that go in, Duffy?" he asked.

"No. And it's *Inspector Duffy* to you, Kenny."

"Your comeuppance has been a long time coming. You know what hubris is, Duffy?"

"A type of pasta?"

"Hubris, Duffy. Mark my words."

"You're going to have to explain yourself better, Kenny. Greek mythology has always been my Achilles elbow."

Fury knitting his brows in a way that you hoped would lead to a stroke but knew wouldn't.

Back to Coronation Road to sleep. Window wipers on maximum.

Park the Beemer, walk down the path in a downpour. Raining so hard it failed to wet me when it hit. Just bounced off . . .

Cat pleased to see me. Neighborhood kids hadn't killed him. Play with him and listen to Peetie Wheatstraw's "Police Station Blues." Sleep upstairs by the light of the paraffin heather. Blue flame, petroleum smell.

Comforting. Comforting as opium . . .

Phone ringing in the hall.

Downstairs in my duvet.

"Yes?"

"Now then, young man, where have you been?"

"Is this Jimmy Savile?"

"It is."

It was either Jimmy Savile or someone pretending to be Jimmy Savile. Anyone could do Savile's voice. He'd been part of the cultural furniture for decades.

"Where have you been?" Savile/faux Savile asked.

"Finland. Where have you been?"

"I've been doing work for Mrs. Currie and Mrs. Thatcher and I told them about you."

"You shouldn't have done that. They're not my type."

"I told them you've been going around asking questions, making innuendos, bothering friends of mine."

"Who told you that?"

"Never you mind, pal! Put a stop to it or I'll put a stop to it for you. You can say what you like about me, but when you go after friends of mine, that's a line you'll regret crossing."

Was this Threaten Sean Duffy Day or something? I was weary of all of this. Ek, Dalziel, and now Jimmy fucking Savile.

"Am I making myself clear, Inspector Duffy?" Savile growled.

"Fuck off."

"What did you say?"

"Why don't you do everyone a favor and just fuck off?" I said, and hung up the phone.

Next to the phone I wrote "this wasn't a dream," in case I thought it was in the morning.

Upstairs to the cold, cold bed.

Sleep.

Cat meowing, low winter sun coming in through the blinds.

Walked to the window and looked out. Coronation Road on a wet February day. Mist rolling down from the Antrim Hills.

Coronation Road. I was making a Deep Map of this street. I knew its nooks. I knew the cracks in the pavement. I knew the parked cars. I was the world expert in its sociology and geography. There goes the man who dresses up as his dead wife. There goes Mr. Grimes, who walks like that because he was tortured by the Japanese in Burma. There goes somebody I don't know. Black Parka again. Didn't like the look of him. I watched him walk around the bend in Coronation Road. Who was that guy?

Later I remembered the footprint in the back garden and one or two other instances of feeling that I was being observed.

Downstairs. A note next to the phone: "this wasn't a dream."

I called Crabbie at the station. "Betty Anderson grassed us up to her mate Jimmy Savile. He called me last night *at home*, warning us off her."

"What exactly did he say?"

I told Crabbie the entire brief conversation.

"So what do we do now?"

"Without making them annoyed, we get the Sex Crimes Unit to redouble their efforts."

"I'll get on to them again."

"Do that."

Kitchen.

Radio 3 playing another Bruckner, which was a bit much for this hour of the morning, the BBC perhaps laboring under the Elizabethan theory that melancholy music could draw out the melancholy humors. The announcer said it was the Fourth Symphony played by the Vienna Philharmonic, but she didn't say which of the various scores the orchestra had gone with. Symphony Number Four existed in five different versions that varied in length from sixty-five to eighty minutes. It was a serious classical-DJ offense not to tell the listener which one it had been. In protest, I flipped to Radio 1.

Shower. Dress. Still pouring, so I got my heavy raincoat.

"Good-bye, cat. Protect the house, don't go near me records!"

Outside to the BMW, checked underneath it for mercury tilt switch bombs, didn't find any, got in.

Key in the ignition.

Hair sticking up on back of neck.

Fear of the unseen. Something menacing, close, terrible.

"Wait a minute . . . Wait a goddamn minute."

Key gently out of the ignition. Car door open. Out of the car again.

Down on my knees. Down on my knees in the cold, hard rain.

Look behind the rear driver's side wheel for a bomb.

A box? A wire?

Nothing. No bomb.

Adrenaline. Heart pumping.

Round the other side of the car. The rear passenger's side.

And there it was.

A brick of Semtex. A bag of nails. A battery. A detonator. A vial of mercury connected to the detonator.

Holy Mary Mother of God.

Shaking.

Inside to the telephone.

999.

Cigarette.

"What is the nature of your emergency?"

"Love, I think we're gonna need the bomb squad."

22: CLOSING THE NET

How to make yourself popular with the neighbors, just when they're finally getting used to you after seven years on the street.

Banging on doors. "Out! Everybody out! Everybody to the end of the street!"

"But it's raining."

"There's a bomb under my car! Everybody out!"

Evacuation of ten houses up and ten houses down from the Beemer. Dirty looks. Grumbling.

"I'm missing the news."

"The weans are at their breakfast."

"I was asleep."

Army Land Rovers and Saracens. Police from as far away as Bally-mena. All of us standing around in the mist and rain.

The bomb-disposal unit of the Royal Engineers arrived and began their work.

A Lieutenant William Cooper, in full bomb-disposal rig, assessed the situation, looked underneath my car, got a tool, snipped the wires of the detonator, thus rendering the explosive device inert. He removed the Semtex block by hand and put it in the Saracen. The rest of the device he left to his sergeant.

Applause from the crowd.

I shook Cooper's hand. "Thanks, mate. That was impressive."

He took off his massive helmet. "It wasn't terribly challenging, actually. These ones are comparatively easy. You just cut the detonator wire. Nothing to it," he said with sangfroid.

"As long as you don't nudge the vial of mercury while you're doing it?" I suggested.

"No, you mustn't nudge the vial of mercury. That wouldn't be pleasant. Listen, old chap, we're going to have to do a controlled explosion on the boot of your car to see if there's a device in there. Hope you don't mind."

"What does that entail?"

"We'll fire a shotgun into the boot, and if there's not a bomb in there, it won't go off. And if there is a bomb in there, it will go off."

"So how is that a controlled explosion? That's just an explosion explosion. You'll wreck my car."

"That's the way we do things."

I shook my head. "No, I'm not having that. You're not blowing up my Beemer."

"We have to."

"I'll open the boot."

"No you won't. I'm in charge here, Inspector Duffy. Not you."

The remote-controlled army robot drove up to the back of the BMW. It waited for a minute, and then it fired its shotgun at the boot.

The little boys who were disappointed that the Brit lieutenant hadn't been blown to bits cheered en masse.

There was no bomb in the boot. And in truth the damage to the car wasn't too bad.

Forensics did their work, and the bomb was taken away for analysis. The good people of Coronation Road went back to their homes. Some of them patted me on the back, others shook my hand. Kyle Acheson, who worked in a garage, said he'd fix my boot for nothing. "It's no problem, you helped with Jeanie's ex and that restraining order. Least I can do. And you've got bottle, so you have. You've got the heart of a tiger, Sean."

"Yeah, that's why they gave me the lifetime ban at the zoo, Kyle."

Kyle didn't get it. But that was OK.

Chief Inspector McArthur came to see me with the number of the divisional psychiatrist and the injunction that I had to take at least three full days off before returning to work.

"Go see Doctor Havercamp, he's very good. We're encouraging our officers to talk about their issues after events like this."

"Maybe I will, sir, maybe I will."

Instead, a day later, I called Forensics for their analysis of the bomb.

A rather crude homemade device. No fingerprints. No claim of responsibility because it was a failed hit.

"Yes, Inspector Duffy, it *was* similar to the device that killed Chief Superintendent McBain."

"That's all I wanted to know."

I'd been given the rest of the week off on full pay, so I did what any sensible man would do on his off-time and drove down to Larne RUC to see how they were getting on with the Ed McBain case.

The station was a morgue that smelled of chips and booze and fear and cigarette smoke. Young men becoming fat old men fast. Police station blues, indeed. The case was closed. Ed McBain had been murdered by an IRA active service unit by way of a mercury tilt switch bomb. End of story.

CI Kennedy wouldn't speak to me, but I found a DC called McGrath who was too new on the force to be completely corrupted.

"Tell me about this bomb," I said, over a pint at Billy Andy's Spirit Grocer (the best pub in Larne).

He furtively handed me the file, which was so thin it was either a case of inept bungling, or a postmodern critique of police methodology.

"The bomb was interesting. Quite different from the usual IRA type. Cruder. Basically just a block of Semtex, a vial of mercury, a battery, and an ignitor. More like a UVF device if you ask me, or even an independent job."

"How long would it take to make a bomb like that?"

"I don't know. If you were working from a plan? Two hours?"

"Tell me about the IRA code word claiming responsibility?"

"'Wolfhound.'"

"Which has been current for about four years. Which means that everyone in the police, the media, the army, and the paramilitary organizations know it. Maybe thirty thousand people."

"What are you suggesting, sir?" the curly-haired, shiny-faced, hazel-eyed, young DC McGrath asked.

"Oh, only that if you wanted to kill Ed McBain for personal reasons, and you wanted to blame it on the IRA, it would be incredibly easy to do it if you knew a little about bomb-making technology and had access to some Semtex, or even a ready-made bomb."

"Who would do such a thing?"

"Who indeed? Maybe someone who had encountered a similar case like that in the past . . ." I said, a dark idea beginning to grow in my mind.

"CI Kennedy never mentioned any of this," McGrath said.

"He wouldn't. Come on, finish your drink. I'll drive you back to the station."

Billy Andy's pub to Larne RUC, to the Coast Road Hotel.

I found Kevin Donnolly behind Reception. "Ah, Inspector Duffy, so nice to see you again. You're looking tan, heard you were away on your holidays," he said, doing his best Julian Simmons impersonation.

"It's not a tan. I was in Finland."

"Oh, nice for some, saunas and all that, eh?"

"No time for chitchat, Kevin. The night Mr. Laakso's wallet went missing. Remember that?"

"Of course."

"The Finns were out late, weren't they?"

"Yes. I think so."

"Do you happen to remember what time they got back that night?"

"Oooh, no, not exactly. I don't keep those sorts of records."

"Roughly, then?"

"Well, it would have been after eleven, because I had to let them in."

"Eleven? Are you sure about that?"

"Yes. I shut the doors at eleven and you have to get buzzed in after that. And they were buzzed in, so they were."

"So it was some time after eleven?"

"Yes, but I couldn't tell you when. Before twelve, probably, but I can't be sure."

Back outside to the Beemer. No bombs underneath. Window wipers on max. Radio 1 on the stereo: "Sonic Boom Boy" by Westworld, followed by "Heartache" by Pepsi & Shirlie, followed by "Rock the Night" by Europe.

"Jesus!"

Stereo off.

The Eagle's Nest on the Knockagh Road.

Mrs. Dunwoody wearing a blond wig today that didn't suit her in the least. "Ah, the brave Inspector Duffy. Can I interest you in—"

"Not today, Mrs. D. I have a question for you."

"Go on."

"The night the Finns were here? Do you remember what time they left?"

"The Finns . . ."

"The Finns. The two young gentlemen were with the girls, you were playing cards that night with Mr. Ek and Mr. Laakso . . ."

"Oh, yes. No, no, I'm afraid I don't remember."

"But roughly. A rough estimate."

"I don't like to be put on the spot," she protested.

"Roughly . . . please."

"Well, I suppose I could check the security footage. It'll take a while. I'll have to ask Ronnie to go through it."

"Please do so."

"All right. You'll have to wait. Do you want to see one of the girls?"

"No, I'll wait at the bar."

"I'll send Niamh down to talk to you."

The bar. Niamh. Red-haired, pretty. Almost as pretty as Beth. She poured me a vodka gimlet, easy on the vodka.

Ronnie and Mrs. Dunwoody together.

"Yes?"

"They left at 9:45 p.m.," Ronnie said.

"Are you sure?"

"We've got a time stamp on the video."

"I'm afraid I'm going to have to take that tape into evidence."

"What about the privacy of our customers?"

"I'm sorry, but the tape is going to be an important piece of evidence in a murder investigation. I'll only need to ever show the bit with the Finns, and they won't be back, will they?"

"No," Mrs. Dunwoody conceded.

"I'll be very discreet. You know me," I said to Mrs. Dunwoody as Ronnie handed me the tape.

"What does it mean if they left at 9:45?" Mrs. Dunwoody asked.

"It means, Mrs. Dunwoody, that it took them over an hour, well over an hour, to make the ten-minute drive from here back to Carrickfergus."

"And what does *that* mean?"

"That means that they went somewhere else first."

BMW to Belfast. Park outside McIlroy Security Services.

Upstairs: the same bored receptionist, the same bored secretary.

"Is Tony around?"

"He's out on a job," Donna said, flipping through the pages of *Elle*.

"Know when he'll be back?"

"Probably back for lunch."

"Lunch is?"

"Twelve," she said, rolling her eyes.

"I'll come back. Tell him Sean was here to see him, please."

"OK."

Beemer to Queen Street RUC, which was a safe place to park and central to everything.

Walk down to the Forensics Unit HQ. Show my ID. Upstairs to the labs.

Prissy, pretty receptionist called Siobhan. Catholic from West Belfast.

"Yes? Can I help you?"

"Waiting for a blood-sample result."

"Case name and number?"

"Lily Bigelow, CRUC Number 333718."

Tapping on a keyboard. Green letters on a computer screen.

"I'm sorry, Inspector Duffy. That case is with the DPP now. You'll have to speak to them for any results."

"Look, I'm in a hurry. I was the investigating officer. We found

blood on one of the dungeon walls in Carrick Castle. I just want to
know if it was Lily Bigelow's blood or not. You've been processing this
case for ages. Please, if I go through the DPP it'll take even more time."

Siobhan relenting.

"It says here that there wasn't enough material for what's called a
'DNA match,' but the blood type was B negative. Miss Bigelow was also
B negative."

"Thank you."

Back downstairs. Quick juke into Matchett's Pianos.

Patrick groaned when I came in. I had been circling this piano
shop for about five years now, occasionally tinkling on a baby grand, or
looking at some sheet music, but never once buying anything.

"What about you, Patrick?"

"Not too bad, you Sean?"

"Days—what are they for, eh, mate? Where can we live but bloody
days?"

"I'll take that as an 'I'm OK.' So are you in to tease me, or are you
seriously interested in a piano?"

I hear you got a bit smoke-damaged from the firebomb at the Athletic Stores."

Pat shook his head sadly. "That we did."

"Entire stock a write-off?"

"Total write-off. You know what heat and smoke does to a piano."

I looked around to see if there were any other customers in the
shop. It was empty. I lowered my voice. "If I was looking to get one of
those 'write-off' pianos . . ."

Patrick smiled. "Well, Sean . . . officially they've all been sent to
Belfast dump. The insurance company insisted on that. No resale or
recycling."

"And unofficially?"

"How much were you looking to spend?"

"Oh, I don't know. Just a good standing piano."

"Somewhere in the region of four or five hundred pounds?"

"Sounds about right."

"We might be able to come to some kind of arrangement."

"I'd have to play it first. See if I like the tone."

Patrick eyed me suspiciously. "Are you sure this isn't some sort of police investigation?"

"I'm hurt, Patrick. Seriously. I thought we were friends."

"I'm sorry, Sean . . . of course you wouldn't . . . look, come over here, out the back."

He took me to a storage room out the back and set me down in front of a gorgeous pre-war Bechstein.

"Go on, then," Patrick said.

I played Liszt's "La Campanella" and, just to annoy myself, Rachmaninoff's "Prelude in G Minor." The piano had a beautiful tone and wasn't damaged in the least. When I played the last bar of the "Prelude," Patrick thought I was money in the bank.

"You play very well, you know," he said.

"I'm rusty."

"No, Sean, you're really good."

I looked at my watch. It was 11:45.

"Well? Will I put it aside for you?" Pat asked.

"Nah, I'll have to think about it, mate," I said.

"I knew it!" Patrick groaned again. "I fall for it every bloody time."

I walked to the door. "Hey, Pat, why could Beethoven never find his music teacher?"

"Why?"

"Because he was Haydn."

"Get out of my shop!"

Back to McIlroy Security Services.

"I'm so sorry, Mr. McIlroy's still not back. He should be here in about half an hour or forty-five minutes. Do you want to wait?"

"No, it's not a problem. I'll come back."

Drive down to Cairo Street. Find number 13 in the middle of a student terrace. Unafraid of clichés, there was a bunch of beardy students hanging out on stoops and front yards, smoking ciggies, strumming guitars, reading Penguin paperbacks. I parked the car and took Beth's records out of the boot; records which I had carefully removed from my collection and put in a milk crate for just such an opportunity as this. Culture Club, The Boomtown Rats, Paul Young, Ultravox . . . nothing that I would miss.

Knock the door.

A sleepy girl with peroxide hair and bags under her eyes.

"Hi, I brought, uhm, Beth's records."

"She's not in."

"Oh."

"So, you're Sean?"

"You must be Rhonda."

"You better come in, I'll make you a cup of tea."

She brought me into an impressively filthy lounge and made me a cup of tea.

"Thanks," I said, taking the mug.

"Should I leave these records up in her room?" I asked.

"I don't think she'd want you going in her room."

"Oh, OK."

Silence. Someone practicing scales on a trumpet outside.

"You miss her?" Rhonda asked.

"I do."

"She has ambitions. She can't be a policeman's wife. She wants to get her master's."

"I know."

"She's a modern woman."

"I understand that. Does she ever talk about me?"

Rhonda nodded. "Sometimes."

"What does she say?"

Rhonda shook her head. "Ach, you know."

"Has she met someone else?"

"Nobody serious. She liked you, Sean. It wasn't you. She just doesn't want to be tied down."

"The last thing I wanted was for her to feel trapped," I said.

A long silence.

I took a sip of my tea and set the mug down on the sofa arm.

"Well," I said, getting up.

"Take the records up and leave them outside her door, if you want. I don't want to carry them up there. First on the left."

Upstairs. Door open. A neat little bedroom. Blue bedspread with clouds on it. Converse gutties tucked under the bed. U2 poster, CND poster, picture of a young Beth on a sailboat, "Free Nelson Mandela" poster. *Sailing? Nelson Mandela? She's never mentioned Nelson Mandela to me.* Desk covered with books: the usual English curriculum stuff and mystery and science-fiction novels I'd never heard of. A brush with long black hairs on it. *Black?*

Back downstairs.

"Better head on, then, Rhonda."

"Yeah . . ."

Out to the BMW. Look underneath it for bombs. Back to Tony's office. Tony there, waiting for me. Charcoal-grey suit, shiny shoes, weird, nervous, pointed look to his face. "I'm so, so sorry, Sean, if I'd known you were looking to see me—"

"Not a prob, Tony, mate. Take you to a late lunch?" I asked. "I'll buy. Crown OK?"

"Thought we were going to go out for drinks? A real old-fashioned session."

"We'll still do that. Late lunch, now."

"OK."

The back snug of the Crown Bar. Irish stew and Guinness.

Small talk for half an hour and then I hit him with it: "Tony, listen, I'm having a few problems with the time line on the Lily Bigelow case. Remember that night you took the Finns to the brothel?"

"Yeah, course."

No change of expression. No flicker.

"You were waiting outside for them, isn't that what you said?"

"Yeah. I didn't want to go in. No temptations, you know? And that place is pricey."

"So the boys did their business and the men played cards and they all came out."

"Yeah."

"Do you remember what time that was?"

"I thought I told you. What did I say? Nine? Nine thirty? Who knows?"

"After they left the brothel, you drove them back to Carrick, yeah?"

"No, they had their own car. They followed me."

"Did you go especially slowly, so they didn't lose you?"

"I drove them back at a normal speed," Tony said a little defensively. "What are you getting at here, Sean?"

"OK, so normal speed then. Ten, fifteen minutes to get back to Carrick?"

"Maybe a little less," Tony admitted. "I'm not an old biddy."

I finished my bowl of stew and stood up. "Well that's tidied that up," I lied. "Drink tonight? Tomorrow night? The famous Carrick-fergus Fifteen?"

Tony's worry evaporated. His face broke into a grin. "The famous Carrickfergus Fifteen? Haven't done that for years. You're on. Tomorrow night."

"Great. Let's meet at the Tourist at six. Early start," I said.

"Early start. Happy days, Sean. Be like old times."

"That it will," I agreed.

"Before you go, speaking of driving, I've got one for you."

"I'm listening."

"Last night the peelers stopped me for speeding and they said, 'Don't you know the speed limit is 70 miles an hour?' I said, 'Yeah, I know, but I wasn't gonna be out that long.'"

I'd heard it before, but I laughed anyway. *It might be my last laugh with Tony for a long time.*

I drove back home, grim-faced.

Tony McIlroy. Jesus Christ.

I thought about telling Crabbie and Lawson what I had learned, but I didn't want to cast suspicion on Tony until I knew for sure. Until the case was rock solid. This was still an impossible crime. An impossible crime and an improbable crime that were linked together—the killing of Lily Bigelow and the killing of Chief Superintendent McBain. And, of course, that little attempted murder of yours truly.

Ek had motive and opportunity and form. To cobble together a plan like that on short notice defied belief, but if he had help . . .

I remembered something Lily's landlady, Mrs. Singh, had said back in London.

"That's what I told all the other detectives. They were very thorough. They came in twice."

I looked in my notebook for her number. I dialed it, apologized for bothering her, and explained who I was. She remembered me.

"Mrs. Singh, you said that two sets of detectives came to ask about Lily Bigelow and went through her stuff."

"That's right."

"Did one of them have an Irish accent?"

"Yes, that's right."

"And was he with another man, skinny, older?"

"No, he was on his own."

"Do you think you'd recognize him, if I showed you a picture of him?"

"I think I would. He was quite handsome."

"Thank you, Mrs. Singh."

I hung up.

A knock at my front door.

McCrabban's long face. Lawson's eager one.

"What are you lads doing out here? Little early for caroling. Come into the living room, it's good to see you."

Lawson glanced at the words "Motive," "Opportunity," "Form," and "Irish detective" in the notebook on the coffee table and gave me a strange look. But I wasn't ready to blurt out my suspicions just yet.

"So, what's up lads?"

"Sean, we just got a weird call from CI Farrow. They're going to make an arrest. They want to know if we want to go along on the collar. Joint publicity. Them and us," Crabbie said.

"Who is CI Farrow?"

"From the Sex Crimes Unit. I've been liaising with her."

"Farrow's a she?"

"She is."

"And who is she going to arrest?"

"Colin Jones from Kinkaid Young Offenders' Institution."

I put down my coffee cup. "Holy fuck! I knew it. I fucking knew it!" I said.

"Aye," Crabbie agreed.

"What are they saying that he did?"

"They're saying that he allowed the Tara branch of the Rathcoole UVF to get access to Kinkaid, to take away some of the boys at night for what the informer described as 'sex parties.'"

"Why would the boys do it?" Lawson asked.

"Coercion, money, drugs?" McCrabban said.

"What did I tell you," I said. "No walls. No security. Anybody could get in and out. How did Farrow get the info?"

"They put the word to grasses they knew in the paramilitaries and one of the grasses was willing to spill for a reduced sentence on an unrelated crime. It's an informer case, so it'll come down to whether Jones confesses or not."

"Any of the boys talking?"

"Nope."

"Of course not. Paramilitaries will keep them in line. The Tara branch of the Rathcoole UVF are particularly ruthless. *Sex parties*— that's a sinister expression. What does that mean, exactly?" I asked.

"Dunno. That's the phrase the informer used."

"It's the rape and abuse of children is what it is. We get an opportunity to talk to this informer?"

"No chance. He's in a safe house. Only Farrow and trusted members of her team are getting access to him."

"It's not our friend Lenny Dummigan, is it?"

"Who knows?"

"Informers, though . . ."

"Yeah."

It was a high-risk strategy. In the early part of the Troubles, informers and so-called Supergrasses were responsible for putting dozens of suspects behind bars, but in the last few years Supergrass testimony without supporting forensic evidence had been increasingly thrown out by the courts.

One informer in a case like this probably wasn't going to cut it.

"Do you want me to tell Farrow we want in on the arrest? It was our tip. It's half of our collar," Crabbie said.

"No, we don't need to be in on the arrest, but I want to be in on the interrogation."

"I'll tell her."

Crabbie and Lawson to the front door.

"How are you holding up, by the way? The lads down the station were asking about you," Crabbie said.

"Holding up?"

"Bomb under your car."

"Oh? That? That's old news. I'm way past that now."

Sunset at 5 p.m., behind thick rain clouds.

Carrick to Newtownabbey in the Beemer.

The interrogation of Colin Jones at Newtownabbey RUC.

Jones had demanded a solicitor, and within forty-five minutes a senior solicitor appeared from McKenna and Wright, and along with her the infamous Charlie McGuirk, a well-known police-hating barrister from the Belfast bar. But that wasn't all. Also in the station was a fuming Betty Anderson and her family lawyer, a dangerous-looking bloke who had just gotten off the shuttle from Glasgow.

"Wise move, not being in on this arrest, Sean," McCrabban said sotto voce. "I think everyone in Newtownabbey RUC is about to experience the wrath of Ms. Elizabeth Anderson."

Wrath indeed, and much shouting.

Writs and threats from each of the disputation of lawyers.

It took a full hour until the interrogation of Mr. Jones was allowed to get underway.

No, Mr. Jones hadn't heard that young men were leaving Kinkaid at night to go to these "sex parties."

No, he didn't think there was a problem with security at night at Kinkaid. No, the paramilitaries did not have access to Kinkaid YOI. Kinkaid was a very secure and respectable place . . .

We watched the efficient and dogged CI Farrow go at it for two hours, but there wasn't any headway. Jones admitted to nothing.

CI Farrow out, McCrabban and Duffy in.

"Mr. Jones, did you know that boys from your home were leaving the institution at night?"

"I certainly did not! I don't believe it. It's a lie concocted by an informer."

"Why would an informer lie?"

"To get us all into trouble. To see this experiment in rehabilitation get destroyed. It's in the paramilitaries' interest that these young men become recidivists, not functioning members of society. And it's in the interests of the prison officers' union that we get closed down. A lot of people don't want us to succeed."

"And if young men in your care are being raped and abused? What will you say then?"

"They're not! It's a lie!"

We asked the same questions again, in a dozen different ways, but got back variations of the same answer. Jones didn't know anything. Jones wouldn't admit to anything. There was no evidence of anything.

"I'll bet you if you ask each of the boys in Kinkaid about these ridiculous allegations, they'll deny everything," Charlie McGuirk said.

"I bet they will, Charlie. One squeak and it's a bullet in the knee-caps, one squawk and it's a bullet in the head," I said.

"I'll remember you said that, that's defamation!" McGuirk said, and had the temerity to write my name down in his book.

We left CI Farrow to it. Her pale, young face, lined and old from ten years of constant defeats. Defeats like this. Because nobody talked. Nobody ever talked.

BMW back to Carrick RUC.

"What do you think, boss?" Crabbie asked in the front passenger seat.

"Her informer better be bloody good. He better be well protected. He better be sturdy as fuck and in a safe house far, far away," I said.

Crabbie nodded.

"They're going to release Jones without charge, aren't they?" Lawson said.

"Yes," Crabbie and I said together.

BMW back to Coronation Road.

A bottle of Lagavulin on my doorstep, with a ribbon around it. A more suspicious man would have left it there, or poured it out, but I brought it in. Doubtless it was for services rendered at some point. A domestic-violence dispute I'd sorted out, or a word in the shell-like of some teen vandal.

I poured a measure of Lagavulin, but I was too keyed-up to appreciate it. This case was coming to a head. They might not be able to pin anything on Mr. Jones, but tomorrow night I'd make Tony tell me everything he knew. He would not be able to lie to me, not when I told him everything *I* knew.

Phone call.

"Yeah?"

"Is this Duffy?"

"Who's asking?"

"This is Chief Inspector Kennedy from Larne RUC. You've been noseying around our files and I don't like it."

"Yeah, you won't like it either when I take a monster shite in that fucking cake-hole of yours, which I will if you ever call me at home again. Then again, you'd probably fucking love it, wouldn't ya, you coprophiliac cunt. Look it up. Furthermore, if you ever embarrass me in front of my gaffer again, you'll end up like your beloved Führer, with a poisoned dog, a Red Army bulldozer through your fucking conservatory, and you lying in a ditch covered in petrol, begging me not to light the fucking match. Ya get me?" I said, and slammed the phone down.

It rang again, five minutes later.

"What now, fuckface?" I asked.

"Sir, it's me, Lawson," he said, sounding hurt.

"Oh, sorry, Lawson. A thousand apologies. I thought you were someone else."

"Do you like twists, sir?"

"You know I don't like twists, Lawson. What's happened?"

"Mr. Underhill. The DPPs investigative team just sent us a fax."

"Oh, bugger. What did we miss?"

"The DPP uncovered an incident he was involved in, in 1962. He was a 'person of interest' in the case of a young nurse who broke her neck falling over the banister and down the stairs of a guesthouse they were both staying at in Glasgow. The Glasgow peelers questioned Underhill and a few of the other residents, but no case ever came to trial, so it's not in our records."

I groaned into the phone.

"The DPP want us to look into it."

"Of course they do."

"If he did it before, it sort of sets a pattern, doesn't it?"

"The previous incident can't be used as evidence in the current case."

"It can't?"

"No, Lawson, it can't, the defense barrister will say that its prejudicial effect outweighs its probative value. It won't be covered by the exception in *Rex v Smith* (1915) the famous brides-in-the-bath case, of which I'm sure you're aware..."

"Uhm..."

"But we'll have to ask him about it. We'll interview him again tomorrow morning."

"Won't we have to notify his solicitor? That woman from the navy?"

"Not if we don't arrest him. Tell Crabbie. See you in the morning."

More Lagavulin. The news on mute. I tried to make sense of things through a haze of booze and images. Blah, blah, fucking blah.

I finished the bottle and went up the stairs, steadying myself on the handrail. I paused at the photograph of me and Muhammad Ali. Me and the Champ. "Me and the Champ, Beth," I muttered. "A 'twist,' he says. I'll twist him."

I flopped on to the bed.
I dreamed Rumble in the Jungle.
I dreamed Thrilla in Manilla.
And I dreamed of the big fight to come tomorrow.

23: THE FAMOUS CARRICKFERGUS
FIFTEEN-PUB CRAWL

*R*ain. *The echoing boom of gunfire. A phone dangling on its wire in a phone booth in West Street, Carrickfergus. Where the Dream Lines crossed. Where I was making the Deep Map. Where one part of this story ended. "Ambulance! Ambulance!" I'm screaming into the phone, trying to make myself heard over the rain. . . . Yeah, I know what you're thinking: gun battle, rain, Ireland. But you don't know. You have no idea. You weren't there. For you, the eighties are: Thatcher triumphant, the Argies bashed, North Sea oil, the unions broke, the Reagan–Thatcher two-step. For you, but not for us. For us, it's helicopters, low clouds, soldiers, curling umbilicals of ash over the great, grey, dying city . . .*

I wish we could spin the clock back to the beginning of the day. Freeze Duffy there, as he drives to Carrick Castle. Let him avoid the melodrama. Let him lose the girl and get the girl and go to Liverpool and grow up and become a man. Let his story be the parsing of the human condition. But, alas, we can't do that, because we're dealing with truth here. Ugly, vulgar, violent, clumsy truth . . .

Carrickfergus Police Station.

I'd been a few days off. In theory, I didn't have to show up for work at all because someone had tried to kill me with a bomb under my car. If this was any other police force in the world, you'd be in counseling for months after something like that. But RUC men and women were made of sterner stuff. Here, this was par for the course, and when I came in, it was a few handshakes, a few slaps on the back accompanied by "it's good to see you still in one piece," and that was it. Sergeant Dalziel with his frizzy hair and yellow raincoat came in to give me Admin grief, and I hit him with a few "where's your mate Keith Harris?" lines, but it was halfhearted from both of us and he left.

Crabbie and Lawson arrived at 9 a.m.

"Shall we go and see Mr. Underhill?" Crabbie asked.

"We shall."

Walk to the castle. Up the castle ramp and under the portcullis to the ticket booth.

"Not you lot again! I'm calling my lawyers!" Underhill said, indignantly.

"Steady on, Mr. Underhill, we just want to ask you one more thing. Give us five minutes of your time."

"What do you want to ask me about?"

"Mary O'Connor. May, 1962. The Fairview Bed and Breakfast on Dumbarton Road, Glasgow. She fell from the third floor and broke her neck. You lived on the same landing as her."

Underhill looked as if he'd been poleaxed.

He sighed and shook his head with infinite sadness.

"Aye, I killed her," he said.

"You killed her?"

"Aye, now that I reflect upon it. I as good as killed her."

"Why don't you tell us what happened?"

"I gave her to understand that we were to be married. And then one day she found letters from my wife in Plymouth. I didnae have the chance to explain that we'd been living apart for years. I didnae know if it was an accident, or whether she went deliberately over the rail of the staircase. I like to think it was an accident. My sea chest was open and the letters were on my bed. Maybe she ran out of the room and she slipped. . . . Aye, I like to think that. I don't like to think that she read the letters and walked to the rail and climbed over . . ."

We spent the rest of the melancholy afternoon checking Underhill's story.

He was the first to find the body, but he arrived back at the guesthouse with a friend whom he had met at Glasgow Central railway station.

The alibi checked out.

The story checked out.

Not *R v Smith*. Not the brides-in-the-bath case. Just one of those awful things that happen . . .

I was still in a melancholy mood when I shook Tony's hand in the saloon bar of the Tourist Inn in Eden at 6 p.m.

"What about you, Sean? We haven't done this in years."

"We're getting too old for this. In fact, I was thinking, what if we got a half a pint in every pub instead of a pint? Fifteen pints is going to kill us at our age."

"A half a pint? I can't go up and order a half a pint. I'll look ridiculous. Half a pint. Who orders half a pint?"

"All right, a pint it is, then. I'll blame you if we get alcohol poisoning."

"Sounds like a plan," Tony said. "I'll get the first one in? Bass?"

"Aye."

And so began the first of the fifteen pubs in the famous fifteen-pub crawl that took you through every bar in Carrickfergus.

From north to south, roughly along the Belfast Road, the fifteen pubs and clubs where you could get a pint in Carrick were: the Tourist Inn, the Royal Oak, Ownies, Dobbins, the Central Bar, the Mermaid Tavern, the Dolphin, the Buffs Club, the Wind Rose, the Borough Arms, the North Gate, the Railway Tavern, the Rangers Club, the Rugby Club, and the Brown Cow Inn.

Technically, there was also the Golf Club and the Yacht Club, but they were off the traditional route and you had to be a member to get served, so fuck them.

The Tourist Inn was a sad venue to begin the crawl. A dreary place with watered-down beer and a reek from the toilets that lingered in the saloon bar. It was the local for only the most desperate of alcoholics and we quickly finished our pints and headed down to the Royal Oak.

Here we had two choices: the downstairs bar, which was full of cops and an older crowd and was quiet, or the upstairs bar, where they played horrible loud music and only served awful lager—but which was full of jailbait and divorcees.

"Upstairs then?" I said.

"Aye," Tony agreed.

We went upstairs and sure enough it was full of seventeen-year-olds drinking cider and rather attractive thirty- and forty-year-olds knocking back gin and tonics. The music on the video screens was Prince or George Michael at eardrum-smashing levels.

I talked to Tony about his marriage and living in England and his father-in-law who was an MP. He told me everything. Tony liked to talk. He was one of those chatty Prods.

"I was just thinking that you're one of those chatty Prods. Not like McCrabban and those boys," I said, sipping my pint of Harp.

"That lot are all Presbyterian and Free Presbyterian. I'm a Methodist," Tony explained.

"And what do you lot believe, then?"

"You know. . . . God, Jesus, the works. No pope, though."

"Saints? All that stuff?"

"I don't think so," Tony said vaguely.

"I haven't been to mass in years. Or confession. I'll be fucked if I get run over by a bus tonight."

"Jesus, it's hot in here," Tony said, taking off his leather jacket. He was wearing a blue striped shirt underneath, white denim jeans, and sneakers. He was trying to look younger than he was, and he did look younger. He could have passed for thirty.

"Loo," he said.

When he was safely in the bathroom, I quickly looked in the side pockets of the leather jacket for a gun and didn't find one. As an ex-policeman he'd have to apply for a license. Sometimes they gave you one. Sometimes they didn't. I, of course, was carrying mine. I was wearing blue jeans, DMs, and my trusty good-luck Che T-shirt—no jacket, but deep in my raincoat pocket I was carrying my Glock 17 and a set of handcuffs.

As an RUC detective you had a choice of firearms: either an ancient Walther PPK .32-caliber semiautomatic, or an even more ancient revolver. Fortunately, I'd been in Special Branch for a brief tenure and had gotten my hands on a Glock. The upshot of all this was that I was armed and Tony wasn't, and I'd brought my handcuffs along, too, to make him come quietly.

"What are you thinking about?" he said, approaching from behind and slapping me on the back.

"Oh, you know, Beth . . ."

"Beth?"

"You didn't meet her. Student. Nice. Funny, you would have liked her."

"Student. Sounds like a pain in the arse."

"She wasn't."

I finished my pint. "Loo first and then do you want to get another round in, or will we head on?"

"You're going to the loo with your raincoat on? Everybody's looking at you. Leave your coat, for fuck's sake, mate."

"My gun's in it."

"I'll watch it. No one'll steal it."

I took the coat off and left it on my stool.

"What about you, Tony? Are you carrying?"

"Of course I bloody am! In this country?"

"You've got a gun?" I asked, surprised.

"Had this made special. Look at this," he said, showing me the secret pocket he'd had tailored in the inside left-hand side of the jacket. Shit. Missed that. Good thing I asked.

"Whatcha carrying?"

".45 ACP. Oldie but goodie. Hollow point. One of those'll stop a fucking rhino."

"Legal?"

Tony winked at me. "Thought you had to go to the loo, mate?"

When I got back, I noticed that the coat had been moved slightly, but when I reached inside the pocket to check, the gun and cuffs were still there.

More videos, more lager, more loud, terrible music.

"Look at that bint over there, she's giving me the eye."

"Sure she is . . . all right, Tony, time to go to Ownies now, I think," I said.

Outside into the cool air. Rain clouds dropping a fine drizzle onto us as we walked down the Scotch Quarter.

Ownies was a different story altogether. Old men in flat caps playing dominoes. No music, roaring fire, good beer.

"Pint of Guinness?" I asked Tony.

"Yeah. Missed a decent pint when I was over the sheugh."

I got Tony a Guinness and a lager for myself.

"Another trip to the loo," I said, and took my pint with me. I poured three-quarters of it out and filled it up with water.

"So, London, eh? The Met? Must have been great," I said, coming back to the table.

Tony sighed. "I was quids in mate, quids in. I blew it over there. A woman will tolerate weakness in a man, but she will not tolerate repeated humiliation. Neither will her father, apparently . . ."

I let him spill it. It was interesting from a psychological stand-point. How the clever, ambitious but honest Tony of five years ago had become this man I saw before me now.

This . . . well, there was no other word for it.

This *murderer*.

If all my assumptions were correct.

"What about you, Sean Duffy? What's cooking in that big brain of yours?" he said, tapping my head. "You always were the nowhere man, the cypher on the outside looking in. You could be thinking anything."

"So could you, Tony."

"No, not me. No back doors to Tony McIlroy. What you see is what you get. But you. . . . You're a deep old cat. Always were. Jesus, this is a good pint."

We finished up and went outside into the increasingly stormy night.

"Did you check the weather forecast?" Tony asked.

"No. Did you?"

"It's a fucking tempest, mate."

"Aye, it's not looking too good. Where to?"

"Central Bar."

Central Bar, Mermaid, Dolphin, Wind Rose, Buffs Club.

A couple of half pints and me watering down my pints on my shout, but Tony holding up his end surprisingly well. He'd always been a heroic drinker. Heroic drinker, heroic fighter, good mate. And I remembered the time he'd decked a guy for calling me a fenian bastard in Newry RUC.

Tony wasn't into music, so we talked football and women. Women and football. He said he still liked the Arsenal and he wasn't banging either his secretary or receptionist.

"I'm a changed man, Sean. None of that anymore."

"How is the business doing?"

"Not too bad, actually. Things were touch-and-go at first, but not too bad now. People don't go to Securicor for finesse work."

We finished our pints in the Buffs and walked up North Street to the Borough Arms, North Gate, and the Railway Tavern. The latter three all paramilitary bars. One UDA, two UVF. Not exactly welcoming places for a cop and an ex-cop. How they could tell we were peelers I had no idea, but they could tell. We went to the toilet together, lest we get a beer keg in the head.

The rain was apocalyptic outside now, and everyone was going home early, before the Marine Highway started to flood.

"You know, mate, I don't think we're going to make the fifteen. I think we should go back down to the Dobbins and end it there," I said as I pissed into the backyard of the Railway Tavern—the only toilet facilities they had.

Tony was outraged. "Not make the fifteen? The whole point of this was to do the fifteen pubs!"

"You fancy hiking up the Woodburn Road all the way to the Rugby Club and the Brown Cow in this?"

Tony looked at me and grinned.

"We gave it a good shot, though, eh? For old-timers. Didn't we? We gave it a run for our money."

Down to the Dobbins Inn in the pouring rain.

We were the only customers in Dobbins, so we got the huge sixteenth-century fireplace to ourselves. It had been stacked with turf that had turned to ash and was giving off a tremendous heat. Steam lifted from my raincoat, my trousers, and even from my shoes.

"You're wetter than the time you fell in the Bann!" Tony laughed. "You remember that time?"

"I remember. And you did nothing to fish me out!"

"Happy days, Sean. Happy days. When we were young and innocent. Another shout?"

"Why not?"

I looked at my watch. It was 11 p.m. Tony wasn't as drunk as I'd hoped he would be and it was last orders now.

Tony came back with two pints of Bass and a packet of fags. Embassy. I lit one anyway and stubbed it out after one puff. Vile.

"Hey, Tony, can I ask you something about the Lily Bigelow case?"

"Jesus, do you have to? You'll spoil a nice evening. Sleeping dogs, you know?"

I looked at him strangely. "That wasn't a threat, was it?"

He laughed. "Jesus, I forgot how paranoid everybody in this bloody country is. That's what living in England does for you. Reacclimatizes you to the Normal."

His eyes. Something about his eyes. What was that look? I couldn't decipher it. Sadness? Exhaustion? What?

"Something about what you said puzzles me a bit."

"Go on, then."

I took out a piece of paper from my wallet and read what I had written there.

"Do you remember you were talking about the case and you scoffed at the idea of a huge conspiracy put in motion to protect the Finns and 'silence her by hiring a nearly seventy-year-old castle caretaker to murder her in a dungeon.' Do you remember saying that?"

"Yeah."

"We found a speck of blood on one of the dungeon walls. B negative. Only two percent of the population has B negative blood. In all likelihood, it's Lily's blood and she was murdered in the dungeon, not the courtyard. How did you know that, Tony?"

"I don't know. You must have told me."

"I didn't."

"Or Crabbie or Lawson. Somebody must have told me. Anyway, Underhill killed her, you proved that. No one else could have done it."

"I think Harald Ek killed her, or had her killed."

Tony paused mid-drink and put down his glass.

"Why would he do that?"

"Because Peter Laakso wasn't happy with what they had on offer at the Eagle's Nest. You knew he wasn't going to be happy with what they had on offer there. You'd already been contacted by Ek and told of Mr. Laakso's particular needs. Maybe he even suggested Kinkaid to you."

"Remind me what Kinkaid is?"

"Almost certainly it took place in a private house near Kinkaid Young Offenders' Institution, where the Tara UVF ran boy mollies from the prison."

"What a load of rubbish! I can't believe you've become one of those fucking queer-bashers. You're a, uhm, what's it called? A *homophobe*," Tony said, using the same tack that Ek had used and becoming suddenly and quite frighteningly sober.

"You know I'm not, Tony."

"You found out Laakso's gay, and you're using it against him to concoct some sort of crazy, convoluted story against him. That's what living in Northern Ireland does to you."

"Harald Ek said the same thing to me. Almost exactly the same thing. It's nothing to do with being gay, Tony. We both know Mrs. Dunwoody caters for both genders. She would have been very happy to sort Laakso out. But Mrs. Dunwoody's girls and boys are all over eighteen. To live outside the law, you must be honest. No, Mr. Laakso has different drives. Drives that you knew could be catered to by the Rathcoole Tara paramilitaries. Heroin, crack cocaine, underage boy prostitutes, underage girl prostitutes. Every copper in East Antrim knows the Tara unit of the UVF are capable of anything. And apparently the opening of Kinkaid has been a whole new avenue for them. As a connected guy, you must have known that, too."

"You're out of your mind, pal. You're trying to be funny, is that what this is?"

"No, it isn't me trying to be funny. You left the brothel at 9:45 p.m. You didn't reach the Coast Road Hotel until well after eleven p.m. It's, at most, a ten-minute run, as you yourself said. You went to Kinkaid, or a place near Kinkaid. And Lily followed you and you, being a good cop, spotted that you were being followed. And you told Ek. And you were thinking that maybe Ek would try and buy her off. But Ek's not that kind of man. He wanted to kill her."

Tony's face was white. His eyes were black points of fury. His hands were shaking under the table. This was it. This was the mainline. This was the well.

"So maybe you arranged a fake robbery to get Lily out of her room and while she was out investigating the commotion, maybe Ek went in there and looked at her typewriter and you pretended to have just arrived as I was leaving. And when Ek knew for certain that Lily was onto him, you two started coming up with a plan. You cooked up a murder plan between you that was designed just for me. The castle was a stroke of genius. A locked room. A suicide, or, failing that, poor old Mr. Underhill as the only suspect. And you knew that I would be the investigating officer and I'd already dealt with a case like that. A case you knew about. A case we'd discussed. The chances of getting two locked-room murders in one career were astronomical. I'd never believe it. I'd insist it was a suicide, or that Mr. Underhill had done her in."

"I'm leaving. You're raving mad!"

I grabbed his arm and pulled him back to his seat. "Hear me out, Tony. If you could kill her in the castle somehow and make it look like a suicide, I would have to buy it, wouldn't I? And if the evidence made it look like a murder, I'd have to believe that old Mr. Underhill did it, because it was impossible to be anyone else. Impossible that I could have two cases like that in a lifetime."

Tony said nothing, but with his free arm he had reached for his leather jacket now. The jacket with the gun inside.

"It *is* impossible," Tony said. "You're drunk."

"DC Lawson told me about Bayesian statistics. I *could* have two cases like that in one career if the deck was stacked. If the game was rigged. Rigged specifically for me."

I felt for my gun in my raincoat pocket, and its shape gave me comfort as Tony poured hatred into my eyes.

"And then there's Eddie McBain. You saw McBain and Bigelow having coffee together in the hotel. You saw him talk to her. You saw him not liking what he was hearing. You knew what Ed was like of old. Very slow to act. Very slow to do anything. But when he got moving, he was unstoppable."

"McBain was killed by the IRA. A random attack. They blew him up. They claimed responsibility."

"Another case you and I worked on together. The McAlpine case. A fake IRA claim of responsibility to cover up the murder of a member of the security forces. I'll bet there's one or two of those every year. Ordinary statistics and Bayesian statistics will allow for that one."

"A bomb? Come on!"

"A bomb that was very crude, the sort of thing Protestant para-militaries who run an underage brothel might have on site, or be able to put together quickly. Or even you, Tony, a dab hand at engineering. All you'd need was the Semtex. And the Rathcoole Tara Brigade could give you that, too."

"And how did I kill Lily?" Tony snarled.

"I don't think you did kill Lily. I think you divided the work between you. I think you took care of McBain and Ek killed Lily."

"How?"

I shook my head. "I don't know, Tony. I don't really know how he did it. But I'll find out. You know me, mate. I'll find out."

"You've really lost it, pal."

"Have I? What size shoes do you take?"

"What are you talking about?"

I grabbed his shoe. "Size 9, by the looks of it. You were in my back garden. You were scouting my house. You planted the bomb under my car."

Tony kicked himself free of my grip and stood up.

"Like to see you prove any of this shite!" he said.

"I'll show Mrs. Singh your photograph and ask if you came to her house and went through Lily Bigelow's belongings in London."

Derek rang the bell at the bar. "Time, gentlemen, please!"

I put on my raincoat. Tony put on his leather jacket. Derek cast us out into the elemental rain and barred the big, heavy door behind us.

"Why does it have to be me? Why didn't Ek do it all? Why drag me into this?" Tony asked, almost desperately now.

I was surprised to see no one on the road, and I began walking up West Street toward the harbor. We might need people. We might need witnesses.

"Ek had to have help from a local source. Someone who knew about Carrickfergus. Someone who knew the ways of the police. Someone who knew my personal history. Maybe you even staged that whole wallet robbery just so Ek could get a good look at me," I said.

"Why would I do all of this, Sean? What possible reason could there be for me to risk everything to help some Finnish guys I barely knew?"

"I don't know. A big stinking pile of money?"

"You have no proof of any of this," he said again. "It's all just speculation."

"We've arrested Colin Jones at Kinkaid. Maybe he'll talk, or maybe we'll get some of the boys and they'll tell us about the night the Finnish guys came."

"Yeah, they'd really defy the paramilitaries to help a police officer."

"Why would they need to defy the paramilitaries, Tony? I thought this was all a load of rubbish?"

He took a big breath and let it go.

Tony's face visibly relaxed.

He was done with the pretense now.

The acting. The fake indignation.

"So all of this is your own little theory, is it, Sean?" he asked.

"For now it is," I said. "If you come quietly with me, get ahead of the curve, tell me everything, I think we can cut you a pretty good deal."

Tony was smiling. "No one at Kinkaid will talk. They're too afraid of the Tara boys. You'll get nothing from them."

"What will I get from you, Tony?"

"You'll get nothing from me, cos there's nothing to get."

I took the Glock out of my raincoat pocket and pointed it at him. I reached in the other pocket and gave him the handcuffs.

"Put these on," I said. "I'm going to have to take you in for questioning."

"No," he said, softly.

"Come on, Tony, it's over. This is the endgame. You thought you were being clever, but it was incompetent right from the start. All you had to do was look in her hotel bathroom. You would have seen that she had sleeping pills and Valium. You should have faked an overdose that night. We probably would have bought it."

Tony shook his head, rain pouring down the face of a drowned man. "No, not you. Not the dogged fucking Inspector Duffy!"

"Was it for money? Was that the reason? Surely you can't have done all this for money?" I said.

"You don't know what it's like to be broke. To have nothing. To be in debt up to your eyeballs. Kicked out of your adopted country. Going home with your tail between your legs."

"How much, Tony? Was it a million? For both McBain and the girl? Is the factory worth that much?"

"What do you care?" he said.

"Why didn't Ek just kill her in the dungeon and walk out with the others?"

"You would have found a murderer. You're good. You would have questioned everybody on the tour, and you would have discovered the killer. Had to be a suicide, didn't it? Only way."

"And if not a suicide, poor old Underhill takes the fall, eh?"

Tony shrugged.

"How did you do it, Tony?"

He laughed. "Wouldn't you like to know?"

He reached inside his jacket.

"No! Hands where I can see them, Tony. Put these cuffs on," I said.

He laughed again. "I knew you were going to pull some shite like this. I knew it. You had a funny look in your eye all night."

"If you make one more move for that gun, I'm going to plug you."

"Oh, for God's sake, Sean. I took the clip out of your Glock, removed all the bullets, and put it back in the gun. Look at it, if you don't believe me. Go on! I'll put me hands up until you do. No tricks, I promise."

He put his hands up, and I released the clip. It had indeed been stripped of all the rounds.

"See?" he said.

I nodded. This was an endgame all right, but it was Tony's endgame, not mine. He took out his big .45 ACP and pointed it at my chest.

"Your mate Ek pointed a gun at me too," I said.

"But this time there's no Lawson to save you, is there? No witnesses around at all."

Cold rain pouring down our faces. Rainwater pooling on the pavement and running into the gutters. The street the color of mud and straw.

How easy it is to love the dead, how easy it is to let life slip away. *Just close your eyes.*

But now I *was* afraid, and fear releases power. Fear is the precursor of action.

Tony's eyes were savagely alive, and so were mine.

Lightning flashed across the lough in County Down.

"Tell me something: We searched every bin in Carrick for Lily's notebook . . ." I said.

"I knew you would, ya big eejit, which is why I wouldn't let Ek toss it in a bin in Carrick."

"What did you do with it?"

"Cremated," he said with a cruel smile.

Thunder cracked like an earthquake above our heads. Tony flinched, and I pivoted and turned and ran.

I ran hard into the rain.

BOOM went the first .45 round. *BOOM. BOOM.*

Those things *could* stop a charging rhinoceros. Even if one of them only winged me, I'd still be a dead man.

I ran down West Street toward the phone booth outside the post office. The Glock still in my hand, dangling there like a phantom limb.

Tony was right behind me.

"Where are you going, Duffy?" he screamed at me. "I have six more slugs in my clip. You're a dead man, Sean. At least die with some fucking dignity."

BOOM and a car's windscreen shattered.

I ducked behind the phone booth.

BOOM and the phone booth glass blew apart.

BOOM and the window of the post office shattered.

BOOM and the phone booth took another direct hit.

"See? See? This is why we can't have nice things!" Tony laughed.

How many shots was that? Seven? Nine in the clip and one in the chamber, so maybe ten all.... Wait a second. One in the chamber? Tony took the bullets from my clip, but did he remember to clear the chamber?

"Sensible that you've stopped running, Sean. I'll make this quick," he said, walking toward me. He made his way round the phone booth and raised the .45.

I aimed the Glock at his heart and pulled the trigger.

24: THE MINISTRY MAN

Morning. Downstairs. Coffee.

Out to the garden shed. Man world. Toolboxes. Paint tins. Assorted Allan keys and spanners hanging on the wall. Two-thirds of a disassembled Triumph Bonneville lying on the floor. Piles of books, piles of cassettes. A bottle of white spirit. A bottle of poteen. Cigarette papers. Tobacco. Cannabis resin concealed in a Ziploc bag in a tin of engine grease. A comfortable leather chair. A space heater for the cold nights. Stolen orange cone, stolen one direction street sign. Old newspapers. Narwhal horn, bookmark in a book of stories by Lamed Shapiro . . .

I sat in the leather chair and sipped my coffee. The cat purred on my lap.

All was safe here—mechanical, greasy, the way I wanted it. Beth had never bothered me out here. She knew.

I thought about her again. She'd been a keeper. Pretty, funny, snarky. I'd messed it up with her. I'd pushed too hard too early. Sure, there was the age gap, but I could have finessed it if I'd played it better.

If, if, if.

Go to the station today?

Have to think about it.

I'd been given another full week of compassionate leave because I'd had to shoot a man. This time I had to take it. This time I had to not come in. A week was the minimum period for Internal Affairs and the union to conduct their investigation before they let me back into a police station.

It was pro forma. The security cameras at the front of the Northern Bank had seen the whole attempted arrest and gun battle.

Phone ringing in the house. Go up the path to get the bugger.

"Hello?"

No answer.

"Hello?"

Dial tone.

Pricking sensation on the back of my neck.

Again.

They knew I was home.

Whoever *they* were . . .

I went to the hall and got my revolver.

My Glock, of course, had been taken into evidence. But I still had my trusty Smith & Wesson. I hadn't put in my range time recently, but unless they showed up with an RPG or something, I could handle it.

The clock said 9 a.m. An odd time for a hit.

Waiting . . .

Waiting . . .

Might as well make a cup of tea and put the stereo on.

Tea. Stereo. Dozing by the fire, listening to *Klavierstück I* by Wolfgang Rihm. Left hand twitching to the music.

A knock at the front door. Nice that *they* would knock.

Peephole. An older man in a tweed suit. Grey hair.

I opened the door, revolver by my side.

"Mr. Duffy?" he inquired, in a been-through-the-wars Home-Counties accent.

"Yes."

"May I come in?"

"Why?"

"I'd like to speak to you for a few moments, if I may? I know it's awfully early."

"What do you want to talk to me about?"

"I'd rather not discuss that here on the porch."

I looked him over. Sixty-five years old. Umbrella. Expensive shoes. A tailored tweed suit. Slight tan, upright bearing, steady grey eyes. I knew the type: service in the war, a respectable DSO, recruited into the Security Services by a chap he knew at Oxford.

"You can come in," I said.

I let him go first.

"Just in to the right there," I said. "Leave me your coat and umbrella, and I'll hang them up in the hall."

"Thank you," he said.

When he went into the living room, I rummaged through his rain-coat pocket and found nothing—not even a tissue—but the umbrella was made by James Smith and Sons, which confirmed my first impression: some kind of high-level British civil servant, or possibly a *very* classy assassin. It had been raining, but the umbrella and the coat were both dry. *He had a car waiting for him.* The umbrella was hickory, with a silver lap band. Extremely faint letters on the lap band. I held it under the light.

"Lt. J Ogilvy COLDM GDS Sept 2 1944," it said.

"Would you like a cup of tea or a drink?" I yelled into the living room.

"Bit early for me. Do you mind if I smoke?"

"No, go ahead."

I went back into the living room, stoked the fire, sat down opposite him, and gave him the ashtray.

"Wolfgang Rihm?" he inquired, gesturing toward the stereo.

"I'm impressed. I thought I was the only person in Ireland who'd heard of him," I said.

"Not my sort of thing at all," he replied. "But one must keep up with the new developments, mustn't one?"

"If you say so, Mister . . ."

"Oh, I've never been one for surnames, if you don't mind."

"What can I do for you then, Mr. X?"

"Oh, you can call me Jack. Everyone calls me Jack."

He gave me a thin smile. We had reached the portion of *Klavier-stück I* that sounded like a demented child practicing her scales.

"Congratulations are in order, of course. Tony McIlroy turning on you like that. You're lucky to be alive."

"Very lucky. Is that what you want to talk to me about?"

"Do you want to go for a walk?" he asked, looking out of the window. "I think the rain has stopped."

"OK."

When I had first moved here in 1981, it used to be that I could cross the street and walk for ten seconds and be in the Irish countryside, but now they had built houses on the Barn Field and the Barley Field and half of the old cricket pitch. However, if I turned right and walked to Victoria Road and kept walking north, eventually Victoria Road became Victoria Lane—a single, unmetaled track used only by tractors—and there, among the wild blackberry, raspberry, and blackcurrant bushes, we were in another Ireland. An Ireland of stone walls and cattle. An Ireland of fortified bawns, passage tombs, and dolmens. In ten minutes we were centuries displaced from the tarmac and the phone lines and TV.

"Cleansing to be outside. Good for the soul," Jack said.

"If you say so."

"I know that you are not an unreasonable man, Mr. Duffy," he said.

"Then you don't know me very well, Jack," I countered.

He sniffed at that and tipped the ash from the end of his cigarette.

"I've read the report you wrote about what happened with you and Tony McIlroy. I've read your speculations about why Tony McIlroy pulled that gun on you. Fortunately, none of those speculations have so far made it into the media. Have you read the papers?"

"No, I haven't."

"They're saying that McIlroy was drunk and depressed over his resignation from the Met. They're saying that you tried to console him as an old friend, take him out for a nice evening, but after too much booze he just snapped and started shooting blindly into the street with an illegal hand gun. Reluctantly, you had to shoot him, to protect yourself and others. You're something of a quiet hero in a way. Maybe they'll give you a medal."

"You know what really happened. He killed Chief Superintendent McBain."

"The team from Larne RUC that searched his house found no evidence linking your friend with McBain's death."

"The sniffer dogs found trace evidence of Semtex."

"But no actual Semtex."

"He used it all. Tony did it. He as good as confessed. He was an engineer. He got the plastique from the Loyalists and he made two bombs. And he conspired with Harald Ek to kill Lily Bigelow."

"It's certainly an interesting hypothesis, but again, there's zero evidence."

"I'm going to find that evidence. He did it. I know he did it."

"Hunches don't count for anything in court."

We walked a little farther up the muddy lane.

"Did you know that Harald Ek is currently in Dublin, helping set up the Lennätin factory there?"

"I may have heard that somewhere."

"You're not going to try and have him arrested, are you?"

"If I can make the case, I am going to have him arrested."

"To what end?"

"To have him tried for murder."

"You really think the Irish police would extradite a foreign national to Northern Ireland to face a murder trial on the basis of your evidence? I mean to say, old boy, what evidence? Not a sausage. You think they would jeopardize a deal with Lennätin to appease you? And you must be aware that Finland and the United Kingdom do not have an extradition treaty; if he's released on bail, Mr. Ek can simply fly back to Helsinki and there's nothing anyone can do."

"Whom do you work for, Jack?" I asked.

"I don't work for anyone, Mr. Duffy. I'm an unpaid advisor to the government."

"Which government?"

"The British government, of course."

I didn't believe him. "Are you MI5?" I asked.

"I work for the government in a private capacity," he insisted.

"Which department?"

"If you must know, I'm an advisor to the Home Office."

"But you used to be MI5, didn't you? Did you know Kate Albright?"

He thought for a moment and then nodded. "I knew Kate. A remarkable young woman. A great career ahead of her. Such a tragedy."

"What do you think Kate would advise me to do with Mr. Laakso and Mr. Ek?"

"Kate would be telling you exactly what I'm telling you. Drop the case, Inspector Duffy. All you have is supposition. Motive, circumstantial evidence, but no proof of any kind. No proof, in fact, that any crime whatsoever was committed in the case of the young lady. What you're doing is stirring up a lot of trouble for no good reason. Is it a question of justice? Is that it? I thought you were a little too cynical for such a sentiment."

"Again, you thought wrong. Or at least, you thought wrong in this instance."

He dropped his cigarette in a puddle and stood on it.

"If it's a question of justice, then perhaps we can make a representation to the Finnish government through the proper channels. We could show the Finns your evidence and perhaps Mr. Ek will be quietly disciplined..."

I looked him square in his steady, grey-blue eyes. He was offering me a deal of sorts.

"How would that work?"

"You would end your inquiry. When a suitable period has elapsed, your suspicions would be passed to the Finns. They would look into it."

I considered it.

It began to drizzle. Sheep baahed in the field to the left. Cows mooed in the field to the right. Rooks and gulls called out warnings as a hawk soared above them.

"No. I've been to Finland. I know how the system works. It's exactly the same there as here. Laakso and Ek are powerful men. Nothing will come of your representations."

"It's better than nothing, surely."

"I'm not beaten yet."

"That's not what I hear."

"Oh? What do *you* hear?"

"I hear that Larne RUC have dismissed as absurd your take on the McBain murder, and I've heard that the DPP is still pursuing the murder case against Mr. Underhill."

"Underhill will get off. I'll testify in his defense if necessary. And if all my inquiries are dead, why the necessity of this little talk?"

"Because a beaten man, an angry, irrational man, can cause a tremendous amount of trouble. Why not just do what your superiors want you to do and let this one go, eh? Do you fish, Inspector Duffy?"

"No, I don't bloody fish."

"Nevertheless, you understand the concept of cutting the line, don't you?"

"I can't do that. This thing is big. There's kids involved. A conspiracy. I'm not letting that go!"

Jack's eyes widened with alarm.

"Conspiracy? What utter tosh!"

"And I owe it to Lily Bigelow."

"You met her, didn't you?"

"Briefly."

"Yes. They told me there was a personal dimension," he mused. "Most unfortunate."

"Says you."

"It's not just that you met Miss Bigelow, is it? You believe that you were—to use the jargon of our times—socially engineered by Tony McIlroy?"

"If that's the way you want to put it, yes. Him and Ek together. They looked at my old cases and designed a murder just for me."

Jack shook his head. "You mustn't blame yourself," he said sympathetically.

I could tell that he wasn't a bad sort. Just another geezer with a job to do. The job, of course, being me.

We turned and began walking back toward the house. He lit another cigarette with a gold-plated lighter.

"So you think Ek did it?" he said.

"I know he bloody did it."

"Why?"

"To protect his boss. To protect the firm. And because he could. A killer kills, and killing's always been easy for him."

"And if you can prove it?"

"I'll have the Garda arrest him in Dublin and we'll at least attempt to get him extradited up here for a trial."

He shook his head. "That will ignite a scandal that will be the end of the Lennätins' investment in Ireland."

"Let the chips fall where they may."

"A cavalier thing to say. Don't you care about the jobs?"

"What jobs?"

"Five hundred jobs in Dublin. Up to a thousand more over the next five years. Jobs in subsidiary industries up here, too. Mobile phones. The future, Inspector Duffy."

"That's what they said about the DeLorean."

He laughed. "That *is* what they said about DeLorean. But this time it's real. Ireland is poised to be the hub of a growing industry. The industry of the twenty-first century. The future isn't in heavy industry. The future is in information. A literate, English-speaking workforce, highly educated and willing to work for a salary significantly lower than their American counterparts. Thousands of new jobs all over Ireland."

"And a human life? The kids in that institution?"

The pupils in his eyes contracted as he turned to look at me. Examining me, perhaps, like a curious specimen in his collection of beetles. "Sorrow is knowledge, Inspector Duffy, those that know the most must mourn the deepest. The tree of knowledge is not the tree of life."

"Says you."

"I can see that I'm not getting through to you."

We had reached 113 Coronation Road now. We went inside and I gave him his coat and umbrella. I did not invite him into the living room for a drink.

"Or perhaps it's pride? Is that what this is about, Inspector Duffy?" he asked, with a slight and rather unbecoming, sneer on his face.

"What do you mean, 'pride'?"

"A determination to prove everyone wrong about you."

"I don't need to prove anything to anyone."

"I think you do. You must be aware of your RUC record. A less-than-stellar police career, no real high-profile convictions. The fact that you never found out who killed Lizzie Fitzpatrick in that other so-called 'locked room' incident when you were with Special Branch. That fact that, for the last six years, you've been treading water here. A constant source of embarrassment to your superiors, a disappointment to your friends."

"Listen, *Mr. Ogilvy*, it never made it into the newspapers or the RUC files, but I did solve the Lizzie Fitzpatrick case. I found out who killed her and how he did it and why he did it. If Tony McIlroy did social-engineer me, he fucked up. Maybe I'm not a great detective, maybe I'm not even a good detective, but I am fucking persistent. And I am going to find out how Ek did it and I'm going to bring the bastard down for it. The UK government might not like it, the Irish government might not like it, but if I can make a case, the RUC will support me, and the police down south will support me, too. Cops everywhere love nicking villains. Have a nice day."

I closed the door and I watched him go down the path and get into a waiting silver Mercedes.

After he'd gone, I sat down on the living-room sofa, shaking.

Frustration, rage, regret.

"Fucking bastards, the lot of them!" I said to the cat and walked out to the shed and opened the bottle of poteen.

I poured myself half a jam jar of the stuff and diluted it with orange juice. I drank it and stared out through the shed window at the black-birds and the starlings and the rain falling slantwise into the garden.

Aye, Ek and McIlroy had used my own case history against me, my own perceived failures. Failures I had aplenty, but not in this instance. I had *not* been defeated by the locked-room problem like the case file suggested. They were the eejits, not me. Not Carrick CID. Not this time.

But the thing that was killing me was, how did he do it? How did he get away with it? While poor, misguided, desperate Tony McIlroy was off killing Eddie McBain, Ek was killing Lily Bigelow.

"How?" I asked the cat.

The cat meowed. It had no idea.

I poured another glass of poteen.

And another.

I put on the radio, alternating between Radio 3 and Radio 4 and when I got bored of news and classical music I tweaked the shortwave and found Radio Albania, which was preaching Maoism and the glories of the Revolution under Comrade Enver Hoxha.

I was drunk and it was pitch black when the poteen bottle was finally empty.

The rain hadn't ceased the entire day.

I locked the shed door, walked up the greasy garden path, slipped, fell hard on to the cement paving stones.

My head cracked.

Blood poured.

You know what the rest is:

The

rest

is

silence . . .

25: BREAKING THE CASE

Pain. Rain. Excited conversation.

"Jonty, call 999."

"Is he dead?"

"No, he is not! I can see him breathing. Call the ambulance. Go!"

"Did somebody shoot him?"

"No! Away and call the ambulance before I take the back of my hand to you!"

I tried to sit up. I couldn't. My head was on fire. A flashlight in my face.

"Lie there, Mr. Duffy, the ambulance is on its way."

It was Mrs. Campbell from next door with, seemingly, all of her kids. Janette was holding the back of my head.

"Wha—what happened?" I managed.

"You fell on the wet path. You've cut yourself badly. Your wee cat was meowing like mad, otherwise you might have lain here all night and bled to death like your man from *Bridge on the River Kwai*, what's his name?"

Saved by the friggin cat.

The ambulance came.

Three-inch cut across my forehead. Only three inches, *but deep.* Eleven stitches. Overnight in the hospital.

Concussion and vision tests. Everything good. But I still had to endure a lecture from a young doctor about my blood alcohol level.

I listened to the lecture and agreed to change my ways. He released me, and I called in at the station with a bandage around my forehead that everyone thought was a practical joke. I filled the boys in on all the latest developments. Crabbie insisted that I go home. Walked me out, leading me by the elbow.

"Home, Sean, and stay there," he said.

I went to the cake shop, bought a thank-you cake, came home, went next door to the Campbells' with the cake.

"Oh, you shouldn't have, Mr. Duffy. There was no need for that."

"If I can ever do anything for you."

"Well, them'uns in here are all too lazy. Could you take Tricksie for a walk some night?"

"How about now?"

"Shouldn't you be resting?"

"No. Fresh air is what the doc said I need."

Down Victoria Road and on to Downshire Beach.

Raincoat, Wellington boots. Black water.

The usual architecture of destruction: shopping trolleys and rubbish and rusting boats and even the odd wreck of a car. Winding mouths of the Mill Stream and the Lagan. Smell of dead seaweed and chlorine.

Dusk over the Antrim Plateau.

A vast, hypnotic murmuration of starlings.

"How many birds do you think there are up there?" I asked Tricksie.

"About a hundred thousand," a bearded young man with binoculars said behind me.

"Really? That many?"

"Oh, yes. Sometimes the Belfast Lough murmuration can swell to half a million birds, but not at this time of year."

"Why do they do it?"

"Some people say it's to confuse the peregrines and sparrowhawks. But there aren't many peregrines in the lough waters these days. Personally I think they just do it for the pleasure of it."

We watched the starlings carve up the red sky in a complex ballet of sudden turns and abrupt stillnesses and radical changes of direction.

"How do they not bump into each other?" I asked.

"Oh, it's a simple scale-free behavioral correlation. The range scales with the linear size of the flock."

"What?"

"The change in the behavioral state of one animal affects and is affected by that of all other animals in the group, no matter how large the group is."

"I see. You're some sort of scientist then, are you?"

"Nick Baker, University of Ulster," he said, offering me his hand.

"Sean Duffy," I said.

"And what do you do, Sean?"

"I'm in the police."

"And you're also a bird-watcher?"

"No, not really. . . . But this is fascinating."

"Isn't it, though?" he agreed.

"It's all simple mathematics, is it?"

"Yes. If you video a flock like this and freeze-frame it, you can see that each bird affects about a dozen birds around it and that way the whole flock acts almost as one organic entity, like one bird."

"You did this freeze-framing?"

"No! I wish. The application of chaos theory to starling murmuration—that's the kind of thing that gets you in *Nature*, that's the kind of thing that gets you a promotion."

We watched for a few minutes more, until the sun finally set and the starlings roosted for the night. I walked Tricksie home and then set off for the station.

Something Baker had said started a cog whirring in my brain.

The police station was empty but for a few reservists minding the store.

I got a coffee-choc from the machine and went upstairs to the CID evidence room.

I wheeled the TV in there and looked out the CCTV footage from the morning of Miss Bigelow's murder.

Freeze-framing through the tape *after* the portcullis had been raised, from 6 a.m. onward.

I sat in a comfortable leather chair, dimmed the lights.

Half an hour of this.

I put on Radio 3, got another coffee.

I watched the footage.

I watched the footage.

I watched the footage.

I watched the—

I stood up. I pressed pause.

I rubbed my eyes. "*Go raibh maith agat*," I whispered and went as close to the screen as I possibly could.

Was I sure?

I was sure.

I called Constable Bennett in from tech.

"How do I print this out?" I asked him.

He told me a complicated answer that I couldn't follow.

"Can you print it out for me?"

"Aye. Who is that? Is he RUC? He doesn't look like one of ours."

"He's not."

Bennett printed out the still from the video. It was surprisingly good. It would need to be. It would need to stand up in court against the most expensive firm of defense barristers in Northern Ireland. Scrub that. Against the most expensive defense QCs in the whole of the British Isles.

One picture.

This.

I walked to my office and set the picture next to the icon of Mary.

I called McCrabban.

"Hello?"

"Sorry, Crabbie, but I had to wake you."

"What's up?"

"I've got Ek."

"How?"

"CCTV."

"How?"

"I know how he got out of the castle. And I've got proof. He's on the tape."

"I'll be right in."

I called Chief Inspector McArthur. "I think we've got him, sir."

I told him about the CCTV footage. He was surprisingly pleased. Didn't care about the politics. Wanted the arrest.

"What's our next step, Duffy?" he asked.

"Go to Dublin immediately and get the Garda to arrest the murdering fucker."

"Sounds good to me."

26: LIFTING THE PRIME SUSPECT

At 3 a.m. Lawson walked into the incident room.

"Good. You're here. OK, let's go," I said.

"Where?" Lawson asked, befuddled, bleary-eyed, *young*.

"Carrick UDR base," I explained.

"What?"

We bundled him outside to the BMW and drove to the army base in Woodburn. Chief Inspector McArthur was waiting for us in his dress uniform. I'd been right: Lennätin was bringing jobs to Ireland, but both the RUC and the Garda loved nicking villains. He grinned at me and shook my hand.

"Good work, Duffy. Very good work."

"Thanks for arranging the chopper, sir."

He patted me on the back. "Proud to do it, Sean. This is going to be good for both of us. High-profile. Coup for Carrick CID and the station. Win-win."

"Don't forget the Garda."

"Oh yes, the Garda. They'll steal some of our credit, more than likely, the cheeky bastards."

We piled into a big RAF Wessex HC2 troop carrier. We put on headphones and headsets. The pilot turned round to look at us. Moustache, helmet, very big grin. "You chaps must be the grand panjandrums. We've got a vector cleared all the way to Rathmines army base in Dublin. This never happens. What's going on?"

"Sorry, that's classified," I said.

The pilot looked miffed. "Oh well, then, I know when to shut up. . . . Last flight check. Air engines go. Vector nine nine. One zero one."

"All the way to Dublin by RAF helicopter. This is the way to travel, Duffy?" McArthur said. "Garda meeting us on the helipad. Joint arrest. Joint presser. Laurels. TV. The BBC . . ."

"Let's not get ahead of ourselves," McCrabban said, as a hedge against fate.

"Always the pessimist, eh, McCrabban!" McArthur said with a laugh.

He was a pessimist, but I saw it Crabbie's way, too. Laurels were a long way away. Ek would fight extradition to Northern Ireland. He could delay the process for years and it would be a tooth-and-nail battle to keep him locked up for all of that time. But it was better than fucking nothing.

"We're approaching the border," the pilot said into our headphones.

"Jesus, that was fast!" Lawson said.

"Normally this would be an international incident!" the pilot laughed.

But there was no incident, and in the blackness through the window the countryside looked exactly the same.

In no time at all we touched down at the army base in Dublin. We were met by an Inspector Burke and behind him a lot of uniformed upper-rank Garda with satisfied looks on their faces.

"Who are they?" I asked.

"Top brass. Here for a kill. If we're going to destroy a man bringing jobs to Ireland, it's going to be because he's a wrong 'un. He is a wrong 'un, isn't he?"

"You've seen the photo."

"That I have."

"The brass know this is hush-hush, right? We don't want Ek to get the drop on us."

Burke grinned at me. "You really think we're fucking bumpkins, don't you? Since you called me, I've had his place under surveillance. He won't be getting away."

Cop car to Merrion Square. Strike that. Convoy of cop cars to Merrion Square. Lights flashing. No sirens.

"Wait in the vehicle, Inspector Duffy. Can't let his lawyers say that we didn't follow procedure," Burke said.

Burke and his boys went in.

Ek came out in his underpants and a jumper between two big detectives.

Handcuffs on, wild, frightened look to his eyes.

I got out of the car so that he could see me.

He was yelling in Finnish, promises, threats—

He saw me across the street.

He looked drab, old, ignominious, humiliated.

I waved at him, grinned.

"You!" he screamed.

"Me," I said.

They put him in a police car and drove him away.

We had the bastard.

27: HOW HE DID IT

Iknew I was in here as a courtesy. This was Burke's arrest, and until the extradition went through, this was Burke's case. Just the four of us in the interrogation room. Burke, me, Ek, and his lawyer, a Mr. FitzGerald (forty, thin, tanned, smooth, grey-haired, with a Chris de Burgh accent—you know the type).

Everyone else on the other side of the glass: Crabbie, Lawson, McArthur, half the peelers in the station.

The interview room? White stucco ceiling, heavy pine chairs, heavy pine table, ashtrays (both kinds: Liverpool and Man United), big one-way mirror, water jug, glasses, notebooks, HB pencils, spools on an ancient tape deck recording a succession of nows in the lives of the four men whose lives had intersected on this particular spring morning in Dublin's fair city. An intersection of four disparate journeys, joined for a few hours on our way to the grave.

Easy to predict the first part of it. Burke will talk. Maybe I will talk. They'll roll in a TV with video underneath it. They'll play the video. Burke will say something. Mr. FitzGerald will ask us to leave the room.

What I can't predict is what Mr. Ek will say. I somehow think it's not going to be the Finnish equivalent of, "It's a fair cop, gov."

The first part was pro forma.

Burke read the arrest warrant and the charge sheet.

"Murder with malice aforethought of Miss Lily Bigelow in Carrickfergus, in the County of Antrim, on February seventh, 1987 . . ."

Burke asked Ek if he understood the charge.

"I do," Ek said serenely. He was fully clothed now. Showered, shaved, and calmed by the presence of his lawyer.

"Do you understand that the following interview is being taped and that anything you say may be used against you in a court of law in this jurisdiction, or in the jurisdiction where the crime was committed?"

"I do," Ek said.

Burke explained that I was present at the invitation of An Garda Síochána and that I had no powers of arrest here and that Mr. Ek was under no compunction to answer any of my questions. Would Mr. Ek have any objection to my presence in the room during questioning?

FitzGerald opened his mouth to say something, but Ek shook his head and looked at me. He was on the edge of his seat, staring at me in an alien way, the way intelligent birds do, head cocked to one side.

"Why do you think I killed Miss Bigelow, Inspector Duffy?" he asked me, in that calm, rarefied, almost accentless voice of his.

"Shall we show him?" I asked Burke.

Burke nodded. "Let's show him."

A constable wheeled in a TV and video recorder. I gave the constable the copy I'd made of the CCTV tape from the Northern Bank. The constable loaded up the video, turned the TV on, and gave Burke the remote control. Burke grinned and gave the remote to me. Nice of him. I was going to get to administer the *coup de grâce*.

"Cheers," I said under my breath.

I had rewound the tape to the point where the sun was just coming up over Scotland and the streetlights were being switched off along the shore of Belfast Lough.

I pressed play on the remote.

"This is CCTV from the Northern Bank in High Street, Carrickfergus, on the morning of the murder. This camera was placed at the rear of the bank, and within its field of view we can see the Marine Highway and the entrance to Carrickfergus Castle. Miss Bigelow was killed in the castle sometime between five p.m. and eight p.m. on the night of the seventh, according to the autopsy report. We know that because Mr. Underhill locked the building up at six p.m. and then lowered the castle portcullis—which weighs two and a half tons and can only be raised and lowered from the inside. The castle was essentially sealed from six p.m. until six a.m. the next morning. Miss Bigelow was murdered in the castle dungeon by someone who entered with her on the evening of the seventh. We know that she entered the building with her murderer because the castle has sixty-foot-high walls and no one climbed over those walls during the night, which we know for certain because there are CCTV cameras pointing at the castle from the harbor and the Marine Highway and the Northern Bank. We have reviewed those tapes and will certainly make them available to you, Mr. FitzGerald."

"Thank you," FitzGerald said cautiously, sensing that something bad was coming.

"Just to make clear, someone could not have entered the main gate of the castle because the portcullis had been lowered from the inside. Furthermore, the main gate of the castle is also covered by a CCTV camera."

"This is Inspector Burke speaking, and for the record, I, too, have reviewed the CCTV camera footage and I am confident that no one entered or left the castle between the hours of six p.m. and just before six a.m., when the body was found."

"That's all very well, but you've said nothing about my client," Mr. FitzGerald interjected.

I nodded and pointed at the TV screen. "I beg your patience for a few more minutes . . ."

I pressed play on the VCR. I fast-forwarded at double speed.

Crisp, oddly beautiful black-and-white videotape. Dramatic early-morning sun throwing giant shadows over the castle gate. A white-coated milkman delivering two bottles and a block of cheese. Starlings flitting in toward the bottles. The sun rising over County Down. The shadows changing. . . . Nothing for a long time, then two constables, WPC Warren and Detective Constable Lawson approaching the gate. Lawson bangs on the gate. It opens. Lawson leaves WPC Warren outside to secure the crime scene. Smart lad, I think, every time. A dozen forensic officers show up from Belfast, clad in white boilersuits. They nod to WPC Warren and go inside the castle. Lawson leaves and goes down to the car park to meet me. Lawson and I walk up the steps and go inside the castle. Nothing for a long time and then . . .

Well then, the whole case . . .

A forensic officer in a white boilersuit carrying a bag walks past WPC Warren and out of shot. The hood of the boilersuit is up, but his face is visible from this angle. WPC Warren doesn't bat an eye.

I stopped the tape.

"You may have noticed the forensic officer leaving the castle," I said.

Ek's lips puckered ever so slightly.

"Let me show you a close-up of that forensic officer."

Burke handed me a folder and I took out the 8 × 10 glossy that I'd had printed up last night.

It was Ek in the white forensic-officer-style boilersuit walking straight past WPC Warren, who didn't even look at him. Didn't even register him. Ek examined the photograph and passed it to FitzGerald.

"You thought you'd committed the perfect crime, didn't you? You thought it would be seen as a suicide, or, if not a suicide, then the only possible killer was the only man in the castle at the time: Mr. Underhill," I said with some small measure of satisfaction creeping into my voice.

Ek smiled and shook his head sadly. "There is no such thing as perfection."

FitzGerald put a hand on his client's arm and looked at Burke. "You are not to take that as an admission of guilt, no such admission was implied or offered."

I unclicked the pause button and rewound to Ek leaving the castle on the morning of the murder.

"You entered Carrick Castle with Miss Bigelow. Tony McIlroy had acquired an RUC forensic officer uniform, which you brought with you in a bag. While you killed Miss Bigelow, McIlroy was going to make or get a bomb to kill Chief Superintendent Ed McBain. At some point in Carrickfergus Castle you must have lured Miss Bigelow to the dungeons, perhaps telling her that you had a story for her about Mr. Laakso. She did not suspect foul play. You killed her in the dungeon with a blow to the head—"

"Mr. Ek is an elderly man," FitzGerald interrupted. I ignored him and continued.

"At that point you had a choice, Ek. You could have left the castle with everyone else. No doubt the body would have been found and you and your party would have been suspects in Miss Bigelow's murder as well as everyone else who was in the castle at the time. But you and Tony both knew that if Lily's body was found before Ed McBain died, Ed would know you killed her. She'd talked to Ed about her suspicions and you knew it. Ed had to die before he knew about Lily's death, before he could set the alarm bells ringing. So you carried out a much more audacious plan. You hid in the dungeon with Miss Bigelow, concealing yourself and concealing her body from Underhill's flashlight. Maybe you watched him and moved the body to a place he'd already searched. Maybe you just stuck it out in a shady corner. Wouldn't matter, anyway, if Underhill found you. You'd just kill him, too and make it look like a murder-suicide. The crucial thing was that Underhill couldn't report the death until you knew Ed McBain couldn't do anything about it. So you hid there until you were sure that Underhill had gone to bed for the night, then you carried her body up to the roof of the keep, removed her notebook, hooked her bag round her arm, put her shoes on the wrong feet, and then threw her off the roof. Then you went back to the dungeon to wait until morning. Tony had told you that forensic officers from the RUC forensic team would soon be on the scene. He was correct. With a dozen boilersuited forensic officers milling about the castle courtyard, it was easy for you to simply walk out of the front gate."

A little groan came from Ek's lips.

"My client admits nothing," FitzGerald said. He patted Ek on the back and whispered something in his ear. Ek nodded, took a deep breath, and regained his composure. He leaned back and looked at me and Burke.

"That is not me leaving the castle. I was in the Coast Road Hotel at the time."

"I think we'll let a jury decide that," I said.

"My client will vigorously oppose extradition to Northern Ireland, where his safety may be in jeopardy and a fair trial cannot be guaranteed in the current terrible circumstances," FitzGerald said.

I nodded and passed the TV remote to Burke.

I leaned into Ek's face. "What was that expression you used in the Go game? *Kami no Itte*—the divine move, was that it?" I asked.

"*Kami no Itte*," he agreed, and gave a little half-smile.

I nodded at Burke and walked out of the office.

An old-school police bar, three hours later:

Guinnesses. Smokes. All the cops. North and South.

Convo:

"See his face?"

"FitzGerald was furious. Red as a beetroot."

"Cross border co-op. This is the way it should be."

"Drinks on me."

I took Burke to one side. "You can't allow him to have bail. He's a flight risk."

"Don't worry, Duffy. This is a very high-profile case for us, now. We'll keep him safe and sound. We're not all messers down here."

"You're wasted in the Garda," I said getting him a whisky.

"You're wasted in the RUC."

"If we'd been serious about police careers, we both should have nipped across the sheugh and joined the NYPD a decade ago."

"I'll drink to that."

Many drinks later, we hit the helipad.

28: THE OAKMAN SURPRISES EVERYONE

Subdued on the helicopter ride back to Carrick.

Let down, somehow. Hadn't everything turned out the way we were expecting? What were we expecting? Fireworks? A teary confession? Not us. We were old stagers. You leave that stuff for the flicks and the telly. But still. . . . That little half-smile of his. As if this was all part of the plan when it couldn't have been. The plan had been to do it and get away with it.

Even so, it niggled.

The idea that possibly he was still one move ahead, when he wasn't. We had nailed him.

Sure, he'd fight the extradition and apply for bail, but the Garda weren't idiots, they'd oppose bail, and if it was granted there would be conditions and he'd be watched. They wouldn't want to lose him.

Chief Inspector McArthur blabbing away the whole flight. Only Lawson was listening to him. I was ignoring him and Crabbie was pretending to be asleep.

Touchdown at the UDR base in Woodburn.

Car back to the barracks.

Grins all around. Lofty talk: the UTV news, maybe the BBC, certainly print media . . .

Agree. Agree. Agree.

Sanctuary of my office with its view of Belfast Lough and Carrick Castle.

Next morning I volunteered for riot duty just to get some action. No one could see the bandage under the riot helmet.

A day of riding in Land Rovers. Of shields and formations and

Molotovs. Cop banter. Milk bottles filled with piss or petrol tumbling through the air. Seen it all before. Too bored even to describe it.

Home. Dinner. TV. *Two Ronnies. EastEnders. Wogan. Newsnight.* The National Anthem. No sleep.

Time went by. Bed. Breakfast. Another day at the office. Lawson's face peeking round the door.

"Cup of tea, guvnor?"

"Aye, why not?"

"Sergeant McCrabban wants to know if it's OK to clear the incident room. Start putting things into boxes . . ."

"Yeah, good idea. Not the basement, though. Keep it handy. The lawyers will want to start extradition proceedings asap and God knows what they'll need."

Lawson came back with the tea.

Good lad. Two sugars, McVitie's plain chocolate biscuits.

"Thanks, son," I said.

"You're welcome, sir."

Standing there. Gormless. Crooked smile—he's not going to ask for a transfer, is he?

"Yes, Lawson?"

"Quite a forty-eight hours, sir."

"Indeed."

"My first time in a helicopter."

"It's exciting, isn't it?"

"Very. When do you think we'll actually get him, sir?"

"For the trial?"

"Yes. I know you don't like us to take it personal, sir, but I can't wait to see that bastard in the dock of the Crown Court."

"It'll be months, Lawson, maybe even years. His lawyers will fight it all the way, and extradition from the North to the South and vice versa is never bloody easy."

Lawson seemed downhearted.

"Don't worry, Young Lochinvar. He can delay it, but he can't stop it. We've got a good case here, and even a dozy old judge is going to see that."

292   RAIN DOGS

More prescience. More Mystic Meg.

And, as usual, I was wrong.

Two days later.

Back home from the chippie and the offie with a pastie supper and a six pack of Bass.

Mrs. Campbell from next door standing on my doorstep.

"Used my spare key to get in, your bloody phone was going mad. Ken couldn't sleep and you know he's on nights, so I hope you don't mind."

"Uh, well . . ."

"It's OK, I answered it. It was a boy from down South. Burke, his name was. Said he would try you later. I asked if he could wait until tea time, when Ken should be up and he said OK."

"Uhm, thanks, Mrs. C."

I called Burke's office number, but he'd gone for the day. I tried him at home, but he wasn't there.

I waited by the phone. Ate my dinner. Drank my beer.

Something was cooking, but what?

I called Crabbie at the station, but as far as he knew, all was quiet.

TV and records. Finally a late-night phone call.

I wasn't in bed yet.

Bring-bring, bring-bring, bring-bring . . .

Into the hall.

"Burke?"

"It's not Burke, it's me, McArthur. Did I wake you?"

"I was still up, sir."

"Aye, no doubt, were you watching the snooker?"

"No, sir, I was listening to a record."

"Yeah, well, I hope you're sitting down. You're not going to believe this, Duffy. He hasn't opposed our request. Nothing. Full cooperation. He's on his way up right now."

"What are you talking about? Who is?"

"Ek."

"What?"

"He didn't object to the extradition request. He's on his way up tonight."

"He didn't object to the—Are you sure?"

"Perfectly sure. I've just been tipped off by newly promoted Chief Superintendent Strong."

"That doesn't make any sense."

"It makes sense if he wants to get the trial over with."

"Only if he thinks he can win, and he's not going to win."

"Are you positive?"

"You've seen the evidence, sir," I said, not completely confidently.

"And if he's planning to cop a plea, Duffy?"

"Cross that bridge when we come to it, sir."

"No, we can't be blindsided. We need a policy in place, now. You and me. We need to have this figured out before Strong gets on the blower again."

I held the phone away from my head.

My thoughts of two days ago.

We didn't want him to get away with it, but could I really risk taking that video to a jury? All it needed was one ignorant fuckhead on the panel to say that one peeler in a boilersuit looked like every other peeler in a boilersuit.

"I want him for premeditated murder, because that's what it was, but if he confesses, I could give the DPP a recommendation of guilty of manslaughter, rather than murder, because of diminished responsibility."

"How so, diminished responsibility?"

"He was in four wars. That's bound to do something to your head."

"Right. OK. I'll see you tomorrow. They'll be taking him to Castlereagh. Presumably the detectives there will give us an interview first thing in the morning. And then we'll need to go to court to oppose bail. So dress up, Duffy. A suit."

"I'll do that."

He hung up. I called Crabbie and Lawson.

They couldn't figure it out, either.

Why would Ek and his lawyers not oppose extradition? He could have held this thing up for years. . . . Every defense lawyer knew that it was always better to delay: the evidence goes stale, memories go bad, all the more opportunity for introducing reasonable doubt.

I had two fingers of Laphroaig to help me sleep, but it didn't work. I tossed and turned and couldn't sleep.

My unconscious knew something my consciousness didn't quite appreciate yet: The devious Mr. Ek was up to something.

29: *KAMI NO ITTE*—THE DIVINE MOVE

Clouds over the Knockagh monument. A storm over the condemned city of Belfast. Elemental rain: cold and tinged with hail. Lightning, thunder, End of Days stuff . . . the usual. The three of us in the Land Rover driving up to Castlereagh Holding Center in East Belfast—the main and most secure remand center for all suspected criminals in Ulster.

McCrabban was driving and I was up front with him. Lawson was sitting all by himself in the back. Rain drumming on the steel roof. Window wipers on full tilt. Hypnotic.

My mind drifting. None of this made any sense. As the Robot in *Lost in Space* was wont to say: *This did not compute.*

Castlereagh Holding Center wasn't far from Mount Stewart, the ancestral seat of Lord Castlereagh himself. Ill-omened place. Ill-omened man. Byron said of his grave in Westminster Abbey: "Posterity will ne'er survey / A nobler grave than this / Here lie the bones of Castlereagh / Stop, traveler, and piss." Shelley said: "I met Murder on the way / He had a mask like Castlereagh."

Murder on the way, indeed.

We drove up the A23, through rainy East Belfast, until we hit the front gates of the notorious holding center. In the bad old days of the 1970s, suspects here had gotten the rubber-hose treatment, and it still had a horrible reputation. Recently the chief constable had taken Amnesty International and the American media on a tour, but all the old suspicions and rumors died hard. Not that Ek was going to get anything but the absolute by-the-book treatment. Even the stupidest reservist wouldn't want to mess with his legal representation.

We showed our passes at the gate and parked the Land Rover by the "bomb-proof" outer wall.

We got soaked in the car park, went through the double doors, and were met by a man with a clipboard.

"Inspector Duffy?"

"That's us," I said.

"This way, if you please."

He led us to a desk sergeant who made us not only sign in but wear name badges and surrender our weapons, too, which was a first. An unpleasant first. Naked without a sidearm even if it was useless against the most likely form of attack up here: mortars or coffee-jar bombs chucked over the wall.

A long, green corridor covered with wanted posters and government warnings about honey traps and booby traps and mercury tilt switch bombs.

Stairs down to the basement. Buzzing striplights added to the ominous feeling. Another corridor, another level. Strobing fluorescent lights sending us messages from the future. What messages? Bad stuff. It's always bad stuff.

"Here," the constable with the clipboard said.

We entered the room.

Bog-standard RUC i/v room. Desk, chairs, tape machine. Three Castlereagh detectives, an RUC stenographer, and a woman who appeared to be the tea lady. Ek was sitting there with his Dublin lawyer, FitzGerald, and a local lawyer, a QC called Sir Evelyn Grimshaw, whom I knew from the telly and the front pages of the *Belfast Telegraph*. Grimshaw was establishment: Inst, QUB, the London Bar, the Belfast Bar. He was a glum-looking bloke with a Deputy Dawg face and a droopy, brown moustache; but looks were definitely deceiving in his case—he was a take-no-prisoners silk who'd worked both sides of the court. Two years back, an RUC motorcycle cop had tried to get him for speeding, and Grimshaw had fucked with the man so badly he'd ended up getting demoted and posted to Strabane.

"It's quite the throng in here," I said. "You think we could maybe clear the room a little?"

We managed to kick out the stenographer, the tea lady, and two of the Castlereagh coppers. Lawson and McCrabban retreated behind the mirror, but Ek insisted on keeping both of his lawyers, or rather, both of the lawyers insisted for him.

Ek said nothing. "Your show, Duffy," one of the Castlereagh detectives said, and smiled.

I looked at the remaining Castlereagh detective, who offered me the lead interview chair opposite Ek.

I sat down, turned on the tape machine, told it who was in the room, the time and date.

I offered Ek and the two lawyers a Marlboro. They all refused. I lit one myself.

"Mr. Ek, you've voluntarily waived your objections to extradition and have thus been brought here this morning to face murder charges in the case of Miss Lily Bigelow. You are being charged with premeditated murder with malice aforethought. Do you understand the nature of the charge that is being leveled against you?"

Ek nodded. "Before you begin your questions, Detective, I wish to make a short statement."

I looked at the two lawyers. Grimshaw was practically begging me to kick up a stink, but I couldn't care less. "Go ahead, Mr. Ek, be our guest. Say what you like."

Ek gave me a little nod.

Could this be it? The confession? Maybe he wanted it over and done with. Sooner or later, they all wanted it over and done with.

Ek pointed at the microphone, and the lawyer moved it closer.

"My name is Harald Ek, I wish to state for the record that I intend fully to cooperate with the authorities in Northern Ireland in their investigation into the death of Miss Lily Bigelow."

"You're not confessing?" I blurted out.

"I do not wish to confess to a crime I did not commit," Ek said.

"Do you deny that's you on the video?" I asked.

"It is not me on the video because I was not there. Clearly you suspect me of being guilty of this crime and have *tampered* with the evidence to produce this tape."

"That's ridiculous," I said.

"Yeah, the RUC's never fitted up a suspect before, especially not here in Castlereagh . . . oh, and for the record that was sarcasm," Grimshaw said. "Mr. Ek came here because he wishes his part in this sorry affair to be done with as quickly as possible, so that the RUC can find the real perpetrator or perpetrators of this crime."

"You are denying that that's you on the tape? That's going to be your defense?" I asked, incredulously.

"That isn't my client on tape. It can't be, because he wasn't there," Grimshaw said.

All this time, Ek hadn't taken his eyes off me, a sad little smile on his thin lips.

The room was spinning and I could feel this little pro forma hearing running away from me. But as Muhammad Ali would say, a great boxer makes his opponent fight *his* fight on his terms. I had done this a hundred times; he was in my arena. Ek was in the chair. My fucking chair. In my fucking room. In my fucking city. I stubbed out my cigarette, leaned forward, whispered: "We know it was you, Ek. And the jury will take one look at that videotape, and they'll know that it was you, too. Do you really want to spend the next twenty-five years of your life in the Maze Prison? Since you're not a paramilitary, you'll be in your own wing. All by yourself. Like Rudolf Hess. Twenty-five years of grey walls and grey food and grey rain while you go quietly mad. Is that what you want, Mr. Ek?"

"That is what *you* want, Detective. I want the truth about Miss Bigelow's death to become known, which is why I have surrendered myself."

"You'll have a bail hearing later on today, Mr. Ek. The RUC will oppose bail and you'll be remanded in custody. You'll be taken to prison and tonight will be the first night of those long twenty-five years."

"You seem to be suggesting an alternative, Inspector Duffy," Grimshaw said.

"If Mr. Ek were to plead guilty and give us a full confession, the RUC would recommend to the director of public prosecutions that he be charged with manslaughter rather than murder, the lesser charge due to diminished responsibility on account of Mr. Ek's traumatic military service in multiple combat theaters."

"Involuntary manslaughter, with no minimum custodial period," Grimshaw said quickly.

"We can discuss that after the full confession," I replied immediately.

Grimshaw looked at Mr. Ek, who still hadn't taken his eyes off me.

"What do you think?" Grimshaw whispered to his client.

Ek said nothing.

"We'd like a few moments alone with our client, if we may," FitzGerald said.

"Certainly, we'll give you the room," I said.

"A different room. Without a one-way mirror and a tape recorder," Grimshaw said.

"Outside, perhaps?" Ek asked. "I think it is going to snow."

The Castlereagh boys led them to a small inner courtyard with a stunted apple tree, a couple of benches, and a pond with sad-looking fish in it.

Ek sat on the bench with his two lawyers while we watched them through the window. All three men in expensive overcoats, expensive scarves, expensive shoes. They talked. We said nothing, waiting behind the glass. Ek turned to look at us staring at him. He smiled and stood and examined the early apple blossom on the tree, and then, to his evident delight, it began to snow.

Snowflakes like the morning of the murder.

"They've had enough fucking time," I said, and pushed the door open and went outside.

"Right, lads. Parley's over. Back to the interview room."

Ek shook his head. "I will go back to the cell and wait for my appearance in court."

I looked at Grimshaw. "What the fuck is this?"

"My client will plead not guilty this afternoon. See you in court, Inspector Duffy."

I restrained a sudden urge to scuff up the leather of his shoe with the mucky bottom of my DM.

"That you will, Mr. Grimshaw, that you will."

Belfast Central Criminal Court, two hours later.

In fight speak: round 2.

All three of us again: McCrabban, Lawson, me.

Three of them: Grimshaw, Ek, FitzGerald.

But the odds weren't even remotely as close as that. A recommendation against bail from an RUC detective inspector would, in most cases, be enough for the judge to remand a defendant in custody.

"The Crown opposes bail. Mr. Ek is from a wealthy family and is clearly a flight risk," the Crown prosecutor said.

"Mr. Ek has voluntarily surrendered himself to this jurisdiction," Grimshaw said.

"Mr. Ek did no such thing. He was extradited from the Irish Republic under an international arrest warrant."

"Mr. Ek did not oppose extradition."

The judge looked at the case notes. "The RUC opposes bail?"

"We do, your honor," I said.

"Considering the nature of the charges against the defendant, bail cannot be set at this time," the judge said.

Round 2 to me, I think.

And yet . . .

And yet, the bastard was still smiling as they led him away in handcuffs.

I didn't like the smile.

I didn't like that smile one bit, but it was over to the prosecutors now.

We drove back to the station.

The snow, as it nearly always does, had turned to rain.

I was uneasy all afternoon. I sat in my office, watching the lough furtive with the movement of birds. The taste in my mouth was acrid and metallic.

"Tea?" Lawson asked.

I drank tea, ate McVitie's digestives, nursed two fingers of Jura whisky.

The clock ate segments of my life on its way round to five o'clock. The day shift went home. I sent Lawson and the reservists home. McCrabban was duty detective, but I stayed with him.

Waiting.

For the bell announcing the next round.

The bell I knew was coming.

Pasta for dinner.

A beer and another whisky or two for me. Lemonade for McCrabban.

At seven, Lawson came back in. "Feeling jumpy, boss. Couldn't stay at home."

Darts in the rec room. Me on double forty to win the game. The phone ringing in the incident room. McCrabban put down his pipe and ran to get it.

Lawson and I followed.

Silent film mode: McCrabban putting the receiver down, looking at us, horror-struck. Me spilling a dart, Lawson dropping a file onto the floor.

"What is it?" Lawson asked.

"He's been released. An 'extraordinary' bail hearing, asked for by Grimshaw, was granted by Sir Michael Havers, and at that hearing he was released into the custody of the Finnish consulate in Belfast."

"What the hell does that mean?"

"I, I don't know. . . . House arrest?"

"Passport surrendered?" I asked.

"I don't know."

"Jesus."

Lawson was the first to react. He picked up the phone and called the airport police at Aldergrove. He told them Ek's details and said that he'd fax them a photograph and the passport number.

"On no account is he to be allowed into the departures area!" Lawson insisted.

He hung up and began dialing the City Airport.

Jolted into life, McCrabban and I alerted the other exit routes: the docks at Larne and Belfast and all the official border crossings.

RAIN DOGS

"Who's Sir Michael Havers again?" Crabbie asked.

"The attorney general of England, Wales, and Northern Ireland!" I said.

"Uh oh. So this is a pretty high lev—"

"Yeah, I don't care! We're finding this clown. Lawson, we need to see if he's really in the consulate, and if he is, a team of watchers need to be put on him twenty-four hours a day. I want a copy of that bail order and the bail conditions," I said.

"Done," Lawson said, and got on the blower.

"I want that bastard found. If he's in the consul's house, I want to know it, if he's in the consulate itself, I wanna know. I want a Polaroid of him, wherever the hell he is, pronto. And while you do that, I'm calling the attorney general and giving that baldy bastard a piece of my mind."

"Sean," McCrabban said, and gave me the look.

"OK, forget that last thing, but all the rest. Until we have eyes on Ek twenty-four hours a day, I don't want any chance at all that he'll give us the slip! Better call Chief Inspector McArthur, too. Christ, call everybody. Get my MP on the line. Get bloody Gerry Adams and the pope on the phone, too."

The High Court faxed us the conditions of Ek's bail. He was required to remain in a private residence, 11 Ruddles Court, White-abbey, until his remand hearing in May. He was allowed to leave the building to shop, exercise, and play golf. He had to remain in 11 Ruddles Court from 10 p.m. until 7 a.m.

I passed the fax to Lawson.

"Find out who owns this 11 Ruddles Court," I said.

"The Finnish consul general owns the house," Lawson told me a few minutes later.

The chief inspector appeared wet and bedraggled and didn't understand the ashen looks. "So he's been released on bail, what's the big deal? They won't let him leave the jurisdiction, will they?" he said.

We glared at him until he left the office, muttering something about needing a towel.

"This police station must lie at the intersection of two evil lay lines," I muttered. "We never get a break."

"More than two. Half a dozen," McCrabban said. "If I believed in such pagan nonsense, which I don't."

The phone rang. It was the airport police at the Harbor Airport. Ek had been held at the second line of security, attempting to board the direct flight to Amsterdam. I grinned at the lads.

"Thank God! That, boys, is a prima facie breach of bail conditions, within hours of being released. The High Court isn't going to like that, attorney general or no attorney general. He'll never be able to pull a stunt like this again."

The chief inspector came in again to share the good news.

"He had us panicking there for a minute, didn't he?" McCrabban said.

"That he did, Crabbie. That he did."

"Now we can lift him ourselves and take him to Carrick Police Station," Lawson said. "We can handle the whole process, cut those Castlereagh guys out of it."

"We'll take the Beemer. You'll not object to a bit of speed, Chief Inspector, will you?"

"Not I," he said, uncertainly.

Downstairs to the BMW.

It's exactly ten miles from Carrickfergus RUC station to Belfast Harbor Airport. Bit of dual carriageway, bit of motorway, a tricky bit through the center of Belfast. Still, it was a Beemer and I had my *Starsky & Hutch* siren, so would you believe eight minutes? Because eight minutes it was. Not quite a complete track on a Yes album.

Screeching tires. White knuckles. Crabbie aged by ten years.

Run through the airport. Meet the airport peelers.

"Mr. Ek? The Finnish guy?"

"This way."

A holding cell in the customs area. A Finnish man.

Not Ek.

"Let me see the passport."

It *was* Ek's passport. What the fuck?

I passed it to the lads.

I walked to the Finnish man. Older than Ek by several years, but not completely dissimilar in appearance. "Who are you? Who put you up to this?"

He shrugged his shoulders. "No English."

I turned to McCrabban, Lawson, and McArthur.

"If we're here, where is he?"

"At that house on Ruddles Court?" McCrabban said.

"Like hell he is. We've got to stop all Finnish nationals from leaving Northern Ireland."

"Can we do that?" Lawson asked.

"We don't want an international incident," McArthur said.

"We'll do it. We'll bloody fucking do it," I said, jabbing my finger into McArthur's chest.

"Why would they do something like this?"

I groaned. "So that we would come here and Mr. Ek would slip out of Belfast International Airport with this joker's passport."

Back to the Beemer.

110 mph to Belfast International Airport at Aldergrove.

Through security.

The BA desk.

"Yes, there was one Finnish national on the six p.m. flight to Copenhagen, connecting to Helsinki."

We looked at the clock.

8:15 p.m.

"Please tell me that the flight was delayed."

"The flight left on time."

"It's supposed to touch down, when?"

"Uhm, round about now."

I looked at McArthur.

"Any ideas?"

"Interpol?"

"Interpol," I agreed with a groan, knowing their bureaucracy of old.

By the time Interpol issued an international arrest warrant, Ek's flight had touched down at Copenhagen and had landed at Helsinki.

We had lost him. Lost him for good.

The next morning, the Finnish consul in Belfast was summoned to a meeting with the secretary of state for Northern Ireland. It was reported to be "cordial."

Cordial?

We sat in the incident room, staring at each other in a state of shock all day. Local TV loved the story, but it was only the third item on the national news.

Lawson did the research and confirmed what we already knew: there was no extradition treaty between Finland and the UK. But there was between Finland and the Irish Republic. If he'd skipped bail down South, he could have been shipped back. But not from here. Not from Northern Ireland in the UK. He'd completely out-generaled us.

"Is this what defeat tastes like?" Lawson said.

"It is. Get used to it," I said.

We went home at quitting time because we couldn't think of anything else to do. I bought a bottle of vodka from the offie and a fish supper from the Victoria Hot Spot. I ate the chips and gave the fish to the cat. I made a vodka gimlet, easy on the lime and soda. I listened to "Master of Puppets" and "Ace of Spades" and "Crazy Train." Yeah, I was in that kind of mood.

At just before midnight, the phone rang.

"Hello?"

"I need someone to go with me to Liverpool. Will you go with me?"

It was Beth. I knew immediately what she was talking about.

"Is it mine?"

"Does it make any difference?"

"I think it does. A bit."

"It's yours."

"And you don't want to keep it?"

"I knew you'd be all Catholic on me. I should never have called. Fuck."

She hung up.

I called her right back. "I'll go with you. When do you want to go?"

"Tomorrow."

"Do you have the tickets booked?"

"No."

"I'll take care of it. You want the night boat?"

"I suppose."

"I'll pick you up at six."

"OK."

30: WHAT DEFEAT TASTES LIKE

City of dreadful night. City of the damned. City of no escape. Rain hisses onto the cobbles and the open drains. The city hums and seethes. The black Farset bubbles to the surface of High Street, oozing human filth. The rusting giant cranes droop over the empty dry docks like the bones of dead gods. Army helicopters sweep the city with a sick white light.

Eyeblink.

Rain.

The Beemer's headlights carving up the black Lagan, shimmering on the forbidding walls of the Westlink. Belfast is the prototype of a new way of living. In 1801 it was a muddy village, by 1901 it was one of the great cities of the Empire, and now Belfast is the shape of things to come. Everywhere is going to look like this soon enough after the oil goes and the food goes and the law and order goes.

Ormeau Road to Rugby Avenue. Rugby Avenue to Cairo Street.

Bottom of Cairo Street, near Agincourt.

There she is, waiting outside in the rain, demonstrating her lack of concern for her personal well-being, for her own body. *I've already made my decision and you're not talking me out of it, Duffy.*

I scope myself in the rearview. *Look at you. Aren't you supposed to be a policeman? Aren't you supposed to enforce the law? Abortion is illegal on the island of Ireland. On both sides of that porous, wiggly-line border. Assisting someone in the procurement of an abortion is a criminal offense under the catch-all clause of the Offenses Against the Persons Act (1861).*

Slow the car, flash the lights.

She's brought a bag with her. Before I can get out to help her, she's in the front seat. Her hair's longer and she's dyed it jet-black. It doesn't suit her.

"Whew!" she says. "Some night."

Some night. Aye.

"Where to, the ferry?"

"Did you get the tickets?"

"Cabin. We're all set."

"Good. Thank you, Duffy."

"No problem."

"You know I can't go to my family."

"I know."

"I knew I could count on you."

"Yes."

Car into gear, window wipers on max. Desperate for the radio, but the mood's not right.

Back up to the Ormeau Road.

"I heard about you and Tony McIlroy. I called you. I called you, but you weren't home. Terrible business. I'm so sorry, Sean."

"It's all right."

"Are you OK? Were you hurt?"

"I'm fine."

"And somebody told me you helped to get that Kinkaid place shut down. Read about it in the *Sunday World*."

"I wasn't responsible for the place shutting down. That was a recommendation of the RUC Sex Crimes Unit in Newtownabbey. It was only a pilot scheme anyway and the Northern Ireland Office didn't choose to carry on with it."

"Look at you, dodging the credit as usual."

"Not much credit to dodge, actually. In theory it was a good idea, but the paramilitaries had infiltrated the place, destroyed it. The prison service won't try anything like that again here. Shame, really."

"What about your murder case? Did that work out in the end?"

"We found who did it. In Ireland, you always find out who did it."

"But . . ."

"But they're never going to go up for it."

She lit a cigarette. Camel. Unfiltered. *Should you be smoking that?*

You know, what with you up the spout and everything, is a line I don't use. This time tomorrow, it won't make any difference.

"Got one for you, Duffy."

"OK."

"Why do anarchists only drink herbal tea?"

"I don't know."

"Because all proper tea is theft."

"You should put your seat belt on."

"You're not doing it."

"I'm exempt."

"Seat belts. Jesus. Nobody ever wore seat belts before Jimmy Savile told us to on the telly. Fucking Jimmy Savile."

"Amen to that."

She's older. She looks older. The BMW drives up Corporation Street and at the traffic light turns right on to Dock Street.

"Ever been to Liverpool before?" she asks.

"Only to Anfield."

A man with a clipboard in a duffel coat. The rain lashing him.

"Where to?" he asks.

"Liverpool boat."

He nods and points.

The BMW joins a queue of cars and vans navigating their way onto the ferry.

We drive up a metal ramp, and a man in a high-visibility jacket tells us where to park the Beemer on the car deck.

I kill the engine, take out the key. "No turning back now," she says.

"I'm a policeman. I can do whatever I want. You wanna go back? Easy."

She shakes her head. "Let me see this cabin you've picked out. I'm expecting luxury."

I look at her forced smile. It just about breaks my heart.

"This way, then."

Out onto the boat deck. Queasy. The deck moving up and down and laterally against the buoys and fenders.

Engine throbbing. The smell of diesel and lough water and the sewage works on Queen's Island and the cigarette factory on the York Road.

"I think I'm going to be sick," she says.

"Not surprised. Let's go up."

Up three flights of metal steps to the cabins. A problem with the steward finding our room that a fiver sorts out.

I've paid for a top-of-the-line cabin, which turns out to be two narrow bunks, a rinky-dink wash basin, and a tiny window that you can barely see through. On both beds there are complimentary copies of the *Daily Mail*, a bar of soap, and a pair of shoelaces.

Presumably to hang yourself with? I think while picking up the laces and chucking them in the rubbish bin.

She sits on the bottom bunk, takes off her shoes, and puts on a pair of slippers.

"I'll never fall asleep in this coffin ship. Is there a bar, do you think?" she asks.

"Undoubtedly."

An hour later, we're chugging past the Copeland Islands and turning south into the Irish Sea. She's had two G&Ts and is the better for it. Smile back on her lovely face. Hair loose. Lipstick off. Eye makeup starting to run. Lips pouty. She's conveying danger in every glance and half the men in the pub are staring at her and then at me. When I get another round, the barman gives me the aren't-you-the-lucky-bastard nod as he brings the drinks.

The G&Ts have loosened her tongue, and she talks about uni and people I don't know. Finally, however, the booze and the boat knocks the fight out of her and she yawns and bums another ciggie.

I walk her back to the cabin and put her in the bottom bunk.

"I used to do a lot of sailing when I was a kid," she says.

"Oh yeah?"

In five minutes she's asleep.

I fix a blanket about her.

"*Sancta Maria, Mater Dei ora pro nobis peccatoribus* . . ." I whisper as she curls into the sheets.

I climb into the top bunk and wriggle beneath the tight white sheets.

The ship gives a great lurch in the sea and settles again.

Don't even know the ship's name. Bad luck getting on a vessel whose name you haven't even bothered to discover. Turn the reading light on. Look in the rubbish bin. Find the shoelaces. Look at the wrapping label. "Compliments of the *Hibernia*."

Light off.

Close my eyes.

Sleep.

Dream.

31: IT'S NOT THE LEAVING OF
LIVERPOOL THAT GRIEVES ME

Throbbing noise. Light. Where are ... oh ... yeah. Glare coming not through a window but what probably should be termed a *porthole*. I swing my legs out and lower them to the floor, or *deck*, if you will.

I look out through the glass. The rain is finished and the Irish Sea is aquamarine and calm.

Beth is still asleep.

Watch says 6:17 a.m. I take out my notebook, rip off a page, and leave a message: "Gone for smoke, back 15 minutes."

I put on my raincoat and find my way up to the cafeteria. Look out of the window. No land, no birds, no other ships.

This side of the cafeteria has at least a dozen single women staring at cups of tea and coffee, tears in their eyes, ciggies in their hands. One of them approaches. She's about fifteen.

"I couldn't get a smoke, could I?"

I give her the entire packet and go up on to the freezing observation deck.

Stand there for a long time, getting cold.

With no landmarks to speak of, the ship barely seems to be moving.

A kid with a crew cut in jeans and a big red sweater opens the door and stands next to me at the rail. "Jesus, it's brisk," he says.

"Aye, it is."

"Have you got a fag?" he asks.

"I gave them away," I tell him.

"Don't be a tight bastard."

"No, really, I gave them to a wee lassie downstairs."

He nods and we stand there, staring at the sea.

"You think that's England?" he asks, pointing at something on the horizon.

"I don't know."

Back downstairs.

Toast and a cup of tea on a tray.

Knock on the door. "Who is it?" Beth asks.

"Room service," I say, doing a Butlerian voice.

I go in to find her dressed. She's wearing jeans and pumps and a black jumper over a shirt.

"Toast?" I ask her, and set the tray down on the bottom bunk. She shakes her head. "Are you feeling seasick?"

"Nah . . . it's just . . ."

"What?"

"Well, I don't think you're supposed to eat anything before surgery, you know?"

"Oh . . . yeah."

"Smells good, though. Is that marmalade?"

"Orange marmalade."

"Yonks since I had marmalade on toast. OK, then, maybe a slice."

Later.

The car deck.

Drivers inside. Engines idling. The Mersey splaying itself against Liverpool's drab skyline.

The boat docks in a grind of gears and backwash. Heavy grain fog. Greasy rain. Cannibalized hulks lying like dinosaur skeletons on Birkenhead. Deserted pubs and rundown hotels and failing seamen's missions. Ancient cranes standing like gibbets over abandoned docks. A city in decline since the outlawing of the slave trade and the embarrassed, hasty retreat from Empire.

We drive off the boat and I'm immediately lost. Cobbled streets, blind alleys, streets that end abruptly at rubbish-filled docks.

I get out the Britain Road Map book, but there doesn't appear to be a Liverpool section that tells you something.

"Do you know where you're going?"

"Uhm, not really, I need. . . . I think the city center must be that way."

But it isn't. Not on the road I'm taking us.

Rows of empty docks and warehouses. Post-Heseltine surrender. Eyeless houses, boarded-up shops. Belfast's got a war going on, what's the excuse here?

"*I've* got a map, got it at the Women's Advice Center at Queens."

I park. She unfolds it. The abortion trail, clearly explained and landmarked. A dotted line leading from the docks to death and back again—at least, that's the way it reads to me.

"There's a couple of places you can go, but me mate Chrissie says the Queen Alexandra is your best bet for outpatient. Fewer Irish nurses giving you the evil eye."

Down at the bottom of the map, I can see the Queen Alexandra Women's Hospital, a blocky Victorian building in smudged black and white, the grim end point for this counter-pilgrimage.

"All right. The Queen Alexandra? Probably find our way there easily enough."

She shakes her head, looks through the windscreen.

"No. No, don't start the car, Sean, we'll walk."

"What's the point?"

"I want to walk, Sean. I want to get some air first, OK?"

Never argue with a pregnant woman. Never argue with a pregnant woman about to become an ex-pregnant woman—an ontological and metaphysical disaster area.

"I'll have to find somewhere safe to park the car, I can't leave it here."

"Then do that. Please."

Car park near the ferry terminal. Fifteen quid a day. Rip-off.

I show her the map again. "Sure you want to hoof it? We're here. Queen Alexandra is over here. No scale on this thing, but it looks like quite a hike. Right through the city center and on to the other side, in your condition . . ."

"I want to walk," she says, with dour finality.

"OK, then, let me get the umbrella from the boot," I say, faux jaunty, ill at ease. Obviously.

Out of the safety of the Beemer, into the greasy rain of Liverpool.

Up Water Street and the Queensway and Dale Street.

I recognize some of the women from the boat. Past St. John's Gardens and Wellington's Column. Along the London Road and Pembroke Place. This is the Great Abortion Trail walked by thousands of Irish women and girls every year. Along the way there are women's health-information kiosks and women's drop-in centers and—in radical juxtaposition—horrific posters of aborted fetuses outside the many chapels and Catholic charity shops.

Outside the strange Christ the King Cathedral there is what looks like a semipermanent encampment of elderly anti-abortion protestors. Some of them are in wheelchairs and some are attempting to play musical instruments.

Many are carrying giant pictures of beheaded babies that you hope are fake.

"Let's get away from here," I say.

Down a side street.

"I need a cup of tea."

Greasy spoon called the Cyprus Café. Checkerboard floor, wonky plastic tables. Beth looking really lovely today. Her black hair tied up in a ponytail. Her green eyes freaked out and vulnerable. Her cheekbones softened.

Radio on in the background. Local Merseyside station. Good stuff. In the time we've been in here they've played Sonic Youth, REM, and the Sugarcubes.

Reviving me a little. Giving me hope. Music can do that. It can lift you out of the present, or perhaps take you into an alternative present.

A present where Beth didn't get pregnant or where Ek didn't escape the jurisdiction or where Tony didn't have to die.

"Come on, we better get moving," she says.

She puts on her coat and we go outside.

"This way, I don't want to go past the cathedral again," I tell her.

My palm being squeezed.

"I'm scared," she says, her voice breaking.

"Everything's going to be fine, really it is."

"I'm really scared."

"Honey, it's going to be fine."

Bodies are dialogues. We tell each other stuff without a word. Her look into my eyes is all trust and faith. She manages a little grin and I kiss her lightly on the forehead.

Finally we make it to the Queen Alexandra.

A redbrick Edwardian façade. Age-blackened. Mossy. Iron bars over the windows. An air of gloom.

"Are you sure this is the one that your friend recommended?" I ask her.

She nods. "This is the one. Definitely."

Up the steps to Reception.

Forms.

"Can I put you as my emergency contact?"

"I would think so."

Forms filled in. We wait. And wait.

"This way," a nurse says, and leads us down a long, bare corridor.

Another waiting room. A No Smoking sign.

She links her hand in mine. I can see tears in her eyes. I'm about to say, *Hey, maybe we should just split* . . .

"Elizabeth McCullough?"

Beth gets up and nods. She takes off her raincoat and hands it to me. She's shivering in her sweater and jeans.

Another nurse leads her through a set of double doors. I attempt to follow, but the nurse—if she is a nurse—shakes her head.

Back to the waiting room. The No Smoking sign.

I'm the only one here. Rain outside again.

A pile of magazines on a small, square coffee table: *Woman, Woman's Own, Cosmopolitan, Just Seventeen, Jackie* . . .

There's a folded-up copy of the *Sun* on a chair near the double doors. A couple of years from now, in the wake of the paper's Hillsborough coverage, you won't be able to get the *Sun* anywhere in this part of Liverpool. But that's in the grim tomorrow and we're still in the grim today.

Back to Reception.

"Is there anywhere I can smoke?"

She nods. "Smoking room's just in there, to the left."

An airless cubby, packed full of doctors, nurses, patients, husbands, and boyfriends. You don't even have to light your own. A whiff of the air in here.

Back down the corridor to the waiting room.

Another bloke's there now.

We steadfastly avoid each other's eyes.

I pick up the *Sun* again. Read Mystic Meg. She claims Leo is going to come into money. I read the sports section and the TV section.

"Done with that, mate?" the bloke asks. He's about twenty-five, with a moustache, cords, and geography-teacher glasses.

I pass him the paper. I wonder how long this is going to take. Should have done some research. I wonder what they actually—

Beth.

Standing there.

"My coat," she says.

"What?"

"My coat. It's raining."

I give her the coat.

"That was it? It's over?"

She puts the coat on. "Come on. Let's get out of here."

We go outside and she walks briskly away from the hospital.

"Beth, you've got to talk to me, what happened? Is it all over? Do you have to go back?"

"Pub? Can we go to a pub?"

I find a pub and get her a gin and tonic.

She drinks it. Smiles. Drinks some more.

"Fuck," she says. "Fuck me."

"You didn't do it, did you?"

She shakes her head.

"You're not going to do it, are you?"

"No. I'm not."

I can't believe it. Tears. Don't ask why, she might talk herself back into it again.

Is that a hint of a smile on her face?

"Don't think I'm going to be some awful hausfrau. I'm not. I'm getting a career. I'm going to be a career woman. You'll be pulling your weight, Sean Duffy. Changing nappies. Everything. You know that?"

"I know that."

"And wipe that stupid grin off your face."

Back to the Beemer. Back on the ferry. Some of the same faces. Girls. Young women.

Changed forever.

Older by a day. Wiser by years.

Ship pulling out. But the landscape . . .

The landscape has changed. This isn't the ruined docks of Liverpool falling into the black Mersey.

This . . .

This is the place where the future begins.

32: *THE HELSINKI TIMES* (5 MONTHS LATER)

A violent summer in Ulster. Marching season. Disturbances. And during one riot in Carrickfergus someone takes the opportunity to steal my car. Livid doesn't describe it.

"Call Interpol! Pull out all the stops! I need that car for the hospital run!"

But joyriders love to play with a BMW and car thieves don't care about terrified, expectant dads.

The riots are bad and it's all hands on deck. Senior officers in short supply. Men with experience of crowd control . . .

Helicopter ride to the observation post on top of Divis Flats. Gap-toothed city sinking into the mud. The black lough lying there like a dead man's mouth. Belfast as Gormenghast, Belfast as Fallen World, Belfast as Cursed Earth.

Glad to be above it. Above the petrol bombs and the half bricks and the bullets. And the words. Too many. Too much. In Ulster every tinker thinks he is the national bard. Words, words, words tripping off tongues like they are going out of style. Not even listening now. Heard it all before.

Weary . . .

This job. This awful job that makes great and continual demands on luck.

Maybe it is time to move on. Leave the cops to the coppers. Leave the robbers to themselves. Aye, if I was on my own . . . but I'm not on my own, am I?

A girl and a baby on the way.

"What are you grinning about, Duffy?"

"I'm going to be a dad."

"You wait and see. It's no barrel of laughs."

Five hours later.

Riot duty over.

Carrickfergus Police Station. Safe behind the rocket-proof fence.

Safe in my office overlooking the lough.

It's raining. Lawson peeking his head round the door.

"Yes?"

"Sir, some good news for a change."

"Good news? Are you sure?"

"Yes, sir. It's Killian, that car thief that we let off with a warning..."

"What's he done, now?"

"He's turned up at the station, sir. He says he found your Beemer. I looked at it. I think it is yours, sir. And not a scratch on it, by the looks of it. I had the bomb dogs go over it, too. Clean."

Down to the car park.

"Is that kid still around, Lawson? I'll give him a finder's fee."

"Oh, he's gone, sir."

"I think I'll take it for a spin to see if it's OK. Wanna come?"

"You're OK, sir."

Wise lad. Knows me of old. On the run to Whitehead and back I hit an even ton past ICI. Back to the station. Pause at the break room to make a cup of tea. Almost six o'clock now. Shift nearly done for another day.

"What's the word, Crabbie?"

"Where have you been, Sean? There was someone came to see you."

"Yeah, that kid. He found my car."

"No, not him. Some English guy. Jack. He said he knew you. He was waiting in your office, but then he had to go."

Into the office. Ash in the ashtray. The smell of cigarette smoke. And there, sitting in the middle of the desk, a neatly folded newspaper.

I unfold it.

The *Helsinki Times*—a full-color English-language newspaper, published in Finland. Obviously a clue in there somewhere. Could it be the tedious lead story on the front page?

Finland to Apply for EU Membership

Finland has always been a cautious player in international politics. The plan to form an economic community among the Nordic countries, Nordec, came to nothing in the early 1950s because the Soviet Union blocked Finland's membership. Finland has resisted joining the EEC. All of this is about to change, however. In the early 1980s about 20% of Finland's exports went to the Soviet Union. This sector has long been in decline and the government has been seeking new markets in the West. Government sources have told us that Finland, along with Sweden, will soon begin the process of applying for EEC membership. EEC membership is not, of course, just about economics. Finland will need to sign up to the Common Fisheries Policy, the Common Agricultural Policy, it will join the Council of Europe and it will need to negotiate a pan European arrest and extradition policy—

I put down the paper. Is that what he wants me to read? To give me hope that the Lily Bigelow case can be reignited somehow? In two or three years, after Finland has signed up to all the relevant treaties, we get a warrant together and go after Ek?

Knock at the door. Crabbie's face. I hand him the paper. He starts flipping through it from the back. "Read that front-page story. I think my visitor was hinting that the Ek case could be brought back to life in a year or two."

Crabbie shakes his head. "Bad choice of words, Sean," he says.

"What do you mean?"

He folds the paper in half and points at a small story on page 17.

Hunting Accident in Lapland

A Mr. Harald Ek, originally from the Aaland Islands, was accidentally shot and killed on Tuesday while hunting in the forest near Nurmes. Mr. Ek, 65, had recently retired from the board of the Lennätin Corporation and was preparing to write his memoirs.

"What do you think, Crabbie? A genuine accident, or did somebody top the bastard?"

"We'll probably never know, but it looks like he's not our problem anymore."

I reach for the bottle of Jura and pour us both a celebratory measure. "I hope it wasn't an accident. I hope it was delayed justice for Lily," I say between sips.

Crabbie finishes his whisky and fills his pipe. "You're a hard man Sean, but in this case I may have to agree with you."

We drink and talk and I dig out the file and type a brief coda to the case of Lily Emma Bigelow. When Lawson comes in, I show him the paper. He says he'll ask Constable Hornborg about it when he sees her next month in London.

"You and Hornborg have stayed in touch?"

"Sort of. Phone calls are dead expensive, but we've written a few times. And we're going to hang out in London next month, on my week off."

"Did you know about this, Crabbie?"

"I try to stay out of people's personal business if I can," he says.

Crabbie goes home and Lawson goes home and I wait for the inevitable phone call. It comes at seven.

"Hello?"

"Ah, Inspector Duffy, I take it you've read the *Helsinki Times* that I left for you."

"Yes. Was Ek your work?"

"A hunting accident. I think it's best to leave it there, don't you?"

"If you say so."

"I do say so. A prudent man minds his own business."

"A prudent man, yes."

"You'd be surprised how fatherhood has the capacity to turn reckless men into prudent men," Ogilvy says. There is a chill in his voice. An unmistakable menace.

"What are you trying to say, Mr. Ogilvy?"

"With the death of Harald Ek, your case is finished, Inspector

Duffy. The investigation into Kinkaid is being handled by the RUC Sex Crimes Unit. The Metropolitan Police's Special Branch is handling the other more outlandish claims of this inquiry."

"So keep my nose out of it?"

"Keep your nose out of it, if you know what's good for you."

"Now you've torn it. I don't respond well to threats."

"That was the old Inspector Sean Duffy. The new Inspector Sean Duffy has a baby on the way."

Click.

Dial tone.

I stare at the phone for a long time.

I dial a number.

"SCU, this is Trish."

"Trish, this is Inspector Duffy of Carrick CID. If she's still in I'd like to speak to Chief Inspector Farrow."

"Hold, please."

"Farrow. What can I do for you, Inspector Duffy?"

"In the Kinkaid case, you'll follow the leads wherever they go, won't you, Farrow?"

"What are you talking about?"

"The Kinkaid inquiry. You'll follow all the leads, won't you?"

"Of course I will."

"Even if they stretch all the way to England and back?"

"Yes."

"Even if they involve the great and the good? Celebrities? Politicians?"

"Are you so arrogant that you think that you're the only competent policeman in Ireland, Duffy? Is that what you think? You know some of us can do our jobs without histrionics, without making waves or without having to shoot suspects in the chest."

That's a low blow. Tony had been a friend.

"Are any of the boys talking at Kinkaid?"

"You know no one's talking, but the place is closed and it'll never open again."

"But if someone does talk. Tell me that you'll believe them and you'll follow the leads wherever they go."

"I'll follow the leads, Duffy. Now don't tell me how to do my bloody job ever again," she says and hangs up.

I sit there, holding the phone.

Sometimes, Duffy, you have to have faith in the competence of others. You personally can't fix everything.

I sigh and put the phone in its cradle.

Beemer. Seafront. Home.

Bacon frying in the back kitchen, Miles Davis on the record player, the cat snoozing in front of the turf fire.

I go into the kitchen and kiss Beth. The hair dye is all gone now and she is green-eyed and glowing and wild-haired and beautiful.

"How was your day? Riot duty, yes?"

"Today was the last day of it. And you won't believe this, I got the car back. Totally unscathed. We won't have to use the bloody loaner anymore."

"That's a shame, I quite liked that little Yugo."

I put my arms about her. "How was your day?"

"I can't wait for this to be over," she said, patting her belly.

"Soon, now. Do you like the name Lily?"

"No!"

"Do you like the name Emma?"

"Emma? Hmmm. I'll have to think about that. . . . Oh, Sean, you couldn't run up the lane and grab some wild raspberries? *Craving* them. Raspberries and cream."

"Of course," I say. "There are blackberries and blackcurrants up there, too."

Beth gags. "No blackcurrants! Just raspberries!"

Outside into the grey remains of the day with a wicker basket.

All the kids are in getting their dinner, so I'm alone on the street but for a dog sleeping in the middle of the road.

Right on Coronation Road and left up Victoria Road. Victoria Road to Victoria Lane and soon I'm up among the wild blackberry bushes, the crab apples, and the hawthorn.

A breath of wind. A hint of brine. Autumn in the sheep and barley fields.

In a few weeks I'll be wheeling my baby girl up here in her stroller. I'll show her this fox print in the mud if it's still here. "Look, it's a fox, Emma. An old vixen, more than likely."

I grab a bunch of wild raspberries and throw them in the basket just as the sky opens and the rain resumes its long-standing war of attrition against Ireland. I run back down Victoria Lane toward those smoky-blue turf fires of civilization where thousands of other souls are huddled on this little green lifeboat of an island that's still somehow floating in the turbulent waters of the Irish Sea.

"I'm back!" I yell, as I open the front door.

Beth is standing in the hall with her coat on and a bag packed. Her eyes are wide: excited, expectant, petrified.

"Oh shit. Is it time?"

"It's time," she says.

AFTERWORD

This book is a work of fiction that explores some aspects of life in Northern Ireland in the 1980s that did not become public knowledge until several decades later. I have drawn on the findings of *Giving Victims a Voice* (2013), the report into the allegations made against the late Jimmy Savile. The report makes chilling reading, particularly in its analysis of police incompetence and complacency across a number of forces in the UK. Savile allegedly silenced some victims by alluding to his "friends in the police" and others by stating that he was "on very good terms with gunmen in Northern Ireland." This book is set in 1987, when Savile's influence had not yet reached its zenith. In 1990, he was ennobled at the personal request of Mrs. Thatcher (her fourth attempt to do so) and in the same year, Pope John Paul II appointed Savile a Knight Commander of the Pontifical Equestrian Order of Saint Gregory the Great (KCSG). The investigation into the alleged Dolphin Square pedophile ring that was launched in the wake of Operation Yewtree is still ongoing.

This book also draws upon the much-criticized *Report of the Inquiry into Children's Homes and Hostels* (1986) into the Kincora Boys' Home scandal. In January 2013, the *Belfast News Letter* reported that files on the Kincora Boys' Home were "conspicuously absent from the routine January 2013 release of 1982 government papers under the 30-year rule." The documents relating to the alleged prostitution ring and MI5 cover-up at Kincora cannot now be released until 2033.

Nineteen eighty-seven was a typical year for the Troubles in Ulster. Twenty policemen were killed in the line of duty, which meant that the RUC—for the sixteenth consecutive year—was the police force with the highest mortality rate in the western world.

That year also saw the beginning of the so-called Tallaght Strategy in the Republic of Ireland that laid the foundations for the "Celtic Tiger" boom. Ireland subsequently became a major center for the manufacture of mobile phones and computers.

The strange military career of Harald Ek is—loosely—based on that of the Finnish officer Lauri Törni, who fought under three flags in four wars and was finally killed on a US Special Forces mission in Vietnam.

Muhammad Ali came to Ireland many times over the years. The two most famous trips were in 1972, to fight Alvin Lewis at Croke Park and in 2005, to visit Ennis, County Clare, which was the ancestral home of his great-grandfather, Abe Grady. He did not, alas, make it to Belfast on either of those occasions, but if he had, I bet it would have gone down exactly the way I described it in chapter 1, above.

ABOUT . . . ADRIAN McKINTY

Adrian McKinty was born and grew up in Carrickfergus, Northern Ireland. He studied law at Warwick and politics and philosophy at Oxford before emigrating to New York in 1993. He lived in Harlem for seven years, working at various jobs, with various degrees of legality, until he moved to Denver, Colorado, to become a high-school English teacher. In 2008, he emigrated again, this time to Melbourne, Australia, with his wife and kids.

Adrian's first crime novel, *Dead I May Well Be*, was shortlisted for the CWA Ian Fleming Steel Dagger Award and was selected by ALA's *Booklist* as one of the year's best crime novels. His Detective Sean Duffy novels have been awarded and acclaimed: *The Cold Cold Ground* won the 2013 Spinetingler Award for Best Novel: Rising Star/Legends; *I Hear the Sirens in the Street* won the 2014 Barry Award for Best Paperback Original and was shortlisted for the Ned Kelly Award for Best Crime Novel and longlisted for the Theakston Best British Crime Novel Award; *In the Morning I'll Be Gone* won the 2014 Ned Kelly Award for Best Crime Novel; and *Gun Street Girl* was shortlisted for the 2015 Ned Kelly Award for Best Crime Novel.